A Dan and Rivka Sherman Mystery

DEATH GOES POSTAL

By Rosemary and Larry Mild

For Les, mysteriously yours,
Rosemary & Larry

Authors of the Paco and Molly Mysteries
- *Locks and Cream Cheese*
- *Hot Grudge Sunday*
- *Boston Scream Pie*

Magic Island Literary Works • Severna Park, MD • 2013

Copyright © 2013 by Rosemary and Larry Mild
Printed in the United States of America by
Magic Island Literary Works.

All rights reserved. No part of this book may be reproduced in any manner whatsoever without written permission except in the case of brief quotations embodied in critical articles and reviews. For further information please contact the publishers at:
roselarry@magicile.com.

Interior book design by Larry Mild.
Cover design by Marilyn Drea, Mac-In-Town, Annapolis, MD.

Original front cover photo by Tyler McLaughlin.
Photo reprinted by permission.

Library of Congress Cataloging-in-Publication Data
Mild, Rosemary P. ; Mild, Larry M.
Death Goes Postal
Mild, Rosemary P. ; Mild, Larry M.
ISBN 978-0-9838597-1-0

First Edition 2013
10 9 8 7 6 5 4 3 2 1

For our beloved grandchildren—
Alena, Craig, Ben, Leah, and Emily

For our wonderful children—
Jackie and Myrna

For our marriage—soul mates, partners, lovers

Acknowledgments

We could fill an entire volume with the names of all the family members, dear friends, and acquaintances who are loyal fans of our books. You are all precious to us and give us the ultimate push to continue our writing.

We especially thank John and Ann Pollack for their wise critiquing of the earliest version of *Death Goes Postal*.

Our grateful thanks also to Judith A. O'Neill, our former mystery course teacher and good friend, for an insightful critique of yet another version of *Death Goes Postal*.

And many thanks to Al Izen, Beth Rubin, Leena Kollar, and Marilyn Drea for their valuable editorial and publishing advice and assistance.

Last but not least, thanks to Go and Manny Nodar for their valued input.

Disclaimer

Death Goes Postal is largely a work of fiction. The plot and the events therein are of the authors' imagination and invention. Only a few select sixteenth-century characters were tapped for their apparent historical realism. All other characters are fictitious and any resemblance to living persons or persons having lived in this century or the past few centuries is purely coincidental.

Contents

Chapter		Page
1	Quest Denied	1
2	Art of Deception	9
3	The Olde Victorian Bookstore	12
4	Decision To Dream	22
5	Go for the Ring	35
6	On the Dotted Line	44
7	Among the Stacks	53
8	On Coming and Going	64
9	A Boy-Scholar and the Critique Group	69
10	Verse and Reversal	80
11	A Move of Their Own	90
12	In Her Defense	105
13	Food for Thought	111
14	Not Enough Clues	119
15	The Petty Manuscript	128
16	Difficult Times	134

17	Confrontations	142
18	Knight to the Rescue	152
19	Snooping and Snatching	159
20	Rude Awakenings	168
21	Interrogation	175
22	Filling in the Blanks	192
23	A Stretch in the Right Direction	204
24	Flight and Pursuit	214
25	Curiosity and Cats	222
26	Undoing	229
27	On the Road	237
28	Splitting Heirs	241
29	City of Squares	252
30	Key Work	262
31	The Stakeout	272
32	Deception and Clarity	280
33	At Nightmare's End	287

Special Printing Glossary

Chase: A rectangular steel or iron frame in which letterpress matter is locked for printing.

Found: To melt (as metal) and pour into a mold.

Font: An assortment or set of type or characters that are all one style and sometimes one size.

Typefounder: One who pours and casts letter type for the purpose of printing.

Printfounder: One who designs and engraves, inscribes, and/or impresses inverse letter molds or dies for the purpose of casting letter type.

Matrix, *pl.* **matrices or matrixes:** Mold(s) from which a relief surface (as a piece of printing type) is cast.

Special Credits

G**othic Leaf** font was chosen by the authors of ***Death Goes Postal*** to represent what Gerheardt Koenig's floral font <u>might</u> have looked like, as in the illuminated first character in each chapter. Many thanks to Rob Anderson and the Flight of the Dragon organization.

"This font was created by Rob Anderson of Flight of the Dragon, using CorelDRAW version 5 and 6. This font is freely available, and may be distributed in any way as long as this message is included.

The author of the font makes no guarantee about the viability and usability of this font and is not responsible for any damages related to the use.

All rights reserved. Copyright 1997, Flight of the Dragon."

Chapter 1

Quest Denied

Bath, England—Friday, April 16th, 2004

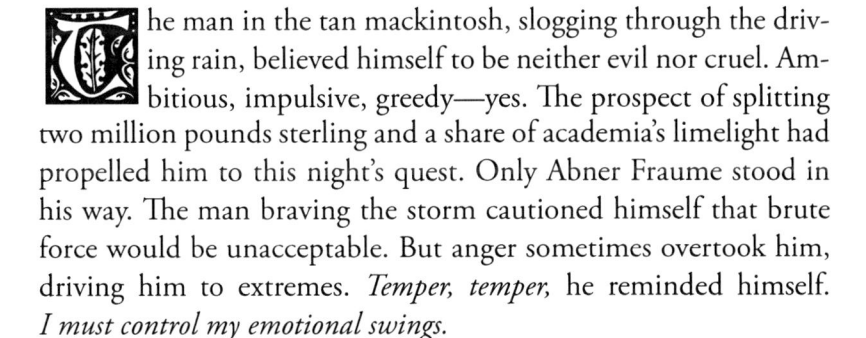

The man in the tan mackintosh, slogging through the driving rain, believed himself to be neither evil nor cruel. Ambitious, impulsive, greedy—yes. The prospect of splitting two million pounds sterling and a share of academia's limelight had propelled him to this night's quest. Only Abner Fraume stood in his way. The man braving the storm cautioned himself that brute force would be unacceptable. But anger sometimes overtook him, driving him to extremes. *Temper, temper,* he reminded himself. *I must control my emotional swings.*

Head down, he made his way across the wet cobblestones of Upper Parke Crescent. A sudden gust heaved him sideways. Holding the upturned coat collar close about his neck, he pushed through the storm. A row of attached brick homes followed the arc of the street—identical except for the wood trim around their doors. Wrought-iron fences separated the stone stoops from the curving sidewalk. The gate at number nineteen stood ajar. *An invitation? Perhaps, but not if the old mule knew who was calling.*

Professor Emil Kravitz climbed the granite steps to shelter under a small peaked roof. He rapped the tarnished brass knocker. No reply. He tried twice more, then peered through the octagonal stained-glass window. A dim light illuminated one room at the far end of a long hall. He brushed away the rain from his gray-black beard and mustache as he waited. *Damn it!* Emil thought. *The old mule's in there, and he's ignoring me.*

Merely lusting after life's finer things, Emil hadn't broken any laws yet. He wanted to be known as a historian of note and a collector of dated artifacts, but lacked the diligence and finances to pursue these passions honestly. He was sick and tired of drilling endless crops of young brats who couldn't care less about a real education. But teaching put food in his mouth, gave him a place to call his own, and left plenty of time for private historical research. Except that his precious research and timing were never quite on the money. Fraume always got there first.

But what's wrong with wanting more? Coercing Fraume into a profitable partnership has got to be the way. He'll come around, I'm sure.

Emil checked the street once more for possible witnesses. No one. Extracting a bi-fold case from inside his coat pocket, he withdrew several tools. The lock-picking technique he'd acquired from one of his more enterprising students. Emil hesitated for a moment as a twinge of guilt rushed through his spine—now he was actually breaking the law.

Inserting a shearing probe and lifting pick into the keyway, Emil set back each of the locking pins until the lock yielded. Pressure on the knob allowed the door to swing inward. He tucked the tools away and removed a Maglite torch from a deep coat pocket. Stepping inside the dark front hall, the intruder listened for any response to his break-in, but heard none. Emil shed the dripping overcoat, leaving it in a heap on the worn carpet. In his black turtleneck sweater and black pants, he melted into the lonely shadows.

The pale light he'd seen from the stoop emanated from the farthest room, four dark doorways down the hall. A quick glance followed the beam of his torch into each room as he silently stole past the smell of tobacco in a sitting room, the clutter of an unmade bedroom, the garlicky aroma of a small kitchen, and a loo that reeked of unlaundered towels. Approaching the final doorway, a floorboard creaked. Emil flattened himself against the wall, un-

Death Goes Postal

sure why stealth mattered. Confrontation was inevitable.

Convinced he remained undetected, Emil put away the torch and pulled on a pair of thin leather gloves before sidling into an office. Stale air irritated his nose, and he suppressed a sneeze. Floor-to-ceiling bookcases lined four walls. A single shaded window faced the rear of the house. Dusty tomes, periodicals, scribbled notes, and cartons lay scattered across the bare floor, leaving only a narrow path for walking. A brass lamp with a green glass shade lit a desk in the far corner.

A noise made Emil stop short. Then he recognized snoring, explosive snorts, and a few murmurs. He inched forward and saw eighty-eight-year-old Professor Abner Fraume, head pillowed over crossed arms on the desk. Thick-lensed glasses lay beside the bald pate. Liver spots on Abner's scalp stood out amid wisps of white hair.

Emil paused to slow his breathing. *Friendly persuasion should be enough. At most, a little arm twisting. After all, the good professor stands to gain as well, and I'll be doing all the legwork. Selling everything will mean certain wealth, and our combined scholarly papers will bring undoubted academic acclaim. I've already got that wealthy German collector who wants to purchase the lot. Maybe I can improve my bargaining position with the old mule if I find either the artifacts or his manuscript first. How can he resist my offer then?*

Emil reached under Abner's left elbow and tried to dislodge a large volume. The old man snorted and stirred. Emil pulled back, then tried again. Gently lifting the elbow, he studied the title: *A History of Sixteenth-Century Medicine,* edited by one of Fraume's colleagues. Not the manuscript Emil sought. He scanned the room for the next place to search, but something stopped him—the snores and snorts had stopped. He turned toward the desk once more. Two gray eyes squinted back at him.

"Who's there? What're you doing in my home?" The old man fumbled for his glasses. He slid one wire temple over each ear and pushed the bridge up his pockmarked nose. Slowly focusing on the intruder, Abner suddenly recognized the familiar patchwork beard and mustache. "Emil Kravitz, how the devil did you get in here? And why?"

"Yes, it's me, Abner. And you know full well what I've come for. Herr Koenig's matrix molds, his chase, and your research manuscript. I mean to have them. You should agree to my generous terms. It can be a profitable collaboration for us. It's still not too late, my dear Abner."

"Don't 'dear Abner' me, you *gonif*. You'll never lay hands on either the block molds or my research. They're my life's work, more than fifty years' worth."

"You're wrong, Abner. I'm not leaving without them."

"You can go straight to hell. The items you want are no longer here, I assure you. I've sent them elsewhere for safekeeping."

"Why would you do that?"

"You bloody well know why, Kravitz. Your nasty threats, that's why. There are some things in this world more important than money. And I'm not afraid of bodily harm. There's nothing you can do to me that hasn't been done before." A tremor raced through the old body. "Remember, I've lived through the Holocaust."

"These are not idle threats, Herr Fraume. I grew up on Chicago's South Side. Learned a few nasty tricks along the way. They're not very nice, Professor." Emil's words fed his own fury.

"Get out of my house before I call the police." Abner reached for the telephone.

But Emil got there first. His left hand pressed down on the disconnect, while his right hand tore the cord from the phone's base and then from the wall socket. Abner pushed away from the desk and tried to stand, but Emil slammed the frail body back into the chair. He folded the phone cord and snapped it on the desk twice to get the old man's attention.

Abner froze. Emil wrapped the phone cord around the scrawny neck and pulled tight. Arthritic fingers tugged at the cord as weakened lungs struggled for precious air.

Emil loosened the cord. "Where are they, Herr Professor?

Death Goes Postal

I've no patience for your child's play. Are they in there?" He gestured toward the maze of cartons cluttering the room. "What did you do with them?" No answer. The victim's gaunt face revealed only fear. Emil tightened the cord, his pulse racing as his anger grew manic.

Abner's feeble fists pounded Emil's forearms, groping the sleeves of the tweed jacket, tugging them inward to loosen the choking garrote. The victim's glasses fell off, revealing red-veined, protruding eyes. Abner's feet, in carpet slippers, kicked and flailed until his whole body sagged. Facial muscles drooped as death bled the fear and rage from Abner's desperate expression.

Emil wiped the sweat off his brow with the back of his hand. He hadn't meant to kill Abner. *Why did the rotter have to be so obstinate? Why couldn't he have just taken the money and shared in the academic kudos?*

The hammering inside Kravitz's chest slowly subsided and a fresh sensation, euphoria, took its place. Propping the body up in the chair, he rolled it back under the desk. Then he began his search in earnest for three items: the sixteenth-century typeface matrices; an engraved and hallmarked antique metal chase; and Fraume's manuscript, documenting the elaborate history of these treasures.

The matrices were pouring molds used to manufacture large decorative typeface blocks that could print the initial illuminated character of chapter text. The chase was a rigid metal frame used to hold moveable type in place during printing.

Three hours later, a frustrated Emil Kravitz sat on a corner of Abner's desk, scrutinizing the office one last time. He'd located five earlier tomes authored by Fraume, but they revealed nothing of the works he sought. After combing through every room in the house, he hadn't found a single trace of Herr Koenig's artifacts nor Abner's historical manuscript tracing them. Scattered notes and an arbitrary reference here and there, but nothing worthy of his murderous quest. He wanted to be done with this mess. The first light of morning squeezed through the Venetian blinds. He knew the time had come to leave. Soon neighbors would be taking in newspapers or heading off to work.

While donning his overcoat and cap, he noticed a sealed, stamped letter, ready to be posted, sitting on the half-round table next to the front door. The address read:

> Mrs. Edythe Bender
> The Olde Victorian Bookstore
> 123 East Franklyn Lane
> Annapolis, Maryland 21401 U.S.A.

Emil slid the letter into his pocket, reset the latch, and left. He had some idea where he might look next.

* * *

Monday, April 19th

"Who's in charge here?" bellowed the newcomer, a large man with a round pink face and curly gray hair. His trench coat lay open. The buttons on his inexpensive blue suit jacket pulled at the waist.

"Constable Sergeant Thorwal from Homicide, sir," the uniformed local constable replied. "'E's in the back room. Kind of an office, I'd call it."

"And you are?"

"Smyth, sir, from Traffic branch. I was the first on the scene."

"Would you inform the sergeant that Chief Inspector E. Howard Winston from Scotland Yard is here to take charge? Oh, never mind. I'll do it myself. By-the-bye, who called this one in?"

"The cleaning lady, sir. Came at 'af past eight this morning. She comes Mondays every fortni't. Poor woman was so shaken, she ran out, leaving the door wide open. Called us from the Boar's Whistle Pub down the crescent, she did." He led Winston down the hall and into Abner's office. "This is the way we found 'im," said the constable. "Looks pretty professional to me."

"And you know that for a fact. How?" asked the Chief Inspector. Winston's patience ran thin, as he'd been at another crime scene most of the morning and nearly half the afternoon. The constable flushed with embarrassment, yet made no response. They picked their way carefully among the books and cartons to the body.

"Where's this sergeant?" asked Winston.

"Must be in the loo, sir."

"Are they done dusting for prints yet? I wonder if they'll get lucky this time."

"Oh, a bundle of prints, sir, but like as not they'll belong to the deceased. That's wha' the crime scene blokes said anyway. Must ha' been a loner, that one. Some kind o' writer or researcher wi' all them reference books and the like."

Winston pulled a handkerchief out of his trench coat pocket and covered his nose. "Whew! Are the photographers done yet? My people want to get him out of here."

"Yes, sir, just finished. They can have 'im. The bloke's bloody ripe, 'e is."

"After a week, what do you expect, Constable?"

A clean-shaven, thirty-something man in a loud sport jacket stepped into the office. "Ah, Chief Inspector Winston. Glad to be working with you again."

"I remember you now, Sergeant Thorwal. The Boxley murder, wasn't it?"

"Yes, sir, you've got a good memory."

Winston's eyes scanned the room, taking in the essence of it. "Who'd you say the victim was?"

The sergeant glanced down at his memo pad. "Fraume, sir, Abner Fraume. He's a retired professor of archaeology from the University of Bath. There's a pile of his published books over there on the shelves. Must have been quite an authority on the subject, according to the endorsements in the front of the first book I picked up."

"Any family?"

"No evidence of any on this side of the pond, sir. There's a bunch of open letters from a sister, Edythe Bender, in America, though. That's Annapolis in the middle of the East Coast."

"I know bloody well where Annapolis is, Sergeant. Anybody notify her yet?"

"Not that I know of…I'll get to it this evening, Chief Inspector."

"Never you mind, Sergeant, I'll handle it myself."

"'Scuse me, gents. Comin' through," said a coarse voice from behind them.

The two police officers stood to one side while the coroner's team laid out the corpse, bagged it, and removed it from the premises. Other forensics technicians continued about the room, collecting evidence, until one made a discovery.

"Chief Inspector! You might want to see this."

The lone word "Kravitz" had been scrawled in pen on the desk blotter.

"Do you think it's the killer?" asked Sergeant Thorwal.

"Quite likely," Winston said. "The handwriting is uneven, scribbled in haste. The man wasn't accustomed to writing notes on his blotter. It has other ink stains, but no other words or names. See how the ink has blurred into it? I believe the victim is naming his killer, but that's merely an opinion." Winston's gaze scanned the room. "Anything appear to be missing?"

"Nothing obvious, sir," replied the sergeant. "The blighter wasn't after money or valuables. Wallet, keys, watch, and the like—all still on his dresser top. Maybe revenge? Our victim was too old to be a lover."

"Don't count on it. Might even be an old feud," Winston surmised. "Or the research. Find out more about Fraume's work. Then check the name Kravitz in major city directories. Try to cross it with fences, dealers, book experts, and universities. What did these two men have in common?"

"Maybe nothing, sir, but I'll get right on it."

"Sergeant, check the planes, trains, and buses. Get some help, too—and someone to monitor the incoming post."

"Yes, sir!"

Chapter 2

The Art of Deception
Annapolis, MD—Wednesday, April 21st

bner's intercepted letter to his sister provided a wealth of information for Emil Kravitz. One, he learned that the British Literary Museum was the sole beneficiary of Herr Koenig's artifacts. And two, Edythe Bender, Abner Fraume's sister, held the key to finding the artifacts and associated academic work. Having resealed the envelope and posted the letter, he then formulated a scheme to penetrate her immediate environs, namely, The Olde Victorian Bookstore in Annapolis. Emil withdrew his entire life savings from the Clydesdale PLC bank in Bath, converted the pounds to dollars, and sewed most of the bills into the lining of his overcoat.

Operating inconspicuously in the U.S., and particularly in Maryland, would require a new persona—a passport, driver's license, and credit cards. All of these he'd stolen from a careless and hapless American tourist in London whose features faintly resembled his own. Renting a car might be tricky, because the rental documents could leave an ominous trail. He had another plan to take care of that problem.

Certain that he would need additional clout in dealing with Herr Fraume's sister, Emil created two more pieces of his new identity on his home computer. He photocopied the British Literary Museum logo from a visitor's pass, added a photo of himself minus beard and mustache, and inserted a solicitor's title with fake legal-department data. Finally, he laminated the composite and behold! A credible ID badge. Printing out a page of business cards came next. He knew it was only a matter of time before this identity would become volatile. Abner's body would be discovered and museum officials might even dispatch their own man to the Annapolis scene. But the rewards appeared to exceed the risks, so he set his plan in motion.

Emil Kravitz deplaned from the last incoming flight to Baltimore-Washington International Airport that night, along with 225 other British Airways passengers. The new persona breezed through U.S. Customs, submitting the stolen passport and answering only basic questions. Carrying one two-suiter bag and a briefcase, he exited to curbside traffic to await the rental car shuttle.

He rented a midsize Mercury sedan for the next two weeks under his assumed name, found the car a couple hundred yards from the office, and threw his belongings in the back seat. What luck, he thought, that the Mercury had been parked in this remote aisle. Unzipping an outer pocket of his two-suiter, Emil removed a small crescent wrench and surveyed the parking lot for witnesses. In the dark, under the lemon light cast by halogen lamps, he saw no one. Even the weather cooperated—a heavily overcast sky with neither stars nor moonlight.

Instead of getting behind the wheel, he loosened four bolts securing the car's front and rear license plates. With the plates under one arm, Emil stepped over a short barrier and walked a brisk half-mile to a BWI public lot, where long-term passengers parked their own cars. In a shadowed section, he chose another Maryland car of a different make and color and quickly swapped license plates. Returning to his rented Mercury, he screwed on the stolen plates. Emil counted on the improbability of most drivers to notice a change in their own license plates.

Sliding into the driver's seat, Emil started the engine and turned on the headlights. At the gate he flashed the rental agreement at the guard, who waved him through onto Aviation Boulevard. He braked at a red light and silently congratulated himself. *The muse of deception must be with me,* he thought. *I wonder if there's one for murder as well.* The light turned green and he accelerated onto I-97 South. From the first Annapolis exit, Crownsville Road, Emil drove to West Street, pulled into an Exxon station, and asked for directions to the Historic District. Cruising a dozen blocks toward Church Circle, he pulled into Loews Annapolis Hotel, where he registered for a single room. He'd look for a suitable flat in the morning. What he needed now was a good night's sleep. He had serious work to do.

Chapter 3

The Olde Victorian Bookstore
Annapolis—Saturday, April 24th

he U.S. Postal vehicle, white with red and blue stripes, hugged the curb in front of The Olde Victorian Bookstore. Instead of placing the stack of letters in the mailbox, the young mail carrier hopped to the pavement and handed them to the elderly man standing on the sidewalk.

"Hi, Mister Bender," she said.

Bernard Bender replied with an empty look. He knew he'd been waiting out front for a reason, but he couldn't have told you why. Bernie clutched the envelopes in his free hand, but had no idea what to do with them. He stared at the mail lady as though he expected something more from her. He didn't know what, but she did. She knew his secret and loved to challenge him.

"Let me see….I have it here somewhere." She fumbled through her jacket pockets until her fingers found a folded scrap of paper. "Ah, here it is." She read aloud.

> *"Wilt thou lay thy frown aside,*
>   *and smile as thou wert wont to do?"*

Bernie's eyes flamed up, as if a match had been touched to dry kindling, and he responded, his words flowing with fresh fire and clarity.

Death Goes Postal

"Fairest maid on Devon banks,
 Crystal Devon, winding Devon,
Wilt thou lay thy frown aside,
 And smile as thou wert wont to do?"

"It's Robby Burns," he said, "from *Full Well Thou Know'st*."

No sooner had the last word of the title left his lips than Bernie's joyous expression collapsed. The fire in his eyes turned to ashes.

"You beat me again, Mr. Bender." The mail lady smiled and reached out to tuck the striped tie inside his navy cardigan. She kissed Bernie lightly on the cheek and climbed back into the postal truck. "See you Monday," she called, and her vehicle rolled to the next mailbox.

The white-haired Bernie shuffled toward the stairs leading up to the bookshop's upper entrance. For him formidable. He needed to get rid of the mail. He couldn't hold onto the railing, his cane, and the envelopes at the same time, so he just sat down on the second step from the bottom. Someone would have to tell him what to do next.

"Bernie!" He still recognized both his wife's voice and his own name. Edythe Bender emerged from a wide doorway underneath a wraparound veranda. The iron-strapped wooden door, suspended inside a large stone arch, bore the name "The Dungeon."

"Ah, there you are, sweets," she said, careful to keep her voice steady. It was Bernie's daily routine to meet the mail lady, but Edythe wondered how long it would be before he wandered off. She took his cane and helped him across the walk to The Dungeon door, which led to a series of rooms filled with books about horror, science-fiction, and fantasy. *Trompe l'oeil* doors, tunnels, spider webs, and ladders randomly interrupted the stacks to provide a delightfully disorienting atmosphere. Several customers perused books in the cozy reading room next to the stairs.

Bernie dropped the annoying mail into a wicker waste basket and studied his empty hands. Edythe retrieved the envelopes, then steered her husband of fifty-three years into a two-passenger elevator. Labeled "For Employees Only," it conveyed them up two floors to their living quarters and deposited them in a high-ceilinged kitchen. He sat down in one of the captain's chairs and stared into the dining room that now served as a reading and conference room and also held the store's Travel section. Customers entered from a stairwell opposite the private elevator.

Edythe prepared tuna salad sandwiches and steeped a pot of English tea. She cut Bernie's sandwich into small squares and patiently showed him once more how to pick them up with his fingers and feed himself. Holding the tea glass for him while he drank, she sighed. His Alzheimer's had reached an almost unbearable stage.

Edythe Bender, once a vigorous, pretty woman with blue eyes, stood five-foot-four and weighed 140 pounds. No way could she continue maneuvering Bernie's five-foot-six, 174-pound frame in and out of bed or bath. She herself was living on stolen time. Her ovarian cancer had spread, and the doctor couldn't predict how long she had left. She needed to provide for Bernie's future. In her most depressed moments, she often asked herself why God allowed this sad state: a mind deteriorating to helplessness inside a body strong enough to survive another decade.

Bernie napped in his chair. Edythe propped her pince-nez glasses on her nose and sorted through the mail until she came to a letter postmarked Bath, England. A welcome message from her brother, Abner. Strangely, the envelope appeared tampered with, as if it had been opened and resealed. Just then, her sales clerk, Liz Nathan, buzzed her on the intercom, asking for help in Technology and Current Events on the main floor. Edythe released the reading glasses, which fell on their beaded chain to her chest. She slid Abner's letter, unread, into a pocket of her smock and attempted to run a comb through her gray wig—out of habit—as if it were her own hair. Hers had fallen out during chemo.

Death Goes Postal

* * *

At eight-thirty that evening, Edythe locked up the shop. Expecting friends, she installed Bernie in his rocking chair in their room, where he would watch television for hours on end. Promptly at nine, she responded to the doorbell and led Daniel Sherman and his wife, Rivka, upstairs to the kitchen table. The house no longer had a living room. She and Bernie had designated it years ago for Best Sellers and Literary Works.

Rivka headed toward the kitchen table, settling her pear shape into one of the four captain's chairs. A certain bounce accompanied all her movements. Dan fitted his large frame into another chair across from her. Slouching, he stretched his long, lean legs under the table. His horn rims rested at the rise of his prominent, slightly crooked nose. Idly, he began to play with the solid wax drippings clinging to the brass *Shabbat* candlesticks sitting on the Benders' table from the night before.

"Coffee? Tea?" Edythe asked.

"Not for me," replied Rivka, a woman of fifty-two, with curly dark brown hair turned out at the collar and pulled slightly back to reveal hoop earrings. Deliberately untamed bangs nearly touched her eyebrows. Full lips with a slight clockwise twist sat in the center of a creamy, unlined face. "It's too close to my bedtime."

Edythe nodded. "Sure, dear, maybe you'd rather have some of this." She set down a plate covered with marbleized wedges of a Middle Eastern sweet made from ground sesame seeds and honey.

"Whoa, Edythe, you're corrupting me, and isn't it wonderful?" Rivka chuckled. Her cinnamon-brown eyes sparkled with every soprano word she spoke. "I wonder what makes *halvah* so popular," she said. "It looks more like a hunk of concrete than a dessert." Munching on a grainy mouthful, she pulled off her navy blue Oxford sweatshirt and laid it across the back of her chair.

"I'll have coffee, regular," Dan said, "but only if it's already made."

"No bother at all," Edythe said. The gas made a popping noise as she turned off the flame under the copper kettle. She measured the instant coffee from a jar, set a blue and white cup and saucer in front of Dan, and brought another one for herself. She passed him the matching creamer and sugar bowl.

Rivka glared across the table at Dan's bushy black hair, a touch of gray threaded through, with a lineup of wisps decorating his neck. He needed a haircut badly. Dan got the message, but figured he'd wait another two weeks just to bug her. A guy had to assert his independence somehow, didn't he?

"Lovely Delft china," Rivka remarked, when the conversation needed a jump-start. "Has it been in the family long?"

Edythe looked pleased. "We bought the set in London just before the war. Not many of our things survived. Our bookstore in Soho was demolished by the Jerry blitz. The dishes were packed in crates, along with a few rare books. Thank God for that."

"London?" Dan inquired. "How'd you wind up here in Annapolis—if you don't mind my asking."

Edythe hadn't known the Shermans socially for long. They were steady customers in the shop and stalwart members of the literary and mystery critique groups the shop had been hosting. But since Bernie's decline two years ago, she'd done no other entertaining at all. Now she warmed to Dan's interest.

"Emigration was Bernie's idea. Horrible memories, so many friends and family members gone. We had to start all over again. Getting an enormous offer for one of our rare books, made the whole move possible. We put *everything* into this place."

"The Olde Victorian Bookstore, what a fantastic concept. And the way you've accomplished it," said Rivka. "An independent bookstore that's so much fun, readers don't want to set foot in a chain ever again."

"That's a bit of an exaggeration, dear," Edythe said, "but thank you for the compliment."

"Edythe, I'm a sucker for Victorian homes. I adore the way you converted this one into your business. It's a delight just to walk in."

"Enough of a delight to consider buying it?"

Rivka's eyes widened behind black-framed glasses. She leaned forward, placing her hands on the table. "Buy your business? Why would you want to sell this gold mine?"

"It's not the gold mine it used to be," Edythe replied. "When Bernie and I ran it together we did very well, but Liz's salary takes a big bite from the take. And I don't blame her for not wanting to put in the fourteen-hour days we did. We did it for love as much as for a living."

Rivka sighed. "I've always wanted my own business, to be my own boss, and work directly for my own success. I'd love a place like this."

"I'm ready to sell," Edythe said. "How serious are you?"

Rivka was about to say "Very!" But Dan crossed his arms over his turtleneck sweater and scowled at her. "Whoa, Rivka, let's not get carried away. We don't know anything about running a bookstore."

Edythe had a ready answer. She'd invited them for coffee, but her ulterior motive embraced this very proposal, and she'd done her homework. "I know I'm stating the obvious," she said, "but please humor me. Dan, you both know more than you think. With Rivka being the feature editor at the *Journal-Gazette* and having her own "Bayside Living" column, she's made a name for herself. She'd draw in customers. And you, Dan, a project manager at Kambrills Electronics. I should think you'd be able to apply those administrative skills to running a bookstore."

"Maybe, but—"

Edythe pressed on. "You've been running the mystery critique group for several years now. The two of you are more than qualified to run this operation."

"That's a bit of a stretch, Edythe," said Rivka. "I just put an ad in the paper to try to get some new blood into the mystery group. We're down to four members."

"See, Dan? Your wife's in the mindset already."

Dan interjected, "Even if we're good at our jobs, we couldn't afford to buy this business. And what's the big rush to sell it?"

Edythe's voice grew shaky. "You've seen my health failing steadily. My cancer has spread. I'm due for another round of chemo at the hospital."

"Oh, Edythe!" Tears welled up in Rivka's eyes.

"I'm so sorry," said Dan, his neck muscles tightening.

Edythe took a deep breath. "It's not for myself that I worry so much."

"Bernie could stay with us while you're in the hospital," Rivka offered.

"Thanks, but that would be only a temporary solution. He needs a nursing home where he can get all the care he deserves."

"Isn't that pretty expensive?" Dan asked.

"Horribly, for anything decent. I need to sell the store to pay for his keep. Sell to you two, preferably."

"Just a minute," said Dan. "What if we decide we're not interested? What's your alternative?"

"If I can't find an earnest buyer before I enter the hospital, it will be the end of the bookstore altogether. I've heard of a *gonif*, a regular thief, over in D.C., who'll buy my stock at an unconscionable discount, then sell everything off piecemeal."

"But Edythe," Rivka protested, "why is it so important to sell to us? We're practically strangers."

"How can you say that, my dear? You and Dan are our closest friends. Bernie and I have no children. It catches in my craw to have to sell everything we've both worked so hard for to some highway robber who'll come in here and coldly dismantle the place." She slumped in her chair. "It would be like we never came to Annapolis or even existed. No, I'd rather give the business away to someone like you folks. Well, not literally, of course, but at least our accomplishments would survive."

Dan took a long drag from his cup and set it down on the table in front of him. No sooner had it clunked on the surface than Rivka reached over and swung the cup to her lips.

"Hey!" he muttered.

"I can make another cup," said Edythe. "There's plenty of

hot water left in the kettle."

"Oh, no thank you," Rivka admitted sheepishly. "I just wanted an infinitesimal sip."

"Don't pay her any attention," said Dan. "She does that to me all the time. We're at a restaurant. 'No dessert for me!' he mimicked in a trilled voice. "I'm usually lucky to get three bites of my cheesecake or whatever." He stole an amused glance at his wife.

Ignoring him, Rivka ran her fingers through her curls. "We can't afford to pay you what this place is worth. Not even if we sold *our* home to finance it—which I wouldn't dream of doing."

"You wouldn't have to. I'd like to propose a partnership," Edythe said. "Of course, the details are complex and it would take time to work out. But basically, the only cash you'd have to come up with is the monthly nursing home bill of around $3,000. Bernie's Social Security and Medicare would cover the rest. The books will show that the store generates a good deal more profit than that. There's no mortgage and all the bills are paid up. After Liz's salary, taxes, new inventory, and a handful of expenses, the average monthly net is about $11,000. I'd be comfortable with about a third of that and I'll contribute to the venture largely as a consultant. When I'm gone, the rights of survivorship pass to you."

"What about your medical bills?" asked Dan. "They must be terribly high."

"Our insurance covers eighty percent, and the rest? Well, you can't get blood from a stone, can you? There won't be any assets left when I sell the store. I don't feel bad about that after the premiums we've paid out."

"Can the hospital refuse treatment?" he asked.

"They won't, but I don't plan to be around when the final bill arrives."

"My godfather!" said Rivka. "What about *your* family? You have a brother living in England, don't you? Maybe he'd want to buy the business."

"No. Abner's eighty-eight, a widower and pensioner. He has an estranged daughter in America somewhere. But she ran off with some rocker musician, and he hasn't heard from her in over twenty years."

Dan looked over at his wife and saw that her eyes had begun to glaze over. He raised one hand, palm out. "Edythe, this is pretty exciting stuff, but it's too much to absorb in one night. We need to go home and think about it and then get into more of the nitty-gritty."

"Of course," said Edythe, not feeling the least bit guilty about springing such a surprise on her friends. "A couple days won't matter. I've had months to think about this, and you've been my number one solution all along."

At that moment a loud snore came from the bedroom. Bernie had fallen asleep in his chair. Edythe stood up, signaling the end of their meeting. As she ushered them downstairs to the first floor, the hallway light picked up the glow of two yellow-green eyes and a furry black sheen prowling along the tops of book stacks, leaping from the end of one to the start of another.

"What a gorgeous cat!" exclaimed Rivka. "Is it yours?"

"Oh, yes, that's Lord Byron. He gets thrown in with the store."

"Here, kitty!" Rivka called. The cat ignored her and padded away. "How did he get that wonderful name?"

"He wandered in here four years ago," Edythe said with a chuckle. "He's always preferred the poetry stacks, where he can sleep mostly undisturbed by customers. Unfortunately, poetry hasn't been that popular lately. The name Lord Byron just seemed to fit."

They exchanged hugs, said their goodbyes, and Edythe locked up after them. She decided to take the elevator and was about to enter it when she stopped, out of breath and nauseated. She sat down hard on the bottom stair, squeezed her eyes shut, and lifted her face to heaven while uttering a prayer for just a little more time. The wave of sickness passed in a few minutes, and she returned to the living quarters and the laborious task of helping Bernie into his pajamas and bed. She looked down into the expressionless face, as he lay there with his eyes closed, and she quoted: "The mind has a thousand eyes, and the heart but one."

A smile danced on his lips as he recited:

> "*The night has a thousand eyes,*
> *And the day but one;*
> *Yet the light of the bright world dies*
> *With the dying sun.*
> *The mind has a thousand eyes,*
> *And the heart but one;*
> *Yet the light of a whole life dies*
> *When love is done.*"

"It's Francis William Bourdillon," he declared.

She laid a tender kiss on his forehead, but not before his face had gone slack once more. He fell into a sound sleep before his wife had a chance to slip under the covers.

Chapter 4

Decision To Dream
Sunday, April 25th

n most Sunday mornings, both Shermans slept in and enjoyed their West Annapolis home in sheer leisure. Not so today. The lady of the house awoke hours earlier, tossing in angst. She regarded her snoring husband and decided to let him sleep. *Nothing bothers him,* she thought. *Dan always sleeps the unworried sleep of innocence—I envy that.* She slipped on a fleece robe over the man-sized T-shirt she wore every night. Dan got such a kick out of her snuggling up to him in bed bare-bottomed that he'd given her several of his favorites. This one was burgundy and gold, the Washington Redskins.

In the kitchen Rivka rattled around loading the coffeepot and from there moved to the front door. Reaching outside, she whisked the heavy bundle of *Washington Post* Sunday papers off the front stoop and plopped them down on the coffee table. Kicking off her slippers, she sank into the flowered sofa and put her feet up. Perhaps the comics would free her from the impending decision-making burden, even for a little while. But instead of reading, she began to reflect on her past.

Rivka grew up an only child in Washington, DC, the good-natured, bright daughter of Leo and Ida Manx. The Manx family had been U.S. citizens for generations. Her maternal grandparents were immigrants from prewar Poland, and so a bit of Yiddish crept into her vocabulary. Much of their lives centered on the synagogue community. Little Rivka was a quiet, respectful child. Growing up she yearned for a younger brother or sister whom she could boss around the way her mother bossed her around. As a substitute, Rivka learned to lie, as if it were a game to entertain herself in her only-child existence. But lying to her mother—and getting away with it—took skill. Rivka had honed it to a fine art. Or so she thought.

The summer she turned nine, Mother enrolled her in Joy Farm Day Camp for two weeks. "You'll be doing a little horseback riding," she announced. The camp was only an hour away, but to Rivka it felt like exile. The summer before, she had fallen off a horse at another camp and broken her wrist. To this day she had a scar on the inside of her left wrist, where the plaster cast had rubbed her skin raw and created an infection. She had no intention of ever climbing on a horse again. But she didn't protest out loud. She hadn't yet learned to rebel. Her first day at Joy Farm she discovered that riding was just about all they did. They rode the horses in an indoor arena, two by two, with the campers on their steeds next to the wall and a counselor riding his horse on their left. No way could they fall off or get hurt. But Rivka was terrified. She sat so high up, and there was nothing to look at but the undulating rear ends of the horses in front of her. At four o'clock on the first day, the bus dropped her off at home, and Mother rushed to the door to ask her how it went. Rivka blurted out, "I fell off five times!" Then she went outside to play. But Mother headed straight for the phone. The next morning, her personal counselor, a huge man with a thick mustache and cowboy hat, hoisted her on her horse and sneered, "You fell off five times." Exposed! Discovered! Nailed! Mother didn't scold her. No, she inflicted a far more subtle punishment. She made her daughter stick out the entire two-week session.

Despite Ida's best efforts, the stage had been set. Rivka emerged from puberty with a cantankerous side her parents had never seen before and certainly did not like. Their daughter's insatiable curiosity challenged every house rule. Strongly opinionated and often flippant, she made both friends and enemies easily.

A side issue, her suddenly pudgy hips, didn't help. Ida had a tough time limiting the delicious cherry varnishkes, kugel, and kasha she served up at dinner. After all, traditional Jewish cooking was what she had learned from her own mother and grandma. But Ida tried, foregoing *schmaltz*—the divine chicken fat—for low-fat cooking oil and serving Jello. Rivka resented her skinny mother's obsession over her daughter's weight.

They clashed frequently. Leo buried himself in the *Baltimore Jewish Times* and *Jerusalem Post*. As far as he was concerned, his little girl was perfect. He supported her through the University of Maryland's journalism school. By graduation, pudgy had become pleasantly *zaftig*.

Rivka's first job placed her in a medical and scientific book redactory with thirty other sedate copy editors. After two years, she saw the job as a dead end and began sending a barrage of freelance feature articles to the local newspapers. Eventually, the *Annapolis Journal-Gazette* offered her the position of feature editor. What a joy. A year later she met Daniel Sherman during an interview covering a defense contract awarded to his firm.

They were married in ten glorious months when Rivka was twenty-three. One year afterward, Jennifer Lynn arrived, and her brother, Leonard Manx Sherman, came on the scene two years later. Despite working full time, Rivka always managed to prepare a Friday night *Shabbat* dinner. She and Jennifer had their special tradition: saying the blessing over the *Shabbat* candles together. Then they'd all pile in the car for eight o'clock services at temple.

Her parents were gone now. She especially missed Ida. Rivka had a flash of her first weekend home from college. She was taking Comparative Religion, and at the dinner table her first night, she announced: "I've decided I'm going to become a Unitarian." Ida retorted: "No you're not!" Subject closed. Secretly, Rivka had been relieved.

She picked up the comics and had just finished "Zits" and

"Prince Valiant" when Dan lumbered through the door in bathrobe and bare feet.

"Hey, love," she said. "I didn't mean to disturb you. You were a bear in full hibernation and making just about as much racket."

Dan leaned over her shoulder from behind and planted a smacking kiss on her smooth cheek. "That chocolate macadamia coffee just wafted into the bedroom and scooped me out of bed. I'm an aroma slave—helpless, even." He took the paper apart looking for Sports and Money.

"Seriously, did you sleep okay?" she asked.

"I don't know, I wasn't there." It was his usual goofy response, but this time his wife didn't laugh.

Dan added, "Same as every night, I suppose. But what you really want is for me to ask how you slept. So, my dear wife, tell me."

"I was up half the night thinking about Edythe's proposition," she said. "God, it's so tempting, something I've always wanted to do."

Dan jumped in. "Sweetheart, it would be great to have a job that's more than a job, something you own. But remember, a bookstore isn't just books and helping people. It's first and foremost a business with requirements for cash flow and profits. Huge inventories, taxes, books to buy. Not all of the work can be classified as fun."

"I understand that, Dan, don't lecture me," she said, sounding a little more snappish than she meant to. "It's just that Edythe has made everything so attractive—a one-third, two-thirds partnership with no initial cash outlay, and she remains on as a consultant."

"I know what you mean," Dan said. "But are we interested in this venture just because we're two bored wage earners? I've grown pretty attached to our regular salaries, and I kind of like eating and paying the mortgage, too. If it doesn't work out, we'll have to start our careers all over again and that may not be so easy."

"I could run the place with Liz until we're sure we can make a go of it. Then you could join me, if needed. Besides, we're both highly skilled professionals. How hard could it be to make a comeback?"

"In our early fifties? Don't ask," he said. "It would depend a lot on the economy and who's hiring. Can't we continue this over breakfast?"

"Sure." She rolled to her feet.

He picked up two gray cloth-bound ledgers from his desk and took them with him to the kitchen table. "I need to have a look at the books before we make any kind of decision."

"Well," she said, "with all your engineering administration courses, you ought to be able to assess our risks intelligently."

"Hey, don't put the whole decision on me. This is something that has to be right for the both of us. All I'm gonna do is check the facts."

Dan spread cream cheese across two poppy seed bagel halves and took a first bite, leaving a smear of cheese at the corner of his lips. The fingers on his other hand slowly leafed through The Olde Victorian Bookstore ledgers for the 2003 business year. He read on and munched quietly for some time with only an occasional "Hmm" here and there. Tucked between March and April, he discovered a balance sheet that absorbed his interest for another fifteen minutes.

"The average monthly profit is just as Edythe told us. Debt is relatively small—comprised mostly of month-to-month stock replacement purchases. A few hundred dollars payable for operating supplies—no outstanding loans. There is one plumber's bill for 278 bucks, though. Of course, there's always liability insurance and taxes, but they seem manageable."

"What about accounts receivable?" she asked.

"With the exception of twenty-six check purchases last month, they are essentially credit card purchases with an extremely low default rate—less than one percent. Only four checks bounced in the last year, and two of the writers made good on them afterward. Annual losses due to bad accounts were less than a hundred bucks."

Rivka began clearing the breakfast dishes while her husband read on to the December statement. Dan made some notes here and there on a lined pad and then closed the second ledger. He waited through the clinking and clanking of dishes as she solved the daily conundrum of fitting every plate and cup into the dishwasher. Turning around, she caught him staring off into the ether.

"What's wrong?" she asked.

"That's the problem—nothing's wrong. It's just as Edythe said it would be. I can't even find a down side to make an argument with. It's almost too perfect. The Olde Victorian Bookstore is a viable business with more than adequate income for both of us. She's right—we'll never get rich, but it's a comfortable living."

"There's more to the decision than the business," Rivka pointed out. "What if Bernie's care costs go up?"

"Some of the care-giving costs are covered by Medicare. They tend to increase as the cost of living goes up. Well, almost anyway. And even if they went up fifty percent, for heaven sake, the man's eighty-two. How much longer can he live? Statistically, he's already dead."

"That's a terrible thing to say, Daniel. Physically, the darling old man's in pretty good shape—could last years yet. Look how he still retrieves all that amazing poetry."

"All that considered, I think the bookstore might be a risk worth taking."

"If that's the case, it makes me wonder why she's offering this grand gift to us, Dan. Why not accept what the *gonif* offered her? Bernie could certainly live on that."

"As she told us: it's a matter of principle. The Benders worked hard most of their lives to build the business to where it is today. Why should she sell at a great loss to a jobber who will resell everything piece by piece? She'd rather know that their bookstore, their creation, will prosper in our hands. I don't blame her. I think I'd do the same if I didn't have any survivors."

"Then you've made up your mind?" she asked.

"I'm not sure. I'd like to sleep on it one more night. How about you?"

"I can't think of any reason not to go for it, Dan. Will you give up your job, too?"

"Maybe. I think so. I wouldn't want you to have all the fun. Besides, I can always do a little hourly consulting work on the side if we need a buck or two more. I've had a few offers in the past." His keen eyes under dark bushy eyebrows casually scanned her body until his gaze made her tingle.

"What?"

"You're awfully sexy standing there with your robe hanging open. Do you want to go back to bed?"

"I could use a few more z's."

"Z's are not what I had in mind."

"I know. I know."

* * *

Sunday lunch-time business at The Olde Victorian Bookstore proved livelier than usual, and Edythe wondered whether she'd get through the day. It was all too much for her. Around four in the afternoon things slowed down a bit. Leaving Liz in charge, she tried to grab a little rest in the bedroom upstairs. She curled up on the bed next to the big rocker where Bernie was napping. He looked so contented there. She closed her eyes, but sleep wouldn't come. Her mind remained alert and fearful lest she forget some minute detail of Bernie's care. She couldn't imagine anything more that could happen to the Benders.

Twenty minutes later the phone rang. *Liz will grab it*, she thought. But on the fourth ring, she assumed that Liz was busy with a customer and picked up.

"Olde Victorian Bookstore. Yes, this is Edythe Bender. Who's calling, please?"

She repeated the caller's identity aloud to make sure she had it right. "Chief Inspector E. Howard Winston, Bath District

Death Goes Postal

Constabulary. What kind of bad news?...My brother? Dead? Murdered? Dear God, no! Not Abner! How?...Oh, no! Who would do such a terrible thing? You think it might be a Professor Emil Kravitz? Yes, I've heard of the man. He was harassing my brother to share his life's research work. So much so that my brother had to hide his manuscripts. You say Abner named his killer before he died...on the desk blotter? I pray you get this Kravitz person and put the blighter where he belongs. My brother wouldn't hurt a fly. He didn't deserve to die like that. When did all this happen?...But that's more than two weeks ago....The cleaning lady?...His solicitor on holiday? I see. Thank you, you're very kind. Goodbye."

Edythe set the phone back in its cradle. A lone tear caught in the corner of her eye, and she wanted to cry, but there were no tears left. She sighed deeply and shoved both hands into the pockets of her smock. Her right hand encountered an envelope—Abner's forgotten letter. With a fingernail she slit the envelope open and stretched out on the bed once more to read what her older brother had to say.

My Dearest Edythe,

I am concerned about your failing health and hope you are not overdoing. The demanding store and Bernard's Alzheimer's are such a *gonsa* burden to bear. Please take it easy for all our sakes.

That no-good fiend, Kravitz, has been at it again. He wants me to sell him the Koenig matrices and chase. He has some Deutsche buyer for my artifacts. I informed him that everything goes to the British Literary Museum. I already promised them. Would you believe he wants to combine his research with mine and share the credit? That *dreck* he writes, I wouldn't put my name to it. The *momser* just won't take no for an answer. He calls and threatens me every few days. No, dear, I'm not being paranoid.

I've hidden everything important and dear to me. Only the clues in this letter (and the two before it) can rescue these items. You must keep this letter with

the others in a very safe place. This is the third and last clue:
>"*And Mark his many long years in space.*"
>   Love and kisses,
>   *Your Abner*

She brought the letter to her lips. Her kiss offered a final goodbye to the loving brother who had suffered so much in his lifetime. He couldn't be forgotten. His artifacts and life's work had to be protected. She'd put this message with the others. The Shermans would know what to do with them. She trusted Rivka and Dan to do the right thing.

Edythe tried to get up, but abdominal pain struck her. She winced and lay back down, this time on her side. Drawing her knees up, she tried to outwait the attack. She knew her time was growing short. The doctor had to be called. She'd make an appointment just as soon as she put the letter away.

* * *

Emil Kravitz slept on into the afternoon, accommodating his jet lag. The adrenaline of the previous night had placed little burden on his ability to sleep. He'd booked the hotel room for a few nights, paying in cash, and a rooming house nearby would serve him after that. He shaved, dressed, groomed, and left the room with a DO NOT DISTURB sign on the doorknob.

Passing up the full brunch in the dining room, Emil ordered two eggs over, toast, and a *banger* in the coffee shop. While waiting for his breakfast, a steeped pot of Earl Grey tea and a free local newspaper from the desk helped him to relax.

Emil turned to the rooms-to-let page of the classified section and circled several possibilities with a pencil. Not having had anything to eat since the previous day, he savored his food and lingered over a second cup of tea. After flirting with his waitress, she gave him directions to the nearest pharmacy. Two items were high on his list: an Annapolis city map and a hair-coloring kit. A Salvation Army used-clothing store caught his attention on the way. *I could use a few casual things for the coming weeks,* he thought. He made several purchases before continuing on to the pharmacy.

Emil returned to his hotel room to find that the maid had ignored his doorknob instructions. She had just finished tidying up, and smiled at him as he entered.

"What in the hell are you doing in my room, woman? Can't you read the sign, you ninny?"

"I knocked first, sir," she mewed. "I go home at three-thirty, but I hadn't done your room yet. I thought you wouldn't mind."

"But I do mind. I paid for privacy and I'll have it. Do you understand me?" He placed his hands, cupped like claws, on her shoulders and shook her. "What did you see? What did you find in here?"

The young Hispanic maid emitted a sharp scream and, knocking his hands free, backed away. She stood there frozen in her tennis shoes, alternately bawling and screeching. Emil's panic quickly melted into caution, his tone turned to sweetness.

"Okay, okay!" he said. His fingers retrieved a twenty-dollar bill from his wallet. "I'm sorry. I didn't mean to upset you. I thought you were burgling my suitcases. Here!" Emil handed her the bill. "Now please leave me alone."

The maid, tempted by the size of the bill, stopped her caterwauling and cautiously snatched the money from his fingers. Eying him with mistrust, she picked the soiled linen up from the floor and scurried out the door, swinging it shut behind her.

Sitting down hard on the bed, Emil admonished himself for losing his temper. *That's how I wound up killing the old man. I wouldn't be in this mess now if I hadn't lost it with him. There's too much at stake for me to be embroiled in maid abuse. I just can't draw that kind of attention.* He nervously fumbled around in his leather shaving kit for a small plastic pill bottle. He found it and popped two of the lithium pills into his mouth. A gulp of water at the sink helped to wash them down. He crossed the room and again sought the bed, flipping his feet up, and lying back on the pillow to allow his heartbeat to mellow out.

His temper had played a big part in bringing about his

separation from his wife. A month after their marriage the two of them were at each other's throats. They had met standing in line for a Beatles concert in Bath and seemed to hit it off right away. Emil had been teaching at a small boy's school and she attended classes at a local college. At first she moved in with him to share expenses, and he enjoyed the natural benefits. They married three months later. Soon after, he began criticizing her paltry housekeeping. She responded by turning her phonograph music up to deafening to drown him out. For a while he'd stand there yelling and threatening her, and eventually his anger came to blows. After one bloody encounter when she actually fought back, he gave up. He stayed away from their tiny apartment more and more often, wrapping himself up in his new hobby: researching early book editions and rudimentary printing methods. One day his disillusioned wife moved out. He hardly noticed.

Emil managed to shake off his bitter daydreaming about his disastrous marriage. He had better things to do. Reaching over to the nightstand, he picked up the bag from the drugstore, removed the coloring kit, and read the instructions on the box. In the bathroom he prepared and applied the solution to his scalp, even more disgusting than the finger-painting he remembered from first grade. For the next hour he sat at the desk with a gooey wet head and a towel over his shoulders. In front of him lay the city map and the newspaper page with the circled rooms for rent. He then chose the two rental possibilities closest to the bookstore. He'd located The Olde Victorian Bookstore on the map according to the address on the letter he'd filched from Abner's flat. It was on impulse that he'd copied the letter before resealing and reposting it from London's Gatwick Airport.

Once the prescribed dyeing time had elapsed, Emil showered, painstakingly washing out the excess color, and dressed in a clean suit. Studying himself in the mirror, he smugly approved. Goodbye gray. He combed the new color straight back with gel, unintentionally looking like he'd stepped out of a 1940s movie.

It took only fifteen minutes for him to reach the first rental possibility—a narrow three-story Victorian home only four blocks from the bookstore with a driveway on the left and small front porch. A white-haired lady with thick eyeglasses answered the doorbell. She introduced herself as Mrs. Irma Riley.

"I'm here to see about the furnished flat to let," said Emil.

"Oh, yes," she said. "Actually, I have two lovely rooms to rent, and they're both on the third floor—one in front, and the other has a nice view of the garden out back. How long would you be staying, young man?"

"Several months anyway, at least until I find a suitable house for my family. But are the rooms private, ma'am?"

"Perfectly private," she assured him. "I rarely go to the third floor in my condition—arthritis, you know. So you see you'll have to clean up after yourself properly and send your laundry out. I'll provide two sets of linens and such. Bathroom's got a combination tub and shower. No meals in the room and no cooking. I won't tolerate a smelly house and I can't abide someone else's food in my refrigerator."

Emil mentally decided on the rear room as soon as he saw it. He listened to Mrs. Riley drone on, listing her tenant rules before he interrupted her. "I'll take this one. It's just what I'm looking for." He would have said anything to keep her from going on.

"But you haven't heard the rent yet."

"I'm certain a nice lady like you wouldn't take advantage of a newcomer in town."

"Oh, you're a charmer, young man, but the rent is still $195 per month, and I'll want one month's security deposit in advance from you."

"I'm sorry, I left my checkbook at the hotel," he said. "Would cash be okay?"

"Better than okay," she glowed. "When will you be moving in?"

Emil counted out $390 in twenties and tens into her open hand. "Around noon tomorrow. Would that be convenient?"

"Anytime. That reminds me—when you come downstairs,

I'll give you the key."

Emil gave her a courtly bow, barely able to contain his triumph. His strategy, his grand plan, was proceeding even more smoothly than he'd hoped.

Chapter 5

Go for the Ring
Monday, April 26th

The bawling alarm clock wrestled the Shermans from their night's sleep at 6 a.m. Dan swung his hairy left arm out in the direction of the offensive sound. The framed picture of their daughter, Jenny receiving her law degree, toppled from the nightstand on the way. It landed harmlessly on his shoes. "Damn!" he grunted as he silenced the alarm and retrieved the picture. He rolled over on his side, fully expecting to encounter the soft, comforting flesh of his wife's *tush*. Nothing but creased sheets. His eyes popped open in time to catch her padding across the cold wood floor to the bathroom, her soft, broad hips wiggling in a way that delighted him.

"Morning!" Dan yelled. The door closed behind her; certain mumblings from inside may have constituted an appropriate response. With only one bathroom, Dan rolled onto his back and locked hands behind his head to wait his turn. Dan Sherman wondered what his father would say about his son ditching his stable profession for such a risky venture.

Dr. Joseph L. Sherman, MD, may he rest in peace, had been a pillar of advice to Dan, who learned well from him. Fanny Levin Sherman fully supported her husband and son, yet rarely contributed anything constructive to their discussions. At work Dan had to make decisions every day. Now, here at home, he had another one to make. He could tell Rivka had already made up her mind. But what did he want?

Dan grew up in the Westville section of New Haven, Connecticut, quite tall and a trifle too thin for his large frame, which made him awkward in group sports. Instead, he found his own place in varsity tennis and swimming during high school. At Rensselaer Polytechnic Institute he came away with a degree in electrical engineering, graduating in the upper third of his class. After three years of being underemployed at Westinghouse, he took his talents to a small firm, Kambrills Electronics, where he designed one-of-a-kind instruments for the Department of Defense. Now a project manager and principal engineer, he faced a whole new and uncertain career. *If we buy the bookstore, maybe I should keep my job for the time being.*

Last night's debate had lasted past midnight, taking several irritable turns. Still lying on his back as the clock hands crept past 6:30, he took up where they'd left off. "I've never sold a book in my life," he argued to the closed bathroom door. "And neither have you. So what makes you think we'll be decent booksellers?" He heard the toilet flush.

"You don't sell books—they sell themselves," she retorted when the water stopped running. "Readers pick up books for three reasons: they've glommed onto an author they know and love, or they're intrigued with the cover, or it's been recommended to them. The sale is clinched by either the jacket blurb or the first few pages. The salesperson is there only to direct traffic and write up the sales ticket."

"So we're trading rewarding careers just to be traffic cops?"

"You might say that. Actually, there's a little more to it. You get to meet some pretty interesting and intelligent people, too." Her voice took on a lilt. "Besides, books are living things. We'd be perpetuating them. Maybe that sounds corny, but anyway…" The door opened, and she stuck her tongue out at him while running a brush in quick upward strokes through her curls.

"I thought you enjoyed being feature editor," he said. "All

that interactive wordsmanship in a newsroom atmosphere. The interviews you do. Isn't that what you always tell me?"

"Yes, but there's stuff I don't talk about," she replied, still standing in the doorway. "Throw in the low pay and a domineering boss and I'm about as content as a kid with measles."

"Wow! That's news to me. I had no idea. Say, when do I get a shot at the bathroom? I'm about to go critical here."

"Now!" She ducked to one side as he dashed past her.

Rivka glanced at the clock, then reluctantly sat down on the edge of the bed. Hunching over, pushing a clenched fist against her mouth, she looked like a female version of Rodin's *The Thinker*. Despite all the hours they'd talked, she had to ask. The splashing rhythms of the shower had stopped, and she called out, "Dan? If we go ahead with this, are you going to keep your job or what?"

Silence. Then he opened the door a few inches, letting a rush of steam out. "I haven't quite decided what to do. I'm not much of a risk-taker."

No kidding, she thought. He'd taken tough night courses at Johns Hopkins and gotten his MS in Engineering Administration. But he'd resisted going for the higher management slots.

"I know what you're thinking, Rivvie," he said. "You're wondering, what was the point of getting my master's? The way I look at it, total responsibility for making profit in a fixed revenue environment is a pretty scary thing. High stress, low satisfaction. I've seen a whole parade of middle managers fall on their faces and get shoved out the door. I love hands-on engineering, designing equipment. It's tangible, creative, something I can put my name to. Especially when we win the bid for a big defense project."

"I hear you, honey, and I'm not being critical." The mosquito-buzz of his electric razor halted their discussion. She jumped up and dressed quickly, in a teal blue top and slate slacks. Rivka didn't do many things in her life slowly. Her M.O., her modus operandi, was perpetual motion, and she liked herself that way. But her mother had always called it *shpilkes,* and her father liked to tease her: "Ants in your pants, Rivvie."

The razor's buzzing stopped. "What about our house?" asked Dan. "You love West Annapolis. Are you willing to trade our three-bedroom town house for cramped, one-bedroom living quarters upstairs from a bookstore?"

"That will be hard, I admit it," Rivka said, "but we're empty nesters now, and I'm just crazy about that adorable old Victorian house. It has so much character."

"It is in pretty good repair from what I can see. Besides, it's paid for. But what about when the kids come?" Dan stepped into the room and began to dress: tan khakis, beige dress shirt, and brown tie arrayed with golden retrievers. He'd grown up with one and still missed her.

"You know what?" Rivka's voice brightened. "We wouldn't have to sell this place right away. And we can't count on Jenny and Mort visiting for awhile anyway, can we? The baby's due any day."

As he threaded his leather belt through pants loops, Dan said, "I guess we could find a place for our sofa-bed and a crib in the mix of things."

Minutes later they emerged in the kitchen, ready to tackle breakfast. Dan turned a crinkled white paper bag upside-down and shook. From the assorted pile of bagels strewn on the Formica counter, he selected a plump sesame-seed one and sliced it through. Popping two halves into the toaster oven, he pushed the handle down to Top Brown.

She handed him a fork. "Here. It's easier to get the hot bagel out than with your fingers."

"Don't give me an extra fork, babe. It's just more work for us."

She sighed. "The dishwasher does the work, dear, and we have to use it. Besides," she brightened, "if we don't, it'll get low self-esteem."

They'd been down this road before. Many times. Dan cracked a helpless half-smile, like *What's the use?*

Rivka bit her tongue instead of carping further, and brushed the excess seeds and crumbs into the sink. She poured the coffee and sat opposite her husband in their cozy breakfast nook. Dan unwrapped a square slice of rubbery, fat-free American cheese, and arranged it on half his bagel.

"You know," he said between munches, "they ought to make a round cheese slice so it would just fit this shape."

"They do. Provolone, great on Italian food, but too salty for breakfast. And you wouldn't have the fun of nibbling it to size. Besides, there is no standard size for a bagel."

"Maybe I could invent one," he said. "But I guess I have a few other things to do."

Rivka smiled. "And another great *Whydon'tcha?* bites the dust. Dear, I know you like things to be standardized, but that's ridiculous."

"No it's not. And not only that, all business invoices should be one size so they fit in my small accordion file. But anyway—"

He lifted his Washington Redskins mug and toasted: "To The Olde Victorian Bookstore."

His wife's body jerked to military-ramrod attention. The jam-laden English muffin fell out of her hand, upside down on her plate. "Darling! Do you mean it? You're going in on it with me? You decided between your shower and coffee?"

"Yeah. Like I said last night, I can do some consulting work if I need an engineering fix. I think I'm ready—it's now or never."

"Seriously, Dan, are we sure enough to let Edythe know our decision?"

"Hey, now you're the one with cold feet."

A flush rose on Rivka's face all the way from her chin to her forehead. "I'm terrified and thrilled all at once. Do you want to call Edythe, or shall I ring her from my office?"

"You do it, hon, I'm expecting one hell of a day. There's so much to wrap up." There would be forms to sign, heavy-duty ones. He'd be required to swear never to divulge critical information involving his Classified work.

* * *

Between ten and eleven a.m. Rivka called the bookshop five times and got only the answering machine. She had no intention of leaving such an important message. Trying once more, Edythe picked up and responded in out-of-breath words.

"It's been absolute bedlam, Rivka. I've never had a morning like it. We've had customers coming out of the woodwork. I shouldn't complain. It's money in the bank, except some *schlemiels* come in to read everything in the store without buying. Others want to return books after reading them, and everyone has questions to ask. So not everything's a sale. Somebody got persnickety with Liz, and she was in tears. I had to console her, too. Don't ask."

"Should I call back?"

"No, no! I'm sitting for a change. So tell me already, what did you two decide?"

"How do you know we made the decision?"

"Simple. Why else would you be calling in the middle of the day and from work, no less. *Nu?* You got something to say?"

"Yes, Edythe, we've decided to make the big leap. We'll do it. I hope we won't regret it."

"I'm sure you're making the right decision. You won't rub elbows with the Rockefellers, but you'll find it rewarding in so many other ways. Unfortunately, there's good and bad: pests and freeloaders. It's a business like any other."

"Whoa, Edythe, you don't have to convince me. We're ready to sign on the dotted line. If we can't make a go of it, we'll make sure there's enough left to take care of Bernie for you. When shall we come over to sign the papers?"

"I spoke with my lawyer. You know Joel—Joel Wise from the critique group."

"Of course I know him," Rivka assured her. "He's a member of our synagogue, too."

"Joel can have a draft agreement ready for tomorrow evening. We could initial the draft and handwrite any codicils necessary until he has a formal document to sign."

"Hmm, you were that sure of us. What time?"

"I'll close at eight. He'll come by around eight-thirty with the draft. We could do it then."

"Fine. See you tomorrow evening."

Edythe heard Rivka hang up her phone, but she sat and stared at the stacks in front of her with an anxious, pained expression until an automated voice reminded her to hang up.

***

At Metheford Academy, Detective Sergeant Fenton Thorwal stood beside the desk of the man he'd just finished interrogating, Colonel Ansel Felsworth. "Mind if I use your phone to call in, Colonel?"

"Of course not, Detective Sergeant." The gaunt-looking headmaster in a faded WWII uniform slid the phone closer to the homicide investigator, watched him dial, and listened for the response.

"Chief Inspector Winston."

"Sergeant Thorwal here. Sir, I've tracked that Kravitz fellow to his place of work."

"And where is that, Sergeant?"

"Metheford Academy, sir, It's a small, military-style school between the A4 Motorway and Camden Road just north of Bath. I'm told the place caters to teenage boys with keen minds and a prior lack of discipline."

"Get on with it, Sergeant, I haven't got all day. What did you find out about him?"

"Well, sir, Kravitz usually teaches English language and history."

"Usually?"

"Yes, except no one here has seen him since April fourteenth. Colonel Felsworth—he's the headmaster—has taken his classes since then, and the school is already advertising for a replacement."

"Have you checked Kravitz's flat?"

"Constable Browden just phoned from his flat in Lansdown Crescent. Kravitz wasn't home. The resident manager let him in. She hasn't seen the man for at least two weeks. As far as she can tell, all his clothes and personal things are still there. She says he's always been pleasant and paid the rent on time. There's no missus, but he keeps the place pretty well tidied up. After going through the place himself, Browden concurs—the man's a bloody neat freak. She told the constable that it's not like the man to go off without telling her. She's afraid that some harm has come to Kravitz."

"Is she romantically involved with Kravitz?" The Chief Inspector cleared his throat.

"The lady says she cooks a meal for him now and then, but no. Somehow, I get the feeling she'd like it to be something more than that. She describes him as dapper, a smart dresser with jacket and tie, and 'always a hanky peeking out of his breast pocket.' According to her, the man is quite distinguished looking with a well-trimmed salt-and-pepper beard and mustache."

"What about height and build?" asked Winston, "Something concrete to work with."

"All she said is 'Taller and heavier than herself.' That would make him something over five-foot-six and twelve stone."

"Any family or friends that she knows of?"

"Browden asked her: apparently none."

"What about his students? Have you interviewed them yet?"

"They're on holiday this week and most have gone home. But I did talk to one youngster from the Continent who stayed on."

"What did he tell you?"

"Not much—something about an argument Kravitz had with one of his other students in the loo. This youngster couldn't hear anything, but the professor had a grip on the boy's shoulders and was shaking the lad like some cocktail. The blighter stopped when he discovered his audience."

"For God's sake, Sergeant, did you get the boy's name?"

"Yes, sir! It's William Petty, sixteen years old. But we're forced to wait until the student body returns from holiday next week."

"And why is that, Sergeant?"

"Because the headmaster refuses to release his home address and phone number without a parent's permission."

"Did you tell him he was impeding a homicide investigation?"

"Yes, sir, I did, but he says he has an obligation to the boy's family to uphold."

"Hand him the bloody phone, and let me talk to the man."

"Here, Colonel, Chief Inspector Winston wants to talk to you."

Colonel Felsworth took the phone. "What can I do for you, Chief Inspector?"

"I'll have a court order for the boy's address and phone number down there first thing in the morning. You might as well release this information right away."

"I'll see what I can do." Felsworth's usual commanding voice shrank before the Chief Inspector's booming demands.

"Thank you, Colonel." Winston ended the call abruptly. He stroked his jowly cheeks with one hand and picked up the open Fraume file with the other. As the breeze from the open window ruffled his wavy white hair, he could only speculate on what would turn a mild-mannered academic into a cold-blooded killer. And what was the lad's part in all this?

Chapter 6

On the Dotted Line
Tuesday, April 27th

Dr. Berthe Helmen's office was on the second floor of the Kimmel Cancer Unit at Johns Hopkins Medical Center. Edythe had always found the long drive to East Baltimore worth the extra effort, but today, in her weakened condition, she had been forced to rely on a volunteer driver. More than just her oncologist, Dr. Helmen had succeeded in fulfilling the roles of friend and personal adviser as well, dispensing a no-nonsense truth in a compassionate package. Edythe added her name to the sign-in list and took a seat along the rear wall. She picked up a magazine and attempted to read. Concentration evaded her altogether, and she put the magazine down. Then she heard her name.

The nurse measured Edythe's height and weight and took her blood pressure. Exchanging her street clothes for a flimsy hospital gown, she waited in an exam room for another five minutes. Anatomical charts covered the walls of the too chilly room.

Doctor and patient embraced for a moment and then, "How are you, Edythe?"

"Eternally tired. I have so little energy. Everything I do is an effort. Dear God! I believe I'm going to need more chemotherapy."

Berthe Helmen said nothing in response and began her examination by listening to the patient's heart. When the remaining visual and palpitation tests were completed, the doctor told her friend to get dressed and meet in her office next door. Edythe expected the worst as she sat opposite Berthe.

"My dear, your cancer has advanced much more than I would have predicted in any similar case. In fact, it's nothing short of a miracle that you're able to get around the way that you do. Yes, chemotherapy might be in order, but I'm not convinced that your system is strong enough to withstand another bout. I want you in the hospital this afternoon—tomorrow at the latest. We need to run a battery of tests to find this out."

"Oh, Berthe, couldn't it be next Friday? There's so many things I have to do to get my house in order. My poor Bernie. I have to make arrangements for him and the store."

The doctor stared at her friend, weighing the danger of waiting ten days against the peace of mind the short reprieve could bring. "Then next Friday it is."

* * *

At eight-fifteen that evening the Shermans came through the front door of the bookstore, climbed the stairs to the reading room on the second floor, and took chairs at the massive conference table.

"Be right with you," Edythe called from behind the closed bedroom door. "Joel hasn't arrived yet. He should be here any minute."

"No hurry," Dan called back. "We're early anyway and we've made ourselves comfortable."

The bedroom door opened and arm-in-arm the two Benders entered the room. Edythe led Bernie to an armchair beside the kitchen wall, eased him down, and kissed him on the cheek before taking a chair next to the Shermans. They chatted for twenty minutes and then heard Joel Wise coming up the stairs. The chubby balding lawyer laid his briefcase on the table and greeted everyone. The level of anticipation rose as Joel slid a sheaf of legal papers out and read aloud. He answered questions, re-read whole sections aloud, paraphrased, modified, and otherwise explained what the two parties were agreeing to. Then the parties initialed each page and signed their commitment to the terms of the document on the last page.

"When do you enter the hospital?" Joel asked when they'd finished.

"I thought I'd get Bernie settled in the nursing home tomorrow afternoon and sign myself into the hospital by the end of next week. The way I'm feeling right now, there's no time to lose. I don't know what the good Lord has in store for me."

"As crowded as those places are, how can you be sure to get him into a decent home so quickly?" asked Joel.

"I've had his name on the waiting list for almost a year now and I've been paying for his reserved room since it became available three months ago."

"Everything's happening so rapidly," remarked Rivka. "It's kind of scary."

"I know," said Edythe, knitting her emaciated fingers together. "If, for some reason I don't come home again, my personal things should go to Liz. Anything else you can give or throw away."

"Hey!" exclaimed Dan. "That's no way to talk. You are coming home again."

"You're a dear, Dan, but let's be practical. It's been written in the *Book of Life* already."

"You are such a brave woman, Edythe," said Rivka. "I have to admire the way you handle so much adversity."

"Not everything," she said as the tears flooded her cheeks. "Not everything. I can only take so much, and now…"

"Is there something else? Bernie?"

"No, not Bernie. About four o'clock this afternoon I received a phone call from Chief Inspector Winston of Scotland Yard. He was calling from the Bath Constabulary in southern England—Homicide, to be precise." A shudder went through her ravaged body as she struggled to continue. "He regretted to inform me that my brother, Abner, was found dead. He was brutally murdered—

strangled with a phone cord. They think robbery was the motive. The police have launched a full investigation and promised to get to the bottom of it." She looked up beyond the room's ceiling. "Dear God, why? My poor brother wouldn't harm anyone."

"Good grief!" exclaimed Rivka. "Oh, Edythe, as though you didn't have enough on your plate. Now *this*!"

"You have our deepest condolences, Edythe," said Dan in a choking voice. "If there's anything we can do…Please…" he couldn't finish.

"Do the police have any idea what was taken?" asked Joel.

Edythe shook her head. "Not really. Abner spent the last fifty years of his life tracking down antique illuminated typeface molds and some gadget used to clamp print type in place during the printing process."

"Do the police have any idea who could have done such a thing?" inquired Dan.

"I think I was able to help them," said Edythe. "Abner had some competition in the quest for these molds, and he was quite worried about the lengths this man might go to to obtain them. In fact, my poor brother was so upset that he hid the treasure. He sent me clues to where it's hidden, but he disguised them in an elaborate conundrum parceled out over several letters to me. He also described and named the man dogging him — a Professor Emil Kravitz of some nearby academy I can't remember the name of. The police seemed particularly pleased with this information."

"Great!" said Dan. "I hope they get the bastard."

"Edythe, I hope you're safeguarding these letters," warned Joel.

"I am, but they won't mean much to anyone else."

"Oh, my dear friend," said Rivka, "I hope this doesn't put you in harm's way."

"I don't think there's any chance of that," she said. "Besides, what more could anyone do or threaten me with? I'm not afraid of this evil Emil character. Eventually, that is, once I've extracted the puzzle clues, I'll forward copies of the actual letters to the Bath

Constabulary as evidence against Kravitz."

"That's another good reason to be doubly careful, Edythe," cautioned Rivka.

* * *

Chief Inspector Winston sat at his second-floor desk in the Bath Constabulary affixing his full name to official correspondence and the lone initial "E" to requisitions and memos. The signature had a flowing broad and narrow flair to it, but the lone letter resembled a backward three, an ampersand with its north and south tails missing. A stack comprising more such paperwork awaited him in his IN tray. Each time he leaned forward with his pen, the large wooden swivel chair complained of his excess weight. But the chair wasn't the only complainer. His superintendent, his doctor, and his wife had all chimed in on the subject. Forty years on the job and he still spent more time pushing paper than solving homicides. The low brown box on his desk emitted a short buzz.

"Yes, Mandy," he said, holding the TALK lever down.

"There's a gentleman waiting to see you, sir. A Mr. Andrew Beecham. He says he's a solicitor."

Winston let loose with something akin to a grumble and came back with, "What's he want from me?"

After a few silent moments Mandy responded, "He says he has some information on the Abner Fraume case."

"Well now, woman, you just send Mr. Beecham on in."

"Yes, sir."

A tallish, scholarly-looking man seemingly in his late thirties preceded Mandy through the office door and briskly strode directly up to the desk. Winston struggled to stand and accept Beecham's handshake.

"Mr. Beecham, what is this information you have on the Fraume case?" Winston indicated a chair for his guest, then dropped back into his own.

"Let me begin by telling you that I represent the interests of the British Literary Museum. One of the curators at the Museum saw Fraume's death notice in the *London Times*, and since our client is heir to certain valuable assets of the deceased, we were, of course, notified to protect those assets."

"Let me ask you, Beecham. These assets: might they be a motive for murder?"

"I can assure you that is the case, Chief Inspector. Though I must admit the thieves would find these assets extremely difficult to fence."

"Ah, museum quality, I presume, but what is the actual nature of these relics?"

"Abner Fraume has willed the museum not only some early sixteenth-century typefounders' collections, but excellent research that documents their historical passage from that period to the present."

"Typefounder? I'm afraid I don't know that term." Winston turned his chair to the bookshelf beside his desk and reached for the dictionary.

"No need for that, Chief Inspector." Beecham, elegant in a three-piece pinstriped suit, crossed his legs and launched comfortably into a lecture. "You may recall that the Gutenberg Bible was most likely the earliest Western book printed from moveable type. By moveable, I mean text was composed by assembling interchangeable type: metal slugs with individual letter faces that could be used over and over again and then rearranged to compose and print other text. These slugs were manufactured from a soft pot metal that picked up and laid down ink on paper in a uniform manner. The manufacture of type involved pouring or 'founding' molten pot metal into inverse letter molds. As the years passed, the demand for books increased; the typeface eventually wore down and needed replacement. Hence, typefounders, respected craftsmen and guild members of the times, hand-engraved the letter face in relief on the end of a hard metal punch. The pounded punch left a sharp inverse letter impression in a hollowed-out brass block called a matrix. In fact, the typefounder supervised the entire replica-casting procedure for new type."

"I see," said Winston. "My wife uses printers' type drawers

for her miniature bric-a-bracs. I'm assuming these relics are collections of printers' type?"

"Yes and no," said Beecham, suppressing a frown to hide his growing impatience. "The relics are typeface molds, actually. This particular collection is quite rare. In order to add to the esthetic value of the early books, the initial character of each chapter began with an ornately decorated, oversized letter. Traditionally, these larger characters were laboriously hand-painted by local monks directly on the finished pen-and-ink page text that others in their order had scribed. As a result, many of the themes were religious in nature. A half-century after Gutenberg, a man named Gerheardt Koenig found a way to create oversized typeface molds in a floral and fauna décor. Eager to replace the costly, labor-intensive handwork, printers turned to Koenig's typeface molds, subsequently called matrices. The man's artistic genius led to fame and fortune. Here, let me show you."

Beecham slid several photographs out of a thin manila envelope and spread them on Winston's desk. In one photograph, two bi-fold wooden boxes lay open with sorted type in partitioned bins on either side. Another shot revealed close-ups of several typefaces and the matrices they came from, all lying on their individual oilskin wrappings. A number of additional photos contained printed proofs of typefaces, demonstrating the ornate details of the oversized font. The last photo was of a gray metal framework abutting two metric rulers that indicated dimensions of thirty-eight by twenty-four centimeters. The two-centimeter engraved border bore an intricate floral pattern that pleased the eye. The frame was hallmarked by Koenig and dated 1507.

Winston picked up the last photo and examined it closely. "What is this thing?"

"It's called a *chase*," answered Beecham, warming to his intent audience. "A chase is used to hold moveable type as a unified cluster on the press during the printing process. Spacers and wedges, called *quoins*, keep the typeface from moving within the rigid frame. What you see here in these photos, together with Abner Fraume's research, is worth a fortune to the museum. It is heavily insured, so naturally we are concerned over the whereabouts of these items."

"I see," said Winston. "You think our murderer has made off with assets bequeathed to the British Literary Museum?" He picked up the Fraume file from the desk and held it toward Beecham. "Your material indicates that he's a thief as well. I can assure you that the crime scene inventory does not reflect any of your so-called assets. Our people were quite thorough."

Beecham nodded, his tone conciliatory. "I'm sure they were, Chief Inspector. We didn't expect that these treasures would be in plain view. Several months ago, Professor Fraume notified the museum's acquisitions director that he was secreting the assets outside the city and that his sister in the United States would inform us where to look for them when the opportune time came. When we saw his death notice, we knew we'd have to dispatch one of our solicitors to Annapolis to meet with the sister. Unfortunately, our assets specialist has been on assignment elsewhere, so I may have to head across the pond myself to sort things out."

Winston's moon face turned a deeper shade of pink. "That might be risky, Beecham. Remember, you're dealing with a killer. And I must caution you further that these assets of your clients are likely evidence in a homicide investigation. In fact, it's imperative that you leave the photos with us so that we can identify the missing items if and when they are recovered. Evidentiary procedures might complicate or delay your client's acquisition; however, if you keep me informed of your progress, I promise to speed things along for you."

Andrew Beecham gathered up the photos and slid them into the original envelope. He pushed them across the desk to Winston. "That's fair enough, Chief Inspector. I've retained copies for the museum. Thank you for your time." Beecham shook the man's hand, snapped his briefcase shut, and stood up to leave.

"One moment, sir," rumbled Winston. "There's still one thing bothering me. Why didn't Fraume just turn the relics over to the museum for safekeeping? Why bother with the secrecy thing at all?"

"We believe it had something to do with the manuscript—some piece of verification he was waiting for perhaps. The old man was still tinkering with his text, too. Could be one of those things where the author is never quite satisfied with his work. I suppose we'll never know for sure."

With a jaunty stride Beecham left the office, taking care not to betray his pessimism. Would these treasures ever see the light of day in the museum?

Chapter 7

Among the Stacks
Tuesday, May 4th

Shortly after lunch, Liz Nathan pushed the tea cart laden with books—some new, some misplaced, but each needing to find its Dewey-decimal lodging among the stacks. She'd collected them from all the reading room tables. Her gray smock, featuring a caricature of the Great Bard, lent her a businesslike appearance. One might even consider the bookstore clerk pretty if it weren't for her mousey-brown hair pulled severely off her too narrow face. The squeaky-wheeled cart came to a stop in the third aisle, amid the current mystery best sellers, between Kellerman and Kemmelman. Liz's petite form darted quickly and efficiently among the aisles, a sparrow looking for seed.

 Liz hadn't noticed the man with tinted glasses watching her from the end of the stack until he asked to squeeze past her in the narrow aisle. She obediently crushed her slight form against the shelves to make more room for him, but he managed to rub against her backside with more than just a brush. She felt her face redden, unsure whether the move had been accidental or aggressive. How could she dare confront a customer with such an accusation? In any case, the sensual contact provoked a certain pleasantness, unfamiliar to her. In a few quick peeks she determined that the clean-cut man stood a few inches taller than her own five-foot-six and that she approved of his camel-colored sport coat and brown slacks. *Not bad looking, either*, she thought.

Without glancing back at her, the man hesitated a few feet beyond the cart, then selected a volume from the shelf. He looked up and caught her staring at him. He smiled. "Don't you just love being in the midst of all this great reading material? I feel like a kid in the middle of a leaf pile. I want to toss armfuls up in the air and watch them float to the ground."

"Oh my goodness, sir," she exclaimed naively. "Not the books, please! I'd have to put them all back again."

He laughed at her expressed innocence, but wondered if it had been put on. "Not to worry, little lady. I wouldn't stir a page on your shelf."

"You're laughing at me, aren't you?" Her face flushed again, and she turned away to arrange more books in a shelf space.

"You wound my sensibilities, ma'am. Why would I make jest of you?"

Annoyed, Liz deliberately remained busy while maintaining her silence and shyness, all except for an escaped sniffle. The next thing she knew, a hand had gently clasped one shoulder and slowly turned her to face him. A droplet broke from the corner of one eye and flew down her cheek. He pulled a folded handkerchief from his pocket and cautiously moved closer with the intent of wiping the tear away. She tried to back off, but he held her shoulder in check.

"Allow me," he bowed in comic fashion. "Dear lady, I have offended you. I want to make amends."

"I'm all right," she said, slipping from his grasp. "And please don't talk to me in that patronizing tone. I *can* manage myself."

"I'm terribly sorry, miss. Is there some way I can have you think better of me?"

"Not necessary!"

"I know. You'll dine with me, say tomorrow evening at…at the Chart House? No strings, I promise." He held his right arm up at a forty-five degree angle. "Boy Scout's honor."

Liz thought for a moment. The Chart House. *This guy sure-*

ly hasn't done anything all that appalling. In fact, he's simply been a gentleman with a sense of humor. A little fun, that's all. What's wrong with me? I've become an oversensitive cat with the man—all too ready to hiss and claw. Besides, he's rather good-looking, in a distinguished way. Smooth, too.

"I really couldn't," she answered. "I don't even know your name."

"Ah, but that's easily remedied. My name is Everet Mark Kantor, but all my friends call me Ev."

"Mr. Kantor. Ev. I, ah…"

"Please!" He held his hands and fingers together in the Asian *sawadee* prayer pose.

Liz stared up into his pleading eyes and relented. "I'd be honored, but you don't know my name either."

"Well, then."

"It's Liz, Elizabeth Nathan."

"Would seven tomorrow evening be a propitious time? I could pick you up here, Liz."

"That would be lovely, Ev."

He handed her Eisenstein's *The Printing Press as an Agent of Change*, the book he'd plucked from the shelf. "Can you tally this up for me?"

"Certainly," she said. "Come with me to the register, and I'll ring it up."

Afterward, she slipped the receipt into a bag alongside the book and handed it to him. He took the bag, winked, and moved to leave.

"Tomorrow, my dear, I'll see you then." He waved from the open door.

* * *

Later that same afternoon Margaret Fraume eased the phone back down in its cradle. It had been some time since she'd answered to that name. And now this weird call. Some solicitor in Bath, England, had telephoned to inform her of her father's death.

How he'd known where to find her was some kind of mystery. Despite the fact that her father had left a moderately sizeable estate, she wasn't even mentioned in his will. Everything went to Aunt Edythe in Annapolis, Maryland. Margaret supposed she deserved that after the way she walked out on her father at age twenty-two to marry that screw-up ex of hers. Living with a would-be rock musician hadn't turned out the way she'd hoped. The only thing she had hung onto was her ex's name in case the bum somehow made it big.

Too many years had passed for her to feel anything for either parent now. She couldn't remember her mom at all—the woman had died when Margaret was still in diapers. *Maybe a good lawyer could get me some money. And maybe I could sidle up to Aunt Edythe for a handout,* she thought. *Auntie Edie couldn't be a young chicken any more. No kids, either. We met only the one time. Probably wouldn't even remember her long-lost niece.* But Margaret couldn't imagine a reason that would induce her to remain in boring Philadelphia. Her present job sucked, and the current boyfriend wasn't any prize either. *Perhaps I could catch the bus down to Annapolis over the weekend. After all, they have lawyers there, too.*

* * *

Mid-morning the next day, Vernon Levant stopped in front of The Olde Victorian Bookstore and looked down at the folded newspaper in his hand to check the address. He stepped through The Dungeon doorway and made a beeline for the cashier's desk. Edythe sat behind the desk making a few notes.

"Hi!" Edythe made a concerted effort to be perky as she greeted the thirty-something customer, sporting a solid rust tie in the V-neck of his patterned sweater. "That's a lovely sweater you're wearing, young man," she added.

"Thank you, my mum knitted it for me," Vernon answered, giving off just a trace of Brut aftershave.

"Well, now, may I help you?" she inquired.

"Yes, of course," he replied. "I'm here about the ad."

"Ad?" she said. "What ad?"

"This one." He held up the folded paper for her to see.

"Oh, for the mystery critique group," she said. "I forgot that Rivka had even placed it. She mentioned it last night, but with all I have on my mind this morning, I let it slip."

"Rivka?" he asked.

"That's Rivka Sherman. She's doing the recruiting. We've lost a few people over the last few months. Never know where our lives are going to take us, do we? A shame, too, such a prolific bunch of writers."

"Sounds ideal. Can I sign up?"

"Sure. Just leave your name and address right here." She pushed a yellow-lined pad and pencil in his direction.

"How about my business card?" Vernon reached into his pocket and pulled out a black vinyl folder from which he extracted a single white card. He laid it on top of the pad so Edythe could read it.

Edythe picked up the card and read aloud: "Independent Insurance Sales, Vernon Levant." She examined the telephone numbers, e-mail and street addresses, and commented, "Oh, you live right around the corner on Lafayette Street."

"That's just temporary, ma'am. This is a whole new territory for me. I'll get around to a more permanent place later."

"Where were you before this?"

"Hartford, Connecticut."

"I thought I detected some kind of accent." She smiled at him.

"I grew up in the Midwest."

"What kind of mysteries do you write? What's your genre?"

"I prefer the police procedurals mostly."

"Well, as the ad says, we'll meet a week from Thursday at 7:30 p.m. upstairs in the reading room."

"I'll be there."

Edythe watched the newcomer leave the premises. *Nice*

looking young man, she thought. Although she was certain they had never met, there was still something familiar about him. Was it his accent or the military shine on his shoes and sharply creased pants?

* * *

Later that morning Edythe left the store in Liz's keeping and climbed the stairs to the Bender apartment. In the bedroom Bernie edged back and forth gently in the wooden Kennedy-style rocker with an expressionless stare. He smiled contentedly at her as she regarded him. The day of reckoning had arrived, and he had no inkling of what was about to happen. Edythe had dressed him as she had for so many months. Her uncertainty of just what Bernie could comprehend made her task more difficult.

One suitcase stood on the floor already closed. Another sat on their bed with its lid open and nearly full. *How do you pack a man's bag for the rest of his life?* Edythe asked herself. *How do you tell the one you love most in the world that he has to leave you and can't see you anymore? How do you make him understand when you don't understand yourself?* Under the circumstances, she decided to tell him a little white lie.

Edythe pulled the small stool from under the vanity and dragged it over to the rocker. Sitting opposite him, she could still see remnants of the handsome, romantic, and intelligent man she'd married in 1941. It was as though their whole life paraded before her, and tears painted her cheeks. Edythe shook her head and wiped them away with the back of her hand. Steeling herself for the job ahead, she regained control.

"Bernie, honey, I've got to go into the hospital for a few days. It's not serious and it's just for a few days. So I've made some arrangements for you to have a little vacation while I'm gone. It's in a nursing home where they'll be able to take good care of you day and night. They're coming at eleven o'clock to take you there in a van. It's almost that now. I love you, Bernie." She took his hand and squeezed it.

Death Goes Postal

Most of what Edythe had told him went beyond his comprehension, but for the first time he sensed that something was about to happen. She helped Bernie to his feet and led him to the little elevator. They descended to the ground floor, and as soon as they stepped out of the elevator, she saw the van and two attendants standing curbside. The Dungeon door had been left open. Edythe shuddered at the sight of it and what it represented for Bernie. She walked her husband through the store and out to where the van waited. She had wanted to go with them and get him settled, but the nursing home administrator told her it was better this way. They were experienced in this sort of thing.

As the two men came to take hold of Bernie, she kissed her husband firmly on the lips and let go of his arm. He turned to look her in the face and a pained expression came over him. *Does he know?*

"Eeeee…deeee…deeee…deeee…deeee!" He reached out for her as the space between them increased.

Even after strapping him in the van and closing the door, Edythe could see the same syllables forming on his lips. Liz came through The Dungeon door with his two suitcases and set them down on the curb. When the attendant finished loading and the van drove off, Edythe sat down on the front steps and sobbed. She felt as though she had betrayed him. Liz helped her to stand and led her up to the bedroom on the second floor.

* * *

At a quarter to five that evening Liz climbed the stairs to the Bender apartment. She found Edythe sitting in Bernie's rocker stuffing giveaway clothing into a black trash-can liner. Piles of his suits, shirts, ties, and underwear formed a moat about her. Liz stood in the doorway, unsure whether she should leave her employer, mentor, and dear friend in such a terrible state. Or, for that matter, whether she should intrude on so personal a mood. Edythe solved the dilemma by sensing Liz's presence and lifting her head.

"Good grief, Liz, don't just stand there—come on in. I was

merely getting rid of some old discards that neither of us will be using any more."

"I was about to close up. The day's receipts and the cash bag are in the cash drawer under the register. You said you didn't mind my closing an hour earlier to get ready for my date with Everet Kantor. I want to go home, shower, and primp a little bit, but first, I wanted to see if you were all right."

"You run along, dear, and have fun. By the way, where's your gentleman friend taking you?"

"To the Chart House for dinner."

"Well, well, sounds nice," said Edythe.

"Yeah, I hope he'll spring for lobster, but I don't want to break the bank on our first date."

"Why don't you lock up on your way out. I'm going to be at this for awhile and I'm in no mood to deal with customers tonight."

"Well, if you're sure."

"I'm sure, so go already!"

* * *

At six-forty Liz returned to the bookstore, rode her Cushman scooter around back, and chained it to the porch railing. She removed a pair of black pumps from the saddlebag and exchanged them for the penny loafers she had ridden over in. The clerk, transformed into a paisley skirt and aqua velvet jacket, walked around to the front. Almost deciding to use her keys to open the store and wait inside, she thought better of it. *No need to disturb Edythe—better wait outside in the pleasant evening air.* Seven o'clock came and went, causing Liz to fret about Ev coming at all. She felt self-conscious standing outside alone.

At nearly quarter past seven, a blue Honda Prelude pulled up to the curb. As she approached the car, Ev got out, ran around the car, and opened the passenger door for her.

"Sorry I'm late," he said, closing the door after her. "Were you waiting long?"

"Not too long," she answered, unsure whether to scold him or not after witnessing such a gentlemanly act.

"I had a business call I just couldn't hurry along," he explained.

Ev threaded his way down Duke of Gloucester Street and over the Spa Creek bridge into Eastport. On the far side he proceeded for a few blocks, and turned back toward the water between two warehouses. They left the car and walked on the wooden pier adjacent to the restaurant building. There were major sailing craft all around them—some even qualifying as yachts. Delicious aromas of foods grilling inside wafted together with the faint smells of the tidal waterfront. Halyard hardware tinkled against metal masts in a chorus of tiny bells while the short chopping motion of harbor waves rocked, lifted, and dropped hundreds of nearby craft.

The hostess informed them that they could wait in the lounge overlooking the water until their table was readied. Ev suggested Frangelico on the rocks to Liz, and without knowing what it was, she agreed to it anyway. She took her first sip only moments after the waitress set down the two thick glasses.

"Ooh! This is yummy," she said. Her eyes lit with delight.

"I thought you might like it." He took her hand in his and squeezed gently. "It's hazelnut liqueur."

"I do, really. Gee, you look so handsome tonight in your gold turtleneck and blue blazer."

"You should wear your hair around your face all the time. It's prettier that way."

"Thank you, you're sweet. Oh, look." She turned to face the massive picture window next to them where a parade of white sails continued gliding to a halt at the yacht club slips on the town side of the water. "It's the Wednesday afternoon sailing races. They're finished now. I haven't watched this in years."

"It's a first for me. I've never seen so many sailboats in my life." Ev sensed the presence of a hostess behind him and turned away from the window.

Their table was now ready, so they followed the young

woman into a huge room with thick wooden stanchions supporting a network of timber arches that spanned the building's width. Planters with tropical flora further divided the room into intimate islands. Waiters and waitresses all wore Hawaiian aloha shirts with bright floral designs. The hostess showed them to a pier-side table and left them to peruse large menus burned into cutting boards. Ev seemed so taken with the overall effect that Liz felt obliged to explain that the building was once a part of Trumpy's Yacht Yard—builders of the former presidential yacht Williamsburg.

Ev ordered prime rib and salad bar. Liz chickened out of the lobster and settled on crab cakes and salad bar. A bottle of Merlot topped off their order. They ate and drank with only a modicum of polite conversation until Ev finished and blotted his lips with his napkin.

"Liz, did you, by any chance, notice some rather large, flat packages being delivered to the store in the last few weeks?"

"Oh, we have large packages being delivered all the time. The usual. Books, magazines, promotional stuff—they're flat. Why do you ask?" She drained the last of her wine.

He poured the remainder of the bottle into her empty glass. "I understand, but packages containing books, magazines, and those other things have a familiar shape. These particular packages would be heavy, a few inches thick and quite large."

Liz bristled. "That describes many books, especially reference and coffee table books, so I wouldn't really find a package of that shape unusual. What are you getting at? I don't understand why you, a perfect stranger until yesterday, would be asking these questions about our store deliveries."

"Uh, sorry, Liz. I, uh, I was expecting a delivery from my boss and I may have given him the store's street address instead of my flat address. Big goof on my part—nothing too mysterious here. Ah, that pendant you're wearing, it looks very elegant."

"It was a gift from my grandmother when I graduated from high school. It's been in the family for years." She held the carved-cameo profile of a woman in a gold filigree oval up for him to have a closer look.

"It's quite old, Italian, late nineteenth century, Neapolitan I should think," he said, turning it over carefully, letting his pinkie brush over her bony neck. "I can tell about these things. Insurance appraisals and that sort of thing."

"You're very thoughtful and sweet," she said.

He released the pendant and watched as she settled it just below her collarbone. She was suddenly aware that his eyes lingered there for a second or two, and this made her blush.

"I'm sorry. Would you like me to order dessert?"

"I'm stuffed. I loaded up on salad bar. Everything was so delicious."

"How about another bottle of wine?"

"Oh, no thank you. I've got a bit of a glow on already and I do have to drive home from the store." Her eyes drifted to the now sunless view beyond the window. "In the dark, too," she added.

"I could drop you at home," he offered.

"Thanks, but then I'd have to leave my scooter and walk to work tomorrow." Liz gathered her belongings and pushed her chair back to stand. She glanced down at her watch. They had been sitting for several hours.

Ev signaled the waiter and paid the check with six twenties. Outside, along the water's edge, they strolled hand-in-hand in bright moonlight for the next half hour and then drove back to the store.

Chapter 8

On Coming and Going
May 8th through 15th

Edythe entered the hospital on Friday morning and was assigned a bed in one of the primary care units. On Monday, instead of the expected chemotherapy, the patient was scheduled for a battery of tests to determine whether she could possibly tolerate any more of the gut-writhing treatments. So, through the following Thursday, Edythe underwent the damnable tests, eerily knowing…yes…even feeling the results before their completion. There would be no new regimen of chemotherapy. Her frail physique no longer had the strength to endure such an invasion. She would never see her dearest Bernie again, nor ever return to their beloved bookstore. Her hospital room would be the final stopping place, and from the pain she felt, the time ticked closer and more personal—a day or two at the most. At least Bernie would be well taken care of.

* * *

Rivka always poured a cup of canned chicken broth over the barbecued chickens she bought at Graul's market. She hadn't cooked a chicken from scratch in years. She had just slipped this bird into the microwave for zapping when Dan walked in the door.

"Well, I gave my two weeks notice today," he announced.

Death Goes Postal

"And they told me I could take them as paid vacation—company policy—something to do with proprietary secrets and such. So, as of now, I'm unemployed."

"I gave my one-week notice on the first. Today was my last day," she replied. "I hope we're doing the right thing with both of us quitting our jobs like this. Maybe one of us should have hung onto rationality—at least until we know if we're going to make a go of it."

Dan clutched a handful of his bushy hair and grimaced. "Hey, that's like wanting to turn back in the middle of a swan dive. Now is not the time." He sniffed the air, then peeked in the microwave window. "Chicken?"

"Are you calling me chicken?"

"Nope, Rivvie, I meant chicken again?"

"Guilty as charged."

"Any mail today?"

"Just the usual *schnorers*. I just gave in December to all my charities, but they're never satisfied. All the trees they're killing." Rivka saw Dan's expression. He'd heard it a hundred times. "Okay," she said, "I'll get off my soapbox."

He grinned. "Until tomorrow."

* * *

Dan and Rivka had been asleep for five hours when the phone jangled them awake. The illuminated digits on the clock revealed eight minutes past four. Rivka leaned over her husband to reach the phone on his nightstand.

"Hey! That hurts," he complained. "Take it easy on my ribcage with that elbow of yours."

"Well, I wouldn't have to lean on you if you'd pick up the phone when it rings." And into the phone she said, "Hello!"

"Is it Jenny?" he asked, noting the tentative look of hope blooming into sheer joy. She responded with a nod and kept talking.

"Hi, Morty. Eight pounds, five ounces? Nineteen inches?

Both are doing fine. Rebecca Ellen Cohn. That has a lovely sound to it. She wants me to come. Right! We're both coming. We'll be there late this afternoon. Morty, you go home now and get some sleep. Hugs and kisses!"

"So we've got ourselves a new granddaughter. I guess there's one advantage to being unemployed. We can go to Jenny without guilt."

"Right. I'll tell Liz we need a week before taking over. So, Daniel, let's put this show on the road. Heave your lazy butt out of bed and get packing. There's a lot of driving between here and Akron. Maybe we can start before the rush hour traffic."

"Sure, babe, but hold on just one minute." Bare-chested, in boxer shorts, Dan swung his legs onto the floor, jumped up, and encircled his wife's waist. He spun her around to face him. When she saw the deep seriousness, his eyes misted over, she responded, tightly winding her arms about his neck.

He whispered, "We're so lucky, Rivvie. We're the luckiest parents in the whole world. And I'm so lucky to have you."

"I'm lucky too, darling, and I love you, you handsome grandpa, you."

* * *

On Thursday morning Edythe's oncologist gave her the dreaded test results, confirming all her suspicions. She watched Dr. Helman make some adjustments to the I.V. drip rates. A matter of days now, and the good doctor had promised to make her comfortable. After Berthe had left her, she lay there in the hospital bed thinking. Abner's letters became the lone piece of unfinished business. Edythe felt compelled to convey their location to someone of trust. Not having been able to reach either of the Shermans by phone at work or at home, she tried Liz at the store and got through. Edythe instructed her to close up the store and come to her room.

Liz didn't care much for hospitals, but she hadn't counted on having to scrub her hands with disinfectant in front of a nurse and wear a surgical mask. Unfortunately, the patient had neither the time nor the inclination to put on her wig, and the shock of seeing Edythe nearly bald drove the petite bundle of sensitivity into tears.

"Liz, darling," Edythe said, "pull yourself together. You'll have plenty of time to simper and weep after I'm gone. I've got something very important to tell you and I must have your complete attention. It's a message, a clue in a fine line of poetry that my Bernie can help decipher."

"Why can't you just tell me what you want to say? Why does it have to be in code? Don't you trust me?"

"I love you, Liz, and I'd trust you with my life, however long that might be. But you sometimes have a loose tongue with strangers. I know you don't mean to, dear, it's just your naive nature. And my hands are much too shaky to hold a pen or pencil anymore."

"Who is this message for, anyway?"

"It's for the Shermans, but I haven't been able to reach them."

"They drove to Akron early this morning. Jenny had her baby."

"Oh, that explains it. I trust Rivka and Dan implicitly, and outside of you and them, in this whole wide world, I don't know who else to confide in. Besides, my brother was murdered trying to protect this secret, and I don't want to put you in harm's way."

"Lordy, murdered you said?"

"That's right. The British police called me last week. His letters name the killer and reveal the location of his precious life's work. His murderer will stop at nothing to get his hands on them. I've hidden the letters in the second floor reading room. However, the Shermans should be able to find them with a little help from both you and Bernie."

Liz started to poke around in the depths of her purse.

"What are you fussing with, Liz?"

"I'm looking for something to write with."

"You can't. I mean you mustn't write this down. I want you to memorize it."

"But I can't remember things all that well," Liz whined.

"It's only two lines, dear."

> *"Her early leaf's a flower;*
> *But only so an hour."*

"Is that it? Doesn't make any sense to me, Edythe."

"It's not supposed to. Daniel and Rivka will make sense of it after they consult with my Bernie. Make sure they take it to him. Now repeat the lines back to me."

* * *

Liz reopened the store that Thursday afternoon after returning from the hospital. She had a lot going around in her head. *Edythe really doesn't trust me after all these years and after all I've done for the Benders. I can keep her damned secrets. I'll show her how reliable I am. I'll take the verse to Bernie myself and find those letters. And give them to the Shermans.*

* * *

Later that evening a floor nurse, responding to a life-signs monitor alarm, discovered Edythe's inert form. The RN had adjusted her patient's morphine drip only twenty minutes earlier to enable her a painless passage. An on-duty oncology intern confirmed her death shortly thereafter. Edythe was buried the next afternoon well before sundown of the oncoming *Shabbat*. According to her own instructions, she was interred without a formal funeral service in the congregational cemetery. Her cantor said the appropriate words while Liz, Joel, and a few others stood silently in attendance.

Chapter 9

A Boy-Scholar and the Critique Group
Bath and Annapolis—Wednesday, May 19th

Winston responded to the intercom on his desk. "What is it, Mandy?"

"There's a Constable Martha Higgins here with the Petty lad and his mum, sir."

"Show the lad and his mother in. I'd like to have a few words with him."

"What about Constable Higgins, sir? She accompanied the lad all the way from Metheford Academy."

"She's got nothing to do with the case. Give her a bloody cuppa or something."

Seconds later, Sheila Petty and her son were shown into the Chief Inspector's office. Winston stood and shook each of their hands. Mrs. Petty, a large woman with light brown ringlets framing her round cheeks, and Will, a tall, bookish boy with rimless glasses, took seats opposite Winston. The Chief Inspector sat and turned on a cassette recorder.

"I'll get right to the point. I've asked you here because you appear to be the only connection between a murder victim and our leading suspect. First, what is your relationship to Professor Fraume, young man?"

"I do—I mean I did odd jobs for the old guy, sir, and he'd pay me six quid a week."

"What sort of odd jobs? Anything unusual or illegal?"

Sheila Petty shot Winston a dagger-look. "M' son's a fine student and 'e wouldn't do anythin' illegal like. Smart, too, 'e gets good grades, 'e does."

Winston cleared his throat. "I was speaking to the boy, ma'am."

"Oh no, sir!" The boy shook his head. "Nothing like that. I'd post letters for him, get groceries, and tidy up the place a tad. Errands and things—that's all, honest."

"I was told that Fraume had a cleaning lady."

"He did, but that old bag only came every fortnight—maybe too long between for him. Besides, I did all the other things, too."

"Other things?"

"Well sometimes he'd send me to the library to copy some reference passage or bring home a book for him."

"He trusted you with his important research, lad?"

"Yes, sir! Professor Fraume said I had all the makings of a fine research scientist. We got along great, sir."

"Now, Will, this is important. Were you ever present when Professor Kravitz paid Fraume a visit?"

"They knew each other, sir?"

"Yes, lad, they did. What was *your* relationship with Emil Kravitz?"

"He was my history and lit teacher."

"Nothing more? I have a police statement from one of your classmates saying he witnessed an argument you had with Kravitz." Winston glanced down at the typed report in front of him. "Yes here it is. '...grabbed Will by the shoulders and shoved him up against the wall.' I should think that's hardly a normal teacher-student reaction. Do you?"

"No, sir!"

"Perhaps you'd care to tell me what that row was all about."

"My term paper."

"What in God's name did you put in that paper to elicit

such criticism? Why would he resort to such drastic means, lad?"

"I really don't know, sir, but it definitely was *something* he read in my paper. He wanted to know all my sources—I'm quite sure about that."

"Go on, lad, tell me about the paper. What was it about?"

"It was a research paper on the history of modern printfounding. All the way from Gutenburg to the present."

"Printfounding?" repeated Winston. Mentally he recalled Beecham's description of typefounders.

"Yes, sir. The casting of individual pot metal type for printing purposes."

"Why would that subject make Kravitz so angry?"

"I'm not sure he was all that angry—more like excited, especially when I told him that Professor Fraume was my major research source."

"Did he think you plagiarized the professor's materials?"

"Oh, no sir. I used all my own words and told it like a series of short stories or vignettes. He may not have liked a research paper done in that form. Or it may be that he didn't read my footnotes and bibliography at the end."

"Apparently he didn't," remarked Winston with a quizzical look on his face. "Isn't that a bit of an ambitious undertaking for a youngster of your age and term? A good deal extra work, too."

"M' son's a bit of a genius, sir," interrupted Sheila Petty. "They tol' m' so a long time ago. Gets it from 'is pa, 'e does."

"Indeed," said Winston. "I'd like to see a copy of this term paper, lad. It sounds as though it might contain some motivational evidence."

"Maybe I could send you a disk or something, Chief Inspector."

"Yes, please do. Did Kravitz harm you at all?"

"Not physically, but he sure did scare me some."

"Thank you for your cooperation with our investigation." Stopping the recorder on his desk, Winston walked around and put his hand on Will Petty's shoulder. He asked his two guests to step out to the reception area and wait while his secretary typed up their interrogatory. He told them he would like them to check the document for accuracy and add their signatures to it afterward.

* * *

The Shermans drove the seven hours from Akron, Ohio, pulling up to the front door of their West Annapolis home close to six p.m. on Wednesday. They unloaded the luggage and sorted through a week's worth of mail before settling down at the dinette table for hot soup and sandwiches.

"Have you checked the phone messages yet?" asked Dan. "There should be a whole bundle of them in a week."

Rivka pressed the PLAY/PAUSE button to the answering machine to scan the incoming messages. The first three were telemarketers followed by a desperate plea from Edythe to phone her as soon as possible. Then two instant hang-ups, another plea from Edythe, and a colleague of Dan's from work calling to wish him well as he'd missed saying goodbye. More assorted telemarketers and hang-ups preceded a message from a troubled Liz Nathan—Edythe had died the previous Thursday. If they got back in time, the interment service would be two-thirty on Friday, the fourteenth, at the Kneseth Israel Cemetery on Defense Highway. Rivka finished with the mail and decided to dial the store number.

"Liz? It's Rivka. I'm sorry we missed the service. Well, we're certainly going to miss her. Did she mention why she wanted to reach us? No? Has Bernie been told yet? I see. Would you like help telling him?…Uh-huh…I understand. What about the bookstore? Closed since last Friday. You planned on opening tomorrow. That's fine with us. Liz, is there something else wrong? You sound like you were about to tell me something else. What's wrong, dear? Are you sure? Okay, then. We'll see you in the morning."

Rivka hung up the phone and looked over at Dan. "I guess you heard everything."

"Yeah, you repeated everything for my benefit. Poor Edythe. She sure was a tough old lady. They don't make 'em like her anymore." Behind his horn rims he blinked away a few tears. "Is Liz going to tell Bernie?"

"Yeah, on Sunday. But when I offered to go with her, the poor girl refused. Several times she tried to tell me something and then backed off. I couldn't get her to open up to me."

"Don't tell me Liz wants to quit on us now. Was she just hanging on for Edythe's sake? Is she afraid to work for us?"

"I don't think so. But something's going on, that's for sure. I'll have a talk with her in the morning."

* * *

On Thursday morning Liz opened the bookstore at the usual nine a.m. She took the CLOSED sign out of the window along with the placard informing the customers of Edythe Bender's death. The Shermans joined her just before noon after tending to their laundry, food shopping, and other pressing errands. Rivka's impromptu *tête-à-tête* with her troubled employee yielded at least two reassurances. Liz needed the job and had no intention of leaving. She also declared herself to be very comfortable with her new bosses.

Pressing Liz further about what was troubling her would only prove upsetting, so Rivka put an arm around Liz, comforting her, and confiding that the store's continued success hung in the balance. "We're depending on you," she said. And this statement educed an upward curl of Liz's thin unpainted lips.

Leaving Liz at the cashier's counter, Rivka spent the entire afternoon learning the layout of the store. If she was to be of any help to the customers, she had to know how to find any book by author, title, or subject. Dan, on the other hand, spent his time getting familiar with outstanding orders, receivables, and payables. He began making lists of things to remember and things needing a change.

Overall, business was a bit slow for a normal Thursday, as some of the regulars weren't aware the bookstore had opened again. That evening Dan sat down with Liz behind the checkout counter reconciling the day's receipts. They resolved all the cash with each of the day's sales, and Liz separated the register change for the next day from the nightly bank deposit. Dan took the small zippered bank bag with him as he and Rivka retreated to the upstairs reading room to wait for the critique group's arrival.

Liz remained to close the store. About to place the CLOSED sign in the tiny window of The Dungeon door, she stepped aside as a man with red-brown hair bounded into the store. "May I help you?" she asked.

"Yes," he said in a loud voice. "I'm here to join the mystery critique group. My name is Levant—Vernon Levant."

"Oh, yes! You're the insurance guy. I saw your card in the drawer."

"That's me, all right." He tipped a hand to his temple in a near-salute.

"Dan and Rivka are already here. You can take those stairs on the left to the second floor." Her gaze followed the ruddy-faced, well-manicured gentleman until he ascended out of sight. *Scary*, she thought. *A bit too sure of himself. And his cologne is a tad too strong.*

"Ahem!"

Liz wheeled around and faced a mature man with sandy-brown bristly hair who had entered the store behind her back. Without a word, he held out a newspaper clipping. Liz immediately sized him up as the strong, silent type.

"Yes?" She recognized Rivka's ad.

"I'd like to be a part of the mystery group. Am I in the right place?"

"Yes. And you are?"

"Edington, Spenser Edington, but most people call me Spence."

"And I am Peggy Morris," said a tall, large-breasted woman who suddenly appeared next to Spence. "Oh no, we're not together," she added. In her mid-forties, dressed entirely in black, her Goth look was broken only by streaks of platinum blonde running

Death Goes Postal

through her jet-black Dutch-boy haircut.

"Nice to meet you both. I'm Liz Nathan. Your meeting's on the second floor." She pointed to the staircase.

In a few minutes the rest of the group started to meander in. Regulars Frieda Forrester and Heather Germain had driven over together, and Joel Wise came in right after them. Newcomer Garry Posner arrived next. Liz had already locked the front door when Everet Kanter showed up and pounded on the wood. Liz let him in, and the two of them climbed the stairs together, conversing amiably as they went.

On the second floor, in the middle of the large reading room, sat a monstrously heavy banquet table in dark unpolished wood. Tonight, only three of the fourteen faded velveteen chairs remained empty. An unmatched pair of antique crystal chandeliers hung over each end of the table, bathing it in readable light. On the cream-colored wall facing the stairs hung four travel posters in clear plastic frames. The first advertised Spain's Andalusia with sandy plains and white-washed, mountain-top villages. The second enticed the traveler to Britain's Cotswolds, featuring thatched roofs and rolling green countryside. The third offered the autumn brilliance of New England's trees in their prime gold amid town squares, quaint shops, and churches. The remaining poster boasted the New Orleans French Quarter during Mardi Gras. Below the exotic posters, ringing the room, bulging bookcases housed close to a thousand books on domestic and world travel.

Rivka came out of the kitchen and addressed the group. "I'm Rivka Sherman, and this is my hubby, Dan. Why don't we go around the table and introduce ourselves while I check on the hot water for tea and coffee. There's cream, sugar, and sweetener on the table."

"Hey there! I'm Garry Posner. That's Garry with two r's. I'm a plumber, formerly of Baltimore," said the man in a black GI buzz cut.

"Hello, Joel Wise here, attorney at law," piped up the round-face man with a smile "And no lawyer jokes, please."

"*Bonsoir!* Heather Germain, high-school French teacher," said the woman with the long, loose red hair, sitting next to Joel.

"Frieda Forrester, waitress over at the Double T Diner," offered the petite lady with the short, bobbed black hair.

"Vernon Levant, Insurance!" said the grinning man with broad shoulders. "I'm an independent adjuster, so if any of you ever need a little adjustment, just let me know."

"I'm Liz Nathan. I work here in the bookstore," she said in her usual timid voice.

"Hey gang," responded the woman with the two-toned hair. "Peggy Morris. Just arrived from Philadelphia a few days ago."

"Everet Kanter, corporate accountant. I just transferred in from Harrisburg, Pennsylvania."

"Spencer Edington—call me Spence," said the man in the last occupied chair. "I'm in sportswear sales."

As though Lord Byron also wished to announce his own noble presence, he suddenly leapt from one of the island travel shelves to the great table, trotted regally across it, and dropped to the floor on the opposite side before retiring to the bedroom.

"Oh, what a beautiful black kitty!" exclaimed Peggy. "Does it live here?"

"Oh yes. That's Lord Byron," replied Rivka. "We inherited him from the Benders. He's the knightly watchcat for the bookstore."

The group chatted informally for nearly half an hour getting acquainted. And then from the high-backed chair closest to the kitchen, Dan called the meeting to order. He introduced himself and asked for a moment of silence to commemorate the passing of Edythe Bender. Dan said they regretted missing the burial service, but that they'd been in Ohio since the arrival of their brand-new granddaughter a week ago Wednesday. After a hearty round of *mazel tovs*, Dan informed the group that he and Rivka had purchased the bookstore from the Benders and that they intended to run the store in the same manner. He added that they would be moving into the second floor residence within the week. He also apologized

Death Goes Postal

for not being able to answer phone responses to Rivka's newspaper ad for new members.

"Did anyone get to see Edythe while she was in the hospital?" he asked.

Liz put down her self-guilt long enough to respond. "I saw her that very afternoon. And she died that evening. I knew she was sick, but I didn't know it could happen all that fast."

She described Edythe's upbeat, businesslike demeanor while a lone tear escaped down her cheek. However, she made no mention of the dying woman's last request. At least not to the group. But the desire to brag about her secret quest was burgeoning, about to burst if she didn't tell someone. On the one hand, telling the Shermans would mean the end of her part in the mysterious poetry game. On the other hand, telling anyone else would be an admission that Edythe had been right about her—she really couldn't keep a secret. Her eyes darted to the head of the table. Rivka had gone into the kitchen, and Dan was busy getting Peggy's personal data on the sign-in sheet.

Perhaps there was someone she could tell after all. Having spent an entire evening with Everet Kanter, Liz decided that he was a man she could trust. Ev was also a man she wanted to impress.

"I've got a mystery to solve myself," she murmured.

Ev looked blankly at her. She decided to raise her voice slightly, certainly higher than she had actually intended.

"I've got a mystery, some poetry clues to solve on my own." Liz tried again.

"What kind of mystery?" Ev's eyes glinted behind horn-rimmed glasses.

"Some letters," she explained. "Very valuable letters, and the poetic clues tell the whereabouts of these letters. Mr. Bender, the former owner of the bookstore, is going to help me with the clues." Her pale, gaunt cheeks reddened as she felt the air suddenly become charged. Both Vernon, seated beside her, and Spence sitting on the other side of Everet, had turned to face her with alert postures.

"What kind of clues are we talking about?" asked Spence. "I'd be happy to assist you."

"Do you know what's in the letters?" asked Vernon.

"Don't answer those questions," Everet cautioned, his words coming out almost as a command. "I can give you all the help you need."

"Gentlemen," she responded sheepishly. "I'm sorry I mentioned this at all. I'm quite certain I can accomplish everything myself. Thank you anyway." Afterward, she noticed she'd collected the attention of Frieda, Garry, and Joel as well. She pulled her unbuttoned cardigan tightly around her chest, as if to prevent herself from spilling even more information. Biting her lower lip, she fixed her gaze on the sheaf of papers spread out in front of her.

Rivka returned to the table, confident and quite striking in her black top, gray slacks, and suede red jacket. Taking over the meeting, she described the goals and procedures of a literary critique group. She told them to ignore errors in spelling or punctuation. "That's for the individual writer to work out, with plenty of literary software available on the Internet if you need it. We have more important fish to fry—if you'll excuse the cholesterol-ridden cliché," Rivka said. She loved turning clichés inside out, as much as Dan reveled in punning. "The main goal of our critique group, my friends, is constructive criticism. We want to always focus on the positive. Of course we'll be pointing out characterization flaws, description deficiencies, plot anomalies, general inconsistencies, et cetera. But please accompany these points with suggestions for sharpening the prose and enhancing reader interest. Above all, be helpful, be kind, and be useful in your criticism. And now Heather Germain is going to present her latest short story, 'Bent on Violence,' for our group's perusal."

"I only made five copies," Heather apologized as she passed them out to share. "I didn't realize we'd have this nice a turnout." She adjusted her granny glasses and read aloud:

"The Morton family had just sat down to a late dinner when they heard a blood-curdling scream, followed by a loud pounding at their back door."

Intent on her reading, Heather didn't hear the low-keyed snicker and a female voice whisper, "Here we go. It was a dark and stormy night."

Chapter 10

Verse and Reversal
Annapolis—Sunday, May 23rd

The Olde Victorian Bookstore felt strange, even unnerving to Liz without Edythe's presence. While the Shermans were in Ohio, she had fretted about her future. *There are two of them, very smart people. Will they still want or even need me after learning the business? Two bosses—how will that work?*

But on their return, Rivka's warm reassurance put her at ease. "Oh, Liz, we couldn't do without you. You are so valuable here with your expertise and you're so good with the customers. We're thrilled that you're staying on."

For a week now Liz had put off her promise to tell Bernie of Edythe's passing. Today, Sunday, her routine day off, she couldn't delay the dreaded task any longer. And Liz thought of another promise she'd made to herself: that she could and would find Abner's hidden letters without anyone's help. *After all*, she thought, *I was an English major, I graduated cum laude, and I'm working in a bookstore. I should be able to get Bernie to decipher a simple poem for me.*

Liz descended to the first floor vestibule of her apartment building and rolled her moped out from under the staircase through the door to the street. Out front, as she put on her safety helmet, her thoughts returned to Thursday's critique group meeting. A knot of anxiety settled into her chest. She'd blabbed too much as usual, and too many members had taken an interest in her letters. Then, something about a book she'd sold crept into her mind, but the title escaped her. Forgetting a title—that alone bugged her. Liz shuddered as she snapped the chin strap in place. Upon pulling away from the red-brick, eight-unit apartment building in the Historic District, she immediately imagined people, cars, taxis, and bicycles following her, but one by one each turned and went its own way.

Arriving at Bernie's nursing home, Liz parked her moped on the sidewalk and chained it to the nearest telephone pole. Strapping her helmet to the scooter, she spun the dial of the combination lock and proceeded up the walkway to the jalousied veranda in front of a sprawling white clapboard edifice. Three steps and a door at one end of the narrow enclosed veranda led to a path between two rows of patients in rockers—each pallid face with its own toothless sunken cheeks and zombie-like stare. Only one of the patients rocked, and he did so at a remarkable rate. Liz stutter-stepped through the lot, bobbing from side to side, eventually reaching the lobby and reception desk without stepping on any toes or seeing a familiar face.

"Mr. Bernard Bender?" she asked the woman at the desk.

"Room 205. He's the new one—second floor," she responded cheerily and pointed. "Elevator's over there."

Liz stepped off the elevator on the second floor and followed the descending numbers to 205. Bernie stood by the bed facing the window, not moving at all. She called his name, and he turned slowly to face her. There was nothing wrong with his hearing. He just didn't seem to recognize her voice.

"What should I do now?" Bernie asked no one in particular. Although he possessed the usual blank expression, a new sadness and a hint of fear had emerged around the eyes, perhaps some degree of knowing.

"Would you like to sit by the window, Bernie?" she asked. "It's sunny and warm by the window."

At the sound of her voice his head tilted in a remote flash

of understanding. He repeated: "Window…sunny and warm." Because he made no move, Liz led him in slow shuffle-steps to it and coaxed him to sit down. She heard him mumble "Dee-dee-dee-dee." Confused at first, she attributed the mumbling to a distortion of his late wife's name. When she didn't respond to him, the mumbles took on an angry tone.

"Edythe?" she asked.

His face turned toward the sound of her voice, but still with a blank expression. "Whyyy?" he drawled. He continued to stare straight ahead.

Liz thought, *Now or never.* She had his attention and she didn't know to what degree or for how long. *I can always tell him about Edythe afterward,* she decided.

"Bernie! I've got two lines for you, honey." She recited:

> *"Her early leaf's a flower;*
> *But only so an hour."*

A fresh gleam lit in the old man's eyes, and a curl of a smile appeared as he responded to the challenge, rising awkwardly out of the chair:

"Robert Frost, *Nothing Gold Can Stay.*"

> *"Nature's first green is gold,*
> *Her hardest hue to hold.*
> *Her early leaf's a flower;*
> *But only so an hour.*
> *Then leaf subsides to leaf.*
> *So Eden sank to grief,*
> *So dawn goes down to day.*
> *Nothing gold can stay."*

Liz wrote quickly and accurately, but missed the last two lines, so she repeated the one before them. Bernie obligingly repeated the entire poem for her, and she got it all down on paper the second time around. The words seemed to proclaim the frailty of life's most precious gifts in the face of time, beginning with the fall of man. But Liz didn't know any more about the letters than she did before. Edythe's intent made no sense to her.

"Is that all?" she asked him.

Bernie patiently repeated the verse a third, then a fourth time, and when Liz failed to acknowledge satisfaction, his expression filled with anger, his cane rose to strike her, and his voice screamed, "Dee-dee-dee-dee!"

A nurse, responding to the ruckus, rushed into the room, took the cane from his hands, and forced Bernie to sit once more.

"Dee-dee-dee-dee!"

The nurse raised her eyebrows and motioned for Liz to leave the room. She took one of his hands in her own and stroked his forehead with her other, brushing the frail wisps of white hair away from his puckered face. She poured water from his pitcher onto a washcloth and cooled his brow and cheeks in slow swipes.

Liz reluctantly backed out of the room, ashamed of the turmoil she'd caused. In the doorway she called to the nurse, "I never got the chance to tell him that his wife died. I wanted to break the news to him gently."

The nurse spun around and gave her a skeptical look. "Yes! Yes! I'll tell him later. Right now I've got to get him calmed down. Please leave now and take your friend with you."

Liz backed down the hall with her hand clutching the collar of her blouse. She was so upset that she failed to register the words "your friend."

"Dee-dee-dee-dee." The pitiful wailing followed her all the way to the elevator.

Liz started her moped and whipped back to her apartment, almost oblivious to the traffic or the route she took. She rolled it into the street level vestibule and into its space beneath the staircase, re-chaining it to the nearest staircase baluster. While bending over and spinning the tumbler of her combination lock, she sensed the presence of another person behind her and attempted to turn. Before she came about, a gloved hand reached around her and clamped across her mouth. She tasted leather and tried to scream, but the pressure against her lips and teeth stifled all sound but a pained moan. Her fingers grasped furiously at the glove. Then something hard poked into the small of her back. A raspy robotic-like voice told her:

"If you want to live and stay healthy, you won't let out a peep. Otherwise, I'll make sure you won't scream. Ever!"

Her muffled wailing continued until the object poked still harder into her back. Then it stopped. The gloved hand released its grip slowly, testing her intent with every relaxing nerve and muscle. The inhuman voice contraption assured her that no harm would come to her if she did everything it said.

A sniffling Liz agreed to cooperate—not to turn around, but to hand over her purse, and remain quiet. Out of the corner of her eye, she caught a fleeting image in the hall mirror of a black knit ski mask over a tan trench coat. When he caught her peeking in the mirror, he shoved her face away with the gun's cold steel barrel. Eyes down, afraid to look elsewhere, she saw a brown wing-tip shoe move close to her right foot. She quickly surrendered her handbag.

While holding his prey under the gun, the attacker divided his attention between watching Liz and searching her handbag. His gloved fingers found her apartment key ring and he held it up to her face, taunting her. "Let's go to your apartment. Now!" With the gun he nudged her forward, up the seven steps, and down the long hall to 2-B, her door.

He handed her the key. "Open it," the chilling rasp commanded. He observed her whole body shake with fear, and her teeth chatter uncontrollably. "You think I'm interested in your body, little lady? Don't flatter yourself."

"Please don't hurt me," she pleaded. Her hand wobbled as she unlocked the door and swung it inward.

He'd had enough of her sniveling. Placing his right foot squarely on her narrow backside, he kicked, thrusting her forward into the living room. She tripped over the sofa leg, landing face down on the rug. Scant daylight illuminated the simply furnished room. His threatening form towered over her, reminding her not to turn over. Liz raised herself on hands and knees and scooted across the room away from where she'd fallen.

Still in possession of her handbag, the dark figure decided to upend its contents on the coffee table. While searching for her billfold, he came across the folded piece of paper on which she had written the Robert Frost verse.

"What's this?" the rasp demanded. "You like poetry? You're not the type."

"No, sir. I'm not. I don't even understand it," she whimpered."

"Then why do you carry it around in your purse?"

"It's supposed to be very valuable," she blubbered.

"Why is that? How valuable?"

"Maybe there's a clue in the verse. I'm not sure." She was more than willing to tell the voice anything to be left alone.

"A clue to what?"

"I don't know. I heard her talking about some letters hidden in the critique room."

"Heard who talking?" he demanded.

"Edythe!" she replied. Liz had turned over and now sat on the floor facing him. She clutched her skirt tightly around her bent knees in defense posture.

"Letters? From whom?" the metallic voice inquired.

"I'm only guessing—Edythe's brother, maybe."

The questions ceased for a few minutes while her assailant thought about this. *Critique room. The verse might be all I need.*

He stuffed the paper in his trench coat pocket.

"Take it!" she shrieked. "It's probably what you want anyway."

He picked up the billfold and spread the leaves to look inside.

"Take my money, too. Just let me go. I won't say anything to anybody about this."

The thief extracted all the currency from her billfold, and dropped it back on the coffee table. Liz shakily got to her feet and bundled her cotton jacket tighter about herself with the idea that it might protect her, then folded her arms across her chest. He took a step toward her.

Now Liz knew for certain that she didn't have the stuff adventurers are made of. *Edythe had wanted me to take the lines of poetry to the Shermans. Why didn't I do as I was told, and nothing like this would have happened to me. God help me. I didn't expect anything like this.*

He edged closer, and she envisioned some lecherous leer beaming out from behind the black mask. Backing away each time he advanced, suddenly Liz realized she stood in the bedroom doorway, a dead-end.

* * *

Emil Kravitz waited for nightfall to make use of the information he'd gleaned from Liz Nathan. On Franklyn Lane, standing on the sidewalk in front of the converted Victorian home, he regarded the mysterious silhouette that towered toward the moonlit sky. Gabled peaks, octagonal turret, Gothic windows—an edifice that nightmares are made of. The dull glow from nearby street lamps wove the quaint wooden detail into intricate gingerbread. Just as he expected, not a single light shone inside. The busy bookstore by day had turned dark, quiet, and intriguing. Muffled sounds reached out from distant traffic on West Street.

Although the Shermans had already taken over the business, they weren't due to move in until Monday. Emil knew that from attending the critique group meeting. He also knew that sloppy breaking and entry had caused him a great deal of trouble in his college days. But those blunders had happened long ago. Calling upon his newly acquired lock-picking expertise, Emil gained access to the vacant bookstore via The Dungeon level door. The old lock gave up easily, but the heavy door groaned painfully through every inch of opening and closing.

Emil accustomed his eyes for a moment to the darkness just inside the closed door. His memory strained to recall the path

Death Goes Postal

from The Dungeon entryway to the staircase somewhere in front of him and to his left. He wouldn't employ the Maglite torch until absolutely sure it couldn't be seen from the street. His carefully measured steps probed through the unsure space until something weird brushed against his trouser leg. Emil reached down to check only to find nothing there. After a few feet more, a similar brushing occurred to the opposite leg. He bent again with the same result. Had it ended there, Emil would have attributed the strange sensations to his own imagination. They continued while he stood in place, and then, while kneeling, he noticed two green orbs in motion, and from these, feline eyes, greenish almonds, he knew he'd encountered the watchcat, Lord Byron.

Emil bent down once more to stroke the cat's fur only to elicit a static spark that momentarily jarred both man and beast. After the electric contact Lord Byron decided to keep his distance, but most obligingly led the way to the staircase. The cat took a number of steps and turned to ensure that he was being followed. Reassured, he repeated the process until they reached the stairs. Within the closed stairwell, Emil pulled the torch from his trench coat pocket and illuminated their path to the second floor critique meeting room.

Lord Byron still led the way, for he hadn't been fed since Liz put out a meager portion of leftover Friskies Saturday afternoon. At the second floor landing they parted ways. Lord Byron turned left into the kitchen and pattered up to the empty bowl in the corner next to the bathroom door. Emil stepped into the critique room and sat down at the massive table. He took out the slip of paper that he'd wrested from Liz and unfolded it. He stared at the entire recorded verse for a few moments and then scanned the room with his torch beam. A book of Frost's poems, he wondered. No, he reasoned: these are the travel stacks. An alphabetic search verified that much.

The burglar could hear Lord Byron meowing in the kitchen. At first Emil tried to ignore the persistent protest, but believing the cat might be giving him some kind of a clue, he took his search to the kitchen. After sliding cans, boxes, and Cellophane packs back and forth on each shelf of every cabinet, the only item hinting of gold was a half-filled bag of Gold Medal Flour. He probed the bag with a table knife to be sure—simply flour. The bathroom off the kitchen yielded nothing of interest, so he contemplated the bedroom as the next place to look. As he attempted to leave the kitchen area, Lord Byron countered to veer Emil back to the Friskies cabinet beneath the sink. His campaign consisted of continual figure eights between the intruder's feet. Emil took the first opportunity to plant a foot under the cat's midsection and lifted it through the air. Howling and hissing, Lord Byron fell out of sight.

Emil resumed his search in the bedroom without success. He returned to the critique room and flopped into a high-backed chair. He laid the Maglite torch, still lit, on the table; being wider at the top, it rolled to another position, focusing its concentrated beam on the opposite wall. The Andalusian plains came alive. Shades of yellow, brown, and tangerine dominated the poster, but nothing he could call gold. He tapped the back end of the torch until the rich greenery of the British Isles flew past the beam and, briefly, something gold, too, before coming to rest in the French Quarter of New Orleans.

A rush of excitement stirred through Emil as he grabbed for the flashlight and trained it back on the skipped *Autumn in New England* poster. This scene of golden leaves just had to be the hiding place of the letters. He lifted the New England poster from its hook and stood it on one side atop the massive table. He removed the squeeze-on plastic bottom strip of the frame, raised the poster off the table, and shook, but nothing fell out, so he removed the right-hand frame section and shook again. The corner of a white envelope protruded between the poster print and the cardboard backing. He pulled the one envelope out and another slid into its place. After removing the second one he shook even harder and then peered up into the bowed recess. Convinced he had discovered all there was to be had, Emil replaced the frame sections and re-hung the poster on the wall. He didn't bother to straighten it. A long triangle of unfaded paint appeared along one border.

Lord Byron chose that exact moment to chomp two rows of sharp feline teeth around the fleshy parts above Emil's Achilles tendon. He drew blood and hung on as Emil swore aloud and tried to shake the cat loose. Emil scraped the cat across the table leg without success. He grabbed for Lord Byron, intending to hurl him against a book stack, but missed. Alert green eyes tracked him and he lunged. Canines ripped through Emil's surface flesh. Emil swung his leg forward in a vicious kick, and Lord Byron sailed clear into the next room. Landing on all fours, he spit and hissed—his own brand of poetic justice.

Kravitz pulled a handkerchief from his pocket and tried to stop the bleeding long enough to make it to the bathroom. Cursing and panting, he grabbed an embroidered hand towel and washed his heel, applied iodine he found in the medicine chest, and dressed his wound. Retreat seemed to be in order, so he rinsed out the towel as best he could and hung it back up. As he left the bathroom, he felt Lord Byron's eyes staring at him from the open door of a closet. The cat hunched up and hissed as he got closer. Emil smiled and slammed the door, trapping Lord Byron inside. The sneak thief then gathered up the two letters he'd found, tucked them into his coat pocket, and let himself out by way of The Dungeon door. In his haste, Emil forgot to mop up the blood that had seeped its way into the critique room's worn beige carpeting.

Chapter 11

A Move of Their Own
Monday, May 24th

The jangling alarm kick-started Dan and Rivka's morning. As they had labored most of the previous day packing, they mechanically sprang into moving-day mode. They made do with one slurpy kiss instead of their usual cuddling before getting up.

Dan plunked a box of Cracklin' Oat Bran and two bowls down on the kitchen table.

"Did you sleep okay, hon?" Rivka asked.

"I don't know, I wasn't there." It was his predictable response.

"How long were you awake before the alarm?"

"About three inches."

She loved his puckish, mischievous humor, especially on this so-stressful day.

After one long sip of coffee, he declared, "Today I am a bookseller."

"Yes," she said, pouring her cereal from the open box. "Isn't that scary?"

"Not as scary as giving up two good-paying careers." He poured milk over the mini-heap in each bowl and sat down next to Rivka.

"I wonder what those messages from Edythe were about.

Such urgency in her voice—something important she wanted to tell us, but couldn't over the phone." Rivka scooped up a spoonful of cereal and slid it into her mouth. After a few crunches and chews she mumbled, "The poor woman died the very same day."

"I'm haunted by the thought that she never got to tell us what she wanted."

"It could be nothing at all, Dan. Maybe she just wanted to say goodbye."

"Hey," he said, looking at the kitchen clock. "It's almost nine. We'd better get moving. I want to tie the trunk lid down with that old extension cord."

Rivka upended the bowl between her lips and slurped up the last of the milk. She saw Dan eyeing her with a smirk. "You didn't see that," she giggled, patting her mouth dry with a paper napkin. "And neither did Miss Manners. You go ahead. I'll wash the few things in the sink and join you in a couple of minutes."

The Shermans pulled up to the curb and parked at The Olde Victorian Bookstore. The tan Toyota Corolla, which Rivka insisted was champagne color, sat low, the trunk nearly scraping the street, overloaded with its cargo of clothes and household items. A dark sky threatened to disrupt an efficient move. They had brought their first carload at 9:30. Rivka tried the door first and then, squinting past her own reflection, pressed her nose to the glass to see inside. Liz hadn't opened on time.

"It isn't like Liz not to show up. Dan, she's a totally reliable employee. At least, that's what Edythe, she should rest in peace, told us."

"Do you have the other key?" he asked. "We'll give Liz a call as soon as we get this stuff inside. I don't want to have to unload in the rain, sweetheart. Besides, this is only the first batch."

Rivka fished around in her purse and produced the keys. She unlocked The Dungeon door and went back to the car to collect an armload. Dan had already stacked three suitcases and an overnighter on a hand cart. He tilted it and wheeled it backward through the open door to the elevator. Bernie's elevator proved so tiny that the packed cart took all the room. Dan reached inside to press the second floor button, hastily withdrew his arm before the doors closed, and ran up the stairwell to intercept its arrival. He off-loaded the cart in their new bedroom. Rivka made numerous trips back and forth from the car, depositing everything in front of the elevator. They repeated this process until the contents of the car found their destination.

Propping herself on the stool behind the register, Rivka picked up the phone and tapped out the number for Liz. After seven unanswered rings, she contemplated hanging up. Then she heard Liz's sleepy voice:

"Hel-looo." It came out shaky and unsure.

"Liz, it's Rivka Sherman. What's wrong? You didn't open the store this morning."

"I'm so sorry, Rivka. I think I was mugged. I went through this horrible ordeal yesterday afternoon. Awful. I didn't sleep a wink last night—didn't doze off until five-thirty this morning. I didn't even set the alarm to get up."

"You *think* you were mugged? Don't you know? What actually happened to you?"

In a choked whisper, Liz said, "I can't talk about it over the phone. I'll tell you about it later. I'm so ashamed."

"Give me your address. I'm coming over to get you right now…I'm not taking 'No' for an answer." Rivka jotted a few notes on the pad in front of her.

Half an hour later, the two women came through The Dungeon doorway, Rivka with her arm firmly around a red-eyed Liz's shoulders. She alternately babbled and whimpered in a semi-coherent stream. Her clothes looked like she'd spent the night in them. The waif-like body shook in spasms.

"Come on upstairs and I'll fix you a cup of tea. That is, assuming I can find the makings in all this mess."

"Where the hell you two been?" asked a hard-breathing Dan, encountering them on the staircase. "I'm ready to go home for another load and suddenly there's no car. Hey, Liz, what's going on?"

"Not now!" said Rivka with Liz in tow. "Can't you see I'm dealing with an emergency here?" The two continued past him to the second-floor bathroom.

"What's up? Is it some big secret?"

"Liz was attacked last night in her front hall."

"Was she—?"

"I don't know yet. Give her a few minutes to pull herself together."

Rivka continued on to the kitchen where she found tea bags, sugar, and a copper-bottomed kettle. She put up the kettle and joined her husband in the critique room. He'd been straightening one of the travel posters and wore a curious look. Carrying a tray of mugs, spoons, and tea bags, she arranged them into three place settings. They sat at one end of the huge table while awaiting Liz and the call of the kettle. Just as it whistled its tune, Liz emerged from the powder room. Though the red eyes and blotchy cheeks persisted, being with the Shermans allowed a new calmness to settle over her. Rivka poured slowly with an unwavering hand and returned the kettle to the stove. Then she leaned over and whispered a few words in Liz's ear.

"No!" Liz exclaimed, her usually timid voice gathering surprising strength. "He did not rape me! Oh how I hate saying that word. He never touched me there. I can't even say that he actually mugged me either. The crud really didn't beat me up—only twisted my arm, hard behind my back so I couldn't run away. That hurt! The guy kept threatening me—questioning me like a policeman—poking me in the back with a gun. He actually kicked me, stuck his foot in my back to force me inside my apartment. I fell face-down on the floor. And when he pushed me into the bedroom I told him everything. Everything I knew, but it still wasn't enough. That's when I thought he was going to rape me. That just about scared me to death. Oh, God. I fell apart completely. I think he actually took pity on me crying on the floor in front of him."

"What happened then?" asked Rivka.

"He stood over me for several minutes staring down at me through those eerie peepholes in his mask. Then, out of the clear blue, he turns around and walks out of the apartment. I didn't know what to think, except he wasn't planning to hurt me anymore." A tremendous shudder overtook Liz, and Rivka hugged her for several minutes.

"So he wasn't after your body after all?" Dan asked.

"No. That lowlife wanted something else, something very specific, but I don't know what."

"Could you recognize your attacker?" asked Dan. "His eye color maybe?"

"No, but I did get a quick glimpse of him in the hall mirror. He wore a black knit ski mask, leather gloves, and a tan trench coat. With a turned-up collar," she added. "Anyway, he was behind me most of the time."

"Did you notice anything else?" asked Rivka.

"Oh yeah! He wore wing-tip shoes. Brown or tan, I think."

"You saw all that, the shoes, too, in the mirror?" questioned Dan.

"I saw them when I looked down."

"He? You're sure it was a man?" Rivka asked.

"Yes. He talked through one of those toy voice gadgets so he'd sound like Darth Vader, so I couldn't really determine gender that way. But the bulk and strength definitely belonged to a man."

"Darth Vader," Dan repeated. "If he used a gadget to disguise his voice, it's someone you know—a voice you'd recognize—a customer maybe?"

Liz's eyes widened. "Oh, my God." Her left hand swung up to cover her mouth.

"Did you recognize any speech patterns—expressions, word choices, accents, or anything like that?" Dan's interest peaked.

"No, I was too scared to notice," she squeaked out. "He seemed to know quite a lot about me, though. He dumped my purse out and went through everything."

"How tall was the man?" Dan asked.

"I couldn't tell much from the mirror, but when I was on the floor, he looked tall, very tall."

"Liz," asked Rivka, "you said your attacker was searching for something specific. What do you think he was really after? Was it your money?"

Liz shook her head. "No. The few bills I had in my purse seemed secondary. He was after something else."

"What then?" Rivka persisted.

"Edythe's letters maybe? It's the only thing I can think of."

"Letters *to* Edythe?" Dan pressed. "Who were they from?"

"Yes, *to* her. From her brother in England. Abner, I believe."

"Why would he think you had these letters or even believe you knew where they were?"

Liz hesitated. She swept her shoulder-length thin hair back around her right ear, then fiddled with the pearl buttons at the collar of her blouse. "I don't deserve all your kindness after the way I've behaved."

"You can't blame all this on yourself," said Rivka. "After all, *he* attacked *you*."

"No, it's not that. I have a confession to make. I've been disloyal to both of you. Edythe gave me two lines of a verse that she intended for your ears only." Liz took a deep breath, and the remaining words emptied like a slot machine in payoff. "She told me it was some kind of code that only Bernie could decipher. It would reveal the location of these mysterious letters. She said that her brother had been murdered trying to protect the secrets in those letters. According to her, those secrets were very valuable, but she wouldn't tell me what they were. Edythe said that I gossip way too much and shouldn't be trusted. Of course, she was right, but I needed to prove her wrong. I didn't do it to be dishonest—I couldn't do anything like that. Not to you guys, especially."

"You mentioned that Edythe was right," said Dan. "So who did you tell about this?"

"The only person that I told outright was Everet Kanter during the critique meeting. I thought he could help me, but then I changed my mind and went to Bernie on my own."

"Could it have been Kanter?" Dan asked.

Liz glanced at the floor a moment while she thought that one over. "I…I don't think so," she said in a small wavering voice.

"Could someone else have overheard the lines of verse?" he continued.

"I didn't tell the lines of verse to anyone. A few people at the table inadvertently heard Ev and me talking about the letters, though."

"But you just met this Everet. How could you know if he's trustworthy?" Rivka scolded, shaking her head in exasperation and lacing her hands together behind her neck.

Liz flushed. "I like Ev and I have a good feeling about him. It couldn't be him. I'd have recognized Ev from his strong aftershave. This guy smelled of talc."

"Still, you're already calling him Ev. He's a stranger, Liz," Rivka said. "And that's a pretty fine distinction, aftershave or talc. Feelings aside, could it have been him?"

Liz frowned and seemed to fold in on herself as a foreign thought intruded: the subject of the book title that had been rattling through her mind; again it slipped away. She quickly dismissed it as a coincidence.

"Liz?" Rivka asked.

"I'm sorry, guys. What was your question? I suppose it *could've* been Ev, but I'm almost sure it was one of the others."

"If it wasn't Everet, what about the others?" Dan said. "Which others?"

"Well, Vernon, Spence, Garry, Joel—and I suppose Heather, Peggy, and Frieda, too, maybe."

"I guess that narrows it down to everyone at the table but us," said Rivka. "Do you remember any of the poem?"

"Bernie said the two lines of verse came from a Robert Frost poem—'Something, Something Can Say,' I think."

"What were the lines that Edythe gave you?" Rivka asked. "Do you remember them?"

Liz rolled her eyes up into their lids and recited:

> *"Her early leaf's a flower;*
> *But only so an hour."*

Dan stood up, pushed his chair back, and motioned with his hand that he'd be right back. He dashed down to the first-floor poetry stacks, pulled three different collections of Frost's poetry, and brought them all upstairs to the critique room table. Out of the three tables of contents, none of the titles seemed to match what Liz had recalled. He then compared the key word indices against the lines that Liz did remember. A single reference in the second collection took him to the exact page and the poem itself: *Nothing Gold Can Stay.*

"The clue can't be in the couplet because that was a given," offered Dan.

Rivka gazed blankly at a spot above the book stacks on the opposite wall, trying to make some sense of either the poem or its title. "The only mention of place is Eden or an idyllic garden. It's all about the brevity of God's greatest gifts, the brevity being a punishment for the Fall of Man—no reference to any sort of cache."

"Golden moments," tried Dan. "How short they are. We could use one here."

Rivka's upward scanning gaze on the opposite wall slowly descended and encountered the posters there. "Wait, *gold*! That's it."

"What's it?" the other two chimed in.

"Frost wrote a lot about New England, didn't he? New England in the fall—golden fall? Just look at the posters on the wall."

"Visit New England in its Autumn Brilliance," Dan read from the poster as he stood and moved toward it.

"Dan! A little while ago, didn't I see you straightening one of those posters?"

"You sure did—that very poster."

"How do you suppose it got so catty-wampus?" asked Rivka.

"Now, Rivvie, don't you go and let your imagination run away with you. Nobody's been in here but us. A slamming door or a dropped box of books on the floor could have done that." He stood, walked over to the wall, and lifted the poster, frame and all, from its hook. The side sections of the flimsy push-on frame sections squeezed together some as he held the poster upright. The squeezed sections made Dan suspicious enough to examine the frame further. A heavy layer of dust coated the entire top frame section and portions of the other three sections, notably places where it wasn't held by probing hands before. Several smudges and far less dust adhered to these sections. He squinted, frowned, and pulled at the lobe of one large ear. "Well, now, you might be right after all," he said. "Someone else has handled this poster and recently, too. Look at the missing dust patches. I didn't make them."

They heard the little bell jingle at The Dungeon door downstairs. A customer had walked in from the street.

"I'll get it," said Liz, rising from her chair.

"Are you sure you're all right, Liz?" asked Dan.

"I'll be fine," she answered with a thin smile. "You two were just what the doctor ordered." She hurried down the stairs and out of sight.

"Dan!" Rivka said. "You've got messy shoes. You've gone and tracked something yucky in on the carpet."

Dan laid the poster down on the table and bent over to check his shoes. Finding more of this thickly congealed dark ooze on the floor than on the soles of his shoes, he concluded that the blob on the floor was the source. He scooped some of the gooey mess on the end of a pencil and brought it up for a closer look in the light. He held it for her to see as well.

Rivka shuddered. "Oh, God, is that what I think it is?"

"Yep, looks and feels like blood. It can't have been here for long or it would have dried to a crust."

Death Goes Postal

"Quite a lot of it from the area of that blob," she noted.

"Maybe it's the stain-resistant carpeting—doesn't soak up much, so it spread. I wonder whose blood it is."

"Whoever burgled the place, that's who. What I wonder is—what's missing?" He reached for the poster and flipped it face down on the table. He looked for telltale adhesive marks to see whether anything had been attached to the backing. Finding nothing there, he removed the individual frame sections one at a time. Rivka lifted off one thin sheet of cardboard backing and laid it on its backside, revealing a significant find. An envelope, addressed to Edythe, and a flat key were taped to the inside of the backing.

"Ah, the 'thlot pickens,' as I always say." Dan grinned, pleased with his remark.

Rivka slid the typewritten letter from its envelope and unfolded it. "I feel like an intruder reading someone else's mail."

"If the old girl didn't want us to read, it she wouldn't have intended the clues for us either. Go ahead and read it already. Aloud," he insisted.

> My Dear Edythe,
> As the years go by I find myself growing fonder of you and closer to you than I have ever been. True, there's an ocean between us, but your weekly phone calls and letters have shrunk that distance to minuscule. Surviving the Holocaust has made me appreciate everything and everyone so much more—especially you, my dear sister. As we were separated over most of our lives, I have enjoyed sharing anecdotes and memories, even the most anguishing, with you. We were never meant to be apart. First, the Nazis forced our lives that way, and then circumstances and choices kept us that way.

"I think I'm going to cry," said Rivka, putting the letter down on the table. She searched in a pocket of her relaxed-fit jeans until she found a Kleenex.

"Haven't we had enough tears for one day?" said Dan. "Do you want me to read?"

"No, wise guy, I'll finish." She dabbed at her cheeks and read on.

> I am saddened to learn that fate will again intervene and take away the pleasure of communing with one another. Cancer! I can hardly believe it could invade that wonderfully robust body of yours. I only hope and pray that expert treatment and time will be kind to you. I do hope that Bernie's Alzheimer's has stabilized enough for him to be of help to you in your time of need. Give him all my best.
> You, my dear Edythe, are all I have in this world now that Margaret has married and severed all ties with me. Even though I know she has made foolish and spiteful choices, I honestly wish her well wherever she is in America. And, as if your current burden weren't enough, I'm afraid I must add one more weight to it.
> Edythe, this is the first of three very special letters I am writing to you. My own life, and more important, my life's work have been threatened by a man named Emil Kravitz. He calls himself Professor, but I think academia would label him a hack. There is little doubt this man would not hesitate to murder for what he wants. I have acquired an extremely valuable set of 520 matrix molds. One of Gutenberg's young associates, an innovative and artistic printfounder called Gerheardt Koenig, used these matrices to cast beautifully illuminated print blocks. Included in my collection is a device called a chase. It is used to secure such blocks and other moveable type in place during the inking and transfer process. I have spent the last twelve years of my life accumulating these artifacts, tracing their history, and documenting both their authenticity and functionality.

"Hey this is pretty interesting stuff," interrupted Dan. "I'd like to know Abner myself."

"We both know that's not going to happen, so please stop interrupting me." Rivka pushed her glasses up the bridge of her nose and continued.

Death Goes Postal

I have called the police several times, but they tell me they cannot act on threats alone. There is nowhere else to turn. Since these threats have become more intense, I have shipped the Koenig set, its chase, and all the accompanying documentation to a hidden destination somewhere in the U.S. where, hopefully, Kravitz can't get his ruthless hands on them. I am entrusting the clues to their whereabouts in a crude verse consisting of three lines. One line of verse will appear in each of three succeeding letters. I believe, by doing this, I can negate any possibility of Kravitz intercepting all the vital clues.

The first line of the clue verse is:

"Pozt a key lime's fare full in face."

Forgive me. All my love,

Your Abner

Rivka put the letter down on the table, and Dan pulled it closer toward him, so he could see it for himself.

"Abner misspelled the first word of the clue line. What do you suppose he meant the word to be? Do you think it was intentional?"

"No. Probably *post*. The s and z keys are next to each other on the keyboard—diagonally, one line apart," responded Rivka.

"It's a common typo."

"There's nothing mysterious about key lime's fare. It's a Key West, Florida, pie delicacy. But is Abner talking about Key West, the place or—with full in face—is it the round shape?"

"No way to tell that with only one-third of the clues," she answered. "Oh, Liz, I didn't see you standing there. Did you make a sale downstairs?"

"Yes, it was Ev Kanter. He bought the new Mild mystery we had on display up front."

"Was there something else, Liz?"

"Yes, ma'am. He wanted to know if I could take off tomorrow. He wants to take me sailing. I told him I'd ask you."

Rivka glanced at Dan to get his reaction, but his eyes were

still glued to the letter. "With all the strange things that are going on, do you think you can still trust the man?" she asked.

"Yes, ma'am. I don't think he'd hurt a fly. He's not my attacker or Abner's killer, believe you me."

Rivka ran her fingers in a jerky fashion through her auburn curls, wondering *What've we gotten ourselves into?* "Things are a bit stressed here with it being our first moving day. We do need someone to watch the store while we're unpacking."

"Oh, lighten up, Rivka." Dan turned to Liz. "You go downstairs and tell that young man you'd love to go sailing with him. We'll use the time to finish up here."

His wife pressed her lips together. *Thanks a lot, husband.*

"Dan! How the heck can we unpack upstairs and tend to the bookstore at the same time?" Because Dan shot her a look like Give-the-poor-girl-a-break, Rivka kept her mouth shut. *Maybe Dan's more sympathetic to Liz than I am. Maybe she hasn't had a date in ages.* "Well, okay, I guess we'll manage."

Liz's face lit up immediately. She spun around and started down the stairs with a bounce in her step.

"Hey, I believe we've got a hot little romance on our hands," Dan said, pleased with himself. "She's a nice kid—needs and deserves a bit of *schmaltz* in her life."

"That's one romantic way to put it, Dan. What's that noise?"

In unison, they paused mid-breath and listened to the high-pitched moan off in the distance.

"I think it's coming from over that way." Dan nodded toward the bedroom, and they both moved closer, but the sound had stopped.

"I don't remember seeing the cat today," Rivka said. "Do you?"

"Nope, but I believe he must have put in a good supply of mice. He hasn't been fed in two days. I wonder if we can be arrested for feline abuse?"

"Lord Byron! Here kitty kitty! Where are you?" The sounds

began again. The moan turned to a whine and then to distinct meows and desperate scratching sounds as they approached the bedroom closet. Dan opened the door and Lord Byron sprang from his mothballed prison like a paroled lifer. Rivka picked up the cat and cradled him in her arms. He started to purr until her hand rubbed his belly fur, and then he let loose one great whine that startled her, to the point of almost dropping him.

Carrying Lord Byron into the kitchen, she set him down on the counter and examined the belly fur more closely. She decided that it was just a tender place, a bruise perhaps. Persistent mewing convinced her that Lord Byron's hunger urgently exceeded any pain. Taking down a can of Friskies Classic Chicken and Tuna Dinner, she noticed that a bag of Gold Medal Flour had been tipped over on the next shelf. Boxes of brown sugar, cream of tartar, birthday candles—all the baking supplies were lying askew, as though a cyclone had passed through the cabinet. While the cat food can spun under the electric opener, she opened two more cabinet doors, and found all the other groceries strewn about. The Cellophane window on a box of macaroni had been punched in, suggesting somebody's frantic search.

"Dan," she said, forking the cat food into Lord Byron's bowl. "I think this whole floor has been ransacked." Minutes later, the lord of the store had wolfed down the whole bowlful and looked up for more. She opened a second can for him, but he quit after only a few mouthfuls. After filling his water bowl, she continued opening and slamming the rest of the cabinet doors. "Oh, no! Every cabinet's been tossed. We've been robbed!"

"You already knew that. We even know what the thief was after. What we don't know is what he made off with."

"At least he didn't get the key or this letter," she said.

"This was the first letter. He could have made off with a second or third letter. I guess we'll just have to wait and see if more turn up. From the missing dust on the side and bottom of the poster frame sections, my guess is that he shook out at least one letter. What are you doing now?"

She had dropped down on her knees in front of the blood spot with an open bottle of seltzer in one hand and a roll of paper towel in the other. "Cleaning up this mess before it gets all over the house."

"Wait! Before you start sopping up, use a kitchen knife and scrape as much as you can into an empty jar in case the police are interested."

"Do you plan to call them?"

"Yeah. They'll file a routine breaking-and-entering form with nothing reported missing. Maybe they'll even come out and have a look around."

"Maybe," she repeated. "Then I should leave the blood there until the police get here."

"Excellent idea."

* * *

On the floor below Liz saw Ev to the front door. They parted with a short hug, and he waved as he walked away.

"Pick you up in a little bit, Liz."

She was really happy that the Shermans chose to let her go sailing with him. *Choose! Choices!* Smart Women, Foolish Choices. *That's it!* The title rattling around inside her head that she couldn't recall. But her brighter thoughts nullified any notion of an omen.

Chapter 12

In Her Defense
Tuesday, May 25th

In downtown Annapolis on red-brick inlaid Main Street, a busty woman in her fifties exited a boutique and stepped into a throng of shoppers. Peggy Morris had just purchased an embroidered beige sweater. Enthralled, she kept peeking into the bag to once again appreciate the pastel needlework. The fresh spring air had triggered an impulse to break out of her Goth mode. Enough black already. She turned to walk uphill and collided with a tall man wearing a brown fedora hat and sunglasses, hurrying toward the City Dock.

"Excuse me, miss."

Peggy clutched her bag's handles tightly and hesitated for an awkward moment, wondering whether he might speak, but with a long stride, he continued on down the sidewalk.

Stirred from her inattention, Peggy called after the athletic young man, "My fault! Have a nice day."

Peggy continued to amble up Main Street, stopping frequently to check the window displays. At Boot-Towne she halted to admire a pair of leather pumps on sale. Angling her head a bit to the right to avoid the glare, her eyes picked up the mirrored image of the fedora, brim turned down, with a feather in it, the man she'd just encountered. *He looks smaller in his downhill reflection,* she thought, *definitely a looker, though. Nicely dressed, too—*

in sharply creased slacks and a turtleneck pullover. The dark glasses, rather dashing. Could this guy be following me? But why? A icy shiver inched down her spine.

Turning her head to look him in the eye, he wheeled about, so Peggy couldn't study his features. Her first instinct was to hurry from the spot. After passing a number of doorways, the urge to peek back at her pursuer just wouldn't go away. A fleeting mirror image in another storefront glass caught the man quick-stepping to keep up with her. She hastened toward Church Circle at the top of Main Street and crossed to the triangular bank building on the opposite corner. Looking over one shoulder from the door, she entered the Annapolis Bank and Trust Company and approached a high narrow desk of deposit and withdrawal slips in front of the Main Street side window. On a whim she picked up a pen and sprawled HELP on one of the deposits slips. A second later she thought better of it, wadded the note, and tossed it in the wastebasket.

From her window view, the fedora man stood on the far side of the street, leaning against the wrought-iron staircase railing to the Maryland Inn. He nonchalantly pulled a lighter from his beige blazer pocket and lit a cigarette, letting it dangle from his lips. *Ugh,* she thought, *he smokes. Strike 1. And he's waiting for me to come out.* A bus passed between them, and she momentarily lost sight of him. Watching the stop-and-go traffic relative to the corner light, an idea struck her. She'd wait for a bus to stop at the corner and then slip out the door on the State Circle side of the bank building.

Peggy had to wait almost a quarter hour and through a half-dozen light changes before a bus actually stood between them for more than a few seconds. Seizing her opportunity, she darted out the door onto School Street, the tiny block that led from Church Circle to the much larger, more prominent State Circle. She peeked back at the light that was just now changing, allowing Main Street traffic onto Church Circle. As the bus's bulk slid past the spot where the fedora man had been standing, she found only an elderly woman and her grandchild walking on that section of sidewalk where she'd last seen her pursuer. She was out of his view! A sigh of relief filled her body with a sense of well-being. He'd gone his own way, perhaps given up.

Peggy trotted a quarter-block to East Street, downhill to Market Street, across Main and into the Hillman garage, the most circuitous route she could think of to her car, repeatedly glancing back to see if the guy would materialize again. Inside the garage, she froze. There he stood, square in front of her, leaning against her Ford Escort. Her sweater bag dropped to the concrete floor. She rummaged through her purse for her can of Mace spray. She popped the safety cap and pointed the spout in his direction.

"D-d-d-don't!" he stuttered. "I can explain." He pulled off his dark glasses and shoved them in his blazer pocket.

"You better not come any closer, you depraved pervert you." She accidentally released a short spritzing mist, a portion of which found its way to his eyes.

"I...I kn-n-ow y-you." His hands flew to cover his eyes. His fingers rubbed furiously. "That burns, lady."

"You had better explain why you're following me. This stuff will blind you if you don't behave yourself, mister."

"I can explain," he said in a much calmer voice. "We've met before. Don't you remember me?" He picked up her fallen package and held it out to her.

Peggy snatched it from him. "Where did we meet?" She studied his face carefully, and the tension in her own relaxed as she did find something familiar there—perhaps the sandy hair, dimpled chin, and the soft gray eyes.

"At the critique meeting. At the bookstore. On the same side of the table down at the far end. You know me. I'm Spencer Edington. I'm a writer, too." The spray-induced tears rolled down shave-scarred cheeks. "Damn! That burns like acid. I can't see anymore."

"If you know me, you'll know my name, too."

"It's Peggy something. But I can't remember your last name.

I couldn't even remember Peggy when we first collided on the street, but I did recall your unusual hair color, the fetching streaks." Spence screwed his face into a tight squint. "Ow, damn it—that hurts." He held his handkerchief to his eyes trying to blot the Mace out of them.

"So why were you following me, Spencer Edington?"

"My friends call me Spence."

"I'll remember that if we ever become friends, Mr. Edington. Which will probably be never."

"I'm new to Annapolis, and I don't have any acquaintances here, let alone anyone I can call a friend. When I bumped into you, I recognized you from the meeting and wanted to strike up a conversation. But I got flustered and rushed off. By the time I remembered your name and got my nerve up, you were already racing away."

"How did you catch up with me the second time?"

"I saw you park in the garage and I waited for you to come back for your car."

"Then the bumping was a setup, too? I was supposed to run into you? Boy, have I ever been duped. That's what I call *chutzpah*."

"If you say so."

"Your eyes still hurt?"

"Yes, ma'am."

"Well, Spence, I guess you're harmless after all. You'd better follow me, and we'll get those eyes taken care of."

"Where are you taking me?"

"There's a hospital emergency room down Franklyn Lane and right on Cathedral."

Fifteen minutes later Peggy Morris held open the air-lock emergency room door for a grateful Spencer Edington. A quick-reacting nurse rinsed his eyes clean and was about to fit him with a pair of cardboard sunglasses for his sensitive eyes to face the sunny outdoors when he fished his own out of his pocket.

"That was nice of you to offer to pay the ER fee, but it wasn't necessary," he said. "As you saw, I had my credit card with me."

"I know, but I felt kind of responsible for my hasty action," she replied.

"You did the right thing in rushing me to the hospital, though," said Spence.

Peggy had intended to leave him standing there when she saw his eyes blinking rapidly again. "Are you going to be all right, Spence? Can you get home okay?"

"Yeah, I can make it fine," he replied. "Only, isn't there some way I can make things up to you?"

"Like what?" she asked.

"Well, dinner and a movie would be nice."

"I don't know anything about you," she answered.

"I could say the same thing about you," he returned. "Yet I'm willing to take a chance on a pretty face with a grand heart."

"Oh, flattery, too." *He is kinda cute*, she thought, *one of those perpetual baby faces that always leave me wondering about his age.* "Maybe I'll consider a drink, and we'll take it from there. How about Fran O'Brien's on Main Street?"

"Sounds great to me."

Peggy slipped her arm into his, and they began to walk over the uneven red-brick sidewalks of Historic Annapolis. She led him straight to two empty stools at the bar, where a ready escape was possible should he turn out to be creepy rather than cute. He eased onto the first stool and, with some amusement, watched her wiggle her rear end onto the adjacent one. They settled in and ordered: a glass of white Zinfandel for her and a bottle of Red Stripe for him.

"You seem to know your way around town for a newcomer, Peggy."

"Been here all of two weeks, actually. I don't like playing the role of stranger, so I get out and mix whenever I can. That's one of the reasons I signed up for the critique group."

"I see," said Spence. "And you had more than one reason?"

"Well, yeah," she said. "I've always enjoyed creative writing, and I wanted to learn a bit more about mystery writing to see if I liked the genre."

"They seem like a great bunch of people," he said.

"You bet," said Peggy. "I sure got a kick out of Liz Nathan, though—the way she blurted out all that stuff about some strange letters. What was she trying to prove?"

"Maybe nothing. But they did sound interesting. I even offered to help her. Say, what made you leave the City of Brotherly Love for this burg?"

"Let's just say I was fed up with my secretarial job and the inappropriate way my supervisor treated me. It was a dead-end position—three wasted years. I need a fresh start away from there."

Spencer reached for her free hand and squeezed it tightly. "Was Annapolis a random choice or a conscious decision?"

"I guess it was on purpose," Peggy replied thoughtfully. "You see, I have someone here I wanted to look up."

A group of entertainers appeared on the small stage and picked up their instruments.

Spence observed her squirming uncomfortably atop the stool. "Oh, there's a live band. Do you want to move to a table?"

Peggy glanced at her watch and declared, "Look at the time. I've got a job interview in the morning."

"But the evening has just begun," Spence protested.

"I'm so very sorry, but there's a bunch of things I have to do to get ready. Another time perhaps," she replied on her way to the door.

"Was it something I said?" he called after her.

"Of course not, silly." She put three fingers to her lips and waved a friendly kiss at him as she disappeared through the door to the street.

Spencer Edington tossed down the last of his beer. Walking past the end of the bar, he slipped into a phone booth.

Chapter 13

Food for Thought
Same Day

Ms. Heather Germain sat at a wrought-iron café table in front of Reardon's on Market Street at the City Dock. The unmarried schoolteacher enjoyed eating here and viewing the steady stream of tourists, shoppers, and strollers passing in the narrow walkway between the curb and where she sat. A heaping platter of mussels sat in front of her, along with a deep bowl of Belgian fries, a mug of dark beer, a basket of condiments, and a napkin receptacle. All of this left little space on the café table for two. The sun's brilliance turned the strands of her red hair and matching brows into a shade of gold, further accentuating the densely freckled islands of her pale complexion. A waiter in white shirt, black bow tie, and apron stood behind her, enticing patrons among the passing crowd. A fork bearing a mussel, newly wrenched from its shell, stopped on its way to her mouth when she noticed a smiling face blocking the sunlight.

"Do I know you?" she said as the mussel, immersed in dipping sauce, slid off the fork back to the platter.

"Vernon Levant!" the stranger volunteered. And when she showed no sign of recognition: "From the mystery critique group the other night. I was one of the fledglings who joined the group."

Heather laid the fork back on the heap of mussels and dabbed slowly at her chin with a napkin, while giving the nicely built interloper the once-over from receded hairline to his New Balance walking shoes. "Of course, now I remember you. You're the insurance chap who's writing killer poetry."

"Tsk-tsk, I'm found out already. Actually, it's crime in verse and nothing worse. Whodunits and all sorts of widgets."

"Oooh! It's unusual, I'll give you that," Heather said. "What brings you down to the City Dock at this time of day?"

"To be truthful, it's sheer hunger. My landlady told me there are some pretty decent restaurants in the market square." He stepped between tables to allow a couple to pass by.

"Please. If you're hungry, I've enough mussels and fries here to feed an army. Won't you join me?"

"I'd love the company, but I had fish and chips in mind." He looked at her nearly empty glass "I'll even supply the wine." He turned to the waiter and ordered before settling into the wrought-iron chair opposite her. "I can see why you like it here."

"It's one of my favorite spots for people-watching. You can catch the whole world parading by from here. And there's nothing I adore more than a parade." Heather pointed out some of the local scenery while they waited. "Off there to the right of the Market House is a bronze sculpture honoring Alex Haley, the famous chronicler of the *Roots* story. His slave character, Kunta Kinte, was sold on the block in this very same market square way back when. Amazing, isn't it?" She continued to informed him of the best places to eat and historical sites to visit.

"Wow," he said. "You sound like some teachers I've had."

"I do teach, high school French."

The conversation halted while the waiter uncorked, decanted, and poured from a dusty bottle into a pair of glasses. He set the bottle down and somehow made room on the crowded table for the additional food.

Heather pushed her half-empty beer mug toward the waiter. You can take this away," she said. "Vernon, you're in for a treat."

"How's that?"

"Wait 'til you taste the batter on your fish. It's the specialty of the house."

"She's right," said the waiter as he set most of the steaming platter on the table, allowing an edge to hang off. "Nobody does the batter better than we do." He winked just before he left them.

Vernon cut off a chunk and raised it to his mouth, noticing he had her complete attention for the entire trip. Her eyes remained on him as he chewed and swallowed.

"Well, how do you like it?"

He licked his lips, delaying the inevitable. "Delicious. The taste is familiar, but I can't quite place it."

"It's potato, a mashed potato batter. Isn't it good?"

"Very," he said, munching away at the next forkful. "I also enjoyed your short story the other night. I liked the title, too: 'Bent On Violence.' I don't think Ms. Nathan's criticism was warranted at all. Everyone else liked it, even the leader, Dan…Dan?"

"Sherman! Did you like my ending?"

"Marvelous! I had a completely different one all picked out, and you surprised me."

"How would you have ended it?" asked Heather.

"I would have expected Beverly to keep on hitting the killer with the pipe wrench until she was sure he was dead. You had her hit him only once and run away."

"That was deliberate. You've got to keep up the suspense. It's one of those gimmicks that's done all the time."

"Oops! I guess I've gone and done it again. It's your story and you have every right to end it any way you like. I'm no better than Ms. Nathan."

"Oh, stop," Heather said coquettishly. "I do have to apologize for the way Liz acted at the meeting. I think she was playing with the lot of us over those letters of hers."

"Didn't she say the letters belonged to the Benders?"

"I believe you're right. From Edythe's brother somewhere in England, I think." Heather fork-wrestled one of her remaining mussels from its purplish-black home and popped it into her mouth. She savored the morsel with a roll of her eyes.

"I wonder what makes those letters so valuable," he speculated.

"I heard it's to do with his historical research papers." Still chewing, she shoved the mussel into one cheek with her tongue so she could say something. "Perhaps he's discovered something new."

"Or old, rather," he corrected with a small grin of satisfaction from behind his glass of Chablis.

"Antique even."

"Would you happen to know just how many letters there are?"

"At least two. Why is that so important, Vernon?"

"Oh, curiosity, I guess. I'm just making conversation." He drew a long sip from his nearly empty glass and refilled it. "I just thought Liz might have said something more to you. You appeared to have an *in* with her."

"No, I haven't seen Liz since the critique meeting." Heather toyed with a dangling pearl earring—a habit when she was trying to think of something impressive to say. "I wonder who the brother's research belongs to now that Edythe is dead and Bernie is *non compos mentis* in a nursing home."

"I should think the ownership would be quite a prize—and who it belongs to might very well be debatable. Don't you agree? Perhaps you and I could team up with Liz." He reached around the table and squeezed her left hand as it rested on her knee.

"Is that a proposition, sir?"

Without speaking he answered by raising his brow and skewing his lips.

"In that case, Vernon, I'll have to give it some thought." *Mon Dieu*, she thought, *this man is pushy. And glib. Are all insurance men like him? Probably*, she decided.

* * *

Two men sat in a corner booth at the Double T Diner in the Parole section of Annapolis. Parole derived its name from

Camp Parole, one of several during the Civil War, where prisoners of war were held until they were sent back to their regiments or their homes.

Even in the hours before the supper rush began, the spacious rooms held coffee-klatching friends, people discussing business, and those just trying to beat the suppertime crowds. Settled into the booth, a much-relaxed Joel Wise unbuttoned his suit jacket and loosened his tie. Joel's law practice included intellectual properties, so Garry Posner had given him an agent's literary contract to peruse earlier in the week. Garry, in jeans and T-shirt, sat across from him, looking relaxed, almost too relaxed as he scratched the short black hair at the top of his head. Joel had chosen this diner to discuss the author-agent contract and learn more about the writer's completed mystery novel, *The Unspun Web*.

"It's been rejected by dozens of publishers—all because I don't have an agent," complained Garry.

"Finding an agent isn't all that easy," said Joel. He had had some of the same responses to his own literary offerings.

"But thirty-three agents turned me down before I got this contract offer. Most responses said 'our stable is full,' 'your genre isn't what we're looking for,' or simply 'not interested.' I admit, the contract offer has been a tremendous boost to my ego. Still, the wording troubles me."

"And rightfully so. This agent is a thief," Joel began. "He's misrepresenting both himself and his services. He charges for reading, editing, and search expenses." The lawyer laid the folded document in question on the table.

"Oh, well," Garry said, taking the document and stuffing it in a rear jeans pocket. His expression never changed. It was as though he had expected this answer. Without a blink, he quickly flipped through the eleven-page menu. "What's one more rejection?" He stopped at the specials—two plastic pages chock full of complete meal inserts.

Joel ran one hand over the shiny trough of his pate between the neatly trimmed side furrows. He hadn't been sure just how

Garry would take it, but now they could relax and enjoy their meal. He looked up to find a chunky waitress standing over them, leaning on one hip while skimming the pages of her order book.

She didn't look at their faces. "Hi, gentlemen, I'm Frieda, your server this afternoon. Can I get you something to drink?"

Returning several minutes later with the hot coffee and iced tea, she set them on the table.

"Frieda Forrester?" asked Joel.

"Uh, yeah," she replied, looking directly at him. "Oh, hi, Mr. Wise. I guess I wasn't paying attention or I woulda recognized you first. Gee! Your friend looks familiar also."

"I'm Garry." He smiled and held out his hand to her, and she shook it. "I was at the critique meeting, too."

"So what'll it be, guys?"

"I'll have a corned beef sandwich and an order of potato latkes," said Garry.

"Bring me the matzoh ball soup, Yankee pot roast, mashed potatoes, and carrots and peas," ordered Joel. "By the way, Frieda, when are we going to hear more of that horse racing mystery of yours? I got a big kick out of the beginning. I especially liked the characters."

"Thanks. It's going kinda slow, Mr. Wise, on account of I gotta work two jobs. It ain't easy being a single mother of two teenagers. I gotta write at night when they're asleep. Maybe I'll have something more in a couple of weeks."

"I can understand that," sympathized Garry. "I'm also raising a teen by myself and that's kind of tough on a plumber's salary."

"I always thought plumbers did well—they sure charge enough," she said.

"Only if you have your own contracting business," answered Garry. "Hey, you seemed to be pretty tight with Liz Nathan the other night. Maybe you know what was going on with her? She seemed all worked up about some valuable letters."

"I didn't hear anything more than you did. Why would letters be so valuable, anyway?"

"I was hoping you knew. Did you happen to hear how many letters were involved?"

Frieda shook her head, turned, and headed for the kitchen once more.

"Letters, plural, has to mean more than one," interrupted Joel. "And from what I heard, she doesn't even have the letters yet, only the clues to their whereabouts."

"You didn't happen to hear anything else, did you?" asked Garry.

"No, I didn't," Joel replied. "But what's all this strange curiosity about some slip of the tongue made by an excitable little chatterbox?"

Joel's stinging question surprised Garry for a moment while he thought of an appropriate response. "I suppose it's the mystery author in me—always looking for a new plot line."

"Sorry, I didn't mean to sound like I was censuring you. It's just that you seemed to be a little excessive on the subject."

"I guess I have to be reined in every so often."

Frieda returned to the table a few minutes later and set a cup of soup down in front of Joel.

"Hey, Frieda—where's the soup? It's all matzoh ball."

"It's inside the ball. Give it a chance—it'll sweat," she chuckled and walked away.

Later, when Frieda brought their orders to the table, Garry touched her hand as she set his plate in front of him.

"Say, Frieda, maybe we could do a movie together sometime?"

Surprised, Frieda pulled her hand back, gave him the once-over, and decided he was pulling her leg. "Sure, we could even share the same sitter. Do you try to date all your waitresses?"

"No! I'm serious. It's not like we're strangers or anything. I liked your sense of humor. If you're not interested, just say so."

She studied his face for a moment and said, "Well, yeah, I'd like that. Call me." She wrote her phone number down on a corner of the paper placemat.

"Great," he said, tearing away the corner with the number.

Frieda smiled and left them to serve a newly arrived couple at a nearby table.

"I'd like to read *The Unspun Web* sometime, Garry. I don't even know what it's about."

"You will, Joel. It needs a mite more polishing, but when I'm finished you can read away to your heart's content."

"But isn't that what the critique group is all about?"

"This one's been through critique already. I'll bring the next draft to the group. You'll see."

Joel began to wonder if the book actually existed. *It could be my imagination, but it wouldn't be the first time some sleaze joined a critique group just to meet new dating material.*

Chapter 14

Not Enough Clues
Wednesday, May 26th

Rivka pushed her way through the front door of the bookstore. An electric air of excitement surrounded her. "Hey, honey, guess what?"

"Hey, yourself," Dan responded. "Where've you been so long? I've been stuck at this register all day. It's almost four o'clock and there's still a ton of work to do."

"Sorree," Rivka managed with false remorse written on her face. She let go of the armful of packages and, for the most part, they landed on a nearby chair across from the counter.

"What happened to Liz?" he said as she leaned over the counter and nuzzled the back of his neck with a kiss.

"Oops! I forgot to tell you. Liz called in sick this morning. Sounded pretty bad, too, all nasal and stuffed up. During their sail yesterday they capsized. She fell into the Severn and caught cold. Doesn't say much for her new beau's seamanship, does it?"

"I guess not," he said. "So where were you all this time?"

"I told you I was going shopping for our new granddaughter. Don't you ever listen to what I have to say?"

"Not very often," he said with a lopsided grin. "I must have been distracted. I hope you didn't devastate the bank account, hon. We do have to run a bookstore now."

"I didn't spend all that much. They had the cutest things on sale. Wait 'til you see them."

"Is there such a thing as Grandmas Anonymous?" he asked.

"I don't know about that, but I was at the post office earlier today mailing a package off to Marvin and Edie. His birthday's next week, and with all the excitement in Ohio, I didn't want to neglect our son. Anyway, I had this brainstorm while I waited in line."

"Ah, front page material. Maybe I should call the *Baltimore Sun* and Channel Eleven and alert them."

"Not quite yet, but wait till I tell you," she said. Two rosy patches appeared on her cheeks, as they always did when she had "exciting" news. "Anyway, I saw this zip code book lying on the counter and I thought about the clue line, especially the word *pozt*. I think it's a double clue, telling us that Abner mailed, or as the Brits say, posted, the package somewhere—in the good old U.S. of A. That is, if the 'z' stands for zip code like I think it does."

Dan asked, "Don't other countries use zip codes like we do?"

"Of course, but I don't think any other country would call them zip codes. Zip is such a terribly American word, don't you think?"

"I suppose so, but we can check that out easily enough. Perhaps our precious package is in Key West like the rest of the line says."

"Why would he go through so much trouble to hide where he mailed it," Rivka asked, "and then, in the first clue, come right out and tell us its destination? No, I believe the clever man would be more subtle than that. I think we have to look to the rest of the clue line for more information."

"Or to the other letters and their clues," Dan added. "After all, he wrote three of them."

"Maybe this line deals wholly with the zip code portion of the address, and the others give other kinds of information. Dan, is there a place called Key Lime?"

"Never heard of it," he replied. "There's an Old Lyme in Connecticut, but it's spelled differently. The *fare* would refer to the pie and *full in face* could mean the pie's shape, like *round or circular*, I'd guess. I've never heard of a Round Key or Circle Key either."

"I think I know where you're going with this. What did we ever do before the Internet?" Her *café au lait* eyes gleamed in anticipation.

"I had a few minutes between customers, so I *Googled* this Emil Kravitz. My first search landed me twenty pages: two pages of Kravitz, ten pages of Emils whoever and eight pages of Emiles. Then I AND'ed his full name with Bath, England. There were seven hits with both names in that area, but two were spelled the French way with an 'e'. Two looked more promising than the others because they worked at schools. I remembered Fraume addressed Kravitz as professor in his letter and figured a treasure of this sort would be sought by someone from academia."

"Hey, hon, that's good. What did you find out?"

He leaned back in his chair with a self-satisfied look. "I got the University of Bath telephone number from their website. They transferred me to the Psychology Department. Their Dr. Kravitz passed on three months ago. The lady I spoke with wouldn't release his home number. Metheford Academy was another story."

"Wasn't it a bit late in the day to be calling England?" Leaning back, Rivka pushed down with her hands and wriggled her rear end up onto the counter to hear more.

"No, there's only five hours difference, and I placed the call a little before nine—two p.m. their time."

"And?" Rivka said when he hesitated a tad too long.

"The Metheford website provided me with a number, so I put in a call to the headmaster of Metheford, a Colonel Ansel Felsworth. He confirmed that Professor Emil Kravitz taught world history and English literature there for the past twenty-one years. At least he did until a month ago, when he mysteriously up and left without saying a word to anyone. It appears that the local police were also interested in his disappearance. Wanted him for questioning. Something to do with a murder, but they wouldn't say anything more. The police interrogated all of Kravitz's students to see if they had any clue as to why he would leave so abruptly. The only thing of note—one class of fifth termers had noticed—"

"Fifth termers?" she interrupted.

"Yeah, their school year is divided into six terms."

"Do you happen to know how old these fifth termers are?"

"I asked the same question, and he told me it varied anywhere from thirteen to eighteen, depending upon scholastic ability. The colonel said this class of fifth termers had noticed Kravitz's unusual reaction to one of the term papers being read in class."

"What kind of reaction?"

"Kravitz began to interrogate the author of the paper quite mercilessly. Shortly afterward, he dismissed all the rest of the class except for this Will Petty kid who wrote it."

"Did the boy plagiarize his work?" Rivka asked.

"Oh, no, reportedly he's very honest. A serious, no-nonsense student. Quite conscientious, according to Colonel Felsworth. Some of Petty's classmates were concerned for the boy, especially when they heard the teacher's tone and intensity growing nasty while the other boys left the room. They said that the man was overbearing and absolutely vicious. One of them hung back outside the door to eavesdrop and he recorded their exchange in his notebook. The headmaster read from the boy's notebook, and I tried to copy as he read."

Dan hesitated and sneezed several times. "Nooo, I'm not getting another cold in by dose."

"Not to worry, sweetie pie," Rivka said. "It's the dust from all these older volumes. What else did you find out?"

"Well, Kravitz demanded to know if any of the boy's so-called research was true. The boy admitted that all of it was, except for the dialogue and some personal stuff he added, like the points of view. Then Kravitz asked for the sources of what he called 'this drivel.' When Will Petty didn't answer him, Kravitz insisted that the young man tell him where he researched his paper. The boy gave in and told him it was some man he knew. To the question 'What man?' he replied, 'Just an old man I do some work for." Kravitz pressed Petty for the name of this man and where he could be found. By this time he was shaking the boy by his shoulders."

"So, Daniel," Rivka urged, "who was the man, for pity's sake? Did the boy answer him?"

Dan took a deep breath and continued. "Will's eavesdropping friend thought he understood the name Adam Fawn, but he couldn't be sure. Approaching footsteps in the hall forced him to leave his listening post. That name sounded just too close not to be Abner Fraume."

"I don't understand, dear. Why would this Colonel Felsworth blab all these nit-picking details to *you*, a total stranger." Dan flashed an impish smile.

"What?" she asked. "What are you not telling me?"

"I told the colonel I was a private investigator working for Abner Fraume's sister."

"But that's a lie, Dan. You could get into deep trouble that way. Why would you do such a thing?"

He merely shrugged. "Why not?" Then, just when Dan needed a distraction, Lord Byron leaped up onto Dan's lap, circled once, and settled in for the stay. Dan scratched the jet-black fur behind the royal ears. "He's been like this for the last few days. I think he's got some security issues ever since his solitary confinement in the upstairs closet."

"Poor kitty," Rivka said, reaching down to get in a stroke of her own.

"Anyway, Felsworth questioned Petty himself after the police left, and this is what he learned. In Will Petty's spare time after school and on weekends, the lad did odd jobs for an elderly neighbor, a man named Abner Fraume, who was a noted historian and a recluse of sorts. Mostly, Will shopped for the man and put away his purchases. Sometimes there were errands to libraries and bookstores. And a number of times he acted as go-between or messenger in other literary and research transactions. Occasionally, he'd tidy up the place when the cleaning woman couldn't make it.

"Abner trusted the boy with a key to his flat and, for the most part, his trust was not abused. But Will had an insatiable curiosity that led him to read snatches of Abner's research work when Abner wasn't around. He grew fond of three stories in particular—three stories that traced the dynamic history of some very old print artifacts dating from the time of the German Johannes Gutenberg to the present. These stories furnished Will Petty with great material to write his term research papers. Felsworth applauds Petty's work. He told me it's an outstanding piece of scholarship and a comprehensive history of some antique printing paraphernalia crafted by a sixteenth-century typefounder named Koenig."

"Amazing! Darling, you're quite a sleuth. It certainly seems as though you uncovered the right man. This Will Petty is a definite link between Edythe's brother and Kravitz. Any chance of getting hold of the boy's term papers?"

"Now you're getting ahead of me, smarty pants. Felsworth told me that the boy's work was stored on disk and, if the boy is agreeable, he'll e-mail us the work. The police also took a copy. Felsworth hinted that a small, tax-free donation to the fine work at Metheford Academy might speed his efforts."

"I hope you didn't promise too much," she cautioned. "We're not exactly the Bill Gateses these days."

"I figured fifty bucks ought to cover it, though I never mentioned a figure to him."

"I suppose it's worth it. By the way did you at least have the presence of mind to get a description of Kravitz?"

"I did," Dan said. "But after you subtract a full gray thatch of beard and mustache, the description of Kravitz might fit any one of our clean-shaven, mystery critique newcomers. They're all close to six feet with medium to athletic builds."

"Why just the critique newcomers?" she asked.

"Someone at the table heard Liz boasting about the letters or she wouldn't have been targeted. Anyway, the colonel didn't have any ideas about eye color or mannerisms and doubted whether a black-and-white yearbook picture of Kravitz in full beard would be of any use, but he'll send it along by snail mail anyway."

"What about hair color? That might be useful," asked Rivka.

"Felsworth said light brown—perhaps even blond, but it's been gray so long that he couldn't remember which."

"But a man on the lam from the police could easily change that with hair coloring dye or bleach," she said. "I'm afraid we don't have much to go on."

* * *

Emil Kravitz set the brown paper bag down on the small table he used as a writing desk, slipped out of his coat, and hung it behind the closet door. A relaxed feeling came over him within the confines of his rented flat. His masquerade needn't be sustained here amid the faded flowery wallpaper and darkly stained woodwork. The smallish space was cramped with furniture he couldn't use and didn't want, but the flat served his purposes quite well. A stingy forty-watt bulb in a table lamp and an opaque window shade made reading a tiresome chore. He spread the curtains back as far as they would go and jerked the sepia-colored shade up to its limit, unleashing the much-needed outside light.

Reaching under both bedspread and pillow, Emil extracted his briefcase, carried it to the desk, and sat down. He probed through a slit in the lining—a cache secreting the letters acquired two nights earlier. He removed both letters and set the case on the floor beside him. A quick examination of the two letters he'd filched from behind the poster revealed that he had already intercepted one of them at Fraume's flat. Emil had posted that letter after photocopying it, so he already knew its contents. But he knew neither the total number of letters involved nor the number of clues each contained. He might have them all, but then again he might not. Unfolding the other letter, the interloper read:

My dear Edythe,

    I hope, with all my being, that you are free of pain and still able to enjoy life. I am that much older than you and yet I grasp at every bit of life's gifts. Some might call it the fear of dying. I'd like to think of it as the love of living. Hang on, dear sister, for all you're worth and savor every minute of it. If there was only something I could do for you. I'd like to hold your hand in mine and walk you through the park again. I'd like to yank on your pigtails one more time. Remember walking to shul holding hands when we were just kids? It was wonderful then, before the Nazis came and took Papa away. As happy as we were, I don't think I could go back and live through that part of life again. We survived, and even today, I have no regrets.

    Emil's threats are coming more often now. My phone rings at all hours, and the frightening thing is that there's no voice on the other end. I get his message in spite of the bullying silence. He is an evil man with a monstrous drive. It's a wonder that I haven't caved in before now. I have come to know that neither I nor my successors shall personally benefit from my discoveries, but I shall do all in my power to prevent that scoundrel from benefiting by my work.

    The next clue is:

> *"At Halley's table set a fourth place."*

I send my best to Bernard and hope he can still think of his old friend.

                              All my love, *Your Abner*

    Emil opened the letter from Fraume that he'd photocopied. He unfolded it and positioned it so the two clue lines were adjacent. He re-read them in the only order that made any sense:

> *"At Halley's table set a fourth place."*
> *"And Mark, his many long years in space."*

    Could Halley be that Roots chap whose statue is down at the Annapolis City Dock? No, that's Haley with one ell. Halley in space could only mean Halley's comet. Perhaps some associated cyclic number carried to the fourth digit. A library might yield information as to Halley's behavior over time. I'll look it up in the morning. But why a capital em in the spelling of Mark unless the old man meant someone's name—perhaps Mark Twain? Ah, the comma seems to bear that out.

He let the two lines flow through his brain over and over until he came to the thought that there might be more clue lines. *That frightened little twit gave up all she knew. I'm sure of it. Still, there might be more she didn't know. Yet Liz could be useful in getting close to the other members of the group. Someone there knows more.*

Emil had experienced a surprising high as he strangled Abner. The risk-taking and sheer power of it fascinated him. He'd discovered the sadistic side of himself and a newfound enjoyment in tasting cruelty. Emil hadn't even minded being rough on Liz. Somehow he'd found a unique pleasure dealing with her.

Emil Kravitz wasn't always this way. In fact, sadism was quite incongruent with his totally insecure beginnings. The path to cheating, bullying, deceit, and now murder began twenty years earlier when he was forced to leave a small Illinois college. What he took away from that bitter experience was a new credo, hard lessons well learned. *Friends can't be trusted, so friendship's not worth the trouble to cultivate, except to suit one's own needs. You put your own goals first and the hell with everyone else.*

Someone in the bookstore critique group *did* know more about the letters, he was quite convinced of it. A fresh thought, a new risk, took root in his mind. He kicked off his shoes and lay down on top of the twin bedspread. Minutes later he fell into a fitful sleep.

Chapter 15

The Petty Manuscript
Thursday, May 27th

Rivka knew exactly where to find her husband. She'd heard the printer at the first floor cashier's station blitzing away with a regimental staccato. At 9:30 a.m. Dan was checking the e-mail on his computer before any customers wandered in. She had some news for him, but instead of bouncing down the stairs in her usual overdrive mode, she balanced her way slowly, step by step. In both arms she cradled a huge, unwieldy tome.

Dan's back stiffened as he heard the unfamiliar heavy feet in the stairwell. When his wife appeared, he sprang up. "Let me help you, babe." He hefted the tome from her and carried it to an empty corner of the desk. He was about to question her, but she got the jump on him.

"Thanks, hon. I'm so excited. This is *Webster's New Unabridged International Dictionary*. The bookstore copy was thirty years old. I'll tell you all about what I've found, but first—" She saw the printer spitting out a pile of papers. "What's going on?" she asked. "What are you printing?"

"Headmaster Felsworth finally e-mailed us copies of the Petty lad's paper on the Koenig research. It'll take a minute or two to finish. Hey, babe, great idea to get that dictionary. We can buy one of those tall scholar stands for it. I get the feeling you found something important."

"I did." Her gold hoop earrings danced back and forth. She

grinned, her cheeks turning rounder the broader her smile. "You're an engineer; you'll love this. I looked up the word pie to see if it had multiple meanings, and sure enough, I found some." Pushing a stack of papers aside, she flipped the tome to her bookmarked page.

"Great, babe. So?"

"For our purposes it can't be short for magpie or chatter pie; nor an old Indian coin. And not a baked fruit or meat dish in a crust; and certainly not the easy-as-pie definition. However, there's one of special interest."

"I'm listening."

"The Greek letter *pi*," she said. "*Pie*: same as *pi*, referring to a jumble."

"*Pi*, is it?" Dan turned to face the computer keyboard. The printer racket had finished. He closed down the e-mail and returned to the online browser. "Yesterday, when you mentioned that old Abner might be trying to slip us a postal zip code, you got me to thinking. What if the word *pie* had a special meaning in the context of printers and printing? So I searched websites on the subject. One from the Melbourne Museum of Printing in Australia had a 'Glossary of Letterpress Composing.' I found this same definition for both *printer's pie* and *printer's pi*."

Dan clicked his mouse on this glossary screen and moved the cursor down the page. "Printer's pie: the mess of types formed when (a) quantity of type is spilt or dropped: a pied job."

"Isn't pi also a symbol used in math?" she asked tactfully. It was about the only thing she remembered from ninth-grade geometry.

"Of course: 3.1415926 and then some—on to infinity, actually. But I'm way ahead of you. I looked up the post office website, http://zip4.usps.com, and typed in the first five fractional digits, 14159, and bombed out. After I remembered 'full in face,' I ignored the decimal point and tried again. Both zips 31415 and 31416 landed me in Savannah, Georgia."

"Wonderful. Now all we have to do is march up and down

the streets of a major Georgia metropolis and knock on all the doors in two zip code areas."

"Don't be so sarcastic," he scolded. "At least we're closer to understanding Abner's conundrum. Every little bit helps."

"Okay, you're right. So, Daniel, let's see what the young man has to say."

Dan picked the sheets up from the printer tray and began reading aloud. Rivka peeked over his shoulder. She tried to focus, but the closeness of her husband's tall, solid body caught her in some unscholarly thoughts. She felt much more like kissing the warm crook of his neck and nibbling his ear. *But hey*, she decided, *we're our own bosses now. We can cuddle any time we want, as long as no customers are here.* She forced herself to listen.

Treatise Part 1 by Will Petty

In Strasbourg, Germany, during March of the year 1503, Gerheardt Koenig found himself staring with fascination at an etching of an old scribe laboriously hand-illuminating a first-character printing block. Koenig knew such soft-metal blocks were used to set off the beginning of each section of printed text. The scribe wielded a sharp, fine stylus in a flowing calligraphy style similar to the moveable *old roman* typeface that filled the rest of the pages. The exception was that the much-enlarged, hand-scripted initial character left room for floral, fauna, and religious designs between the outlines. Repeated strokes with the stylus deepened the design. This extremely patient man, truly an artisan, applied a period-popular religious theme to the illumination of these characters.

"Hey, this is pretty sophisticated stuff," Rivka said. She rolled an office chair on casters over so she could sit alongside her husband. "How old did you say this kid was?"

"I didn't. Felsworth didn't know for sure without looking up Petty's personal records, but he did think the boy was a good deal younger than most of his classmates. Can I continue now?"

"Sorry," she said.

> Mr. Koenig realized that, like the moveable type, each block had a limited life use because of the soft pot metal employed. These blocks, requiring so much labor to produce, had to be used sparingly. As he watched the old engraver at work, an idea began to ferment in his mind. Like the smaller type, large illuminated type could be reproduced by pouring heated pot metal into brass molds with inverse typeface. But it would be two years before he would find a way to punch the mold. A single punch would require an inordinate amount of force.
>
> Gerheardt knew that the old scribe's finished text must be intended for one of the wealthy. Since literacy had barely spread through Europe in those times, many of the wealthy depended upon others—educated employees and servants—for actual reading. The illuminated characters helped these privileged illiterates to associate with particular passages on the pages.
>
> After learning to read and write from the monks at a nearby monastery, Gerheardt apprenticed in his father's trade as a typefounder, a man of metals and tooling. Young Koenig proved quick to learn, and in time he supplanted the senior Koenig in the foundry end of the print shop's business, taking the craft to innovative ways for improving the production of typeface and printers' metallurgy.

"Wow!" said Dan. "This paper appears to have been thoroughly researched. No wonder Kravitz challenged the kid."

"Didn't you say that Petty worked for Fraume?" she asked.

"Yeah," replied Dan. "He had access to all of Fraume's research, but it takes a superior mind to understand it well enough to write a paper like this. This Petty's quite a scholar in his own right." Dan continued reading.

> The elder Koenig, a former blacksmith and pi-

oneer in typefounding, had worked for Peter Schoffer in a print shop obtained through the foreclosure of Johannes Gutenberg's enterprise a half-century earlier. Johannes Fust, who financed Gutenberg, was Schoffer's father-in-law. Gutenberg had pioneered the use of moveable individual typefaces in a converted worm-screw wine press to render his forty-two-line (per page) Bible, but he was hardly a businessman.

Koenig's latest idea envisioned a font set six times the size of Gutenberg's typeface, covering four lines of indented text and compensated for with appropriate inter-line spacing. The entire initial character would be too difficult to punch at once, so he engraved a portion of an elaborate design into sixteen separate punch heads made of hard metal. The smooth-sided punches were aligned in a small frame. Pounding the individual punches into a common brass matrix block collectively formed the inverse image of an oversized character. Filling the matrix with molten pot metal, a largely lead/tin alloy, many pieces of type with the designed character face could then be cast from this larger-than-normal mold. A reasonable amount of trimming, shaving, and adjustment was necessary, but this was true of any cast typeface of the day.

He had to work the project on his own time, because the shop's owner wouldn't allow him the hours needed. As a result, the first character took nearly six months to achieve the desired degree of perfection.

The jangling bell on The Dungeon door signaled the arrival of a customer. Liz, working the lower floor, responded, enabling the Shermans to read more of the Petty papers.

The remaining set took over four years to complete, but by1507, everyone in the foundry showed interest in the brass matrices that history would come to know as *Koenig's Original Floral Font Matrices*. The set comprised forty brass matrix blocks, including the upper-case alphabet, numerals, special characters, and punctuation. Koenig's fame spread, and the demand for the new type grew, so he designed and produced two additional sets employing different floral designs. All of the soon-popular Koenig font sets burgeoned into extensive use until the 1600s, but fell into decline thereafter, only to be abandoned by the end of the eighteenth century, when serif and modern *roman* styling became the norm.

The Koenig matrices, preserved in oiled rags, wound up on forgotten shelves in a stone wine cellar beneath the print shop of one Manfried Heinswaller and stayed there for another two hundred years. Only Heinswaller's diary chronicled their existence and history, but not their exact whereabouts. Interested collectors, stimulated by his diary, soon became frustrated with fruitless searching.

"Wow," exclaimed Rivka. "This is exciting. I don't think even Eydthe had any idea of the value or history behind these things. It's a shame she and Bernie couldn't be a part of all this. Weren't you surprised that the sets are made out of brass and not carved from wood?"

"Not really," Dan said. "Wood isn't that durable, and they were already using brass alloys of copper and zinc long before the sixteenth century. Besides, brass is a pliable yet durable metal, very suited to the task. It also conducts heat away from the molten metal very well."

Rivka grabbed the pages from him, and she would have read on, except that the door jangled twice more. Liz was busy with the last customer, so the Shermans parked the Petty papers in a drawer beneath the counter and assumed their role as booksellers.

Chapter 16

Difficult Times
Same Day

At 5:45 only one patron remained in the store, and Liz waited on the elderly woman in the language section. Rivka, in need of a break, took the opportunity to sit down at the cash register. Pulling open the drawer beneath the counter with the intention of snacking on a Butterfinger candy bar, she discovered it wasn't there. *Dan must have gotten to it first, but that would be weird*, she thought. *He doesn't usually eat candy bars.* She picked up the sheaf of papers there to look underneath, and while they still remained in her hand, Rivka remembered they were the Petty papers. Each of the pages they had already read was stacked in succession behind the previous one.

Rivka had read only two lines before she felt a gentle breath on her nape.

"You weren't gonna read that without me, were you?" Dan bussed his wife on the neck, slid a chair over next to her, and sat down. A warm shiver tickled her insides. Together they read more of the Petty boy's work.

Treatise Part 2 by Will Petty

Eventually, in the year 1909, a bookstore replaced Heinswaller's print shop, and three years later a stationer took it over. The entire complex was demolished in 1916 to make way for a small clothing factory of two dozen employees. The new construction covered the top of the same wine cellar, using it as a partial foundation, without ever disturbing its precious cache.

Sometime during World War I, Lili Ostreck descended to the factory's basement level to fetch special bolts of cloth to make German flag-officer uniforms. As Lili pushed her cart along the basement floor, one wheel struck a hole in the floor, temporarily hobbling the cart. She lifted the wheel out of the rut and started to go on, but the hole had a ring in it, and this attracted her further attention. On hands and knees, the young woman brushed away a layer of straw and debris to find a wooden door attached to the ring. Surprisingly, the door swung open freely and revealed a set of stone steps, leading down to a sub-cellar with a dry stone floor. She started down the steps, but abandoned the idea when the cobwebs, musty odors, and lack of lighting overtook her. She promptly retreated and covered over her discovery before delivering the cloth to her workstation on the floor above.

The next day on her lunch break, Lili returned to the sub-cellar with a torch, a broom, and some gloves. The cache comprised mostly rubble and a few bottles of visibly turned wine. Her disappointment would have been complete except for three wooden cases with fine brass handles. Inside these cases she found curious brass cubes wrapped in oily rags. The nineteen-year-old woman could see the strange mirror-imaged letters inside the brass cubes, but didn't know what to make of them; however, she thought Herr Sigmund Stein might be able to help her. He collected old books and things. And Lili worked for Herr Stein on weekends as a maid. She unwrapped a few of the blocks and put them in her apron pocket before replacing the cases and restoring the sub-cellar floor as she had found it.

On the following Saturday, Lili waited until the Steins had returned from synagogue and then brought the brass cubes to her weekend employer. Herr Stein examined them quite carefully and told her that they were very old. Asking if there were more where these came from, Lili explained about finding the cache with three cases full of them. Herr Stein became extremely excited. When she asked whether these things were valuable, he smiled and assured her that they were indeed, but only to someone who could appreciate their value—a fine collector like himself. Herr Stein refused to discuss price until he saw the entire collection.

The following Monday Lili remained in the factory after work, and when everyone else had gone home, she let Herr Stein into the building via a rear door so as to avoid the cranky night watchman. The clandestine pair quickly made their way to the ancient sub-basement, where Sigmund Stein became overwhelmed with joy. The wooden cases contained thin brass nameplates with dates and distinct Koenig hallmarks, tiny K-shaped anvils. Each case contained eight rows and five columns—forty neatly compartmented, brass matrices. But to Stein's further amazement, he discovered a printer's *chase*—a flat four-sided metal frame obviously designed to lock a print project in place—a device to prevent even the most immeasurable movement among the individual print type in the job. The experienced collector knew that smooth wooden bars normally occupied the larger spaces around the print type within the *chase,* and a system of wood and metal wedges, called *quoins*, were usually driven between the chase and its spacers.

This was no ordinary *chase*. Although the inner surface was just as true, square, and smooth as the day it was manufactured, the outside bore an intricate filigreed design, the date, and Koenig's hallmark anvil. In itself, the *chase* was a work of beauty created by a master artisan and craftsman two hundred years before. The two interlopers settled on a generous finder's fee, and Lili helped Sigmund carry their newfound treasure back to the Stein country manor.

So pleased was he with their discovery that Herr Stein offered Lili full-time employment, and eighteen months later, she married Deiter Hoffmann, son of the Steins' current butler. A fatal heart attack took the elder Hoffmann in 1921. Deiter assumed his father's duties in the Stein household.

Fine wood and glass cabinets were constructed,

and both matrices and chase were proudly displayed, along with other lesser antiquities in the Stein collection. They remained there until October of 1940 when it became more than apparent that the Nazi regime intended to pilfer the wealth of their *Yuden* population. Sigmund, with Deiter's help, bricked over several small caches in the basement walls. One of them held the brass matrices and cast iron *chase* throughout the Second World War.

While Herr Stein wasn't arrested until February of 1942, his home was raided on a continuing basis. Deiter and Lili chose to leave, rather than be arrested for fraternizing with known Jews.

"So much for loyalty," Rivka mumbled.

"I don't think there was much of a choice the way the Nazis were arresting people right and left in those days," answered Dan. "Employment or any association with the Steins posed a danger to the Hoffmans. At least that's the way Deiter and Lili must have seen it."

Treatise Part 3 by Will Petty

Near the end of 1943 Allied bombers had left the once-palatial Stein home in piles of brick, stone, and glass rubble. Stein's wife and daughter died in the same attack, but Stein wouldn't know that for sure until years later. Stein, in his sixty-third year, was found fit enough to serve in a slave labor camp. Forced to carry heavy bags of chemicals used in the making of munitions, the frail man survived on a broth produced by boiling potato peelings and a thick gruel made from stale bread, rotten vegetables, and spoiled dairy products. With hundreds of others, he slept on the top tier of a massive communal bed constructed of raw wooden beams and stretched gunny-sack material.

It was here in the communal bed that Sigmund Stein met Abner Fraume. Although Fraume was a much younger man, the two men forged a fast friendship, sharing intellectual exchanges and prewar stories. Their camaraderie made life slightly more bearable until

Stein's health took a turn for the worse twenty months later. Sigmund guessed from the incessant coughing that he had contracted tuberculosis. He began avoiding Abner for fear that he might infect his friend. The Allies were already on the way across Western Europe, but Sigmund Stein knew he wouldn't live to see the day of liberation. However, Abner might last until then, and Abner was the only one Stein could trust, so he told him of the Koenig treasure and its history. He even drew a map for him in the dust so that he might find the cache after the war. Sigmund Stein passed out of his misery only a few nights later.

"That's so sad," Rivka said, choking up on the words. "But at least Edythe's brother knew where to look for the chase and sets."

"We assume that's how he wound up with them."

"Do you think there are any clues in the boy's papers?"

"There's only one way to find out. Let's read on."

Indeed, Abner did survive the carnage of the terrible war and was liberated by the advancing Allied Forces that spring. A much weakened, older, and very susceptible refugee, he convalesced in a tuberculosis sanatorium in Frankfurt, Germany, for three years immediately following the war. When fully recovered, finding his only sibling, Edythe, became a priority. He discovered she had married Bernard Bender early in 1939, and the two had emigrated to England. The Benders' London-Soho bookstore and home had taken quite a beating during the Jerry blitzkrieg, so immediately after the war they found a fresh start in the United States.

In 1953, after a lot of paper chasing and near misses, Abner and his sister were joyously reunited in Annapolis, Maryland. They resolved to stay close and in touch for the rest of their lives. Afterward, Fraume boasted that never a week went by without a letter or a phone call. In 1955 Abner moved to London and a year later he relocated to Bath in the south of England.

Death Goes Postal

A childhood mastery of the English language enabled him to teach European history at the local university there.

"How could Petty know all this personal stuff about Abner and Edythe?" asked Rivka.

"Either the lad had access to Fraume's personal correspondence or it's a little reality-based fiction," replied Dan.

"It's so smooth," Rivka said. "It might be a little bit of both. Even though it sounds as if he's writing a scholarly dissertation, we're still dealing with a youngster seeking a good grade on a term paper. And who knows? Maybe, in a conversational moment, Abner actually told Will a bit about Edythe "

"Turns out, there's even a plot to follow," said Dan. "The boy's got imagination. I'm hooked. Let's go on."

Abner never forgot his friend Sigmund and said *Kaddish* for him on a regular basis, even though there was no known grave. He made frequent trips to the Continent in search of the Koenig treasure and any related documentation. He visited the remains of the Stein home and, amid the rubble, found the cache which once held the Koenig matrices, but someone had beaten him to it. Only a small brass nameplate with the anvil hallmark identified the empty cache. Unknown to Abner, this particular cache had been cleaned out by Deiter Hoffmann in 1947. Other caches lay open as well—some due to looting and others exposed by repeated bombing.

Abner did have some success in locating the Heinswaller diary and some notes by Peter Schoffer. He also found some original research on Gutenberg, Fust, and others in a German library. He'd acquired some minor relics—an old converted wine-to-printing press, some *old romans* type, and a few early books, including one of Gutenberg's forty-two-line Bibles. Each of these he'd turned over to the British Literary Museum in London. He had Stein's own words on how he might find the treasure in the first place. All he needed was the Koenig treasure itself and he could present his entire work to academia—a lifelong ambition. Abner spent almost fifty years in that pursuit, and as time went on, he felt that dream gradually slipping away from him.

"I wonder how much more *Evil* Kravitz knows than we do," Dan said.

Rivka nodded ruefully. "*Evil* Emil's got one or more clue-filled letters that we don't have."

"And maybe a whole lot more," Dan added, frowning. His dark eyebrows, knitted together, took on the look of a fuzzy caterpillar. "Hey, babe, this scenario is beginning to take shape. Remember, a man attacked Liz at her apartment. And somebody—we don't know who, or even if it's a man or woman—broke into the bookstore at night."

Rivka's eyes gleamed under flickering lashes. "And whoever it was got those letters from behind the poster." She jumped up, chunky body quivering with excitement. "That's it, Dan!"

"That's what?"

"What if it was a disguised Emil Kravitz at the last mystery critique meeting?" Rivka breathed in deeply, trying to slow her thumping heart. "Oh, my God! He had to be…to pick up the information that Liz blabbed about the letters. How else would he have known about the cache behind the poster? So, the way I see it, if he already has enough information to find the chase and matrices, he'll be the one who doesn't show up at the next meeting."

"If you're right, Rivka, that's good news and bad news. The good: we'll be rid of him. The bad: he'll get away with theft—and murder!"

"Kravitz has to be one of the newer male members. There's Everet Kanter, Spencer Edington, Joel Wise, Garry Posner, and Vernon Levant. What do we know about these people?"

"I'm surprised you didn't put my name on the list."

"Naw, I've been letting you get away with murder for years," she jested. "Why would I suspect you now? Besides, you're too cute. Joel's been in practice for years in Annapolis. So we can eliminate him pretty easily, but what about the others?"

"We can't eliminate anyone yet," Dan said. "Lawyers are crafty and sometimes they act as agents for some pretty shady clients. But it's difficult to believe that about Joel. And if you think about it, Everet Kanter is the most logical—his name is the closest to Emil's. If Emil is Everet, I'd say that's a pretty clumsy name disguise for a thief and murderer."

"Hey, it's getting late," said Rivka looking at her watch.

"So what's the hurry?" asked Dan. "We could finish this thing in a half-hour."

"Tonight's the critique group," she replied, shoving the Petty papers back in the desk drawer. "And there are a few things I still have to talk to Liz about."

Chapter 17

Confrontations
Same Day

Liz Nathan whined, "I won't do it. I don't have to come to the meeting. I just know he'll be here." She leaned over the book cart, gripped the rails tightly, and tried to push the cart toward the rear of the first-floor stacks. It wouldn't budge.

Holding onto the cart from the other end, creating a tug-of-war, Rivka argued, "Even if he is, why would he bother you? He's already squeezed out all the information you had."

"I suppose so, but how would *he* know that?"

"He let you go, didn't he?" Rivka persisted. "Besides, I don't think he's going to show up. The way I figure it, the guy who mugged you will be long gone by now. Dan and I think he'll be the no-show. That's how we'll know who he is."

"Why wouldn't he come?" Liz asked.

"He already knows where the artifacts are and should be well on his way to recovering them. What would he want with any of us, especially you?"

"What do you mean, Rivka, 'especially me'?"

"Like I said, he's done with you."

"Then why do you need me to be there?"

"Well, there's that slight chance he might show—you know, just in case. You're the only one who's been alone with the man. We're counting on you to recall something useful about him. His voice, his size, or a mannerism, maybe."

"You just said he probably won't come."

"He probably won't. Anyway, how can he hurt you if we're all there beside you? Besides, he didn't really hurt you the first time—just a scare, wasn't it?"

"Just a scare, huh? He pushed me around, kicked me, and threw me down. Wasn't that more than just a scare?"

"Of course. You're right. He did get rough with you." Rivka's voice softened, realizing how insensitive she must have sounded. "Liz, you won't be alone. We'll be there to help you. Especially Dan. He's really strong. Will you come?" Rivka had to wait a few seconds for her answer.

"I suppose so." Liz bit her lip and looked away.

Rivka released her grip on the cart, allowing Liz to complete her journey to the Horror and Fantasy shelves. Rivka returned to the register, stopping to help a customer locate a used translation of *Dante's Inferno*. She found Daniel ringing up a sale comprising one trade paperback and two mass-market books. He thanked the patron and turned to Rivka.

"Dan, I just had a talk with Liz. She's still pretty rattled over the mugging. It took a lot to convince her to come to tonight's critique meeting."

"I don't blame her, hon. Neither one of us has ever been unfortunate enough to be either a mugger or a *muggee*. Why is it so important that she be there?"

"I don't know. I just thought she might remember something about *Evil* Emil."

"I still think our man won't show. Why would he?"

"Maybe to get more clues or to keep up appearances."

"Come on, girl. Out with it. You've got something else brewing in that gorgeous head of yours."

"Well! I wondered if Liz would be capable of minding the store while the two of us took a little vacation. She's such a bundle of nerves that I doubt whether she'd stay in the store alone for even ten minutes. Frankly, I don't have the chutzpah to ask her."

"Sweetheart, what makes you think we could afford either the time or money to take a vacation right now? We've got everything we own tied up in this place and we haven't shown much of a profit yet."

"Not exactly a vacation—more like a two- or three-day weekend in, say, Georgia?"

"Rivka, you devil you. What do you have in mind?"

"You know that flat key we found?"

"Yeah!" She had his attention now.

"It looked so much like a post office box key that I took it over to try in one of the boxes at the Church Circle post office. It fit several of the slots, but of course it wouldn't turn in any of them. I think *pozt* and *pi* refer to a post office zip—not a residential zip. We're looking for a postal box, Dan."

"Of course. If it looks like, feels like, smells like, and fits like, it surely must be one. But there's no number on it. Abner must have sent a copy rather than the original key. How do you expect to—" Her silence led him to a conclusion. "You mean you want to try this key in every box in the Savannah post office?"

"Two post offices!" Rivka nodded so vigorously her glasses slipped down her nose. "Plural. Remember, there are two possible zips, depending on whether we use the actual number sequence or round it off."

"Two is right," he said. "Hey, aren't the school kids due for a break soon? Perhaps we could get Heather to help out for three days."

"Even French teachers need time off," she said. "So why would Heather want to fill in for us?"

"Well, she adores books and browsing in the store, and I suppose we could pay her a few days' wages. That might be reason enough. Most teachers need extra cash."

"Wait a minute, Dan. Aren't post offices closed on Sundays and holidays?"

"Absolutely," he replied. "But the box area is always open to the public—all the better for us. Less traffic and less chance of being noticed."

"I'll speak to Heather tonight." Rivka nodded, then cocked her head. "It's awfully quiet in the back of the store, don't you think?"

Just then, they heard the sound of books tumbling to the floor, followed by a frantic voice. "Oh, hell!"

* * *

Every one of the male suspects did show up at the meeting—every one, that is, except Joel, who'd called to say he had a client meeting, but would try to make it later. Liz purposely took the seat at the conference table between Rivka and Daniel for whatever protection she thought that might offer. She slunk way down in her chair, trying to make herself smaller, if not altogether invisible. Heather chose to sit between Peggy and Vernon on Dan's side of the table. Everet and Spencer sat farther down. Frieda, sitting opposite them, was pleased when Garry chose the seat next to her.

"Vernon's kind of distinguished, don't you think?" Heather whispered to Peggy.

"Yeah, intellectual looks, but maybe a bit old for you. Nice bod, though. I can see why you're interested."

"Who said I'm interested?" Heather said coyly.

"You're the one who brought him up," Peggy reminded her.

Heather grinned sheepishly and turned to find Vernon looking her way. *Did he hear what I said? Hopefully not.* She took a deep breath and launched into a conversation with him about her story, in a sort of confidential murmur. "I reconsidered your suggestions about the ending to my story. Now I have the heroine striking the villain several times before running away, but the creep eventually recovers and resumes his threatening chase. It actually adds to the suspense this way."

"I didn't mean for you to compromise your story just for what I had to say."

"Oh, no, Vernon," she replied. "It's just that I respect your opinion. After all, isn't that what a critique group is all about?"

"I suppose you're right," he said. "But remember, it's only an opinion—my opinion."

Heather smiled. "By the way, I've given some thought to your other proposal as well, but I haven't had a chance to talk with Liz yet. She's been a bit of a recluse since her mugging experience."

"Really? I would enjoy teaming up with the two of you, especially you." He winked at her, eliciting a broad flush in her cheeks.

As Rivka called the group to order, Lord Byron bounded up onto a nearby bookcase. Maintaining his security barrier behind Dan, the black furry body arched, the cat bared his teeth, and directed a mean series of whines and hisses toward the opposite end of the table. His Lordship was visibly upset over something—enough to divert the attention of everyone in the room. Because of the distance over the table, neither Dan nor Rivka could determine who the rage was directed at. Only Spencer squirmed in his chair.

"What's the matter, Spence?" asked Dan. "Don't you like cats? Seems like Lord Byron has taken an extreme dislike to someone at your end of the table. Is it you, by any chance?"

"The feeling is mutual!" Spencer responded irritably. "I'm hyperallergic to cat fur. Keep him away from me. I could go into convulsions."

"How about you, Vernon?" asked Rivka. "What's your take on cats?"

"Oh, I can take 'em or leave 'em," Vernon said. "But I prefer a dog. They're so much more dependent and substantial—a pet you can roll around on the floor with. I get bored with just petting, feeding, and cleaning up after cats. I don't have the patience for them."

"Garry?" tried Rivka one more time.

"Don't ask," Garry snapped. "My ex had cats all over the house—fourteen of them to be exact. You couldn't even walk in the house without tripping over them. She treated the damned things better than she did me or my kid. So every time I see a cat, I think of my ex. I can't stand any of them, including my ex."

"Before you get to me," interrupted Everet. "I'd like to know why it's just the men's opinion on cats that you're soliciting?"

"Two reasons," replied Rivka. "One, Lord Byron has a particular dislike for cat burglars. As you may know someone broke into the store the night before we moved in. During the break-in, Lord Byron was attacked and locked away in a closet for almost two days before we found him. And two, Liz, at the very least, recognized her attacker as a male."

"That still doesn't give you the right to suspect any one of us," responded Everet. "It could have been any stranger."

"I'd say it couldn't be," Rivka shot back. "A complete stranger wouldn't have known that Liz had any information to give unless that person sat at this very table on the night she misspoke."

Out of the corner of his eye Dan caught Liz wincing and squirming.

Rivka put an arm around Liz's shoulder, gripping tightly to comfort her. "And the thief wouldn't have known where to look for the letters."

"The four of us are truly suspects then," said Garry. "That's absolutely fantastic—a real live mystery for the critique group to consider."

"Then it's letters that were stolen?" asked Peggy. "And you believe it's the same man that attacked Liz?"

"We must be dealing with a desperate and determined man," said Vernon.

Rivka nodded and watched Everet approach Lord Byron, but before he got close enough to confirm or deny, the bundle of fur calmly retreated from his bookcase perch and slowly descended the staircase without any apparent emotion.

"Just how many letters were there?" asked Spencer.

"Did the thief get all of them?" queried Vernon.

"And was there any part of the cache that the thief didn't get?" Everet added.

"I'm afraid I can't answer any of those questions, gentlemen," replied Rivka.

"Can't or won't?" asked Garry. If we're going to solve a mysterious mugging and theft, we need to have a few clues to ponder, don't we?"

"Who has literary work to be critiqued tonight?" asked Rivka, trying desperately to get the meeting back on track. She had no idea how to get the culprit to expose the wound from Lord Byron's bite, short of asking outright.

"I started a new chapter in my novel," offered Frieda. "I got this idea talking to Garry. The beginning almost wrote itself, but midway through, I got stuck again. Maybe someone here can help."

"Do it!" Rivka urged. "That's why we're here."

Frieda read her chapter start, stimulating a lengthy discussion. Help came from all quarters, and she seemed pleased with the result. Peggy read a first draft of her short story, and the group agreed that it had a good deal of polish to it already. They suggested a few magazines where she might try to have it published. Lastly, Vernon read from several of his *Just Punishment* poems with lines that went like:

> *"Hematologists are circulated*
>   *and educators are matriculated.*
> *So if idols can be adulated,*
>   *why shouldn't mimics be emulated?"*

Vernon claimed he had a million of them and found writing them enjoyable. His rhyming amused the group, but several smirked and squirmed, refusing to take him seriously.

While the others chatted over cups of Dan's special blend of hazelnut coffee, Rivka took Heather aside. "I'm not sure I have any right to ask you this, but I don't seem to have anywhere else to turn." She hesitated, then seeing Heather's okay-by-me shrug, continued. "I wonder if I might call upon you to mind the store with Liz while Dan and I take an extended weekend. It would be during one of your regular school breaks." Rivka outlined what was expected of them and promised to phone each evening. Heather agreed, sloughing off the idea of payment, but Rivka insisted, and so the arrangement gelled.

"Heather, on another subject, how well do you know Vernon?" asked Rivka.

"Not well. We met here, then I bumped into him at the City Dock the other day, and we had a bite together."

"Do you know anything about him? Like where he's from?"

"Vernon told me he's from Connecticut. The man's sensitive, writes poetry, and he is kinda cute."

"Are you involved with him, Heather?"

"Now you're beginning to sound like a mother hen."

"It's just that I'm concerned. Dan and I believe that one of the new men in our critique group is the mugger-slash-thief. He is far more dangerous than we've let on."

"What do you mean?"

"This same man probably killed Edythe's brother, Abner, in England to get his hands on some very old and rare relics. And because he came up empty-handed, we think he's desperate enough to kill again to achieve his ends. Be careful, Heather. Go slowly."

"And you think it might be Vernon?" Heather's green eyes widened and her jaw dropped.

"No more so than the other three. But remember—one of them is very likely a thief and even a killer."

"He'd be wasting his time. What possible information could he get from *me?*" asserted Heather in her best bravado voice. She hugged Rivka, thanked her for caring about her safety, and then disappeared down the staircase.

When Rivka's attention returned to the conference table to pick up her things, she found Liz still sitting in her chair. Everyone else had gone.

"He *was* here, wasn't he?" demanded a trembling Liz. "And don't try to tell me that Joel was my mugger. He was the only no-show."

Rivka slid into a chair beside her. "I assume your mugger *was* here, and no, it's not very likely that Joel Wise did it. He's had a law practice in Annapolis for at least fifteen years."

"Well, don't lawyers do other peoples' dirty work? Couldn't he be doing just that?" asked Liz.

"Anything's possible, Liz," answered Rivka. "but Dan and I have known the man too many years. We believe our killer came from England."

"Did you just say 'killer'?"

"Oops! Just a slip, I assure you." Rivka felt like biting her tongue.

"I'll *bet* it was. Don't lie to me, Rivka. Who did he kill and why?"

"I'm sorry, Liz. Dan and I think he killed Edythe's brother in England before he came here. He was after the letters and mugged you to find out where they were."

"And to think I let you talk me into coming to this meeting. I trusted you, and you still persuaded me to come, in spite of knowing what this man is."

"Guilty as charged, Liz. I'm truly sorry. But you have to admit, you did lead him to the poster with the letters whether you wanted to or not."

"Who's guilty and of what?" asked Heather, reappearing at the head of the stairs.

"What are you doing back here?" Rivka demanded.

"I forgot my briefcase with the changes to my story in it. Ah! There it is on the table—right where I left it." She snatched it up and headed toward the stairs once more.

"Good grief," said Liz, trying to ignore Heather's return. "Can I spend the night here? I don't want to go home to an empty apartment. I'm afraid of this guy."

"I guess so. You could sleep on the couch in the other room," Rivka said. "I'll get you a pillow and some sheets and blankets. But it's just for tonight. You have to pull yourself together. Remember, the man wanted the letters. He doesn't need anything more from you, so you're safe, even at home."

"Wait!" called Heather from the top step. "Liz, honey, you could come home with me. I doubt if anyone would think of looking for you there. I've got plenty of room—twin beds, in fact, and besides, it's still early. We could stop off at the Maryland Inn for a few minutes and listen to some Charlie Byrd imitator play classical guitar. A glass of wine might be just what you need to loosen up."

"That's a great idea," offered Rivka, not especially anxious for a brooding overnight guest. "A little night life might be just the thing for you, Liz."

"Gosh, I suppose it couldn't hurt. The wine might help me get some sleep. I haven't been sleeping too well lately."

"Well, honey, if that's all the convincing you need, grab your things and let's get going," said Heather.

Liz picked up her floppy purse and followed Heather to the first floor and the street.

Rivka stared at the empty stairwell, reflecting on the evening's events. *God! What am I doing, exposing my friends to danger like this? Is it too much chutzpah to expect them to mind the store while Dan and I go gallivanting off to Georgia? Am I being an alarmist frightening Heather that way? I've opened a real Pandora's box.*

Chapter 18

Knight to the Rescue
After the Meeting

The sharp night air struck Garry Posner with a bone-chilling shiver as he left the bookstore. It jolted him out of lethargy instilled by two hours of sitting in a warm room. He'd gotten stiff, too. His sixty-four-year-old body needed to move about more often. Being with other writers opened a whole new feeling of camaraderie, especially with that cute, dark-haired waitress. The perky little lady seemed genuinely attracted to him as well. Her speech, odd selection and phrasing of words, came out a little rough sometimes, but that gave her character and interest. Maybe he'd use her in one of his stories.

Garry halted under the bookstore gas lamp long enough to collect his bearings and then quick-stepped toward his Chevy pickup. After a few steps, a loud grinding sound assaulted his ears. The raspy whine reared up and demanded attention a second and third time, too, but the last time it waned like a dying creature, begging for his assistance. He finally recognized both the sound and its direction and responded to the starter's cry for help. Frieda Forrester's car sat curbside with Frieda leaning over the steering wheel in a definite gesture of frustration.

"Hi, Frieda. I'm Garry. From the meeting. Remember? Sounds like your car is misbehaving, little lady. Mind if I give it a try?"

Death Goes Postal

The unexpected voice startled her into sitting upright. Instinct led her to push down on the door locks button. Then she recognized him and started to roll down the window. But remembering the discussion about the thief and mugger, she stopped the glass partway down. He repeated his offer to help. She could hardly refuse—the alternatives being to spend the night in the car or walk some unknown distance to a service station. She scrutinized his face, looking for some kind of reassurance.

"Release the hood," he called to her.

As soon as the hood popped up in front of the windshield, Garry disappeared from her view. Underneath, she imagined him jiggling linkages, messing with wiring, and sniffing for signs of carburetor flooding. His re-emergence minutes later lacked promise as he shook his head and pursed his lips into a tight scrunch. The problem remained elusive. He slammed the hood back into place and approached the quarter-open window.

"Don't know what else I can do under there. You want to give it one more try?"

The starter gave up a desperate uh…uh…uh…before switching to a death-defining click.

"Oh, no," she groaned.

"How about I give you a lift home, and you can call someone more capable in the morning."

Frieda nodded, rolled up the window, and got out of the car. While she locked up, he told her he'd parked in the next block. They strolled past century-old homes in the sprinkled light of shaded street lamps. Most of the way they conversed in sparse, halting words—she searching for any reason to mistrust him. But he revealed a kindly, chivalrous side to his nature. An offer of his windbreaker bolstered a more reassuring opinion of him. Frieda accepted and covered her goose bumps with his jacket. And when he held the door to his pickup for her and helped her inside, that act of thoughtfulness sealed her trust. She studied his profile during the ride down Duke of Gloucester Street and over the aging drawbridge into suburban Eastport. Conversation became easier as they made the last few turns and her house came into view. He parked out front, and the words kept coming. As they talked, Frieda glanced at the upstairs window and knew the girls were in bed, if not asleep already.

"After your chivalrous deed, the least I can do is invite you in for a cup of coffee," she offered. "I'm afraid I can't promise you anything but plain old instant. It's all I keep in the house—all I generally have time for these days."

"It's late," he said, "and I should be getting along home."

"Ten-forty's not too late, Garry. Besides, the kids are asleep, and we can have the parlor to ourselves. That is, unless you have to get home to your gang."

"No, Phyllis is an only child, thank goodness. She's spending the night at a friend's so I don't have to report in."

"Then you'll come in for a little bit?"

"If you don't think I'm imposing too much. After all, we're practically strangers."

"How old is Phyllis?" she asked, climbing down from her side of the pickup before he had a chance to get there.

"Sixteen going on twenty-five," he quipped as they walked up to the tiny porch.

"Then she's a difficult child?"

"Oh, no. Just that she's making a fashion statement and experimenting with makeup and doodads."

"Be grateful it's not tattoos and body piercing—the nose, the lips, the belly button, wherever."

He surprised Frieda, taking the key from her and opening the door. She led him inside and deposited him in the parlor while she put the kettle on in the kitchen. By the time she returned, he'd settled in at one end of the sofa examining a paperback potboiler she'd left on the coffee table. Frieda slid out of her shoes and sat against the opposite end of the sofa, facing him.

"So what attracted you to the Annapolis area, Garry?"

"I'd heard I had some long-lost relatives here and since I got laid off from my last job, I figured this was as good a place as any to start over. Besides, my ex decided she wanted to harass us some more. I just wanted to get away from all that."

"A messy divorce then?" she asked.

"You better believe it. Without warning, she runs off with some furniture salesman, leaving Phyllis, fourteen cats, and myself to fend for ourselves. Six months later she returns and wants alimony to support her new lifestyle in her own separate apartment. Can you believe the balls on that bitch? Whoops, sorry!"

"I understand. Believe me, I do," Frieda said, as a shrill whistling sound beckoned from the kitchen. "Cream and sugar?" she asked, bounding up to respond.

"Neither."

"So where are you guys hanging your hats these days?" Frieda called from the other room.

"It's a tiny two-bedroom flat in an older, neglected building—about all I can afford right now. Sea Bright Apartments. Number 107."

Frieda returned with a tray and set it down on the coffee table. Besides the mugs, she had set three slices of chocolate *babka* pound cake and a few oatmeal-raisin cookies. He watched her every move—perky, yet graceful and efficient. More than that, he liked the woman he saw—petite yet curvaceous, with a kind of homespun prettiness. Frieda settled on the sofa much closer this time, and Garry could sense her nearness, a faint mixture of perfume, soap, and heat. Or was the heat his own? His reaction unsettled him.

"Did you find your long-lost relatives okay?" she asked. Garry took a cookie and bit into it. "Yum! These are good. Where do you buy them?"

"I bring home the day-old cookies from the case at the Double T. Now you know all my secrets." She put her hand on his leg and gave it a small squeeze. Inwardly, she wondered, *What's so secret about a bunch of dumb lost relatives?*

Garry placed his hand over hers and squeezed back. "I never knew day-old cookies could taste this good. They're not stale at all.

I'll bet Phyllis and I could eat through a barrel of them in nothing flat." He took a second cookie.

There were crumbs left on his cheek and Frieda leaned over and brushed them away, one by one, with her forefinger. Her face, intent on the task, had drawn close—so close that on impulse, Garry bent forward and kissed her lightly on parted lips. She didn't seem surprised at all, and in fact, provided added gusto. They continued for several moments until he felt an equally impulsive need to break off and to apologize.

"I'm truly sorry," he said. "I can't do this."

Frieda put her fingers to his lips and tried to squelch his protest. She leaned still closer, intending another kiss, but he deflected her wrist and backed away.

"I'm just not ready for this. It's happening too fast. We've only just met."

"I know it's rather sudden, but I thought we both wanted the same thing. You've been such a dear. I am really fond of you, Garry. I wouldn't want to jeopardize our friendship."

"This is all so foreign to me. I haven't been this close to a woman for some time. I don't even know how to behave. I feel like a schoolboy, wondering how far this sort of thing will go. I'm fond of you, too. Be patient with me. Please!" Garry got to his feet and slowly walked to the door. "Thanks. I'll call you." He disappeared into the night.

"Thank *you*," she whispered through the door after he'd gone. The fact that he'd promised to call her was encouraging. She was glad she'd written down his address. Maybe she'd take some cookies over to him in a few days. It might be a chance to meet Phyllis as well.

* * *

The next morning Emil Kravitz started up the walk leading to the Riley house with a small package in hand. He had hardly reached the front door when his landlady met him with a declaration and a barrage of instructions.

Death Goes Postal

"My sister Agnes is having an operation, and I have to go up to Albany and take care of her during recuperation. I'll be gone at least two weeks. If you wouldn't mind, I'd like next month's rent in advance. God knows, I could use the money. Take in the mail and stack it on the dining room table. Stay out of the kitchen while I'm gone, but you're welcome to watch the television if you promise to water the plants and not make a mess in the living room. Not too much water now. Oh! And be sure to lock up, young man."

"Yes, Ms. Riley."

"It's Mrs. Riley. I don't hold with this modern Ms. business."

"Yes, Mrs. Riley."

"Don't just stand there, young man. I can't carry this valise to the curb by myself. Make yourself useful."

Emil picked up the weathered valise and carted it to the taxi waiting at the curb. The driver took it from him and stowed it in the trunk. She climbed in the back seat and waved as the cabbie drove off. Emil waved back, even though his mind had begun to refine his plan, a plan that would get things moving again. He couldn't afford to use his present identity much longer. Someone from the British Literary Museum would be arriving in Annapolis shortly, and certainly the car rental charge would be contested before long.

The boarder used his key to the front door and climbed to his room, where he laid the package on the desk. FRAGILE, in red, appeared twice on the white wrapping. The label bore only an Annapolis P.O. box address, no return specified. Emil pulled up the lone chair and sat down while he tore the paper away. He undid the packing to reveal the contents: four hypodermic needles and a foil-covered bottle marked Trichloroacetaldehyde Monohydrate plus accelerant. Underneath, he found paperwork containing dosage, cautions, and directions for use. A note intended for Kravitz appeared on the back of the information sheet: "We're even now. Don't ever try to contact me again." The note had been signed with the initial "G."

A grin of satisfaction grew on Emil as he leaned back in the chair. He now had a way to ensure that the little critique group had given up all the information it possessed. His heart beat louder and blood raced through his veins.

Chapter 19

Snooping and Snatching
Saturday, May 29th

Two hours before her eleven-to-seven work shift began, Frieda drove slowly down Marina Street until the Sea Bound Apartments rental sign caught her attention. Checking the apartment name against the name she had written on the scrap of paper, she found the two differed, but only slightly. *Could I be mistaken:* Sea Bright *instead of* Sea Bound, she thought. *Done that a lot lately.* Several apartment complexes occupied the park-lined street, but the building with the sign appeared distinctively different from the others—older and poorly kept. It fit Garry's description, so she parked and walked into the nearest of two entrances carrying a partly wrapped box of oatmeal-raisin cookies.

The mailbox numbers ran from 105 through 108. Frieda checked the name plate on 107—P.J. Whooten. *Strange,* she thought, *but there's still the doorbell to try.* She rang, heard the chiming inside, and waited for a response. None came. A vacuum cleaner turned off in apartment 108, and logic led her to inquire there.

A tall bony-faced woman answered the ring. "Yeah?" She wiped her glasses with the end of her apron.

"You know the people next door in 107?" Frieda asked.

"You looking for old man Whooten? He's gone out of town for a few days. In sales, you know."

"No, ma'am. I'm looking for the Posner family—Garry

and his daughter, Phyllis. Do you know them?"

"Nobody but Pete Whooten lives there, and he won't be home until much later this evening."

"What about these apartments?" Frieda asked, indicating the remaining two doors in the hallway.

The tall woman shook her head and pursed her lips. "Don't know them very well, but well enough to know there ain't a man and a girl in either one of those. Maybe you should check with the rental office. Next entrance over. Ms. Lyle, I think, could help you."

Frieda tried the office, but Ms. Lyle, after scanning the card index and files, couldn't find any trace of the Posner family either.

"Are you sure you got the name right—the address?"

Frieda wasn't sure about anything anymore. She absent-mindedly left the cookie package on the office counter and walked back to her car. *Why would Garry lie to me? Who is he really? If he's a killer and thief, why would he be so nice to me?* Her eyes teared, and then her disappointment, her apparent loss, turned to anger. She pounded both hands down on the steering wheel. *Why? Every time I come across an eligible mensch, or someone I thought was a mensch, he's out of reach.* After stewing in the driver's seat for some ten minutes, she collected what was left of her composure and pride, started the car, and drove off to her shift at the Double T.

* * *

Sitting at the kitchen table, Rivka finished the last of her tuna sandwich and washed it down with a swallow of one-percent milk. Her body suddenly felt weighted down. *How can I be tired? It's only noon.* But she knew the answer. Owning the bookstore, being in business for themselves, meant being married to the bookstore. She knew it would be like this. And yet she didn't, not in the flesh. Something she certainly hadn't counted on was missing Friday night *Shabbat* services at temple. Maybe they could up Liz's pay to work Friday nights. Or hire a sub.

Missing too was time to read. Here she was, surrounded

by thousands of books, and she hadn't had five minutes to pick up even one of the novels she'd started. *A Separate Peace* by John Knowles. That was her bedside book. And Dorothy L. Sayers' *The Nine Tailors,* that was her bathroom reading. She'd had it with thrillers for the moment. Too much violence.

Rivka made a sandwich for Dan, covered it with Glad Wrap and put the lettuce, mayo, and bread back in the refrigerator. When she shut the fridge door, she saw Lord Byron's empty water bowl. She washed, refilled it, and set it on the floor. Next the litter box. *Ugh.* It hadn't been cleaned or changed in days. Forgetting to also put Dan's lunch in the fridge, she grabbed the litter box and carried it down to the backyard. Outside, she pried the lid off the lined garbage can and slid the soiled kitty litter into it, wrinkling her nose at the pronounced stench. Using a garden trowel, she scraped more of the reluctant litter into the can and replaced the lid.

The small backyard had a slatted fence and featured a modest patch of greenery: grass, weeds, an azalea bush with a few disheartened blossoms, and a tall honeysuckle hedgerow. As secure and deserted the yard seemed, Rivka sensed the weight of interested eyes. *Is someone watching me?* After surveying the stillness of her surroundings, she dismissed the wayward ESP as her overactive imagination.

Eyes *had been* watching her from the third-floor rear bedroom of a house facing the back street, opposite the bookstore backyard. Edythe would have known it was a rented room in Mrs. Riley's house, but Rivka couldn't know that.

Next door a radio played Sheena Easton's "My Baby Takes the Morning Train." Its catchy melody reverberated through Rivka's head and whole body. She felt like dancing, but a more grubby task awaited. Using the garden hose, she power-rinsed the stuck-on residue from Lord Byron's litter box, and a few paper towels torn from the roll removed the last drops. In the midst of working and humming the familiar tune, Rivka didn't see or hear approaching danger.

Without warning a strong gloved hand clamped over her

mouth, stifling all her feeble attempts to scream for help. A strange outer-worldly voice commanded her complete compliance under threat of bodily harm—even death if she cried out. She struggled fiercely until a sharp object, presumably a needle, pierced her jeans and entered her right buttock. Instantly, fright kicked in. Skin-crawling perspiration sprang from every pore. Rivka felt suddenly light-headed. Her own thumping heart echoed loudly, and then the beat seemed to fade farther and farther into some distant grotto. Her vision swirled and blurred. Objects moved. Her legs folded. Within minutes, the daylight disappeared altogether, and then—nothing.

* * *

Dan didn't relish spending any more than the noon hour behind the register. The bookstore had become busy in the past half hour, and Liz had been rushing around answering questions and fetching books for customers. He stepped out from behind the counter and poked his head down several rows of book stacks. Rivka was nowhere to be seen. Her last words were: "I've got a few chores to do upstairs. I'll relieve you in half an hour." That had been more than two hours ago.

As he looked up, Liz flew past him with a customer in tow.

"Liz," he called after her, "have you seen Rivka lately?"

"I saw her a couple hours ago, going out the back door with Lord Byron's litter box. Haven't seen her since." Liz disappeared around the corner out of earshot.

It took another twenty minutes for Dan to corral her and install her behind the checkout register. Having accomplished this, he set out to look for his wife, fully expecting to find her dawdling over something she'd just unpacked from the recent move. Upstairs in the bedroom seemed to be the logical start, but their bed was still unmade and none of their packed cartons had been opened. Rivka's Jewish star and chain lay on the dresser. *Odd,* he thought. *She'd never leave that behind. She'd worn it round her neck every day since they'd gotten engaged.* The bathroom smelled of fresh 409. In the kitchen, the breakfast dishes had been washed and left to dry in the drain basket. A plate with a tuna salad sandwich had been left on the table for him, the bread a bit dry now. Rivka's purse lay on the counter by the door. But there were no other signs of his wife having been there—except that Lord Byron's litter box should have been on the floor in the hall. It wasn't. He concluded that she must be out back with the litter box, as Liz had suggested, or taken the car on some errand. *But she wouldn't leave without telling me.*

Dan tried the next floor up and still no sign of Rivka. A call up to the mystery loft went unanswered. *Not to worry,* the troubled husband convinced himself, *just some household errand.* Reaching the back veranda, he found water running from the garden hose. The empty litter box sat upended on the flooded concrete walk. Dan shut off the hose faucet and re-coiled the outstretched length onto a reel fastened to the house. A number of crushed flowers caught his attention. Finding a half-used roll of paper toweling piqued his curiosity. A gouged-out stretch of mud convinced him that something or someone had been dragged there. *Rivka's been hurt and gone to the hospital,* he thought. *The car—she's taken the car to the hospital. But that's impossible. She'd have asked me to drive her there.*

Dan dashed down the narrow alley to the street out front. Their Toyota Corolla sat where they'd parked it the night before. The driver's seat remained in the position for his longer legs. She hadn't driven it. He pushed his way into The Dungeon entrance and trudged up to the checkout register.

"Liz, I can't find Rivka anywhere. I don't know what to do."

"Did she have any appointments that you forgot about?"

"Not that I know of. I can't believe she'd go anywhere without her purse. Besides, the car is still out front."

"That's not likely," Liz said. "I've never known her or any other woman to go out without their purse. Their whole life is inside. Unless—"

"Unless what?" he urged.

"Unless she went to a doctor in the neighborhood or to the hospital. It's only a few blocks away."

"Could she have run into trouble? Maybe she's hurt."

"Oh God." Liz blanched. "Could it be that Kravitz guy?"

Dan ran up the stairs to the living area and started phoning Rivka's doctors and dentists and the emergency room. Then he tried some of her friends. None of these shed any light on her disappearance. Even the police needed forty-eight hours before they could react to a missing persons report. Dan returned to the checkout counter and relieved Liz to go about her other duties. *There must be something I can do*, he thought. Waiting was not his strong suit. The distraught husband didn't have to wait long.

Dan was startled to hear "Yankee Doodle" being played in synthetic tones nearby. It came from a cell phone lying on the counter close to the door. It didn't belong to him, yet he compulsively reached for it.

"Hello!"

Somehow, Dan expected to hear Rivka's voice. Instead, he heard a strange mechanical voice telling him: "Your wife has been apprehended and taken to a secure place and will remain safe and healthy as long as you comply with my instructions."

As soon as Dan tried to intervene, the voice threatened to hang up. The instructions were precise and well thought out. "Do not call the police if you want to see your wife alive again. Speak to no one. Let me remind you that Abner Fraume died for not cooperating. You must gather all of Fraume's letters and slip them into the fly leaf of any book. Then take the book, stand outside the bookstore door, and wait for further cell phone instructions. You have four minutes to accomplish this."

Taking the phone with him, Dan darted up the stairs to the *Autumn in New England* poster and retrieved the remaining letter. Sliding it into a book called *Madrid on $200 a Day*, he scribbled a quick note to Liz and flew down the stairs to the front of the store, dropping the note on the counter as he passed by.

Death Goes Postal

The phone began its "Yankee Doodle" ring tone again as soon as he emerged from the store. The voice told him to walk left to the next corner and wait. He complied, and when the cell phone beckoned again, new instructions took him two blocks right to a deserted residential neighborhood. There Dan was told to place the letters and book beside the base of a telephone pole and immediately walk another block in the same direction.

"When do I see Rivka again?"

"Do as I say and you'll see her before nightfall. Now leave the book and get going before I change my mind."

Dan did as the voice ordered, and the succeeding instructions led him back toward the bookstore. He was told to wait there until the letters had been verified. Then another call would tell him where to find his wife.

As Dan approached the store, Liz flew into his arms sobbing, thinking *he'd* been kidnapped as well. As tactfully as he could, he released her and ran to the car, saying he'd explain later. The obsessed husband screeched away from the curb, burning rubber on the smooth street. Nearing the block with the drop site, he drove with far more caution. He scanned in every direction looking for any sign of the kidnapper or Rivka. The book and letter had already been taken, and no sign of anyone remained.

Dan returned to the bookstore to wait. Logic told him he should wait patiently until nightfall, but this was his wife! Her life was at stake! In his neat Oxford button-down shirt and creased khakis he found himself surrounded by customers on this warm spring Saturday. Normally, he'd have been elated by all the business. But focusing, concentrating almost eluded him. The customers had so many requests: where were the travel books, the biographies, the self-helps; and on and on. He diverted those he could to Liz, but he had to man the register. His entire body went rigid, stone cold from his toes up to his heart. His chest constricted. He felt all his engineering training and experience evaporating in a cloud of choking fear. His years of mathematical solutions that evolved into valuable equipment for the Department of Defense; chalk talks with his brilliant physicist colleague; irrefutable logic that led to a simple device and lucrative commercial contract. What did it all mean now?

Darkness fell. Ringing up the last sale, he faked a jolly farewell to the last customer and locked up the shop. At eight o'clock Dan allowed in the idea that the kidnapper's cell phone might never ring. Sweat stained the armpits of his light blue shirt. The thought, followed by bizarre images, gnawed at him. He called the police.

The detective listened carefully. Upon hearing the ransom details, he referred Dan to the Federal Bureau of Investigation field office in the Baltimore Federal Building. An after-hours answering machine yielded an emergency cell number to call.

Special Agent Kenneth Robards responded to the number and listened to Dan's plea for help. Ken agreed to come to the store right away and meet with Dan and Liz.

Just after 9:30 p.m., Robards arrived. At six-foot-two, the man still could have played nose tackle for any professional football team. The agent's dark brown hair ended squarely across his forehead. Though thick brows made the fortyish man's eyes seem larger and more intense, his demeanor was friendly and attentive to Dan's story. He retraced the day's events and obtained a briefing on the letters, clues, possible motives, and new faces. An examination of the backyard area confirmed Dan's suspicion of a kidnapping. He accepted photographs of Rivka and Kravitz. Hers was recent and pretty close to true. But the bearded and scraggly likeness from the Metheford Academy yearbook was tiny and out of date. The lenses in the suspect's horn-rimmed glasses bore the camera's flash, obliterating any eye area characteristics. The picture conveyed no real sense of height or bulk. The hair coloring appeared dark—perhaps also the camera's doing. The agent thought he might do better sending for a photograph and description from Kravitz's British Isles driver's permit. It was already 3 a.m. in Britain. That would have to wait until morning. Dan, in his disoriented state, couldn't remember exactly what Rivka had been wearing, but Liz contributed a good description of her outfit: white blouse, tan sweater, faded

Death Goes Postal

blue jeans, a wide man's belt, and penny loafers with no socks.

Meanwhile, Robards alerted the Savannah FBI field office to keep an eye on the post offices bearing the two zip codes. He promised to forward the photos and Rivka's description from the office fax later that night. The agent also apologized that he couldn't give them any kind of timetable or anything on their mode of transportation. Since Dan and Liz insisted that Emil had been at their critique meetings, Robards wanted to interview every attendee. Liz called the numbers on the critique group list, but on a Saturday night, the only person she could reach was Frieda on her shift at the Double T. The interview calls would have to wait until the following morning.

Chapter 20

Rude Awakenings
Sunday, May 30th

In the wee hours of the following morning, Heather rose up on her right elbow and stared at the sleeping figure lying next to her on the queen-sized, pull-out sofa-bed. The decision to reject the twin beds in the bedroom was an easy one. But the decision to bed down with a complete stranger staggered her mind. She hadn't any plausible explanation—it just happened. *Good grief, it amounted to only one step above a one-night stand.* The sometimes prudish schoolteacher in her knew better, but couldn't stop—never even wanted to stop. It had all started with thick prime ribs at Fran O'Brien's on Main Street, accompanied by wine and music, followed by dancing, more wine, and sweet talk. By the time they'd gotten to the Irish Cream coffee, heated chemistry had already convinced Heather Germain to share her bed.

Vernon had proven himself to be an accomplished seducer and lover—gentle, fierce, and loving all at the same time. His voice possessed a convincing quality, a certain assuring tone, an alluring message. Her eyes traced and remembered the shape beneath the sheets. *His smooth muscular body wasn't bad either*, she thought. Heather smiled and blew a quick, unseen kiss across the sheets at him, while swinging her legs off the sofa-bed to a sitting position.

The humming timepiece on the nightstand soon lost some of its fuzziness, revealing the time as 3:20 a.m. They'd dozed off just before one o'clock with her head in the crook of his shoulder and, without recalling when, the duo had somehow separated afterward. Heather picked the beige nightie up from the floor and slipped it over her head. Standing and wriggling, the lacy garment clung at first and then slid down beyond her chiseled hips. On her way to the bathroom she stumbled into an out-of-place chair. Vernon had used it as a clothes tree. In her stumbling, a dull thud sound convinced her that something had dropped on the carpet. Looking back, she saw that he slept on. Pushing the lowered shade slightly away from the window allowed enough street light into the living room to see that Vernon's wallet had fallen from his pocket. She scooped it off the carpet, but, before returning it to the errant pocket, another thought struck her. Heather, the French language arts teacher, became Heather the snoop. Carrying the wallet into the bathroom, she eased the door shut and turned on the light.

    Heather rifled through the contents, finding $153 in bills. The wallet didn't seem to belong to Vernon Levant. She didn't see any cards with his name on them. But this wasn't the only surprise. She then expected the wallet to belong to Emil Kravitz. It didn't. An automobile insurance card inside belonged to someone named Fenton Thorwald. So did credit cards and other cards. *Odd,* she thought. *No driver's license or anything with a photo on it.* Heather restored the contents of the wallet and refolded it to pocket size. She recalled that Vernon had removed a credit card from his wallet at the restaurant to pay for their meal. He had signed the Levant name. She searched the wallet again for a credit card in the name of Vernon Levant. None. *Could the man have two wallets?* she wondered. After a thirty-minute bathroom sojourn trying to decide her next move, she opted to return the wallet to its original trouser pocket.

    Heather turned out the light, opened the bathroom door, and waited until her eyes grew accustomed to the darkness. Approaching the chair where Vernon had draped his clothes, she discovered that his things were gone. At the sofa-bed the sleeping form was gone also. In a panic she ran for the light switch and flipped it on. *Alone! He had left nothing—not even a note.* It was the same throughout the rest of the apartment. *Wouldn't he check his trousers for the wallet and the money inside?* Or did he suspect she'd uncovered his secret? *Why did he lie? Who was he, really?*

* * *

Around 1 a.m. Sunday morning, the first sensation Rivka felt was a sore shoulder, hip, and forehead. She must have fallen. And that place on her butt, it hurt too—like someone had given her a shot. A strong urge to rub all the places that ached, to see, to breathe through her mouth, to shout, all gave way to the realization that she had been bound and gagged. She lay awkwardly prone on some hard surface. She had no idea how long she'd lain there. The last she could remember was just before noon on Saturday. But time didn't seem to be the problem. Darkness inhibited any vision. A shroud covered her head and stuck to her cheeks, pressing her sweaty hair in tightly about her head and face. *Kidnapped?* She had trouble thinking. *Who? Why?*

Slowly her thought process restored itself. She opened her eyes to suffocating blackness. I can't see! The next sensation was a horrid, bitter taste in her mouth. *Drugged! Oh, my God. I've been drugged, bound, gagged, and carted off somewhere to be dropped on a cold, hard floor like so much baggage. It's not like cement. Only a bare wood or linoleum floor could be this smooth.*

Rivka whimpered, grunted, stiffened, stretched, and shrank—testing the bindings in every way imaginable, using all the strength and slack she could muster, but to no avail. Her anger grew, she trembled with frustration, but then she realized she needed to try brain power in lieu of the futile brawn efforts. Forcing herself to relax, she then felt the presence of someone else in the room.

Fear displaced her anger and sharpened her senses. More than merely the sound of another person breathing, Rivka became aware of someone's amusement at her expense. She heard an otherworldly rasp, certainly the product of some eerie mechanical or electrical voice-disguising device. The voice told her: "You can be made a great deal more comfortable if you're willing to cooperate."

She nodded yes as vigorously as possible with the shroud covering her head. In response, two powerful arms lifted and conveyed her body to what felt like a bed or at least some kind of mattress, leaving her head propped up on pillows. A slash of light leaked in as her assailant lifted the shroud as far as her mouth.

He hesitated. The weird rasp warned, "You are in a third-floor flat at the rear of an abandoned house on a deserted street, where it is extremely unlikely that anyone will hear you. But for your own sake you had better not scream when I remove your gag. Do I make myself clear, lady?"

Again Rivka nodded, so he tugged at the tape and drew it slowly across her face. A final yank on the tape stung her lips and cheeks. She cried out in pain. The raspy voice cautioned once again, and when she rewarded him with her silence, the shroud dropped to shoulder length once more. As the perspiration beaded on her forehead it was absorbed by the rough, smelly fabric of the shroud.

"Do you have any idea *why* you're here, Mrs. Sherman?"

"No I *don't*. You drugged me, didn't you? What on earth did you inject me with? It's making me sick to my stomach." The mixture of anger and fear wrestled for dominance in her speech.

"And take this dirty wet rag off my face. I can barely breathe."

"Just a little cocktail to immobilize you," the voice rasped at her. "Quite harmless, I assure you. The nausea will subside shortly and you'll be fine. Fine, that is, if you tell me what I need to know."

"How much of that putrid cocktail drug did you use? Do you really understand what you're doing? You could have *killed* me with an overdose."

"See here, miss, if I wanted you dead, I wouldn't have kidnapped you. As for knowing what I'm doing—the instructions are quite explicit about dosing. A hundred forty pounds, I'd say. Right?"

"A hundred thirty-three," she corrected. "But that's beside the point."

"As for the product, it's bloody amazing what can be found for sale. My only concern was the on-time delivery, but then you already know I needn't have worried."

"I…I demand that you let me go immediately or you'll be in a lot of hot water."

"Look, Mrs. Sherman, you're in no position to be demanding anything of me. I don't think you know what's at stake here. I know that you and your husband have been hiding Abner Fraume's letters. I'm not sure just how many of them contain his clues, but I want them—all of them. I mean to have them. In fact, I will kill to get them. Do you understand me?" He poked her deep in the stomach with his finger after each declaration for emphasis.

"Yes sir!" she snapped.

"I'm going to ask you just once where they are. If I get the right answers, you get to remain on the bed. Otherwise it's back on the floor with a fresh gag in your mouth." With that he poked down hard and twisted with his forefinger.

"Hey, Kravitz, or whatever your name is now. That hurts!"

"Oh, so you do know my name."

"Yes, I know, and the police know the name of the man who killed poor old Abner Fraume. You're a murderer and you're probably going to kill me as well. Oops!"

"Wrong! Most likely, you are going to live. On the other hand, Abner was uncooperative, and unfortunately, I had to take his life. You are going to tell me what I want to know, and then I will leave a note for your husband to tell him where to find you. But before I start, I want to show you I mean you no harm. Let's just say it's a gesture of good faith. I've prepared a peanut butter and jam sandwich and a glass of milk for you." He held the sandwich under the shroud for her to eat.

"Aren't you going to free my hands so I can eat and

drink."

"That much faith I haven't got." He snickered and gave her a sip of the milk.

"Now then, how many letters did Abner write to his sister?"

"I think he wrote her at least twice a month. Sometimes more."

He rubbed the peanut butter on her nose to show his dissatisfaction. "That's not what I meant and you know it," he rasped. "Let's try the question again. How many of the clue letters are there?"

"I only saw the one. It said others would follow. I don't know how many."

"Now Mrs. Sherman, where did you find that letter?"

"On the back of the same poster where you stole the other letters. We saw the tape marks, but you'd already taken them. This one was higher up, so you missed it."

He tilted the glass to her lips under the shroud while she took a long pull on the milk. "Perhaps you remember the clue line, then."

"I'm not sure, but I think it read 'play for a key lime pie in the face.' Yes! That's it." She repeated the clue a second time for certainty.

He gripped her shoulders and shook them. "Mrs. Sherman, would your memory improve if I told you that I already have the first letter?"

"No, I'd say now *you* were lying to *me*."

"On the contrary, my dear. Try, 'Post a key lime's fare full in face.' However, Post is spelled with a zed instead of an ess."

"Wow! Well, yeah. How could you have gotten hold of that letter?"

"Your husband left a present for me last evening."

"Daniel wouldn't do that…Unless…"

"Unless he thought his lovely wife was in danger. Yes?"

"Wait a minute here. If you already have the letter and its

clue line, why do you still need me?"

"I'm going to ask you one more time—how many of the clue letters are there?" He poked his finger deep into her stomach once more.

"Ow, you're hurting me."

"Well!" His finger jabbed again.

"Three!" She cried out. "If you'd read the damn letter, you'd already know that."

"Of course. I was just testing you. Do you have any idea of the line's meaning?"

"No," she insisted, but something inside said he wouldn't be satisfied with a simple No. "Not really, although key lime pie is a delicacy served in Key West, Florida."

"That's all you could make of it. Where in Key West?"

Although a million useless suggestions flowed through her brain, only one seemed worthy of an all-out bluff. "Well, Daniel did suggest that the word *play* could mean a theater location and *pie in the face* would imply slapstick. So I think we're…I mean you…are talking about a comedy theater in Key West. Honest, that's as far as we got. We've never actually been to Key West. Since you have all the rest of the clues, I'll bet that information means a lot to you."

"Hmm! Of course. I'll have to think about this."

"So what happens now? I've done my part and told you all I know. Are you going to let me go now?"

"Not just yet."

"Untie me, you brute!"

"Not just yet, lady. And now I'd like you to shut up."

She felt gloved hands roll her on to her side and then a sharp needle prick once more. She jumped with the pain. The needle had penetrated a muscle, and much of the sera leaked about the wound. She was still awake when she heard the door close and the stairs creak with his footsteps.

Chapter 21

Interrogation
Sunday, May 30th

Dan feared the worst for his wife of twenty-six-years and visualized her undergoing all sorts of distasteful treatment and even torture. He had endured a sleepless, mind-wandering Saturday night tossing and turning. The anguished husband hadn't spent a night away from Rivka since they had moved to Annapolis in '98. Just before dawn, a troubled sleep took over from fatigue, but not for long. He awoke in disbelief and then saw the empty side of their bed. Despair and fury replaced disbelief—fury because neither the police nor the FBI seemed to be acting quickly enough. If he had his way, he'd be almost to Savannah by now. *What's the matter with those people?* he thought. *I'd better not antagonize the only ones who can help us, though.*

The information gleaned from Dan and Liz had led Special Agent Ken Robards to believe that Emil Kravitz had been present for at least two of their critique meetings. He agreed that the four men were the most likely suspects, but wanted to interview everyone who'd been in attendance anyway. Robards requested that Liz contact the members of the critique group and have them assemble in the bookstore as soon as they could. Heather and Peggy promised to come at once. Frieda would be available when she got off work at eight that night. Of the men, only Spence and Garry could be reached. Spence agreed to drop everything and come right over, but Garry couldn't come until afternoon. Joel's secretary informed Liz that Mr. Wise was expected back from an out-of-town interrogatory session around 9:30 that evening. She promised to leave a note for him to call the store as soon as he got in.

Liz offered Robards a choice of two reading rooms on The Dungeon level to hold his interviews, and he selected the larger of the two. Dan rearranged the tables and chairs in the room to appear like a court of inquiry and sat down behind the table to await the interviewees.

Spencer Edington arrived first, and to Liz's surprise, insisted on speaking with the FBI agent immediately. The agent showed no objection to seeing him first, and twenty minutes later she became even more curious when Robards came to the doorway alone.

Liz, gripping her canvas shoulder bag almost to the point of white knuckles, asked to go next.

Robards agreed to interview her before Heather and Peggy, who had arrived in the meanwhile. Prior to taking a seat at the table opposite Dan and her FBI interrogator, Liz acknowledged Spence seated on an upholstered bench along the rear wall of the room. Not understanding the meaning of his presence nor where he'd chosen to sit, she became even more unnerved. She couldn't keep an eye on him as long as he sat behind her. Still in the gray smock that covered her cotton blouse and long skirt, she crossed her arms tightly over her chest and pursed her lips firmly. She knew the terror of being attacked and understood that her closest friend was going through that same terror. An icy wave shimmied down her spine, and poultry skin popped out on both arms.

Robards, detecting Liz's red, swollen eyes and high-strung demeanor, kept the questions both impersonal and unpressured. Still, probing her solo search for the poetry clues provoked another round of tears. Her description of the mugger skittered around anything useful, telling him little except that her attacker was certainly a male. And yet her descriptions of the four men at the critique table were remarkably specific, especially that of Everet Kanter. In fact, Liz became animated when asked to talk about her rendezvous with Ev.

"I don't really know what he does for a living, but I think he's some kind of accountant or bookkeeper," answered Liz.

"Has he ever tried to convince you that he is someone or something that you know he isn't?"

"Gee, I…"

"Something to make you suspicious perhaps?" he coaxed.

"Uh, yes. A few days ago I introduced him to a friend from Chicago and I mentioned that they both were from the same part of the country. Ev outright denied ever having been in the Midwest."

"What's so suspicious about that?"

"Well, when we went sailing a week ago, he bragged to the boat rental person that he had spent a lot of time sailing on Lake Michigan."

"Did you try to get an explanation?"

"Yes, but he put me off. Said he'd tell me later. When I pressed him, Ev said he just told the boat rental girl that so she wouldn't give him a safety lecture."

"I see. Have you ever detected any kind of an accent, say British, in the man's speech?"

"He has a slight accent, but I assumed that he came from New England. I never even thought of him being British."

"Is there anything else you want to tell me about the case?"

"No sir."

"Ms. Nathan, thank you. Would you ask Ms. Germain to step in here, please?"

Liz turned away to leave and glanced over at Spence. He never looked up from writing in a small notepad. In the next room she spoke quietly to Heather and then went to sulk behind the cashier's counter. Somehow she felt her interview hadn't gone well.

Heather strode confidently into the reading room, then hesitated, taking notice of Spence sitting along the opposite wall. "What's he doing here? I thought I had some expectation of privacy."

"I shouldn't think Mr. Edington would compromise your privacy."

"Why not?" Heather demanded.

Robards suppressed his annoyance at her challenge. "Mr. Edington is sitting in with us at my request. As an insurance investigator, he has provided us with some valuable information in this case. I'd like his take on all of your responses."

"Isn't he in sportswear sales, a likely suspect—same as the rest of us?"

"Yes and no." The FBI agent chose to acknowledge her question rather than answer it. "Ms. Germain, I've asked you here so that we can ascertain what has happened to Mrs. Sherman and to collect and develop any clues to her current whereabouts."

"Of course, I'll do anything I can, but I'm not aware that I know diddly about Rivka's disappearance."

"Please let me be the judge of that. Were you in contact with Mrs. Sherman either yesterday or today?"

"No. Shouldn't you FBI types be out there looking for Rivka and the creeps who took her?"

"Ms. Germain, I'm the one conducting the interview here," groused Robards.

"Sorry!"

"Did you know of any appointments or engagements she might have had for Saturday?"

Heather shook her head emphatically to this and several other related questions. She responded to the description of the four male newcomers with less detail than Robards would have liked. However, her description of Vernon Levant carried with it an altogether different attitude and a slight smile, reflecting a definite personal involvement. And for a moment, her mind wandered. Its absence was duly noted.

"You seem to have a bit of insight into Mr. Levant. What do you actually know about him?"

"He's a very nice man—so intelligent, so gallant, so handsome, so attentive, so—"

"Ms. Germain!" Robards interrupted. "I wasn't asking for your feminine assessment of the man. I want to know something more specific, more tangible. Is he who he says he is? Where is he from? What does he do for a living?"

"He says he's an insurance rep from Hartford, Connecticut. We've really had only a few dates."

"Your earlier praises of the man implied you two were more intimate. Can't you tell me any more about him?"

Heather's deep blush confirmed the agent's assumption. She looked over her shoulder to see if her admission registered with Spence. He never looked at her. Robards pressed her harder until she told him the story of the wallet belonging to Fenton somebody. As she spoke, Robards looked over her shoulder and made eye contact with Spence. He nodded back.

"So why didn't you come forward with this information beforehand?"

"I wanted to confront Vernon first and see what he had to say."

"And did you?"

"No, I never had the chance."

"Why is that?"

"He left before I had a chance to."

"Without his wallet?"

"Uh-huh."

"When was this?"

"This morning, early, around 3:40 a.m." Her face flushed again.

Robards softened his voice "Not to worry. Does this mean you still have the wallet?"

"Uh-huh. I wanted to confront him with it, like I said."

"I'd like you to bring it here to me, but I'd appreciate it if you would handle it as little as possible. Put it in a paper bag—use tongs if you can, so I can get some untainted fingerprints."

"I'll bring the wallet in, but as I told you I've already handled it a bunch." Embarrassed, her anxious fingers toyed with one teardrop earring.

"The less you handle it, the more we have to work with," he cautioned.

"It'll take about fifty minutes to go get it in this weekend traffic."

"Fine. And thank you for your cooperation. On your way out would you have Ms. Morris step in here, please?"

Heather rushed from the reading room and motioned to Peggy that Robards wanted to see her next. Passing the checkout counter, Heather informed Liz she was going home for something and would be back in an hour.

Peggy gathered up her purse and slipped into the reading room, closing the door behind her. She found Dan Sherman and Special Agent Robards engaged in a heated discussion. Robards beckoned her to take a chair at the table, and as she sat down, she noted that Dan looked terrible with a less-than-perfect shave and deep shadows under his eyes. Intent on making sense out of their conversation, Peggy didn't notice Spencer Edington sitting behind her.

"Ms. Morris," asked Robards, "do you have any knowledge of Mrs. Sherman's whereabouts?"

"None at all, sir. By the way, It's still Mrs. Morris even though I'm divorced."

"How long have you known her, Mrs. Morris?"

"A little over two weeks, at the mystery critique meetings only. About three-and-a-half hours altogether I should say."

"I see. At one of these meetings, were you able to overhear a certain conversation between Ms. Nathan and Mr. Kanter where she spoke of some letters written by Mrs. Bender's brother?"

"I think so—at least part of the conversation. It was certainly loud enough for everyone to hear."

"Did you convey that information to anyone else?"

"Of course not! Who on earth would I tell?"

"Your ex, for example."

"I haven't seen that creep in eighteen months. Besides, Liz's idle chatter didn't mean anything to me, so I didn't pay much attention to it."

"Are you a long-term resident of the Annapolis area?" asked Robards.

"No, I just moved here from Philadelphia three weeks ago."

"Why Annapolis?"

"I was trying to find some long-lost relatives here."

"Did you find them?"

"Yes, sir." Peggy looked away. "But it was too late. My auntie had already passed away."

"You have my condolences," the agent said while searching her body language for some expression of her personal loss.

"Thank you, it's been ages since I last saw her. I was no more than eleven then, so I can't say that I really knew her."

"I see," acknowledged Robards.

* * *

While the interview with Peggy continued in the reading room, Heather returned with the unexplained wallet. Following the agent's explicit instructions, she had handled it with care and deposited it in a brown paper bag. The reading room door was still closed, so she placed the bag on the counter beside the cash register in plain view for Robards to find. Seeing no one around, she left the bookstore and returned home. Minutes later, Liz came across the paper bag and stowed it under the counter, believing it to be a lunch some customer had left behind.

* * *

At 8:20 that evening Frieda Forrester waited her turn in the leather recliner across from Liz. Lord Byron lay curled up in Frieda's lap. The off-duty waitress stroked the royal feline in slow, soft moves. The laird and master of the bookstore stretched and grinned, slightly turning his head up and to the side, with each stroke. A medley of his tympanic purring accompanied the store's background elevator music. If he sensed the air of urgency about the place, he gave no sign of it.

The street door swung open, jingling its tiny bell, and Garry Posner entered. At the sight of him, Frieda's body stiffened, relaying this distress to her feline charge. Lord Byron rolled over, let out one great mew of protest, jumped to the floor, and leapt to the third shelf of a nearby book stack—all in what seemed a single effort. The laird's desertion seemed to solidify Frieda's hostile suspicions about Garry. He was, in her mind, the mugger/murderer Emil Kravitz.

"Hi, Liz…Frieda. Hey, Frieda, why the glum looks? It's a beautiful night full of lovely stars and bright promises."

"You lied to me, you dirty bastard. I actually felt sorry for you. And after I opened my home and heart to you. How could you be such a lowlife?"

"Whoa! Just how in the world did I lie to you? What actually did I say?"

"You told me you lived at the Sea Bound Apartments—Number 107, in fact." Frieda's voice turned strident. When I got there, nobody had ever heard of you. Liar, liar—especially at the rental office. So there!"

"I never said I lived there," Garry replied smoothly. "I told you: Sea Bright, the small apartment building behind Sea Bound. It's the tan stucco building with the brown shutters. I rent cheap because the lease is short term, and the place needs to undergo a bunch of renovations." Garry smiled and assumed a comic wide stance with hands on hips. "So there…right back at you."

"How do I know you're not lying to me now?"

Garry was saved from further excuses by Dan, who flung the door open with Robards behind him.

"What's all the racket going on out here?" Dan asked. "You're disturbing the interviews."

"Dan!" Frieda shouted. "That's him!"

"That's who?" Dan asked.

"Emil Kravitz!" she replied. "Garry is Emil Kravitz."

"How could you possibly know that, Ms. Forrester?" asked Robards.

"He lied to me."

"That's hardly a fair indictment of the man," declared Robards. "What did he lie about?"

"Where he lives and who knows what else. How do I know I can trust him?" Frieda's eyes blazed.

"She misunderstood the address," Garry responded. "And I can prove it."

Robards turned to Garry and eyed him sternly. "Mr. Posner, *are* you actually Emil Kravitz?"

Garry spit out a wise-guy, amused laugh. "Hell no!"

Robards faced Frieda. "I promise you, Ms. Forrester, I'll get to the bottom of this when I question him. For now, let's cut out the name-calling, if you don't mind." He and Dan returned to the reading room to finish their interview with Peggy.

"Thanks a lot, Frieda. You're sure going out of your way to make me look bad. It's not my fault you got the apartment names wrong." Garry turned on a pouty look.

"I still think you lied to me," she said.

He fumbled through several sport coat pockets before bringing out a greasy, crumpled envelope. He flattened it out and shoved the address label in front of her. "Here!" Sure enough, Garry Posner was the addressee, and the second line read, 'Sea Bright Apt. 107.' He took one step toward her. She backed away.

"You could have typed that up just for my benefit," she said smugly.

"And arranged for the BGE electric company to bill me at the same address? Sure! Boy, you are one hard sell."

She bit her lip and tried to think of something else to test him. "What about your daughter, Phyllis? Does she even exist?"

Garry walked over to the counter, picked up a pen, and

wrote a telephone number on the back of a store business card. He handed it to her. "Here, dial this number."

Frieda inched up to the counter and reached for the phone so as not to get too close to him. She dialed and waited, but the ringing never stopped.

"There's no answer," she said quietly. Garry merely shrugged his shoulders.

When the reading room door opened again, Peggy emerged and hurried to the front of the store. A jingle told the others that she had stepped out into the evening. And when Garry and Frieda looked back, Dan and Agent Robards stood staring at him.

Dan spoke first. "I don't really think you are Kravitz, but there is something that would go a long way toward proving you didn't have anything to do with the break-in and robbery."

"What's that?" exclaimed Garry, Frieda, and Liz almost in unison.

Robards called out. "Mr. Posner, would you please step into the reading room so I can ask you a few questions?" While Garry entered the room ahead of him, Robards regarded the two ladies with a look of severe officialdom. They were both disappointed at being excluded.

"Garry, can I get you to pull up your trouser legs and roll down your socks to expose both ankles?" Dan asked once Garry had settled into the chair.

"This is ridiculous," responded Garry.

"Just do it," boomed Robards as he shut the door for privacy. His face had taken on a lineman's scowl.

"Yes sir!" Garry bent forward, removed his shoes, and exposed both ankles. "There! What's my hairy gams got to do with anything?"

Dan examined the left leg first, but other than some discolored veins and a bruise mark well above the ankle, he found no signs of either a cat's bite or major scratch. The right leg bore a suspiciously jagged gash across the ankle—long and deep enough that it could be construed as a cat's clawing. "I'm not sure if this is proof enough that Lord Byron attacked you. Tell us the truth, Posner, are you our poster burglar?"

"Wait one cotton-pickin' minute, people," Garry protested. "I'm no burglar. I cut that ankle on a piece of hack-sawed pipe a week ago. I'm a plumber and I'm always cutting myself this way. Look at all the cuts and scrapes on my hands and arms. That scratch doesn't prove a damned thing."

"The blood types will," Dan fired back.

"You mean the blood sample I sent to the lab?" asked Robards.

"From the amount of blood puddled on the floor," Dan said, "he'd have to have a sizeable wound. I hope the sample I gave you is sufficiently preserved."

"Don't worry about that, Mr. Sherman. The forensic labs can work with a lot less, and sometimes, a good deal older sample."

"Hey!" clamored Garry. "Are my ankles free to go? Can I put my shoes on again?"

"Yeah!" said Robards. "But first tell me what you know about the letters."

"What letters?" he asked. "I don't know anything about any letters."

"Weren't you in the room when Ms. Nathan spoke about the letters from Professor Fraume?"

"Oh, those letters."

"Yes, *those* letters, Mr. Posner." The agent scowled at the stalling tactic.

"Same as everyone else at the table," replied Garry. "Only what I overheard Ms. Nathan say—something about how she had clues to finding these letters—nothing else that I can remember. Even if I had them in my hot little hands, I wouldn't know what to do with them."

"Did you know either the Shermans or the Benders outside of the meetings?"

"Nope. I'm a newcomer to town. Am I still a suspect for

the kidnapping?" Garry asked.

"To tell the truth we haven't established any positive connections among the burglary, the kidnapping, and the murder. Although it's still highly plausible," admitted Robards. "I'd say you are. But I suppose you're somewhat less of a suspect by reason of your very presence here."

"Lucky me. Is that it?"

"One more question. Before coming here to Annapolis, what was your last place of residence?" asked Dan.

"Baltimore, I rented a loft over on Paca Street. I figured a loft so they wouldn't complain about me keeping my tools in the place. As I said, I'm a plumber."

"Do you live alone?"

"My sixteen-year-old daughter, Phyllis, lives with me."

"How long did you live in Baltimore."

"About two-and-a-half years. Then I went—"

"And just why did you relocate here?" asked Robards.

"Well, my ex-wife found out where I was living and started to harass me. Besides, the construction job I'd been working came to a close."

"What was all that ruckus between you and Ms. Forrester before?"

"It was a natural mistake on her part. She wrote down the wrong address, I guess. The names of the two apartment complexes do sound alike."

"Why don't you write the correct address down for me and we'll simply check it out." He pushed a lined pad and pen toward Garry.

Garry took the pen and pad and began to write.

"Can you furnish us with a name and an address for your ex as well?" Robards asked.

"I wrote her telephone number down, too."

"Why Annapolis?" Robards pried further.

"Why? It could have been anywhere, except that I got this strange phone call from an estate lawyer about inheriting some property in Annapolis. I was supposed to meet the lawyer here to explain, but the guy never kept the appointment or even called back. No, I don't remember his name."

That's mighty peculiar, the FBI agent thought. *Not to pursue the possibility of inheriting property? Not normal. What else is he hiding?* "We'll be in touch, Mr. Posner. I may have more questions for you."

He ushered Garry out and closed the door. Garry, in relaxed slouch, ambled through the stacks, examining books along the way.

Inside the reading room, Dan griped. "Damn it, Robards! All this questioning is getting us nowhere. Isn't there something more we can do? They're probably on their way to Georgia by now."

"I know how frustrated you must be, but we're doing all that we can right now. I've got agents in Savannah holding down the fort at that end. Right now what we need is more information."

"Can't we fly down there and intercept them?" Dan argued. "This is my wife! Can't you understand that?"

"We don't know for sure if that is the kidnapper's destination," said Robards. "And even if it is, they might not have even left Annapolis yet."

* * *

Meanwhile, outside the room, Liz hurried down the aisle between the stacks to the first floor restroom when the phone began to ring. "Would you get that for me, Frieda? I'll be out in two shakes."

"Sure thing, Liz," Frieda called after her. She picked up the phone. "The Olde Victorian Bookstore. Please hold for assistance."

A female voice asked for Garry Posner.

Frieda hesitated. "I believe he's somewhere in the bookstore, but I'm not sure where. There's an investigation going on here right now."

The voice ordered: "If you see him, ask him to call his wife tonight."

A frown dug deep ruts in Frieda's brow. "May I ask who's calling?"

"His wife, Anita Posner," snapped the voice. "Who else, lady?"

Frieda said she'd try to deliver the message and hung up. *He's lied to me again.* The call left her with a sinking feeling in her stomach. *He never said he still had a wife. He called her his ex.* She felt the acid reflux rising and falling in her throat.

"Who was that on the phone?" asked Liz when she returned to the front of the store. "Did they leave a message for me?"

"It was for Garry. He needs to call his wife tonight."

"Oh? I didn't know he was still married."

"Unfortunately, neither did I!"

When Garry finally emerged from the stacks carrying two books to buy, Frieda passed him on her way into the interview room. "Call your *wife* tonight," she said pointedly, and quickly closed the door behind her, leaving no room for any response from a totally stunned Garry.

Frieda's interview didn't take long. First, she knew nothing of the kidnapping. Mainly, she was asked about her impressions of Posner, and she quickly repeated her suspicions and told them about his continual lying. She claimed to be a long-time member of the critique group and a good friend of Edythe Bender. As far as her interrogators were concerned, she had furnished no new information. They dismissed her. Left alone in the reading room, Dan, Spence, and the FBI agent assessed the information they'd acquired during all the interviews.

"Do you think I acted stupidly in returning to the scene of the drop?" asked Dan. He splayed his long legs out under the table.

"No," Robards said, adjusting his striped tie, looking crisp in his agent's "uniform": white shirt and charcoal-gray suit. "Under the circumstances, I might have done the same thing. Still, there's always the risk he might have seen you. But if I'd been in his shoes, I'd have kept you in sight during the drop and been long gone soon afterward."

"What I mean is," Dan persisted, "do you think I put Rivka in any greater jeopardy?"

"That's hard to say," replied Robards. "But I have a feeling she's still safe. It would be foolish for Kravitz to burn any bridges and harm her, especially when the man can't be sure he has a clear roadmap to whatever Professor Fraume was trying to hide. None of us know how much information or how many clues lie ahead of him. I believe he's too clever to do anything to her just yet."

"I want to believe you, Ken, but I repeat: Shouldn't we be on our way to Savannah already?"

"I understand how hard this is for you, Dan. You want to feel like you're taking positive action. But running off to Savannah might be a little premature," Robards said. "You've assumed that was their destination on the basis of the zip code association. That assumption is a little thin, don't you think?"

"I don't care how thin it is." Dan pounded the table. "It's the only lead we have. I'm going to Savannah even if you don't want to come along."

"Not so fast. We've got agents covering both post offices. I alerted airline, bus, and train terminals with copies of Mrs. Sherman's picture last night, and Kravitz must realize that. So whatever their destination, there's a damned good chance that they're driving."

"Then maybe we can intercept them if they're driving."

"It's possible, but we don't know anything about the car he's driving. I'm also concerned about a direct confrontation. It could put your wife at risk. I'm expecting the picture from Kravitz's international driver's permit. It would be handy to know just who we are dealing with. A description helps a lot in these matters."

"You're the professional," said Dan, his expression sagging. He already had a stubbled chin from a hasty morning shave. "I guess you know better how to handle these things."

"Yes, of course," Robards said. "But perhaps I've been a little hasty here and missed something. Didn't you say your wife had come to the same conclusion on the Savannah clue?"

"Yes, we used the same logic, and I don't see why he's taken her unless he believes Rivka is right about the clues. God forgive me if she's leading him on a wild goose chase."

"What if we can confirm that Professor Fraume sent the artifacts to Savannah?"

"How are you going to do that?" asked Dan.

"Let me make a few calls. I have an idea. Do you have the number of the Metheford Academy?"

"Sure," said Dan. "Come with me." They left Spence in the reading room and headed to the front of the shop, where Dan rummaged around in the wooden drawer beneath the cashier's counter. He handed the agent a slip of paper with the colonel's number.

Robards asked to use the store phone. He wanted to know if Will Petty had ever posted a sizeable package to a Savannah, Georgia, address. The phone rang and rang, and just before he was about to give up, a man's voice answered.

"Colonel Felsworth?" Robards asked. "I'm with the U.S. Federal Bureau of Investigation."

"Ain't no one 'ere but me," said the voice. "It's bloody four o'clock in the morning, it is, an' the colonel and everyone else 'as gone 'ome t' bed."

From their conversation Robards learned that he was speaking to the night watchman. The agent apologized and said he would call back the next morning at 9:30 London time. He hung up and scowled as he realized he'd have to get up at 4:30 a.m. local time to make the call.

Another idea hit him. "On the off-chance that the Petty lad *did* mail Abner's package to Savannah, I'd better make an airline reservation." Robards thumbed through the directory pages for an airline number. "I'd much rather have eliminated some of the suspects beforehand. But I'll have someone continue working on this end if we wind up going." As he began dialing, "You're right, Dan—time *is* growing short."

A few minutes later he laid the handset back in its cradle. Turning to Dan, "I've booked the two of us on an 11:06 flight tomorrow morning to Atlanta, with a 1:23 p.m. connection to Savannah."

"Let's see. Today's Sunday," Dan said. "I'd better ask Heather to come in and help Liz in case we're not back by the weekend. Liz will have to go it alone for a few days."

Dan, Spence, and Ken Robards waited around for Joel's call until almost midnight. It never came, so the others left, and Dan closed up for the night, wondering, *What else can go wrong?*

Chapter 22

Filling in the Blanks
Monday, May 31st

Rivka woke with a start—a bitter cottony taste in her mouth and a groggy, confused, and spinning mind. Her sight was still impaired by the coarse, soggy shroud. She was still gagged, and she tried once again to struggle with the bonds cutting into her wrists and ankles. She had no idea how many hours or even days had passed. Her cramped bones complained. Her body cried out for potty, water, and food. The much softer bed had given way to the hard floor again, and a sixth sense detected the proximity of her silent abductor. *This creep's an unhappy camper again*, she thought. *Oh God, he must not have liked my explanation of the clue lines.*

Emil pulled the gag from her mouth, untying and lifting the baglike shroud only as far as necessary, but not far enough for her to see her captor.

"You weren't quite honest with me, Mrs. Sherman. As you can see or rather feel, I have rewarded you accordingly."

"You brutish thug. This floor is damn hard. Your cords are cutting into me. Please, you're hurting me. I told you what we knew. Can't you let me go?"

"*Pozt* a key lime's fare full in face," the mechanical voice read aloud.

"What did you say?"

"You heard me, and you now know that I have checked out your lame suggestions. So there's no cause for you to lie anymore."

"I didn't lie. I may have misled you a bit, but I didn't lie."

"There's a difference?" he mocked.

"I didn't mean to. Can't you let me go now? Everyone knows your name, Mr. Kravitz. I don't know what you look like, and I sure can't help you any further. Please! At least, let me use the bathroom. I've already peed in my pants twice."

"Well, if you absolutely can't help me," he said, "I could leave you here to die a very prolonged death without any effort at all. If you think being trussed up like that is painful, consider this in concert with hunger and thirst. Of course there *are* alternatives, my dear. Well, ta-ta!"

"Wait, wait, let's not get hasty now. I don't mean that I *can't* or *won't* help you. It's just that I don't know *how* I can help you. I only read the one letter." She felt the prickly sensation of fear, goose bumps popping along her arms and legs.

"In that case," the croaking voice said, "I can help you with your most immediate problem." He picked her up, carried her to the bathroom, and stood her on her feet in front of the toilet.

"Now what?" she questioned. Her embarrassment remained hidden under the head shroud, but her fear manifested itself in her shaking. "You're not going to take advantage of me, are you?"

"Rest easy, woman. I never mix pleasure with business." Emil undid her belt and pulled down her jeans—only her shirttails and panties remained. He was determined not to untie her.

"This isn't going to work either," she blurted out.

A much annoyed Emil gripped the waistband on both side of the panties and yanked them down. "Now sit," he commanded.

She sat. "You're inhibiting me. Leave me alone for a minute."

He left the room and shut the door behind him. Several minutes later she called to him, and he returned to find her standing, barely balanced, and completely helpless. He started to pull up the panties."

"They're wet," she complained.

Emil let them drop to the bound ankles once more. He opened the medicine cabinet door, searched for a moment, and then slammed it shut. Next he examined the contents of a commode drawer and extracted a pair of cuticle scissors which he used to cut away the wet panties. After tossing the piece of lingerie in the sink, he stuffed a hand towel between her knees and pulled it up to form a diaper. Her belted jeans held the towel in place. "How's that? Are you ready to cooperate now?"

"Uh…Do I have any choice? Yeah, sure. I guess you must have gone to kidnappers' school." It was nervous humor.

"Very funny, I didn't enjoy that any more than you did."

"Sorry!" she said. "Does that mean you don't find me attractive?"

He picked her up, carried her back to the bedroom, and bounced her down on the bed. "On the contrary, Mrs. Sherman. I do find you attractive as well as vivacious. But there's no room in my life for that sort of thing any more." He didn't say it aloud, but he wished she were twenty pounds lighter.

"Are you gay then?"

"No, damn it! I'm not gay. For your information I was even married for some time. I never imagined a kidnapped person could be so talkative."

"Have you kidnapped a lot of people?"

"No! You're the first. Stop that! Stop trying to distract me from the business at hand."

"Sorry," she muttered.

"I believe you and your cohorts have already translated the clue line from the first letter. You could save me considerable time, and for that, I might be grateful and turn you loose. You see, it's only a matter of time before my full description arrives. That makes my current identity rather fragile with the authorities."

"They say there's honor among thieves. Does that hold true among murderers as well? I mean how can I trust you? Especially with this horrible bag on my head."

"I see you have a sense of humor, Mrs. Sherman. I can also

see your dilemma. But surely, you can see that the choice is yours. If you want my reassurance, that too is all yours. I intend to spare your life if you translate the line in question. If I catch you in any lie, regardless of size or intent, it's all over. There you have it."

"You said spare my life. What about turning me loose?"

"You're quite astute as well. Your life for the translation. Your freedom for Abner's chase."

"Chase?" she asked.

"Actually, Gerheardt Koenig's *Original Floral Font-Matrices and Chase*. When I am in possession of this treasure, I will personally guarantee your freedom. Now, how about the first word *pozt*. The zed's a misspelling, is it not?"

"Not," she responded quickly and emphatically before he changed his mind. "We believe it reveals two things. The first tells us we are dealing with the postal system, and the second, a zee, reinforces the first by suggesting a particular postal zip code."

"But there aren't any numbers in this clue line."

"Oh, but there are. Take the next phrase—key lime fare. What does that suggest?"

"Don't give me any nonsense about Key West, Florida, woman. I've had a private investigator check that one out for me—comic theater indeed."

"No, no. Key lime fare refers to a kind of pie. Very good eating, I might add."

"And just how is that relevant?" he asked.

"Printers spell pie two ways: *pie* and *pi,* and it means a printer's mess, a dumped composing box, for example. We looked it up."

"So where is this going?"

"The last phrase is 'full in face.' That would mean round in shape or a circle. I think both words are apropos here."

"I get it—the Greek letter *pi*—the circle ratios—3.14 something."

"Exactly!" she answered. "According to Dan, 3.14159 or 3.1416, depending whether you round off or truncate the next digit. Ignore the decimal points and they become zip codes for U.S. post offices in Savannah, Georgia."

"That's it? Nothing more?"

"Well, Mr. Kravitz, I've covered the entire first line. If there's more, it has to be in the other letters that you have. In fact, to show my good faith, I'm willing to help translate those as well."

"I am counting on that. You must understand that's why I can't let you go until after I've made off with Abner's collection."

"I see. You hinted as much even before I volunteered."

"How about this line, for example. 'At Halley's table set a fourth place.' "

"I'm not sure which Halley this is—perhaps the astronomer or his comet. But 'set a fourth place' might limit the zip to just the fourth place fractional part of *pi*. But since zips have five digits it's more likely that the whole number, three, is included in the zip code."

"What does the word *table* mean to you, Mrs. Sherman?"

"Oh, I guess you'd better call me Rivka since we're going to be spending lots of time together."

"Fine. Rivka it is. Now the word?"

"It could be some math table or timetable or some table of elements. Are there any more clues? I thought there was another letter."

"One more clue line, my fair lady. 'And Mark his many long years in space.' The strange thing is that Mark is spelled with a capital em. Mark, by itself, suggests a biblical source or a familiar literary pen name like Mark Twain."

"What was the rest of it?" she asked. " '…his many long years in space.' Space suggests we are talking about the comet, Halley's comet. I think *his* refers to his comet and a timetable for its return, the comet's orbital time in years. I once read that Samuel Clemens, aka Mark Twain, was born when Halley's comet was still in the sky, and he predicted his own death on the occasion of its return to the Missouri skies. The problem is—I don't recall the number of years involved."

Death Goes Postal

"I looked that up in my landlady's encyclopedia," he said. "Its orbit is seventy-five years long, but what does that mean, practically speaking?"

"Well, Mr. Kravitz, I'd say you have a box number in one of two post offices with the *pi* zip codes."

"Couldn't it be a street address within those zips?" he asked.

Rivka shrugged her shoulders. There wasn't any way to tell him without acknowledging the existence of the mailbox key and its whereabouts. She had kept her word and hadn't lied to the man. Starting now might jeopardize their fragile pact.

"Well, my dear woman, we are about to embark on a long journey. About 600 miles, I would guess. I'll try to make the auto boot as comfortable as I can."

"In the trunk for 600 miles?" she complained. "Still trussed up like this?"

"With you in the passenger seat, how would I explain your hostage status if we stopped for gas or food?"

"I can give you my word, my parole. If I behave, you might be more disposed toward granting my freedom when the time comes."

Emil puffed up the pillows under her head. In a small way this acknowledged her cooperation. Suddenly Rivka realized that Kravitz hadn't been using his mechanical voice device. He'd abandoned it altogether some time ago. She wasn't sure if this was a good sign or not, or whether to bring up the fact at all. *What the heck,* she thought. *I might as well know where I stand.*

"You're using your own voice now. You must realize that it's a dead give-away. I already know what you look like, Emil. Or do you wish to use your other name?"

"No, Emil's fine." He bent over and pulled the untied shroud from her perspiring head, spring-releasing a crop of tangled hair.

Rivka instantly saw that her identification had been precise. Looking down, her wrists and ankles were bound with tie-straps, strong plastic bands employing locking teeth devices that permitted tightening yet prevented removal. Other straps loosely fastened each wrist strap to the belt in her jeans, severely limiting her movement to the loop's size. Originally one of Dan's, the belt's strength was never in doubt.

"Is this the way I'm to travel…in the trunk, too?"

"For the time being. I'm going to accept your word. You'll ride in the passenger seat bound pretty much as you are." He cut through the tie-strap holding the two ankle bands together and replaced it with a much larger one, but did not bother to snug it tight. "Okay, stand up. This should allow you about a ten-inch step. A little more comfort, but impossible to run."

"What about food, water, and an itch?" she said, trying out her new reach.

"I guess you'll just have to depend on me, won't you? If you become meddlesome, I can always rely on the needle. A quarter-dose will keep you awake, yet for the most part, nonfunctional."

"I'll behave."

Emil left her lying on the bed while he made use of the bathroom. As soon as the door closed behind him, Rivka rolled to her stomach and smeared three crude letters on the white pillowcase using her lips as a pen. The dry lipstick left only a faint trace, but it was definitely legible. When she heard him flush, she rolled onto her back again and, wiggling over, covered the message with her hair. Her captor didn't seem to notice anything suspicious upon his return to the bed.

One of Emil's arms slipped under her knees and the other behind her back. Her body swung through space and then upright until she stood on her feet once again.

"Can you make it down the stairs this way?"

"I think so if I step sideways one step at a time."

Emil tucked a bed pillow under one of her arms. Collecting his overcoat, briefcase, and valise, the two started down the stairs and out to the waiting rental car, a brand-new Mercury Bearcat sedan. He unlocked the passenger side door, rolled down the window, and sat her inside. Reaching through the window, he passed another large plastic tie-strap around the heavy waist belt and through the door's armrest, affixing her to the door. From the driver's side of the car, he tie-strapped the opposite ankle to the seat frame closest to her foot. He tilted her seat back, took the pillow back from her, and placed it behind her head.

"That better?" he asked giving it a quick fluffing.

With great effort she kept her voice steady. "First class," she quipped. *Don't lose control now,* she warned herself. Choking back tears, she wanted to cry, to scream with despair. The tie-wraps cut into her wrists; the skin had turned red and raw. *When will this end? And why is he suddenly so considerate? He's not threatening me like a thief, kidnapper, and murderer.*

Emil threw his overcoat on the back seat, dumped the valise and briefcase in the trunk, and started the car. Two hours later they left Maryland and crossed the Potomac River Bridge into Dalgren, Virginia.

* * *

The yellow cab nosed into the short driveway on Maple Street at 10:30 Monday morning. The driver hurried to open the trunk and rear door for his passenger. In her hand Irma Riley clutched the exact fare from the BWI train station to her house, plus her usual miserly ten percent tip. She handed the money to him, then waved another two dollars in his face—his, if he'd tote her old leather suitcase up to the front door. She paid the man for his effort and watched him move down the walk, shortcutting across the last piece of lawn, much to her displeasure.

The moment she entered her tiny foyer and locked the door, shutting out the outside world, Irma developed a crawling sense of foreboding. Not that she could put her finger on what was wrong. Peering through her thick lenses, a tour of the first floor revealed nothing suspicious. She opened her suitcase, scooped up an armful of packed clothes, and started up the stairs. At seventy-eight, she could never drag the heavy thing up. Now she wished she hadn't been too cheap to buy one of those new canvas ones with wheels.

The door to her master bedroom was the first out-of-place indication. It stood half open. It should have been tightly shut as she had left it, especially while she rented to that strange man in the third-floor rear room. She elbowed her way into the room and, at the sight of its condition, dropped her whole armload of clothes on the floor. The chenille bedspread and top sheet were strewn across the floor. Blood—or was it lipstick?—stained the pillow. Rubbed-off black shoe polish streaked the white fitted sheet.

The fuming Riley temper, rather than reason, governed the actions that followed. The irate landlady marched up to the third floor rear and pounded on her tenant's door until her fists hurt. Hearing nothing, she turned the knob slowly and entered the room. She found the bed unmade and dirty damp towels thrown over the chair. The air smelled of stale sweat. Not only was her tenant absent, but all of his things were gone, too. *At least he's paid up in advance,* she thought. Then realization set in, and minor trembling turned into the shakes and dizziness. Her head felt hot and her scalp showed pink under thinning white hair. Irma had to sit on the edge of the bed to avoid passing out.

Several minutes later Irma Riley gathered up all her strength and slowly maneuvered her way back down to the first floor and the telephone. She reported her findings and suspicions to the police and then lay down on the sofa for a good cry while waiting for them to come.

* * *

Across the single-span Potomac River Bridge lay the state of Virginia. Behind, the state of Maryland. Rivka's seat had been tilted for comfort, but she had to bend over to even scratch her nose. God forbid she needed to scratch somewhere else. However, the tilted position allowed her to see out both the windshield and the side windows. Emil didn't say much, and she chose not to antagonize him. She noticed signs for the gates to the Army's Fort A.P. Hill flying by. And then U.S. highway 301 became extremely rural and divided. Fewer and fewer roadside stops. She licked the dryness pasted to her lips. The foul taste of the drugs he'd been shooting her with still lingered there.

"Any chance of stopping for something to wet my lips?" she asked. "I'm dying of thirst."

"If I stop for a drink, you'll want to pee again."

"And why not?" she snapped. "I'm no machine. I can't hold it forever."

Emil didn't answer but kept on driving. Roughly ten minutes later, he pulled into a service station devoid of cars and drove around to one side where there were two restroom doors. Finding the ladies room door locked, he disappeared around front and returned with keys to both rooms and two Mountain Dews. He put one key in the ladies room door and, with a pair of fingernail clippers, cut her free from the car seat and door. She struggled, but couldn't reach the buckle to let her jeans down. When she protested, he laughed and undid her buckle three notches. He reminded her that she'd given him her word and cautioned her again as he led her to the restroom. "Besides," he sneered, "where're you going to run to in this God-forsaken spot?" He waited until she had finished, re-wrapped her, and shackled her to the seat and door once more.

Emil left one of the Dews with her to drink while he used the men's room. Thirst had become her first priority. Rivka could easily hold the soda can in one hand and pull the tab with the other, but it was another thing altogether to drink from it with both hands tethered to the belt around her waist. Turning her head sideways, leaning way over between her knees, and using one leg as a steadying pivot, she tilted the can until it poured onto her face. Just as she feared, little of the liquid made it into her mouth, and the remainder spilled onto her jeans' leg and the carpeted floor. A second plan proved slow and arduous, but slightly more successful. Leaning over a little less, she poured the drink into a cupped hand, then sipped, and finally licked the hand dry. Repeating the process provided her with some relief.

Her captor returned to the car and witnessed the pitiful scene. Emil broke into a belly laugh. He watched Rivka's anger rise. Because his captive had remained true to her word and caused him no real bother, he assumed a much calmer and friendlier demeanor. Emil took the can from her and held it to her lips as she drank—a bit too quickly. She gasped, gagged, and coughed as soda dribbled down her front.

"You should have waited for me," he said, grabbing a handful of tissues from the dashboard box and wiping her cheeks, chin, and sweater front.

"Hey, you're running the show, and so far the script is pretty ugly."

"Let's put it this way: You've got star billing."

"Can I use an understudy?"

"You know better than that. But you sure are spunky. I like that in a woman."

"Oh, no," she moaned.

"Just a casual remark, Rivka. Don't go ballistic on me now." Emil reached around in back of the passenger seat for his overcoat. Fumbling around in an outside coat pocket, he retrieved the stolen cell phone, the one he'd used to handle the ransom messages to Dan. His finger tapped out thirteen tonal digits and waited.

It was an overseas number. Rivka heard the lengthy string of double tones, a distant phone ringing, someone answering, and really wasn't that surprised when she heard Emil speaking in German. She understood a few German words from the similar Yiddish language her parents spoke when she was young. Emil spoke to his buyer. Although his face spelled anger, his words came out hesitatingly chosen, his tone attentive, and his speech soft. Apparently, the two parties reached some sort of agreement just before Emil turned off the cell phone and shoved it back into the overcoat pocket.

Emil sat in the driver's seat contemplating—staring blankly at the windshield for several minutes; then his brows lifted and a nod followed. He'd made up his mind to something.

Death Goes Postal

Rivka heard him restart the engine. She had used the down time to retest her bonds—tugging to learn her latest confinement limits. Then her eyes scanned the immediate environment for anything that might aid her escape.

Chapter 23

A Stretch in the Right Direction
Virginia and Annapolis—Same Day

Rural Virginia in all its greenery rushed by the windows, but Rivka kept eyeing the overcoat on the seat behind Emil, particularly the pocket bulge. If she somehow could reach his coat and the cell phone within, Dan, the police, or anyone could help her out. But she didn't have the reach to the coat as things now stood. The hard plastic tie-strap bonds had etched ugly red welts into her wrists from the intensity of her prior attempts to free herself. She tried to focus on not giving up. Her morale needed a swift kick in the behind and something extra to plant a viable plan of escape in her brain. Despite all efforts, noticeable despair and fear leaked into her outward expression.

"You hungry?" he asked. "Would a hamburger and some chips help you along?"

Rivka nodded, "Yeah, that would be good." Sure, hunger had crossed her mind, and an internal pang had already nudged her stomach. And stalling their progress to Savannah might offer some yet unforeseen opportunity for escape. Rivka tried to think of the possibilities. She didn't want to spiral backward into drugs and trunk accommodations by betraying his trust. She had no compunction about lying to and cheating a criminal, but needed a significant margin of success before attempting a run for it.

They pulled off the main highway into a major truck stop

for gas. Emil chose the self-service pump farthest from the pay island and got out to fill the tank. It took a few additional minutes for him to scrub, squeegee, and dry the windshield with gray paper toweling. He paid with another stolen credit card and drove between the refueling lanes out to the center of a huge parking lot. It was well away from the sprawling Iron Skillet restaurant, despite the huge number of empty parking slots much closer in. A cardboard sun barrier, unfolded and stuffed in the windshield, left her out of sight from the restaurant patrons. By lowering her seat all the way back, her entire view comprised the car's tan ceiling fabric. Leaving her in this out-of-scrutiny, out-of-trouble position, Emil left for the restaurant.

Rivka found the new position added a slightly different extension to her reach. The bond to the door's armrest pulled tightly on her belt, giving her body a left-side twist. Her left hand could now reach the carpeted floor about eighteen inches from the targeted overcoat. It might as well have been eighteen feet because the absolute finger reach stopped considerably short of the mark. However, her view of the carpeted floor extended somewhat farther. In fact, her eyes spotted something shiny protruding from the recess in the carpet cut-out surrounding the driver's seat strut, the place where the frame attached to the deck. She tried to focus and determine the nature of the object. And then it came to her—a paper clip! She imagined just how she might gain her freedom with such a tool. Her fingers couldn't get there, but her upper body could stretch that far. The problem would be to fit her face beneath the low fitted seat so that tongue and teeth could extract the clip.

Before Rivka had a chance to try, she heard someone approaching the car—footsteps crunching on the gravel parking lot. She lay back flat on the seat and closed her eyes momentarily as though his return had awakened her. Emil slid into the driver's seat and dropped a white paper bag on the floor between the seats.

"Lean forward," he commanded as his hand found the lever driving the seat back into the full upright position. "That's better."

Emil unwrapped a hamburger and set it on her lap with the

waxed wrapping underneath to guard against dripping and soiling her jeans. He pulled out a built-in cup holder from the dash and set a large drink cup and protruding straw within its grip. When she hesitated, he picked up the hamburger and held it to her mouth for a bite. Rivka bit off a chunk and chewed away at it like she had all the time in the world—like it would be her last meal—something to savor. Besides, the one-third-pound burger proved to be quite tasty. The problem turned out to be his lack of patience. Emil then placed the burger in Rivka's own hand and pushed her body forward to where she could take her own bites and sip through the straw. Once he saw that she could manage on her own, Emil took a second drink and a sandwich from the same white paper sack and began to eat and drink. After a few bites and sips he started the engine and headed for the highway.

"How'd you know that I like chocolate shakes?"

"All women like chocolate," he answered. "I hear it has something to do with a feeling of wellness. Some even say it's an aphrodisiac."

"Now don't you go getting any ideas, buster. Our agreement is one thing, familiarity with my body is another thing altogether."

"Don't worry, I haven't any designs on you," he said. "Why can't you just respect the status quo?"

"Fine," she said, leaning forward for a long draw on the straw. Then an idea slurped in along with the shake. "I suppose there's no reason why we can't be civil until this horrible thing is over with."

* * *

Later that same morning Special Agent Robards came through the front door of the bookstore and found a red-eyed Dan waiting for him with a small overnight case.

"Have you heard anything yet?" Dan asked while his voice cracked.

"The word from Bath is that Will Petty vaguely remembers

posting four heavy packets off to someplace in the U.S.A. He *thinks* it might have been Georgia, but doesn't remember the city.

"Anything else, Ken?"

"Not really," he replied. "I did receive Kravitz's driving permit photo, but it turned out to be no clearer than the yearbook picture we already have."

"What about the other two men?"

"According to a rental agency in Baltimore, a man answering to Vernon Levant's description rented a car yesterday morning. It's possible a woman waited for him, but the witness and local police can't be sure. As for the Kanter fellow—no word yet."

"Agent Robards! Agent Robards!" Liz called to him. "You have a phone call at the counter."

Robards took the handset from her. "Special Agent Robards speaking. Uh-huh…right, restraints, yeah…uh-huh, uh-huh. What's that she wrote on the pillow? A lipstick smear? Yeah…tell 'em thanks for the heads up." He put the phone down on its cradle.

"Any news?"

"As a matter of fact, yes. It seems the Annapolis police were called to a potential crime scene this morning. A landlady reported that a disgruntled tenant had wrecked her place. When the local police got there, they discovered a badly tossed bedroom with clippings of tie-strap restraints all over the place, shoe polish marks on the sheets, and lipstick smears on a pillowcase. A black cloth bag with a drawstring lay in the bedclothes. It might have been an over-the-head shroud. The landlady claimed that a second pillow was missing. The officers concluded that someone had been held there against their will and called in the detectives. Our missing persons bulletin caught their attention so they gave us a heads-up on the case."

"That's it? No sign of Rivka?"

"Well, the distance from the pillow to the shoe marks indicate a height between five-foot-five and five-foot-seven."

"That's consistent with Rivka's height," said Dan. "She's

five-six. Anything else?"

"Yes, the report mentions a cut-up pair of soiled ladies panties they've determined came from someone with an 'A' blood type. The DNA is expected to take some time as their lab is backed up."

"That's Rivka's blood type," Dan declared. "It must have been her."

"Possibly!" said Robards. "Another thing: the pillow smears spelled out 'S-A-V' which the detectives construed to mean—'save' as in save me."

"That may not be what she meant," Dan said. "There's nothing to be gained with such an obvious message. I think Rivka's telling us he's taking her to Savannah, Georgia. And that's where I think we ought to be going right now before we miss our plane."

"Considering that the Petty lad remembers posting Abner's packages, it's not as much of a leap of faith anymore," responded Robards.

"Not when you couple it with everything else we know. Savannah is what Rivka deduced."

"Oh, before I forget—the coffee pot was still a tad warm, so they couldn't have left more than two hours earlier, say between seven and eight this morning."

* * *

Less than a mile after the Iron Skillet stop, Virginia Route 207, the modest two-lane, pastoral link between U.S. 301 and I-95, had deposited the white Mercury sedan into the multi-laned interstate with all of its accompanying traffic. Out of sheer nervousness Rivka, like an old yenta, chatted away, telling Emil about the Shermans' transition from editor and engineer to bookstore proprietors. Emil, concentrating on the almost bumper-to-bumper driving, contributed nothing to the exchange.

Failing to lure him into conversation, Rivka entertained herself by people-watching and car watching. Complaining about her sore wrists seemed futile at this juncture. A preteen lad peering out of a side window made a face at her, and by way of a return message, she screwed up her expression into a distorted horror mask. She raised her brows at a young GI and winked at an elderly gentleman, eliciting wide smiles from both. The game seemed almost fun, and then she wondered whether eye contact could be employed for communications purposes. Mouthing her plight with single word facial communiqués like *help* and *kidnapped* became another possibility. These were limited by the short attention span of a passing motorist or passenger. And if, somehow, such attempts backfired, what could she expect from her captor in terms of retaliation? She wanted to gamble, so she continued with the outlandish expressions until Emil glanced past her to a passing car and caught a screwed-up face cast back at them.

Without warning, Emil's right hand flew off the steering wheel, grabbed her left ear, and twisted. The stinging pain stunned Rivka into frightened silence. His steely grasp had crushed down on her diamond studs, cutting their sharp edges into her earlobes. Her face flooded with tears. She finally found her voice.

"What the devil was that for?"

"If I catching you making eye contact again, I'll do more than that. I'll stuff you in the trunk, or at the very least, lower your seat again. It's a much longer journey if you have to stare at the ceiling fabric for the duration."

Her first reaction was to shout *Go to hell, you maniac!* But in her helpless state she suppressed the urge and took a new tack. "I-I don't mean any disrespect, but you're n-not exactly the most talkative man I've ever met." Her shaking body interfered with her speech.

"Well, if it's conversation you want, what do you want to talk about?"

"It seems you know a lot about Dan and me. I don't even know if there's a Mrs. Kravitz."

"Not any more."

"You mean you did your wife in?" *Oh-oh,* she thought, *I shouldn't have said that.*

"No, no, nothing like that." He laughed without mirth. "The bitch just wearied of the academic life and wandered off one day. I never heard from her again. I didn't much care then. Still don't."

"Academia?" Rivka asked timidly. This flipping between brutality and friendly banter scared her. Was he a paranoid schizophrenic? She took a deep breath and listened, determined to keep calm.

"Yeah, it was my day job. I wasn't always a criminal."

"You mean you were a college professor?"

"No, nothing that glamorous. I taught reluctant young boys European history in a very exclusive academy in England."

"You mean Metheford Academy?"

"Yes. I see you've been doing some research on me as well."

"Actually, Dan looked you up," she said. "It was his idea."

"I see. And what do you have against teaching?"

"Nothing," she replied. "Teaching's a noble profession. Done right, it's extremely rewarding."

"You're mistaken. It's boring and the pay's not all that great either."

"So why the extracurricular activities?"

"Well, opportunities knocked at my door. Moderate risk, high payback. So with no obligations to anyone but myself, why not?"

"There are plenty of reasons why not, but I don't think you want to discuss them with me."

"Oh, I don't mind," he answered. "It can't do any harm now. It's a life I'm not going back to. Sheer boredom with my day-to-day work. Humdrum can be a mighty impetus. Many have risked much more for a lot less. I suppose my love of beautiful objects and the spectacular histories they reveal had a great deal to do with my decision. I can't afford to lose sight of the monetary gain either."

"I've read a good portion of the Will Petty manuscript," Rivka said. "It's quite fascinating. Your school forwarded it to both the police and to us. I can't understand why you left such an obvious trail."

"Sometimes I'm the cool meticulous planner. At other times I'm the hyperimpulsive overachiever. The latter gets me into lots of hot water. Doctors tell me I have a bipolar disorder. Excitement drives me to do foolish things and take actions I've sorely regretted. I'm afraid my past is paved with those impulsive blunders."

Emil took the 295 bypass around Richmond and rejoined I-95 South once more. Traffic became less congested as they headed toward the North Carolina border.

"Have you ever seen the actual matrices and the chase?" Rivka asked after a long period of silence.

"Only in a very poor photograph, but even there, I could tell they were magnificent. I did come close to owning them once. I answered a classified ad in a Munich newspaper placed by one Deiter Hoffmann. He sent the faded picture to me for verification. The man claimed to have the actual merchandise and agreed to meet with me. However, at the time of the meeting, he informed me that both the print sets and the chase had already been sold to someone else. He wouldn't tell me who it was. I later found out it was Professor Fraume."

"And you couldn't press him?"

"We met at a *biergarten* in a very public square—no opportunity for rough stuff."

"How'd you find out about printing type sets in the first place?" Rivka asked.

"Quite by accident. I stumbled on a photocopy of the Manfried Heinswaller diary in a small printer's museum in Mainz, Germany, maybe twenty-five years after World War II had ended. Thereafter, I joined a group of fortune-hunting collector fools, who thought they could undercover the whereabouts of the matrices. I spent a year and a half researching everything relating to the subject, but I, like the rest, failed miserably. That is, until I came across the Petty lad's paper. That led me straight to Abner Fraume. I knew he had what everyone else had failed to find. I tried to make a deal with him—share both the money for its sale and an equal amount of credit for the research. However, he already knew of me by reputation and refused outright."

"What exactly could you bring to that deal? Why would he let you in on something he had exclusive rights to anyway?"

"I had the buyer—an extremely wealthy private collector. Most generous, I might add, as well as discreet. Besides, my research would have saved Fraume quite a bit of time, and the man wasn't getting younger by a long shot. I could have filled in some of the missing historical information and add several lesser-related artifacts. But no, the man was going to give the whole treasure away to a museum in return for publishing his pitiful manuscript. He literally wanted to trade away everything for nothing: his piece of immortality. Damn, the man was obstinate." Emil's shadowed face had reddened, and his road stare intensified as though Abner hovered somewhere outside the windshield, taunting him.

"Is that why you killed him?" Rivka asked calmly.

"That old fart was flushing opportunity down the loo. He made me angry, and I got flustered." Emil's voice rose and the words came faster. "I lost it—just too much. Can you believe it? Fraume tried to call the police. I got so mad when he picked up the phone that I ripped the cord out of the wall and wrapped it around his neck and…"

Emil pulled out of his lane and picked up speed.

"Spare me the details, please!" Rivka watched him weave between cars, from lane to lane, at breakneck speed until she feared for her life. "And slow down or you'll get us both killed." Rivka wondered if she'd triggered more than she wanted to know. "Of course, if you just want to attract a highway patrolman for speeding, that's your business." Then she thought, *Why am I telling him this? A patrolman is just what I need.*

Emil moderated his speed to seventy and fitted them back into the slower lane once more. "Thanks for the reminder," he muttered. "Say, aren't you the least bit afraid of me? Your very life is in my hands and yet you sit there conversing with me, even cracking jokes. What's going on in that busy little brain of yours?"

"I'm trying very hard to stay out of the trunk," she replied. "What would you do with me if I made a fuss, got hysterical, and started to whimper or even bawl? The conversation helps. Besides, you left me with a bit of a reminder, too. My ear still hurts."

"You've got a point there."

"A number of people, besides myself, know exactly who you are and what you look like. The police might even have figured out where we're going. Dan certainly knows. Assuming you acquire the matrices and get your price for them, then what?"

"Then what?" he repeated. "Then I assume my next identity and make myself scarce. It's already taken care of, and I won't discuss any more of those details."

Petersburg, Emporia, and the North Carolina border came and went as dusk settled in around them. Emil turned on the low beams, then rubbed his cheeks and chin vigorously to stave off the tedium-borne drowsiness. A green road sign informed him that the city of Wilson, NC, lay eleven miles ahead. He glanced down at the open map and then across at Rivka.

"You getting hungry yet?" he asked.

"Hungry, tired, and sore—sitting like this for so many hours. A potty stop might be in order too. You think I'm a camel? That I can go all day?"

"Okay, okay, I get the message. We'll look for the next comfort-stop signs and get off the highway." Sounding reasonable, he was thinking less so. *This woman is getting on my nerves. She's too logical and too bloody inquisitive.*

Chapter 24

Flight And Pursuit
Same Day

Special Agent Ken Robards and Dan Sherman were among the forty-seven passengers boarding Delta's Commuter Flight 1366 to Atlanta just after ten-thirty that morning. They pulled their only luggage, rolling carry-ons, behind them and stowed them in the overhead bins. Dan settled into a window seat in row 15, and Robards took the aisle seat next to him. Dan had been far too anxious to get any sleep the previous night, so he caught some much-needed, yet interrupted, shut-eye right after takeoff. Meanwhile, his traveling companion spent the time catching up on the Petty manuscript.

In the waiting room just prior to the flight, Robards had used his cell phone to keep in touch with the two surveillance teams working out of the Savannah field office. He hadn't expected pertinent activity at either of the two post offices quite this quickly, but he didn't want to take a chance. The consensus was that Emil had taken Rivka with him; public transportation was too risky for a kidnapper transporting a victim. Using the warm coffeepot found by the landlady as a guide, his best guess placed them in a car somewhere between Annapolis and Savannah, no more than five-and-a-half hours into an eleven-hour drive. That would put them in Savannah around seven-thirty that evening if they drove nonstop—much later if our victim didn't share any of the driving;

or figuring in gas and pit stops.

Dan had been asleep for fifteen minutes when the agent's cell phone jingled a tune and woke him. He heard Robards answer, exchange words, listen for a few minutes, and then hang up. "Anything new?" Dan asked.

"I'm not sure," answered Robards. "The Baltimore field office informs me that a man fitting Everet Kanter's description booked a flight to Fort Lauderdale via Atlanta around noon yesterday. There was no sign of any woman accompanying him. The ticketing agent was pretty specific about his description because he flirted with her, but airport security had no photograph to show her, so she couldn't be certain."

"I don't know if that's good news or bad," said Dan.

"Hard to say at this point," said Robards.

"You finished with the Petty lad's dissertation yet?"

"I've got a few more pages to go," Robards answered as Dan leaned over his shoulder to read with him.

> By the year 2001 World War II was over a half-century in the past, and Abner Fraume had reached the age of eighty-four. One day, while the professor sat reading the classified ads in a German language newspaper, his eyes lit up at the mention of the words 'sixteenth century' and 'Koenig' in the same sentence. He rang up the international number given and spoke to a man named Deiter Hoffmann. Hoffmann refused to say much over the phone, but did agree to meet with him at a beer hall in Munich the following Wednesday.
>
> On that particular Wednesday Fraume rode a train to London and Gatwick Airport, where he caught a flight to Munich. A cab took him to the beer hall and, after thirty minutes, Deiter Hoffmann approached his table and inquired if he was Abner Fraume. The two men introduced themselves and both spoke politely yet vaguely for some time before getting down to business. Each sized up the other, considering the amount of trust to be extended. First, Deiter explained that he had been the Stein butler. Abner then

enquired if Deiter was the lawful owner of the property he intended to sell.

"Did you take the treasure from its hiding place?" Abner asked him bluntly.

"*Yah!*" said Deiter, "but it vas only for safekeeping until Herr Stein returned. *Und* I never heard from him after the war."

"But Sigmund Stein died in concentration camp," declared Abner. "I witnessed my dear friend's demise."

"After all, Herr Stein trusted me to bury zis treasure," replied Deiter. "He must have intended me to have it if he didn't return. Also, he had no survivors, and ve vere almost family. In fact, my late wife actually uncovered zese things that were hidden for hundreds of years. Who should have them, the government? My lawyer tells me I have an excellent legal claim."

"I see," Abner said. "But why did you hang on to it for so many years and only now try to sell it?"

Deiter explained that he'd helped Stein to bury other articles of value and had lived off those over the years. Recently, he had been bankrupted by an accidental death lawsuit. The accident had not only taken the life of his wife, Lili, but the life of the man whose auto she'd hit. He had not thought of parting with the Koenig treasure because of its public recognition, but now he had become desperate and needed the money.

"Do you know the monetary value of the Koenig pieces?" asked Abner.

"At least a million euros in the right market. *Und* I'm not making guesses."

"I'm not a rich man," said Abner, "and I have only limited support from the university and the British Literary Museum. How much are you asking?"

"A quarter million euros. It's easily vorth at least three to four times that to certain collectors."

"You mean illegal collectors, Herr Hoffmann."

"*Yah!*" Deiter agreed. "I wait for someone, honest or not, to answer my ad."

"A quarter million euros—that's quite stiff, isn't?"

"Two hundred thousand then and not a pfennig less," Deiter announced. "It has to be vorth that much to you. *Yah?*"

"I'll let you know when I see the actual Koenig matrices and chase," Abner answered. "I also have to contact the museum and university."

The next afternoon Abner examined and verified the three cases of matrices and the engraved chase. He was ecstatic and sought an arrangement with Deiter for the mentioned amount. After a good deal of give and take, the two men agreed that Abner would take delivery in Bath, leaving Deiter obligated to supply an export license and bear the costs of shipping and insurance. Abner could now complete his treatise on the Koenig pieces.

"This is quite a story, Dan," said Robards. "I wonder how much is really true?"

"If the lad used the Heinswaller diary and the rest of Fraume's research material, I'd say a good portion of it is fact. Of course, he added dialogue and must have romanticized a good deal. You know? The boy will make a first-rate novelist someday."

"I agree," said the agent. "At least now we know something of its value and relative size. I'm not sure what more we can glean from these papers."

"I don't think we missed any clues, Ken. I didn't see anything that jumped out at me."

"I believe you're right," Robards said. "I'm surprised Abner entrusted the whereabouts of the treasure to the boy after taking so much care to hide the location from the rest of the world."

"I don't think Abner knew of the boy's connection to Kravitz," said Dan.

* * *

On the southern outskirts of Wilson, North Carolina, Emil slowed and turned off to follow the directions on billboards hawking service stations and restaurants. He selected the least busy restaurant and parked some distance away from the door as he'd done at the previous stop. Rivka protested when Emil reached to dispose of her drink cup in the holder. She leaned forward and feigned sipping the remaining liquid from the cup. He cut her bonds from the armrest, and as he turned away to get out of the car, she lifted the straw out of the cup with her lips and intentionally dropped it between the front seats. He skirted the car to open the passenger-side door and helped her to her feet.

This time the lone unisex restroom was situated inside at the rear of the building next to and behind the fast food counter. Other than the short-order cook and the order taker, only one couple occupied the establishment, and their affectionate behavior, feeding catsup-dripping fries to one another, indicated that they were oblivious to the room around them.

Emil held onto Rivka as they traversed the room in quick ten-inch steps—the limits of her tie-strapped stride. At the restroom door, hidden from the counter, he loosened her belt, enabling her to complete the rest of nature's mission on her own. He checked inside beforehand to assess the risk, and again afterward to be sure she hadn't left any kind of message. Then Emil led her back to the car and tied her into the submerged seating position. He returned to the building and took some time to use the facilities himself.

In the car, Rivka wrapped her fingers around the straw on the nearby floor and managed to raise one end of it to her mouth. She hoped and prayed that it would remain rigid enough for the job she had in mind. She eyed the paper clip lying in an indented well beneath the driver's seat. The clip became her ultimate target—the key to her escape. Knowing that her face could not fit under the driver's seat, she manipulated the opposite end of the straw underneath the seat to the well. Bumping the clip proved easy, but nudging it out of the half-inch-deep well around the seat leg proved to be more difficult. The clip stood at a 45-degree angle at the perimeter of the indent, and the straw had too large a diameter to fit in the eye of the clip. Rivka bit down on the end of the straw in her mouth, flattening it in her teeth, until the screwdriver-like flat end held its shape.

Dropping the straw on the floor once more allowed her to switch ends of the straw with her hand. Back in her mouth, the flat end of the straw easily slipped into the eye of the protruding paper clip. She slowly raised the clip entirely out of the well and free of the seat's underside, but she still had to deposit it back on the carpet in front of the driver's seat. In order to pull the clip any closer, she needed to get above it and drag it toward her. The process was slow and sometimes disappointing when the flat end bent the wrong way or slipped out of the eye altogether.

Rivka heard Emil coming back and had to abandon her quest while he asked her preference between a fried catfish sandwich or crispy chicken and fries. She chose the latter, and he hesitated for a moment. *Was he suspicious?* He tilted his head before leaving as though there was something else to be said. But there wasn't. She waited another thirty seconds before resuming her task. *Was he testing her somehow?*

Despite all the misses and misdirections, the clip found its way to the space between the seats where her left hand could actually reach it. Rivka dropped the straw and retrieved the clip from the floor. Now if only she could utilize her husband's concept of how to reuse locking tie-straps. He'd perfected just such a tool to accomplish that feat. It was another one of his inventive *Whydon'tchas*. The first step involved bending one leg of the clip away from its main body, but before the open point could be inserted in the tie-strap locking device, the rustle of a paper sack could be heard approaching the door. Quickly, Rivka stowed the deformed paper clip under her belt for future use. Both hands would soon be needed to feed her face.

Emil tossed the old cup out on the open parking lot and set the new drinks down in the double cup holders extended from the dash.

"Hey!" she cried. "That's littering!"

"So add it to my list of crimes," he grumbled, setting the empty drink tray on her lap.

He raised her seat upright and then shook a partial bag of crispy-fried chicken parts and loose fries into the tray. From a second white paper sack he produced a catfish sandwich with oozing tartar sauce and an outcropping of lettuce.

Rivka took a few bites and munched for a while. *A little greasy, but serviceable,* she thought. "Not exactly diet food," she commented aloud.

"You don't have to worry about your figure. I like my women Rubenesque," he mumbled between munching.

Her stomach began to boil. What ghastly nerve calling her one of *his* women. She took a deep breath to keep from gagging. But she was determined to focus. *Get a grip,* she warned herself.

"I'm surprised your wife left you. You know how to treat a girl. First feed the stomach and then the ego."

Rivka received a disapproving glare for her intrusion into his private life. She continued to eat her chicken parts and fries while Emil silently chewed away on his sandwich. When she suggested that some catsup would have been nice, he ignored her.

Emil finished the catfish sandwich, crumpled the bag, and threw it on the floor behind him. Spotting another reproachful look from Rivka, he admitted, "So I'm not the neat freak I used to be. I'm not a lot of things I used to be. In fact, the old Emil will soon disappear altogether."

After a long drag on his drink Emil turned on the ignition, and the engine came alive. He drove on into the night. A few hours later rain sprinkled lightly on the windshield in front of them, and wipers became necessary. The rain intensified and visibility declined. His concentration required more effort. Now and then, Emil ran the window down, grabbed a handful of rainwater, and sloshed it across his face, forcing himself to stay awake. Somewhere between the North Carolina cities of Dunn and Fayetteville, Emil surrendered to the torrential onslaught and pulled into a roadside rest stop.

* * *

Death Goes Postal

Ken Robards and Dan Sherman deplaned from Flight 1366 to Atlanta just after one p.m., pulling their only luggage behind them. After checking in with the gate agent, they settled into black vinyl waiting room seats.

"How about you watch the luggage while I go over to the newsstand and pick up a newspaper?" asked Robards.

"Sure," Dan said as the agent made his way toward the satellite gate concourse.

Dan got up to take off his sport coat and laid it down on the next seat to his. On second thought, he reached into a pocket and retrieved Abner's postal box key.

When Robards returned, Dan showed it to him, and admitted he'd been extremely careless, leaving the key loose in an outer pocket. The key, even without a number stamped on, was the only way they'd find the exact box containing Abner's chase and matrices. With the key intact, they could try it in all the suspect boxes. This time Dan stowed the key in his wallet. Robards had taken Dan along for two reasons. First, Dan wouldn't surrender the key unless he was allowed to come along. Second, Dan knew what each of the suspects looked like in spite of the fact that he didn't know which one would actually show up.

"Damn! I forgot all about it," said the FBI agent.

"What?" asked Dan.

"The other wallet, I forgot all about Levant's other wallet. I sent Ms. Germain all the way home for it, and somehow she never got back to us."

"I don't have a personal number with me for either of the ladies," Dan said. "Of course, you could try the bookstore." He removed a business card, pointed to the phone number on the bottom right, and handed it to Robards. The agent dialed several times, but a busy signal responded each time. Forty minutes later, the two anxious men boarded the connection to Savannah.

Chapter 25

Curiosity and Cats
Baltimore and N. Carolina—Same Day

Stopped at a Baltimore traffic light, Frieda's thoughts drifted to Garry and the phone message she'd taken for him. The last four digits were all that she remembered writing down. *The woman's name would be Posner as well,* she thought. *Shouldn't be too hard to look up.*

The light changed to green, and it took a honk from the car behind to get Frieda to move. In her mind she had already made the decision. Hopefully, it wasn't as rash as it sounded. At the next corner, a public telephone stood at the back of a Sunoco station lot. She drove in and parked alongside. It was the phone book she was most interested in. "Posner…Posner," she mumbled. "Ah, here it is: Mrs. G. Posner and the number ends with 4163, too. It's 1302 West Marlbury Street. Not too far from here."

Frieda wrestled with the idea of a telephone confrontation, but decided against it. However, the phone could be used to determine if Mrs. G. Posner was at home. She dropped in the coins, dialed, and waited. A woman picked up after three rings and shouted a raspy hello. Frieda said nothing, hung up, and returned to the car. She sat there for several more minutes, contemplating whether to go through with a face-to-face meeting. In the end, wanting to know where she stood with Garry and having the nearby address in hand proved sufficient for her to start the engine and drive there.

The small gray house wasn't hard to find; the numerals 1302 loomed large on the left of two pillars flanking the door. Frieda parked, climbed three marble steps, and rang the doorbell. A thin woman in a print housecoat answered the four-tone summons. She wasn't at all what Frieda had expected—the voice had been so much bigger.

"Mrs. Posner?"

"That's me," the woman answered. "What do you want?"

"I'm not exactly sure," Frieda stumbled. "Maybe I should explain."

"Maybe you should!"

"I'm a friend of Garry's," she began.

"Oh-oh, another one of his girlfriends?"

"No, I'm not that kind of friend. At least not yet."

"Then who are you, woman?"

"Let's just say I tried to be his friend, but I caught him lying to me."

"He'll do that," the woman declared. "Would you like to come in? It's chilly out there on the stoop."

"Sure!"

Frieda stepped into the front hall and the odor of kitty urine nearly overtook her. There were at least a dozen cats in the front hall. More on the staircase leading to the second floor. Uncountable cats moved among each of the front rooms. She followed the woman through a series of doors until they reached the kitchen where fresh-perked coffee made a desperate attempt to wrestle the litter smell down.

"Coffee?"

"Yes, thank you, Mrs. Posner." Frieda looked around the kitchen. A calico stared down at her from the top of the refrigerator. Two more cats lazed on the counter, and another had just jumped to the floor, which was covered with an array of porcelain and stainless bowls.

"Most folks call me Nita. Otherwise, it's Anita." She gently nudged an all-gray out of her way with the toe of her foot to clear the path.

"I'm Frieda, Frieda Forrester." She hadn't meant to use her real name. It just slipped out.

Nita motioned for Frieda to have a seat at the dinette table while she poured two mugs of coffee. Placing them on the table, she pulled up a chair for herself. Her visitor smiled, for she had noticed that the cups bore two incompatible logos—Redskins and Ravens.

"Mixed loyalties, I presume?"

"Yeah! One more thing Garry and me never agreed on. He sure liked them 'Skins. I'm a Ravens fan myself." She pushed the sugar bowl closer. "Got no milk or cream in the house—sorry." She finished stirring in her own cup and dropped the same teaspoon into Frieda's cup. "So what did you want to know about him?"

"Is he still married to you?"

"I'm not quite sure."

"I don't understand."

"Well, we've been separated for more than three years. Actually two years. The first was sort of on-again off-again. Five or six months ago Garry filed formal divorce papers. I got the final papers to sign last month, but I've never signed them. Oh, I told him I would, but I just never did."

"Are you contesting the divorce?"

"I wasn't going to until I got that phone call from an uppity English lawyer type, telling me that my husband might come into some legacy from his birth father. I always thought he never knew anything about his birth parents. Anyway, I'm not about to give up on anything that's rightfully mine. Would you?"

"I don't know. I'm not in your shoes. If you don't mind my asking, why are you two divorcing? Did he abandon you financially?"

"No, nothing like that. He sends me money regularly and pays the rent on the house. But we fought a lot—mostly over the cats. He couldn't abide them. Sometimes we fought over disciplining Phyllis. That's our daughter. Never could get her to toe the line.

That one has a mind of her own. Lazy, too—couldn't get her to do a thing around the house. Garry kept saying she wasn't my slave. What did he know? A girl's gotta help her mom."

"Then he sends you enough for child support."

"No, no. Phyllis lives with him, always has. Them two are from the same mold."

"Don't you miss her, Nita?"

"Not really. We couldn't get along. She was always talking back to me, and Garry would take her part every time. I do get lonely, but things are better off this way. A lot quieter, too."

"I see." Frieda drained her cup and set it down. "I want to thank you for the coffee and conversation, but I must leave now. I've got the two-to-eight shift at the diner where I work."

"You never did say why you came. Not that I didn't enjoy the company. I get so little of it these days."

"Let's just say I came to commiserate over Garry. We have a lot in common." Frieda knew it wasn't true, but she couldn't admit that she had come to spy on Garry. They were walking toward the front door when Frieda noticed an antique vase on the hall table.

"Say, that's a beautiful vase. Aren't you afraid one of the cats will topple it?"

"Oh, of course not," Nita replied. "Cats are sure footed—even more so than people. Garry sent it from England a few years back."

"England?"

"Yeah. He and Phyllis tried living over there for awhile. Told me they respect plumbers in that country."

"Why England?"

"He used to visit some friend—a guy he met in the army. They went every year or so."

"Didn't you ever go with them?" Frieda asked.

"Nah, I don't like flying. Scared of them things. Besides, the cats would miss me."

"Why'd they move back?"

"How the heck should I know?" replied Nita.

"How long ago was that?"

"A couple a years—maybe more. Hey, you sure ask a lot of questions. Why don't you ask Garry if you're so all-fired curious about his past?"

"Bye now," said Frieda, sensing Nita's change of tone.

"Bye."

* * *

The roadside rest stop comprised one tiny restroom building, a billboard-mounted roadmap, and about thirty parking slots. A tractor-trailer stretched out for the night some distance off at the egress to the interstate. Two street lamps struggled to illuminate the park amid the torrential downpour. Parked in the shadows away from either lamp, Rivka and Emil lay back on their reclined bucket seats staring at the darkness overhead and listening to the invasive pounding on the steel roof. Suddenly, the night disappeared in a huge white flash. Deafening claps of thunder dwarfed the drumming on the roof and prevented either one of them from even snoozing.

"I'm sorry for the crack about your ex," said Rivka, trying to jumpstart the conversation. "I know these things are touchy."

"I should be over it by now," he responded introspectively. "I suppose I wasn't the best husband around. She needed friends—lots of them, and I've always been a damn loner. I wanted her. I didn't need anyone else. It's hard to be social with someone while you're questioning their motives, and guarding against being used and abused. Everybody's got their own agenda, looking out for number one."

"Hey, that's a pretty narrow view of people in general. You've got to open up to people and they'll open up to you."

"Yeah, and they'll step all over you." He rolled on his side to face her. "I learned that lesson a long time ago."

"You've worked with youngsters in the past and in some ways you've been almost decent with me."

"Well, that's different," he said. "I was in control—no trust involved."

"You accepted my word."

"Did I? I guess you took me by surprise. Maybe you just look trustworthy."

"Careful, your hard shell is showing signs of a major crack. What on earth happened to make you think like that?"

"It's a long story."

"I don't think I'm going anywhere tonight, and you weren't planning to get any sleep with all that racket going on out there, were you?"

"I've never told this story to anyone since it happened over thirty years ago in Chicago. I never knew my father, and my mom didn't make much in a retail dress shop. I was a pretty good athlete in those days, good enough for a full varsity football scholarship at Northwestern University. I pledged one of the rich-boy fraternities and readily accepted their friendship and gifts. Because I was a perfect rube, a trusting, beholden fool then, they used me. Sent me on all sorts of crazy errands. The usual hazing, I suppose. On the other hand, I enjoyed a busy life full of social and athletic activities and that left little time for actual study. My grades were beginning to reflect my lack of attention.

"Four of my teammates/fraternity house brothers suffered the same academic affliction. Just before finals they enlisted my help in stealing Professor Mortimer's physics exam. Being the agile cornerback—I weighed considerably less than the linebacker, the tight end, or either of the two linemen—I was the one boosted through the professor's office window. Unknown to me, that window, whose sill was a mere eight feet off the ground, had been clandestinely left unlocked during the afternoon. No sooner than my foot had touched the floor, the window slammed shut behind me, and lights flooded the room.

"As it turned out, this was not the first time students had attempted to filch Professor Mortimer's precious exam. He'd seen the unlocked window, and sat on his swivel chair in total darkness awaiting his prey. The man of science told me that he was disappointed in me because I had shown some promise. But the disciplinarian in him couldn't let me get away with blatantly invading his domain.

"Outside the window, my loyal *four housemen* had vanished, leaving me to take on the wrath of the whole physics faculty and the departmental investigation by myself. I accepted responsibility for what I did, and I implicated none of the others. Absolutely no one of my so-called brothers stepped forward either to surrender themselves or to speak on my behalf. Even before the honor board met, my own fraternity disavowed themselves of me and tossed me out of the fraternity for dishonesty. When called to testify, one of the four brothers even lied, saying I'd tried enlisting him in the plot and, of course, he refused. He was asked why he hadn't reported the incident. He replied that he didn't think I'd go through with it. So much for friendship, loyalty, and trust."

"I can see why you'd be angry," said Rivka. "But it was years ago. Why let that anger rule your whole life?"

"I was willing to take on the whole blame," Emil said, his tone bitter. "They didn't have to turn on me like that."

Rivka watched his right hand scrunch up into a ball and anger dominate his whole face. Her fear returned, and she needed to calm him before he took his volatile mood out on her. "But that was only a few mean-spirited people and one isolated incident," she offered in a small voice. "Surely, you could have made a friend or two since then."

"When I got married I thought I could depend on my wife. But you know how that mess ended."

"Yes. I see the rain is lessening—not as loud as before," Rivka said. "Maybe we can catch a few winks before morning." Not daring to make eye contact with this maniac, she watched him with a sidelong glance as he considered her proposal. *The longer I can delay his destination, the better my chances of being rescued,* she thought.

"Yeah, get some sleep," he grumbled, staring off into his own past.

Chapter 26

Undoing
Same Night

Nestled in a forest of scrub pine trees, the off-road rest stop sheltered them from risky driving in a prolonged downpour. Hours later, when the rain had turned to an interminable drizzle, Rivka convinced him he needed to sleep 'til daylight. Emil lowered both front seats and made himself comfortable facing her. He focused on her for several minutes before closing his eyelids. It was a softer, kinder stare. It was as though he'd begun to care for her. That notion worried Rivka and made her even more uncomfortable, actually creeping her out. She closed both eyes and feigned slumber. There wasn't any chance of her actually falling off to sleep. The blood rapidly coursing through her veins pumped her to an emotional high—an edginess peaked by her decision to take the ultimate risk.

Rivka had developed an escape plan dependent on one of Dan's *whydon'tchas*. She prayed that she would be able to recall every detail about his gadget for reusing tie-wraps, which he preferred to call tie-straps. According to Dan, the lock within the sheath of a tie-strap utilizes an internal plastic spring that rides easily up a ramp, then drops back on the plastic strap in one direction, but hangs up on the steep vertical face in the opposite direction. Dan had mounted a thin steel tooth on one jaw of a pair of gas pliers. When the pliers closed about the sheath, the inserted tooth bent the internal spring out of the way, permitting him to slide the strap in either direction. *I bet I can use this paper clip to hold off this same locking spring. Please, dear God—let it work.*

When Rivka heard Emil's steady deep breathing and recognized a sound that faintly resembled a snore, she barely opened one eye and regarded him suspiciously. *Is the man still testing me or is he so tired and so absent from any self-guilt that sleep consumes him easily?* She saw him stir and then turn his head and shoulders toward the driver's door, clumsily dragging and bumping his legs along. Soon the heavy breathing resumed, along with frequent snores and the occasional explosive snort. Believing the entire night now belonged to her efforts, Rivka waited another half-hour according to the dashboard clock. She'd decided on releasing her right hand first. The interlocking loops—one around her wrist and the other over the belt—would give her the longest possible reach. She removed the clip from its hiding place beneath her belt. But no matter how she scrunched her body and stretched her bonds to reach the opposite wrist with the clip, at least three more inches had to be conquered. She could, however, touch fingertip to fingertip. Plan B fell into place.

Rivka wore Dan's old belt in the loops of her jeans. At least eight inches of overlapping belt length had been tucked into the left-side loops. She bent the clip into a crude hook and transferred it to her mouth. Keeping the sliding belt section anchored to her waist with her left elbow, her right hand pushed the overlapping belt flap toward her midsection, causing a major-sized hoop to form inside the buckle. After nearly twenty minutes of wiggling, pushing, and tummy sucking, all but the flap at the bitter end had gone through the buckle's outer ring—simply, there was nothing left to push on. Transferring the hook-like clip to her left hand, Rivka snagged one side of the hoop close to the outer ring and pulled the remaining flap length through. The length of belt sought its natural shape, flapped open, and came to rest extended to her right. Now the clip slipped along the stiff leather until it found and fell into a punched hole close to the inner ring of the buckle.

Death Goes Postal

Tugging on it only bent the clip until she sucked in her tummy to reduce the friction. Then the buckle itself moved until restrained by a jeans' loop. Rivka could now reach, grab, and pull on the belt flap. She leaned backward and sucked in as hard as possible.

Then the miracle happened. The belt spike popped from the punched belt hole and lay at an angle below it. At this point the entire belt released, and she slid it out of the loops bit-by-bit, freeing her left hand entirely, but leaving her right hand still shackled to the door and her left foot shackled to both her right foot and the seat frame.

Emil snorted in his sleep and shifted position, alarming her and reminding her of her tenuous situation. Her body and breathing petrified on the spot. *Had he heard the belt buckle slam against the glove-box door?* Only when the odd sleep noises dwindled to near silence once more, did Rivka dare continue. She straightened the clip into a probe once more, and with her free left hand tried to insert the probe under the strap within the locking sheath of the strap about her right wrist. Cold perspiration sucked her shirt against her armpits as she encountered more frustration. With each push the tie-strap slid away around her wrist. Friction wasn't enough; she needed a hard edge to stop the sheath from moving. The bond restricted movement to somewhere on the door. The inside door release handle fitted this task. Holding the sheath against the handle with her wrist, this time the probe went in snugly and protruded from the opposite side. A small adjustment centered the probe between the ramped strap and the locking tooth. Rivka tugged at the freed strap until it grew to a size to free her right hand. She tried sliding it on again and held it against her waist to see whether she could fool her captor into thinking his victim remained hooked to the door. With newfound maneuverability, the left-hand strap proved easier to release, and she tried that loop on for size as well.

First light began dancing under dawn's doorstep, tripping through the pines, illuminating wet needles as it leapt. First sounds invaded the silence of waning night: tractor-trailers rolling over early morning roads still damp from the rain. Rivka suddenly realized that she hadn't replaced the belt around her waist. With two oversized hand loops and her hands free, replacing Dan's belt became quite simple. A good deal of time would be needed to free her legs, more than she believed she had, even though Emil hadn't stirred for some time.

Rivka's next thought was to retrieve the cell phone from Emil's pocket—more important even than her hobbled legs. Deciding to chance it, she tugged on the coattail hanging off the back seat and slid it forward until the clunky phone in the side pocket struck the floor with a thud. Before she could slip her hand into the pocket to retrieve it, she heard a groan from the driver's seat. A quick glance in his direction found him still facing toward his door. The back of his head was all she could see. As she slid the phone out, her trembling hand bumped into the plastic on the back of his seat and dropped it onto the floor, making noises that seemed louder than they actually were. Another unintelligible sound warbled from him, and his head moved back and forth a few times.

Slowly and quietly she slid the coat back into its original position on the rear seat, picked the cell phone off the floor, and deposited it in a seat crease beneath her. But when she turned to face forward, the coat slid to the floor again. Emil began to move, to turn over. Rivka abandoned the coat and slipped her right hand through the door side strap and hugged both her wrists to the belt—hopefully replicating the image of how he'd last seen her. *Will he notice the coat on the floor?* Emil faced her now, but his eyes remained shut. Then, as though someone had pulled the handle on a one-armed bandit, both eyes rolled open wide. He stared at her eerily for several seconds and then smiled, presumably over the fact of her presence.

"I'll be back for you in a few minutes," he said, as he opened his door and stood on his stiff legs.

In the postdawn wooded surroundings, the car's dome light came on, then off again when he shut the door. Literally, the light bulb overhead struck Rivka with another idea. Waiting until Emil had gone up the walk and disappeared into the rest-stop building, she tested the three-position switch associated with the dome light by opening and closing her door. The original position worked with the door. A second position set the light to remain on all the time. A third position disabled it, regardless of the door. She left the light switch in the disabled position. If an opportunity presented itself during another sleep-out, she didn't want the light to awaken her abductor.

Emil returned to the car and snipped the bonds to the chair frame and armrest while she held her wrists tightly to the belt. He undid her buckle several notches and led her up the path to one of two ladies rooms. As soon as it became vacant, he motioned for her to enter. When Rivka shut the door, Emil picked up a folding sign from an empty mopping bucket and stuck it in front of the restroom: CLEANING—USE OTHER RESTROOM. After Rivka came out, he led her back to the parking space and restrained her to the car once more, never noticing the enlarged loops about her wrists. He started the engine and pulled out into the ever-increasing daylight and traffic on I-95.

"You're a spunky lady, Mrs. Sherman," Emil declared once they had reached cruising speed. "Aren't you the least bit afraid of me?"

"You had better believe I'm scared," she replied. "No one has ever threatened my life before. It's not like this sort of thing happens every day. You think I like being abducted by a thief and murderer?"

"You call me all kinds of names. Yet you seem so calm, and there's no sign of tears. I can't even find fright in your eyes. I've never met anyone quite like you."

"I'm trying to think. I can't think when I'm excited or blubbery." *Oh-oh, I shouldn't have said that.*

"You wouldn't be thinking about escape, would you? I don't recommend it." He shook his head as he spoke. "I'd have to take drastic precautions if you attempted anything."

"Of course not. A deal's a deal," she lied.

Two hours later they crossed the border between the two Carolinas.

* * *

On the way home from work, Garry stopped at the Giant food store in Festival Mall. He picked up bread, milk, coffee, a ready-roasted chicken, and an assortment of side salads. Leaving the checkout counter, Garry thought he noticed a familiar woman's face. He quickly rolled his shopping cart outside in pursuit. He hadn't the least idea what he'd say once he'd caught up with her, but they needed to talk. Their last meeting had ended in such a mess of anger, confusion, and mistrust.

"Garry?" Frieda's voice rose with an element of surprise. "I didn't expect to see you here."

"Well, a guy's gotta eat, doesn't he?"

"Of course, I didn't mean…"

"Car running okay now?"

"Yeah, fine." She finished loading the groceries into the car trunk.

"Girls well?"

"Uh-huh. Uh…Garry?"

"Yeah?"

"I've got a confession to make. It's not easy for me to tell you this."

"So tell me already!"

"I went to see your wife in Baltimore, and we had a nice long chat over coffee."

"My ex-wife! Well, I already heard all about your little tête-à-tête. She called me."

"It's still wife, according to Nita. The way she told me, she hasn't signed the final divorce papers yet. She said she might be entitled to some money you were going to inherit."

"Nita was just pulling your leg. My lawyer got her to sign a few days ago, so it really is ex-wife."

"How'd he do that, if you don't mind my asking?"

Death Goes Postal

"Well, the lawyer threatened her by placing my voluntary house payments and generous alimony in jeopardy. He pointed out that we haven't even been notified of whose legacy it might be or if I'm considered a legitimate heir. Any claim to this inheritance would be shaky as a result of the long separation between us. It could be months or possibly years before any of the probate gets settled, and even then, there might not be much in the end. So, as of last Thursday, I'm a free man with no more secrets. Do you believe me now?"

"I guess it was all one big misunderstanding," she said, closing the trunk lid. "You'll probably never forgive me for mistrusting you."

"I think we're all under a bit of stress, considering the mugger and murderer in our midst." He watched her park the shopping cart in the stand and return to the car.

She appeared to be quiet and introspective until she stood before him again. "You're being very generous with me, Garry." She opened the driver's door and slid behind the wheel.

He closed her door and leaned in on the rolled-down window. "Maybe I find you worth it. By the way, did you ever try calling Phyllis? I hope you hung onto the number I gave you."

"I'm sorry," she said. "I'd forgotten all about it. I've become such a ditz."

Frieda opened her outsized leather purse with its silver studs and dug deep inside. Triumphantly, she held up Garry's business card. Holding it in one hand, she rummaged again in her purse, pulled out a cell phone, and tapped away with the tip of her thumb. On the fourth ring a young woman's voice answered.

"Who am I speaking to?" asked Frieda.

"You're the one that's calling," answered the voice.

"Hi, my name is Frieda Forrester. Your father and I—"

"Hi, Frieda. I'm Phyllis. Dad's told me so much about you. I can't wait to meet you. I'm sorry. He's not home right now, but I can have him give you a call when he gets in."

"No, that won't be necessary. You see he's here with me right now. Do you want to speak with him?" She handed the phone to Garry before the answer came back.

"Hi, sweetheart. Did you finish your homework? Uh-huh... Yeah, she is, isn't she? I'll try not to be too late. Love ya." He kissed into the phone and returned it to Frieda. "Well!"

Frieda hesitated and then coyly motioned for him to come closer. He stuck his head well inside the window. She planted a hot kiss on his lips and ran a caressing hand across his cheek. Leaning inside at a forty-five degree angle quickly turned more awkward than romantic. He backed out and straightened up.

"I've got a great idea," he said. "Why don't I go back inside and pick up another ready-roasted chicken, plus some extra trimmings, and meet you at your place. On the way I'll stop at home and bring Phyllis along. How does that sound?"

"Like a party," she said. *Like a long overdue party.* She started the engine, blew him another kiss, and drove off.

Chapter 27

On the Road
S. Carolina—Tuesday, June 1st

An extra lane eased the truck traffic for awhile in South Carolina. The peaceful overnight had left Emil in a pretty decent mood. A tune running through his mind escaped in the form of a hum so that Rivka heard him. She, on the other hand, was bored.

"You're in a good spirits," she said. "Mind if we talk some?"

"Fine, but you know the rules."

"How'd you wind up in England?" Rivka asked.

"I wanted to finish college, but every transcript the schools requested carried my blemish along with the grades. It found its way into all my records. Many of the schools I applied to didn't even bother to reply. So I started applying overseas in any country that spoke English or Deutsch."

"Deutsch?" she questioned.

"Yes, Deutsch. My mother was an immigrant, so we spoke German at home. I'm still fluent. I also began life as a bastard. My so-called father had been a rotten bully. Had his way with my mother and left her cold afterward. I never knew him. I'm named after her father. Kravitz was her family name, so it became mine. She was a pitiful thing. Knew nothing of what you people would call love. I was all she had. Died during the summer between my junior and senior years of high school. Maybe I'm telling you more than you wanted to know?"

"No, no," she responded, "I'm interested. So you had better luck in England, then?" *I'd better keep him talking,* she thought. *It seems to have a calming effect on him.*

"No, not at first. The schools still wanted my transcripts, and the ones that replied did so with short and curt form-letter refusals."

"Wasn't there anything you could do?"

"I tried," he said. "At one small college in Scotland, I intercepted my transcript in the mail bag at the registrar's office and retyped the page carrying the damaging information. I resubmitted it and waited. A week later I received a letter from their provost's office accusing me of tampering with the mail. They even threatened me with prosecution."

"Wow! How'd they find you out?" she asked.

"Apparently, the weight of the paper bond I used was different enough to be detected. After quite an extensive search and several thousand dollars of application fees, I found Haverley College, a small school that would accept me as a freshman solely on the basis of academic testing. I'd told them my high school was no longer in existence so they wouldn't see that I had matriculated to any college previously. I repeated two and a-half years and completed enough additional studies to obtain a bachelor's and a master's degree in six. After graduation with honors, I had no problem finding a position at Metheford Academy just outside of Bath."

"I told you we know about Metheford. Dan spoke with the headmaster there a few days ago. He also sent along Will Petty's term paper."

"Then you know something about Koenig's matrices and chase."

"Yes. How long did you teach there?" she asked.

"It would have been twenty-two years in November. Teaching history and literature to young lads was a natural for me, and they had some sort of rapport with me, too."

Death Goes Postal

"That's quite a stretch between beloved teacher and—you should excuse the expression—'murderous villain.' How'd that happen?"

"Well, I'd have to say there are two things involved. I've always had this terrible temper when I didn't get my way. I told you one doctor diagnosed me as bipolar. He told me my extreme anger was triggered by moments of stress. I took lithium for awhile, but I didn't like the side effects, so I stopped. I've got some other pills now."

"And the other thing?" she prompted as he pulled out into a passing lane.

"Being poor encouraged a sticky-finger habit. I stole things whenever the opportunity permitted. Got away with it mostly." He passed two slower moving cars and returned to the right lane.

"How did you get interested in this particular quest?"

"I've a natural flair for world history and once, during my fourth term at Haverley, I even viewed one of Gutenberg's forty-two-line Bibles. I became instantly attracted to it—not for any religious, ethical, or moral reasons; but more for the mechanical genius of the man. I performed some academic research on the history of printfounding. I published a number of papers on the subject in historical journals and made a name for myself in the field.

"Then, about ten years ago, Abner Fraume recovered the Heinswaller diaries and turned them over to the British Literary Museum. As an established researcher on the subject, I had access to the diaries and Professor Fraume's notes. I began to see how my own research dovetailed beautifully with Fraume's findings. I also became obsessed with finding the actual relics, but had no success until I read the Petty lad's papers. I consulted with Fraume about a possible collaboration, but the man wasn't interested in fame and fortune. His entire motivation was purely academic."

"How unreasonable," she said.

"Are you making fun of me?" he asked as his expression cast a stern look.

"N-n-no," she stammered. "I merely wanted to agree with you. Abner should have at least explored the possibilities with you." *Whew,* she thought, *I nearly pulled his chain.*

"Yes, the man wouldn't listen to reason. I even had a buyer and a very tempting price, one million euros."

"Who would pay such a price and why?" she asked.

"Let's just say he's an anonymous collector with a large bankroll and an even larger ego."

"Your buyer's German or Austrian, isn't he?"

"German, yes. If you expect me to supply his identity, *that*, my dear, would be your undoing. I'd have to renege on my promise to set you free."

Rivka tried to swallow the lump in her throat. She hadn't expected to be reminded of her eventual plight so bluntly. The stark idea of death raised goosebumps on her arms. *He still intends to release me,* she suddenly rationalized. *Or is he just saying that to keep me in line?*

"And what if we don't find Koenig's relics?" she asked nervously. "Are you still going to kill me?"

"Perhaps and perhaps not," he answered slyly.

"What kind of an answer is that? Have the decency to tell me where I stand."

"I don't know the answer."

Chapter 28

Splitting Heirs
Annapolis and S. Carolina—Same Day

Frieda burst into the house with the news that there would be guests for dinner. She flew though the rooms, shedding layers of her uniform as she went, hesitating only to mobilize her daughters with specific tasks while she showered and changed into fresh clothes. Trudy the thirteen-year-old—surprisingly agreeable for her age—dialed the oven to a 450-degree preheat and went about setting the dining room table. Marcia, seventeen, slammed her book shut, grumbled the unintelligible, and moved around the room with a dust cloth, gathering out-of-place clothing along with stray school books and papers, empty glasses, and assorted dirty dishes.

"Who's this guest?" asked Trudy, from outside the bathroom door.

"Just some guy I met," Frieda answered from inside. "A real gentleman. He's nice and we hit it off real well."

"And where'd you meet him?"

"Probably some lonesome bozo from the diner," Marcia interrupted. "She's always picking up strays."

"I heard that," Frieda screamed through the door. "For your information, young lady, we met at the mystery writers' critique group. And as long as I pay the bills around here I'll bring home whom I damn well please. Is it too much to ask you to do a few things for your working mother?"

"What's his name?" asked Trudy.

"Garry. Garry Posner. He's new in town. Oh, by the way, he's bringing his daughter over, too. So make sure you set enough places."

Trudy started to ask the age of his daughter when she heard the shower water drowning out her words. She slipped one of Mrs. Swiff's thawed berry pies into the pre-heated oven and, after filling the coffeepot, switched it on to dark brew. Several minutes later the shower went silent and the doorbell took its turn. In fact, it rang several times.

"Will one of you get the door? Please!" Frieda, wrapped in a towel, darted out the bathroom door and slipped into her bedroom, closing that door behind her.

"You're closer," Trudy called to her sister with her wet hands under the faucet.

Marcia, still grumbling, headed to the front door, pulled it open partway, and faced the two visitors.

"Hi! I'm Garry, a friend of your mother's, and this is my daughter, Phyllis. You must be Trudy."

"Wrong! I'm Marcia the troll. But hi, and welcome anyway." She swung the door wide for them, and they stepped into the living room.

"Hi yourself and thank you," answered Garry.

"Say, aren't you the new kid in my A.P. English and history classes?" declared Marcia.

"Hey, you're right," said Phyllis. "I just transferred in from Baltimore. I didn't recognize you right away, but sure."

"Just your luck to get stuck with ole prune-face, Mizz Guthrey," quipped Marcia.

"Does the wicked witch of the classroom ever smile?" asked Phyllis.

Marcia giggled. "Not once since last September."

"Hey," said Garry. "You two gonna stop gabbing, or am I gonna have to hold these groceries all night long?"

Death Goes Postal

"I'll take one of those," said Marcia. "We can put them on the kitchen counter."

As soon as the bag bearers entered the room, Trudy greeted and welcomed them. "You must be Garry and—"

"Thank you. It's Phyllis, Garry and Phyllis Posner." Phyllis began unpacking the bags as soon as they were set on the counter. Sliding the two roasted chickens closer to the oven, she suggested that they might need reheating before serving.

"Yep," agreed Trudy. "We'll heat 'em in the oven when the pie comes out."

Everyone turned when they heard the bedroom door squeak open. Frieda emerged in a pale yellow blouse and brown tailored slacks with sharp creases. She greeted the guests, and after stealing an embarrassing peck on Garry's cheek, she took both of Phyllis's hands in her own and then, with a change of mind, hugged her instead. When Trudy refused to surrender the apron, Frieda led Garry and the older girls back into the front room to get acquainted.

Dinner went without a hitch, and when Trudy retired to her room to do homework, Phyllis and Marcia pitched in to do the dishes. Afterward, the two disappeared into Marcia's room, where they listened to her collection of music CDs.

Left alone, Garry and Frieda seized the opportunity to become more comfortable with each other. Then, as they moved toward intimacy, she was pleased to find him much less inhibited and far more receptive this time. But before they had to slow for propriety's sake, Garry's cell phone began its "Row Your Boat" tune. They separated, and he answered.

"Oh hi, Joel. Well, to tell the truth, it's not the most opportune time. We're guests for dinner at a friend's house. It's that important?"

Garry looked across at Frieda with uncertainty. He put his hand over the mouthpiece. "It's Joel Wise. He's got someone in the office that I need to meet with. It's a legal matter. I really don't want to break up such a lovely evening."

"Something to do with the divorce?" she asked.

"No. He says it's about my birth father and a possible inheritance. There are some papers to sign."

"Sounds pretty important to me although I fail to see why it couldn't wait 'til morning. You'd better go. I'll tell Phyllis. In fact, if you're not back by ten, I'll drive her home. The girls seem to be enjoying themselves so much, I hate to break it up. Go ahead. She'll be fine."

"Okay, Joel," he said into the phone. "I'll see you in fifteen or twenty minutes. That's upstairs second door on the right?"

Garry hung up, shrugged his shoulders, and then held out his arms for her. She came closer, and he wound them about her.

"He has to be in DC in the morning, so it's got to be tonight. Anyway, I'm looking forward to a lot more evenings like this one, uninterrupted ones, that is." He kissed her full on the mouth, their lips lingering as they separated. "Now, lead me to the girls. I want to explain to Phyllis that I'm leaving and that you are kind enough to drive her home later."

Frieda waved as Garry pulled away from the curb, and her eyes followed him to the next intersecting street. *I feel like a schoolgirl again,* she thought.

* * *

Rivka glanced at the Mercury's gas gauge, hovering in the red zone. *Should I tell him? Surely, Emil won't knowingly risk stranding us on the interstate. But if he does run out of gas, what choices will he be forced to make? Abandon me? Kill me? Kill a highway patrolman or anybody else who stops us? He can't very well let me go. Not yet, anyway. I know too much.*

"You'd better stop and get gas soon," she said.

Emil nodded and took the next turn-off—Hardeevile, South Carolina—the last town of consequence before the Georgia line. Savannah lay just beyond the border, marked by the river of the same name. He had been driving continuously from their overnight rest stop.

Death Goes Postal

Emil gassed up the car first, then orchestrated the restroom routine once more. From the station's mini-mart, he purchased two egg salad sandwiches, two tuna sandwiches, and a bag of Sun Chips. It also occurred to him that he needed directions to the Oglethorpe Station Post Office without eliciting any unnecessary suspicion.

"I-95 is back that way," Rivka reminded Emil as he drove off slowly in what seemed to be the wrong direction.

"I know!" he snapped.

Emil turned into the heart of Hardeeville and crept along Main Street, seeming to search for some particular business or place that Rivka certainly couldn't fathom. Apparently having found just what he'd sought, Emil pulled alongside a parking meter and got out, leaving Rivka in the upright position. He fed the meter and entered what appeared to be a café.

The broad window out front displayed NED'S INTERNET CAFÉ in large blue letters. A short gauze-like curtain stretched across the glass expanse, transparent enough for her to see him take a seat at a terminal facing the street. *What's he doing in an Internet café? What's he got in mind?*

Inside, Emil deposited the required quarters and immediately logged on. After several Google searches, he arrived at the U.S Postal Service URL www.zip4.usps.com. Entering the 31416 postal zip, it linked him to the city of Savannah and the default Oglethorpe Station at 1348 Eisenhower Drive. MapQuest yielded not only the pertinent series of maps, but step-by-step instructions for getting there. He printed out what he needed, paid for the printed pages at the desk, and purchased two coffee lattés. The researcher left the café as matter-of-factly as he'd entered and returned to the car.

Emil retrieved the brown bag of sandwiches and spread a large dinner-style napkin over Rivka's lap. He upended the bag and shook an egg salad and a tuna on rye onto the napkin. Dumping the remainder into his own lap napkin, he tore open the chip bag and shook chips over the tops of the sandwiches. While Emil and

Rivka shared the coffee and sandwiches in the car alongside the curb, she maintained the charade, hiding her enlarged wrist restraints by turning more toward the passenger door and scrunching down to eat and drink.

When they'd finished, he turned to face her: "Do either you or your husband have the key to box number seventy-five?"

"Dan, my husband, has the key. It was taped on the back of the *Autumn in New England* poster with the letters, only you seem to have missed it."

Emil scowled. "One more question: Was the key marked with an actual box number? One would have to doubt it when a whole clue was devoted to that number. We determined the box number from the coincidence in the span of Mark Twain's life and the return of Halley's comet."

"No, it wasn't marked. You have that advantage over Dan, but remember, he has the actual key."

Satisfied with her answers, Kravitz started the engine and made a sweeping U-turn back toward the interstate. Instead of taking the up-ramp, he drove past the interstate altogether. Emil turned at route U.S.-17 North and drove until encountering the Hardeeville post office. Parking out front, he slipped on a pair of mirrored sunglasses, and left her once more. He entered the government building and rented a postal box of a size he might encounter at Oglethorpe Station. Giving the postal clerk a temporary address at the Dunes Motel down the street, he told the man some important packages just couldn't be entrusted to a motel desk clerk. Emil forked over the minimum one-month rental. Emerging with the key to his new box, he walked one block down and across the street to Curen's Hardware, a store that advertised: KEYS MADE WHILE YOU WAIT. The large sign in the shape of a key was hard to miss.

A young man with thick, round glasses, straw-blond hair, and a myriad of freckles waited on him at the counter. "May I help you?"

"I'd like to buy a key blank for this," Emil said, handing

over the newly acquired key.

"Hey, man," the clerk said, turning it over and over in his hand. "This key's special. I'm not supposed to sell 'em to just anyone."

"My good man, would an extra twenty bucks take care of your ailing conscience?"

"It ain't so much my conscience as it's the law I'm worried about."

"How about another twenty, forty altogether for a second blank and a valid excuse: you simply lost them."

The man spun the key carousel, lifted the key blanks from their hook, and handed them to Emil: "Remember, you didn't buy 'em here, mister."

"With a few extra blanks, I'd surely forget where I acquired this thing," replied a smiling Emil. Two more blanks clinked down on the counter. He paid the clerk with a fifty and pocketed the four blanks. "Keep the change," he added as he left the store.

Rivka looked up just in time to see Emil re-crossing the street to where they were parked. She had enlarged the strap loop around her left foot, but had not yet begun to work on the other leg shackle. She quickly re-hid the paper clip and slipped her hands back into their recently oversized rings. It took concentration on her part to maintain stress on these bonds so he couldn't tell how close to freedom she'd progressed. Feeling pleased with herself to finally be taking charge of her predicament, she hadn't noticed a policeman approaching her curbside window. The encounter came as a shock. She looked first at the smiling man in uniform and then through the windshield at her captor. Her heart pounded, *surely loud enough for him to hear.*

Emil stopped abruptly when he noticed a policeman approaching the passenger side of their car. Through the windshield he found Rivka glaring straight at him. Her confused and terrified expression told him that she needed to be reminded of her promise and a whole lot more. He began with an impromptu sign language: a lip-tapping shush; a finger drawn across his throat; his hand shaped like a pistol, its trigger finger in motion; followed instantly by reaching into his pants pocket. He hoped that she would translate all of that into: "If you blab to the cop, I'll have to shoot him and cut your throat."

He watched Rivka's head vacillate between the policeman and himself. *Would the cop notice this?* he wondered. Emil stepped into a doorway where he could see and not be seen. He saw the cop take off his sunglasses. *Will he see her restraints? They're talking now. Will the bitch tell the cop everything?*

* * *

Joel Wise maintained a small but well-furnished law office on State Circle in Annapolis opposite the oldest state capitol building in the country still in use. Nighttime spotlights on the stately dome lent it all the prominence due. At eight p.m. the lights in Joel's office were also burning. Seated in a wing-back chair at a polished oak table in his paneled conference room, Joel pulled a sheaf of documents from his briefcase and studied several of the sheets before he addressed the two visitors sitting across from him. Both appeared impatient—wondering why they were summoned to his office, especially at this late hour.

"Peggy…Garry, I'm terribly sorry to keep you waiting, but I've just recently acquired a bit of information from the Annapolis police that is of specific interest to each of you. I'm just getting familiar with the material myself."

"What could we two possibly have in common?" interrupted Peggy. "We only met a few weeks ago, and the only thing that comes to mind is the critique group. We haven't said a dozen words to each other in all that time."

"That's true," Garry confirmed.

"Oddly enough, there may be a major connection," said Joel. "Let me explain. A few days ago I received a packet from an estate barrister in Bath, England. Although you may not be aware of these facts, the packet contained documents attesting to a possible connection between the two of you.

"I don't understand," said Peggy.

"Is Peggy Morris the name you were born with?"

"No, it's my marriage name. I was born Anna Margaret Fraume. What's this all about?"

"Was your father the late Abner Fraume?"

"Yes."

"And your mother—the late Ilse Fraume?"

"Yes again. Please, are you the lawyer who contacted me in Philadelphia?"

"No. I'm afraid not," he replied. "That gentleman has been taken ill and couldn't be here in person. He extends his apologies. He works for the British legal firm responsible for executing and administrating Abner Fraume's last will and testament. Edythe Fraume Bender was the sole beneficiary. Because I've already represented the Benders in the past, and realizing the difference in laws between Great Britain and Maryland, the British firm has asked me to intercede for them in the interim. Abner Fraume died leaving a modest estate and a rather large legacy. With the death of his sister, his designated heir, and the legal incapacity of her husband, Bernard Bender, there remains a question of possible alternative beneficiaries. You, my dear, among others, are under consideration. By the way, are you still legally married to that rock musician, Ritchie Morris?"

"No sir!" Peggy replied enthusiastically. "I got rid of that drug-ridden creep in 1998. I should never have married him. My father warned me that if I did he would disown me. My divorce was made legal and finalized on July 7th,1999."

"Then your father and you were estranged right up until his death?"

"Yes. Even though I got divorced, I was always afraid to return to Father after the way I acted."

"There is an alternative death and incapacity clause covering any of Mr. Fraume's children. That might include you, but only if you are drug free," said Joel.

"I've been clean since before 1998."

"Wonderful," said Joel. "And now you, Garry. Would you state your full name, please."

"Garry Mark Posner, but what's this got to do with me?"

"Do you know anything about your biological parents?"

"Not really. All I know is I'm adopted and that I was born in Germany in 1939. I was adopted after the war by the Posners, and they moved to New Jersey when I was six. I've been living in the Baltimore area for years. A few weeks ago some barrister fellow called my ex-wife from England. He gave her a telephone number and told her that if I came to Annapolis, he would meet me here and tell me about my early years. She passed the word on to me. I guess the caller would be that same guy, the one that's ill. Right?"

"Right! Supposing I told you that your real name was Gormond Fraume and that you were the pre-Holocaust child of Abner and his first wife, Hilde Fraume. What would you say to that?"

"What in blazes is going on here? If it's true, this comes as quite a shock to me. I haven't got a shred of memory to dispute what you're saying. One question, though. Why didn't my father make any effort to find me after the war? Didn't he want me anymore?"

"Oh, but your father did search for you right after his release from the tuberculosis clinic in 1946. He checked every major city and refugee camp listing until he found your name included in the deceased column. You see, someone—probably some hasty vital statistics clerk—had mistakenly checked off the wrong column. He should have checked off the ADOPTED column."

"Does this mean I'm one of Abner's heirs?"

"Possible heirs. There's still a good deal of legal preparation and verification to be done."

"Does this mean there's still some doubts about our origins?" questioned Garry. "That is, mine and my, um, stepsister's?" He glanced over at Peggy and raised his eyebrows.

"No doubt in my mind," replied Joel. "And she's not your stepsister. She's your half-sister. You share the same father."

"What happened to our mothers?" asked Peggy.

"Hilde, Garry's mother, died in a Nazi death camp in 1943. Ilse, your mother, died giving birth to you. Your father remained a widower after that, married to his research work and teaching."

"What do you think the estate will amount to?" Garry's body stiffened with tension as he leaned forward to hear the answer, defeating his effort to keep calm and not appear overeager.

"Well, all of Mr. Fraume's research and artifacts—roughly two million pounds sterling—will go to the British Literary Museum, but there's a sizeable bank account. He lived frugally on his university salary. However, he kept investing his reparations and social security checks from the German government. The man I spoke with at the firm mentioned a figure of nearly 140,000 pounds."

Peggy felt slightly dizzy from exhilaration, tinged with a shred of disbelief. "When do you think we will learn any more about the estate and its distribution?"

"Oh, perhaps in a few weeks. I think we need to get past this terrible kidnapping incident first. Make sure Rivka Sherman is safe and freed." Joel shoved the sheaf of documents back into the briefcase and snapped the latch. "I'll be in touch in a week or so." He intentionally left the conference room for his office to enable the newfound half-siblings to get better acquainted. When he returned forty-five minutes later, they had already gone.

Chapter 29

City of Squares
Savannah—Same Day

The policeman's flushed face loomed large in the passenger side window. "You all right, ma'am? Awfully uncomfortable to be sitting there in the hot sun." He removed his sunglasses to see her better, but it didn't help; he still looked directly into the bright light.

Rivka felt a gagging sensation in her throat. She'd watched all of Emil's threatening gestures. Was he actually carrying a gun? If he even had one, she hadn't seen it. But who knew? He was a killer. She uttered a few words, trying hard to be convincing. "Why, yes, officer. Just fine."

The policeman replaced the glasses on his face and tipped his cap, "Have a nice day," and continued between the cars to cross the street.

Emil waited in a doorway a few minutes and then returned to the car.

"What did you and the cop have to say to each other?"

"He asked if I was okay, and I said, 'yes.' Then he said. 'Nice day' and I agreed. Honest!"

"You didn't ask him for help or tell him about me?"

"And risk you killing both of us? No. Certainly not. I got your meaning, all right."

Emil scrutinized her face for several moments and then his

eyes followed the policeman's casual stroll down the opposite side of the street. Satisfied, he went to the car's trunk and popped it open. She couldn't see what he was doing, but when he slammed the trunk shut and returned to stand by the driver's door, his looks had somehow changed. Nothing drastic—more on the subtle side. A different pair of shoes made him appear taller; a polo shirt gave him a casual look. His hair parted on the opposite side, and thick-lensed glasses added an intellectual touch. Emil, delighted with the result, opened the door and slid into the driver's seat.

"Ah, the new you," she said. "I suppose that means a whole new identity, too. Do I still call you Emil?"

Emil, without a word, started the engine. Releasing the brake, he made another major U-turn back toward the interstate on U.S.-17 South. Again, choosing not to use I-95, he remained on U.S.-17 all the way over the Savannah River bridge into the city itself.

* * *

"Damn it, Robards! You can't expect me to sit on my butt in this two-by-four office all afternoon while Kravitz is out there doing God knows what to my wife." Even the crisp air-conditioning in the Bureau's Savannah office didn't help the desperate husband.

"Calm down, Dan! We're doing all we can. The Bureau has three good agents babysitting both post office buildings, one inside and two more outside in cars. They're working four six-hour shifts to cover the clock."

"Shouldn't we be there, too? I'd feel a lot better if I were at least doing something."

"I can't allow that. Kravitz knows exactly what you look like from your critique meetings. One peek at your face in broad daylight might either spook the man or drive him to take extraordinary measures. Your Rivka's very safety is at stake. In any case, our agents don't want to lose the element of surprise. Our strategy is based on the fact that we possess the only key, and even if Kravitz knows which postal box to open, it would have to be breached forcibly. This is not likely to happen during normal post office hours."

"How are your agents going to know which box to open?" asked Dan. "You can't try them all, can you?"

"I'm hoping we won't have to. The postmistress is cooperating completely by running a search for the original rental box agreement. With any luck, Fraume will have used his own name on the agreement. If that fails, we can at least narrow the search considerably. From the Petty lad's description of the artifacts, it's very likely letter-size boxes can be eliminated right off. It's the larger or, possibly, the jumbo-size postal boxes that will have to be examined. Also, we're momentarily expecting exact dimensions, weights, and photographs from the British Literary Museum by request of the Bath Constabulary. That should help in confirming the authenticity of the relics."

"Why the British Literary Museum?"

"The constabulary's investigation of the Fraume murder led them to learn that the British Literary Museum was the intended recipient of the artifacts, as well as the scholarly tome associated with them."

"I sure hope it arrives on time, Ken."

"So do I, but that's not the only problem, Dan. Judge Davis won't sign off on a limited search warrant until we have the descriptions."

"How or why is the search limited?" asked Dan.

"The judge tentatively agreed to the warrant, but stipulated that the FBI has to specify exactly what we're looking for. Otherwise, nothing can be removed from the box. We can't even open any sealed packaging unless it precisely fits the size and weight description."

"Hey, Ken there's a call for you on line three," said a newcomer to the room. "From London, I believe."

Robards left to pick up the extension in the next room, thinking *This may be what we've been waiting for.*

Death Goes Postal

The newcomer turned out to be FBI. "Hi, Mr. Sherman. I'm Agent Elliot Landow. I've been coordinating your case from the Savannah office."

"It's Dan, and I can't thank you enough for all the attention and resources you folks have been giving our case. I just wish I could be more proactive. I hate sitting around twiddling my thumbs."

"It's the same in most kidnapping cases. We spend most of our time waiting, either waiting for the kidnappers to make their next move or for information to exchange hands. Your turn will come this evening," said Elliot. "Remember, you're the only one who can recognize Emil Kravitz."

"I know he's one of three or four people," said Dan.

"Gentlemen," said Robards reentering the room. "That call was the one we were expecting from the museum: a Michelle Painter, the assistant director of acquisitions. Ms. Painter was quite familiar with the Abner Fraume bequest and able to describe its contents. She called to alert us that the description and photographic attachments have been e-mailed to us. I checked and found that everything we need has already arrived. I immediately forwarded a copy to Judge Davis and I'm in the process of printing out several copies of the material as we speak."

"Why so many copies?" asked Dan.

"I want to put this material in the hands of our current agents inside the post office via messenger, ASAP. We'll send it over with one of our staff secretaries. With the judge's approval and the postmistress's permission, the two inside agents can begin their searches. Fortunately, the new descriptions will limit the search to actually rented boxes. Seventy oversized boxes—twenty-four at one of the two post offices and forty-six at the other. So we'll know *which* post office in an hour or so."

"Couldn't you set up roadblocks or something?" asked Dan. "I'm worried about Rivka. She must be terrified."

"I understand what you're going through, Dan," explained Robards, "but Savannah is a fair-sized city with many access roads.

It would take almost the entire police force to cover every one of them. Besides, the sight of a roadblock might spook our kidnapper. No, I'd advise against that. We know the artifacts are a virtual magnet to one of the post offices. I prefer confronting the man in a place where we can control the situation much better."

"You look terrible, Dan." said Landow, noticing the tense, fidgeting body.

"I'm fine. Really I am," Dan protested. "Actually, I feel like hell. It's all this waiting around and feeling useless. Rivka would call it *shpilkas*. Yiddish for ants in my pants." His voice choked. His big strong body suddenly felt small, shrunk. Bottom line, he feared for his wife's life. What was that monster doing with her? Or to her?

Elliot Landow gave him an understanding nod. "Dan, why don't you and I leave the details in Ken's capable hands and get some fresh air. Nothing's going to happen in the next few hours. We're only a few blocks from the historic district. I think a little walk is what you need right now."

Dan hesitated. "I'm not so sure about leaving. Supposing something happens while I'm gone?"

"Go ahead," said Ken. "Elliot carries a cell phone, and I can reach you in a hurry if something unexpected turns up."

"But…"

"But nothing. We don't expect anything to go down until after dark tonight, and I promise, you will be in on the stakeout."

Landow nudged a reluctant Dan Sherman outside the office and down the hall to the elevator. At street level warm sunshine and fresh air greeted them. The two men walked a few blocks into the historic district.

"Nice wide streets here for such an old part of town."

"Great observation," said Elliot. "Early Savannah grew out of a plan of wards and streets proposed even before the first settlers arrived. Originally, squares of land were sold or granted to settlers, and four of the largest were set aside for government and religious purposes. In fact, Savannah is known as the city of squares."

Death Goes Postal

"You'd make a great tour guide," said Dan. "I take it that Landow is Jewish."

"You got that right, and you?"

"Through and through," replied Dan.

"How much do you know about our history here in Savannah?"

"Not much. Oglethorpe. Early 1700s. Prisoners from the English jails."

"Debtors actually…from London. They came over with Oglethorpe on *The Ann* in 1732. A year later forty-two Jews arrived on a ship, but were refused landing in Savannah. While the ship lay at anchor, a contagious disease raged ashore. Doctors were in short supply. Among the passengers, a Portuguese-Jewish doctor by the name of Nunez volunteered and proved instrumental in halting the spread of the deadly virus. As a result, a grateful colony welcomed Jews ashore and allowed them to purchase land."

The two men turned toward the riverfront after passing the last of the historic squares. Agent Landow pointed out the site of the first synagogue, a home rented from the Morgan family on Telfair Square. Eventually, they reached Factor's Walk and the Chart House Restaurant set in a 1700s cotton warehouse.

"Dan, how about some lunch?"

"I guess so. I'm really not that hungry."

Both men lunched on the salad bar. Over a second cup of coffee, the ring tone on Elliot's cell piped up with "Green Sleeves" and he responded, "Landow. Right. I'll tell him."

"Was that Ken?" Dan asked anxiously. "Does he have any news?"

"Yes, he had an e-mail from the bookstore informing him that Heather Germain had forwarded the Fenton Thorwal wallet and that it should arrive by FedEx this evening. Apparently, Ms. Germain had left it in a brown paper bag on the counter for me, but Ms. Nathan mistakenly put it under the counter, thinking it was someone's lunch."

By the time the two men returned to the gray stone office

building an hour later, they found Ken and another agent, Bob Miller, busy formulating a stakeout strategy.

"Good news," said Robards. "The Oglethorpe station search has turned up the printfounding artifacts. The search at the other post office has been abandoned, allowing those agents to beef up our twenty-four-hour surveillance at the Oglethorpe post office. With the postmistress looking on, the contents of box number 191075 are being inventoried and verified right now. Agent Miller and myself are leaving for the scene and should be back here around six o'clock. Stay put, and I'll brief everyone on their stakeout assignments when we return."

* * *

With the onslaught of evening and the limited illumination from distant street lamps, the regiment of live oak trees arching over the road reduced the visibility even further. The black SUV down the street from the post office doubled as an FBI stakeout vehicle. A second FBI vehicle, a white pickup truck, sat across the street facing the opposite direction. Agents Bob Miller and Elliot Landow sat in the back seat of the SUV. Special Agent Ken Robards sat behind the wheel, leaning sideways with his back against the door in order to face the others.

Dan Sherman sat in the passenger seat with a pair of binoculars because he alone could identify Emil Kravitz. For him, Kravitz was one of two people who had crashed the critique meetings: Everet Kanter or Vernon Levant. He was betting on Kanter because of the similar initials. Perhaps he was being a bit naïve.

The normally manned postal windows had closed at five-thirty, and the number of patrons frequenting the building dwindled to an occasional few. The lack of activity made the agents' wait seem interminable, but their effort was soon rewarded. A black Ford Bronco passed them, U-turned, and parked on the opposite side of the road several hundred yards away. Dan trained the binoculars on the car and twisted the focus knob to sharpen the image. A lone man, with a cap pulled low over his forehead, got out of the

Death Goes Postal

Bronco and walked toward where they were parked. Dan tracked the man as he approached. The man turned left and crossed the street to the post office. His profile proved more revealing.

"My God," exclaimed Dan. "It's Levant."

"Are you sure?" asked Robards.

"Yes! I'd recognize that face anywhere." Dan's binoculars followed Vernon up the front steps and inside the door. "Aren't you guys going to apprehend him?"

Robards looked to the back seat. "Men, we'll take him when he comes out. Wait until the doors close behind him before you move in. We don't want him ducking back inside and endangering others. Go!"

The two men slid out of the SUV and took up stations on either side of the door. Satisfied with the arrangements, Dan trained the binoculars back on the Bronco. A woman sat in the driver's seat. He wondered if his Rivka was the driver. Suddenly the Bronco's door opened, and the woman got out. She was about the right height and build, but he couldn't be sure if it was Rivka.

"The driver of the Bronco is coming toward us," announced Dan.

"Do you recognize her?"

"No, damn-it, never seen her before."

"Hey, let me have those glasses." Robards snatched the binoculars and aimed them at the approaching brunette in a pinstriped pants suit.

The woman didn't stop opposite the post office, and instead, kept coming toward them. At thirty feet Robards dropped the glasses, pulled his gun from a shoulder holster, and cautioned Dan to get down. About fifteen feet from them, the woman slowly reached underneath her jacket.

"That's far enough, ma'am," Robards called to her. "Open your hand, remove it slowly from your jacket, and interlock the fingers of both hands over your head. Now!" He slipped out of the car to confront her directly.

"Take it easy, Robards," she yelled at him. "I'm Special

Agent Justine Burgess of the Atlanta field office. I was about to produce my credentials when you interrupted me."

He took several steps in her direction. "Hold your jacket open so I can see the pocket, please." She complied, and he removed the black vinyl folder. He also noted the straps to her shoulder holster, even though the gun was not yet visible. He flipped open the folder and authenticated her credentials. "Sorry! But you were transporting one of our suspects—Vernon Levant."

"I just received the message briefing me that you were staked out here," she said. "Vernon Levant is only an alias. He's really—"

"Emil Kravitz," Robards interrupted.

"No! He's not the man you're looking for. He's Sergeant Fenton Thorwal of Bath Constabulary's Homicide section. We've been asked to cooperate with him on the murder of Abner Fraume. I thought it best that I give you the word before Miller and Landow pounce all over him."

Robards clicked the button on his walkie-talkie to get the attention of the two agents on the steps. He waved the men back to the SUV. Ten minutes later Vernon left the building, and Justine called him over to the SUV. After the introductions, Robards became curious.

"Say, Thorwal, what led you to this post office?"

"Several weeks after the Fraume murder, a registered receipt came in the post for him, telling us that his package had been delivered to box number 191075 at this post office with a zip code of 31416. Apparently, the package went by ship. The notification was forwarded just yesterday. I would have been here sooner except that I lost my credentials and had to wait for duplicates to arrive."

"I believe that a Ms. Heather Germain has found your wallet. It seems that it dropped from your pants pocket while you were asleep in her apartment. It should arrive here sometime this evening by FedEx."

"Gawd, this is bloody embarrassing," he admitted.

Robards smiled. "I'd say when you British chaps go undercover, you take that sort of thing literally."

"I guess I deserved that."

"You could always say it lay in the line of duty." Robards had the crack of a smile on his face.

"Honestly, it started out that way, but I soon grew rather fond of Heather. One thing led to another. Of course, I would never compromise the investigation."

"Hey, don't worry. Your secret's safe with me." Helplessly, he broke into a loud guffaw. "Maybe."

Chapter 30

Key Work
Three Hours Earlier, Same Day

A highway's view of any city offers the best and worst panoramas, and Savannah proved no different. Here great white Georgian mansions, green parks, formal gardens, patina'd monuments, and its extraordinary Riverwalk served up in old Southern charm. They all vied for space with serious traffic, light industry, and plaguing slums.

Emil glanced at his watch. *4:30 p.m.—the post office would still be open for business.* Following the Internet instructions, he turned south on White Bluff Road, along the security fence of Hunter Air Force Base, and then east at the beginning of Eisenhower Drive, where it was less likely they would miss the 1348 address. Just past the post office branch he parked on the opposite side of the street. Before getting out of the car, Emil used a black Sharpie Marker pen to coat and recoat an even layer of black skin on the shanks of each key blank he'd purchased. After several minutes of using his breath to dry the key blanks, he carefully wrapped each individual blank in several protective folds of paper. After lowering Rivka's seat to the lowest angle to keep her out of window view, he opened his door to leave.

"Hey!" she cried out. "Lower the windows! I could die in here in this heat!"

He gave her a stony stare. "I won't be long, Miss Prima

Death Goes Postal

Donna."

"Are you kidding?" she shrieked. "It's ninety degrees out. The temperature in a closed car can reach 130 in ten minutes. And don't you dare talk to me like that!"

"I'll talk to you any way I want." Sullenly, he slid back into the driver's seat, started the engine, and lowered the four windows about an inch. Without waiting for what he knew would be a protest, he left the car and climbed the stone steps to the post office.

Her body felt as if it were caving in on her. Her brain swarmed with random thoughts. *What could I have done that I didn't do? What else should I do now? Am I being too namby-pamby? Please, God, help me out of this. Help me get free. If you just let me escape I'll never ask you for another thing. Well, you know what I mean. Of course I will. But I'll do anything you want. Do you want me to keep Kosher? I'll do it. And I promise we'll go to services more often. I'll never again snitch blueberry muffins during Yom Kippur fast. But please help me. We have our first grandchild. I have a bookstore to run. Dan needs me. And I promise not to argue with him so much. I'll be nicer. I'll eat a piece of chocolate before opening my mouth. Or am I being punished for getting a D in Judaism in Religion 101? It was a mistake, my thinking I knew it all without studying…Emil Kravitz is a German name. Is he anti-Semitic? Would he have killed Abner if the old man hadn't been Jewish?*

In utter exhaustion coupled with the suffocating heat, she dozed off.

* * *

Inside the post office, Emil stood in the service line and purchased a book of stamps, all the while casing his surroundings. Only one person seemed to be out of place in the lobby area. A well-dressed, clean-cut man in his thirties hovered over a stand-up desk reading an Atlanta newspaper. *In the middle of the afternoon? Not the most comfortable place to absorb local, world, or even sporting news,* Emil thought. He walked toward the section where the postal boxes were arrayed. Passing close enough to the man to observe that the paper's date was three days old, Emil pegged him as a definite FBI agent. The agent glanced up at him. Emil gave him a friendly nod and quickly turned away.

Continuing on toward the boxes, Emil began observing the box numbers: all six-digit numbers between 190300 and 191999, meaning at least sixteen ended in 75. Five of these were in plain view from where the agent had chosen for his surveillance. Emil hoped it wouldn't be one of those. Several double banks of six-foot-high, back-to-back postal boxes stood in the way of the agent seeing the remaining eleven. Much larger boxes, for oversized packages, stood against the rear wall behind the last bank of standard boxes. Stacked across that thirty-foot-long rear wall were boxes two feet high and eighteen inches wide. Kravitz knew none of the other boxes could possibly house the wooden cases that held the chase and matrices. The jumbo box numbers ran from 191050 through 191180; only two ended in 75.

Standing slightly back out of the way, he waited for a kneeling woman in a gray suit to empty her box. Keenly observing her key's shape, he saw that it was similar to the four blanks in his possession. From prior experience, he knew the lock was too small for his set of lock-picking tools. The amount of mail she withdrew led to the assumption that she might be a business person, perhaps an owner or a secretary. She somehow felt his fixed attention and turned to look at him.

"Too nice a day to be working," he commented.

"Why, yes, it is," the woman returned, drawling out the last ess like a question, while she filled a shopping bag with the acquired mail. Then she took a second key from the bottom of her box and walked over to the rear wall. He watched her remove several larger packages from one of the jumbo-size boxes.

"Good day," he said. Casting him a dubious look, she hurried out with her stuffed bag clutched in both arms. Emil reached into his pocket for the folded paper packets. Now alone at the rear wall, he tried all four key blanks in the nearest candidate slot: 191175. Surprisingly, only one of the four blanks actually fit. And only that blank fit the lock of 191075. It occurred to him that he was missing another piece of information. He tried to remember the line from the last letter—"And doubly Mark his long years in space." *Doubly,* he mulled. *Either a birth date or a death date plus the number of years. Mark Twain died in the early 1900s, so it has to be the year he died. There are no 1800s here.* He vaguely remembered Rivka telling him the year. He usually had no trouble with important historical dates. He knew it had to be either 1910 or 1911, as the box numbers were confined to that range. The more he repeated the two years to himself, the more the year 1910 ran through his brain. He had to take a chance since only one of the blanks fit both lock slots. He hadn't noticed any difference in the shanks before this. He swore under his breath—once, at the locksmith clerk for pulling a fast one; and again, at himself for not being more careful.

Slipping the key back in the lock of 191075, he rotated the coated shank back and forth several times as far as the blank would go. The shank lost its black coating in just those places where the surface encountered resistance: the stops and palls within the lock. Afterward he removed and rewrapped the key blank, taking care not to disturb the coating surrounding the newly made rubbings. Palming the packet, he left the post office and returned to the car.

He found Rivka staring up at the ceiling, breathing heavily, beads of sweat collected on her upper lip, her curly bangs damp and plastered against her forehead. Emil started the engine and turned the air conditioning on High. He did not, however, raise her seat up.

"Did you find it?" she asked, refusing to look at him.

"Yeah. By the way, what year did Mark Twain die?"

Go to hell, you bastard, she wanted to say. "Let's see—1835 plus 75. That's 1910. Why?"

"The actual box number turned out to be 191075. It's the 1910 part."

"Ah, the year. It's the double meaning," she acknowledged.

"But what would have happened if the post office had assigned a totally different box number?"

"I'm sure the old buzzard would have come up with an equally clever conundrum." He turned on the ignition and pulled away from the curb.

Rivka feigned sleep, fighting tears. Her lower back ached from the forced prone position. Her belly throbbed with anxiety. An acid taste of despair crawled up to her mouth. The tie-straps around her wrists, even though she'd secretly loosened them, still scraped her flesh, especially against the scar on the inside of her left wrist, where she'd had the compound fracture when she was eight. And two-and-a-half days in the same sticky clothes, the same humiliating makeshift diaper. How much more of this could she take? *Is Dan here in Savannah? The FBI? Is anybody here who can save me? Get a grip!* she scolded herself. When she felt sure her voice wouldn't whine, she asked, "Can't I sit up now? I'm getting so sore."

Impatiently, roughly, he raised her seatback, but only halfway.

The Mercury roamed the neighborhood in ever-widening squares in search of two objectives. A hardware store fulfilled her captor's first set of requirements. A bench vise, a pair of lock-jaw vise grips, a battery-operated Dremel tool kit with half a dozen spare batteries, plus an a/c converter, and a nine-piece set of metal jeweler's files. He paid in cash for the key-making tools and returned to the car.

The second objective—finding a facility to accomplish the blacksmithing chore—proved more difficult. *Far too much noise for a motel or hotel,* he mulled. And just about the time he considered setting up shop in the car, a tow truck passed him, going in the other direction. *Perfect!* Emil made a U-turn, closed on the truck, and followed it until it pulled into a small service station. The truck's driver, a gray-haired but muscular man, parked beside the building and entered the office, where he spoke to a young crew-cut version of himself. As Emil's Mercury approached the fueling pumps, the crew-cut came out to service the car.

Death Goes Postal

"Fill 'er," said Emil, "Regular, and check the oil." He popped the hood and spread a newspaper across Rivka's lap and arms to hide her restraints.

"Yes, sir." The crew-cut, in a Carolina Panthers T-shirt, removed the gas cap, inserted the nozzle, and started the pump. Moving to the front of the car, he disappeared under the hood long enough to check the essential auto fluids. "Oil and transmission are good to go, sir." Slopping the windshield full of water, he squeegee'd it free of bugs and smears. With the other hand, he paper-toweled the remaining streaks from the glass.

"The two of you run this place?" Emil asked.

"Yeah, just my dad and me. That's him inside. It's his night to work, and I'm outta here just as soon as I'm finished with y'all. Takin' my kids fishin'." He replaced the nozzle in the pump housing. "That will be $23.96. You interested in a glassware coupon?"

Emil shook his head, paid him with a fifty-dollar bill, and watched him go to the office to ring up the sale. Rivka jerked her head up and toward the office. Emil's malicious glare warned her not to make eye contact.

"Is your father a good mechanic?" Emil asked when the son returned with his change.

"He used to be, but all that crawling around under a car got to be too much for him."

"I think I've got an electrical problem, an intermittent short, maybe."

"If it's something small, y'all can pull into the end bay, and he'll have a look-see."

"Thanks!"

Emil pulled away from the pump and stopped at the farthest service bay, continuing to idle the engine. Behind dark glasses, his weasel eyes tracked the young man, who climbed into his pickup truck and drove off. Emil got out of the car, opened the driver's side back door, and grabbed his briefcase off the seat. A curious Rivka turned her head. "Eyes front, lady!" he ordered.

Flipping the case open and unsnapping a pocket, he pulled

out an already-filled syringe. Despite his attempt at concealment, Rivka saw it all. "Hey! You promised!" she blurted out. "We had a deal, buster, and I've kept my part of the bargain."

"And I'm keeping my part. This isn't for you."

"Who's it for then?"

"*That* is none of your business, Rivka. If you persist, I might change my mind."

She shrank deep into her seat. A double toot of the Mercury's horn alerted the older man inside to open the bay's overhead door, enabling Emil to drive in. The middle-aged mechanic, in jeans and tank top, turned on the lights and came over to the driver's door. "My name's R-J. Got a problem under there, have ya?"

"Yeah! I think it's an intermittent short in the lighting. Every time I hit a bump, the lights blink. I'm afraid they'll go out altogether." Emil popped the hood.

Emil stepped out of the car, purportedly to assist in diagnosing the problem. As R-J bent over the front right fender to have a look, Emil plunged the syringe needle deep through the denim into the soft part of his butt. The mechanic roared for at least thirty seconds before collapsing into a heap on the garage floor.

Witnessing her abductor's savage act, Rivka screamed. She whimpered and cringed as Emil dragged R-J by his shoulders and deposited him in a tire storeroom behind the office.

Stepping to the front of the bay, Emil turned the keyed wall switch and brought down the overhead door to seal them off from the world outside. He surveyed the heavy workbench and nicely equipped open tool chest along the inside wall of the service bay. Intent on producing a workable postal box key, he pulled the pertinent key blank out of his right-hand pants pocket. Securing the handle of the unwrapped key blank in a bench vise, he plugged in the a/c adapter for the Dremel tool. Selecting a rotary metal cutting blade, he fitted it into the Dremel's chuck and tightened it with the chuck key. Forty minutes later, the blank began to take on the shape of an actual key as a result of grinding away metal where broad shiny marks had existed.

Death Goes Postal

The beeps of customers' cars interrupted Emil twice. He emerged from the office to pump gas and wipe windshields. Emil serviced them with a smile and told one of them that R-J and his son were off on a fishing trip. He pocketed the cash the first time and pocketed the remainder of the cash register when he had to make change for the second customer. He'd already taken $43 from R-J's wallet earlier, replenishing his declining bankroll by almost $800.

Returning to the workbench and key he was fashioning, a penknife and three cornered files removed all the burrs from the edges, and he recoated the surface black with Sharpie Marker ink. He'd never expected to make it on the first try—several would be needed. While washing his hands, Emil noticed a pair of greasy coveralls and a dog-eared Atlanta Braves baseball cap in the washroom. After donning both items, he returned to the car to find an agitated Rivka trying to hold back her tears.

"Did you have to kill him?" she cried.

"Nothing of the sort," he replied. "The man will simply be taking a nap for the next twelve hours. He'll wake up fit as a fiddle with a slight headache, that's all. It's the same stuff I gave you."

"Where are we?" she asked.

"In a roadside garage where no one can hear you," Kravitz snickered. Rivka took up his offer for a restroom, and when she resettled in the car seat, he left her with two vending machine candy bars, saying, "I'll be back in ten minutes." Emil turned off the inside lights, removed the keys that operated the bay doors, and exited the service bay to the office. There he plucked a key ring marked TRUCK from a wall hook, flipped over the BACK IN THIRTY MINUTES sign, and locked the office door as he left.

Rivka heard the tow truck door slam, its engine start, and even imagined him driving off. She removed her hands from the tie-strap loops, but left the seatback in its half-upright position and reached under her seat for Emil's cell phone, the one she'd lifted from his coat and hidden there. Flipped open, the phone revealed three pre-programmed numbers. Punching in the first yielded no answer. The second resulted in someone speaking German. She hung up.

She punched in the third number. After several long rings, her husband picked up: "Sherman!" And when he didn't get an answer fast enough he added: "That you, Kravitz?"

"No," she answered in a loud whisper. "It's me, honey. It's Rivka. I'm okay. Don't worry. I'm using Emil's cell phone, but I don't have much time before he comes back. He said ten minutes."

"Sweetheart, are you in Savannah?"

"Yes!"

"Where are you?"

"I don't know. All I know is that I'm tie-strapped into a car that's locked in a small roadside gas station, probably somewhere at the southern edge of town. I think I remember seeing two initials in the name on the window. But I can't see that front window from here."

"Where is Kravitz now?"

"Most likely, he's gone to the post office on Eisenhower Drive—the 1300 block. He cased it this afternoon. I think he's trying to manufacture a key to the box."

"How'd he know which box number, honey?"

"He…Oh-oh. Gotta hang up. I see some lights coming into the station now. I'll call again when I get another chance, honey. I love you."

Rivka closed the phone and shoved it under the seat once more. Her first thought was to slip back into her tethers. But she decided it must be someone else out there, looking to gas up. Listening more carefully, she realized this idling engine didn't sound at all like the truck that had driven off earlier. Yelling for aid to the wrong party bore a great risk. She feared what would happen if Emil caught her at it. Minutes later, she heard the car drive off. Keeping an ear attuned to outside sounds, Rivka slipped out of all the enlarged tie loops and used the paper clip to loosen the tether about her left ankle. She freed herself by stepping out of the last remaining loop.

Death Goes Postal

Rivka opened the passenger door, stepped into the service bay, and headed for the door leading to the office. On the front window she spied the reverse name of the station—R-J's Towing & Service. Just as she got to the door, two bright lights turned into the station. The big towing truck had come back. Ducking down and out of sight quickly, she looked around for another exit and found none—nothing to use as a weapon either, at least nothing worth the level of risk she'd have to take in return. Throwing something at him, anything, meant she couldn't miss. And swinging a blunt object meant she had to be swifter, stronger, and more accurate to succeed. *No,* she thought, *I'd better wait and survive to try again.* Rivka flew back to the car, lowered the seat, and slipped into her tethers before Emil opened the door.

Shedding the borrowed cap and coveralls, Emil found Rivka chewing on one of the candy bars he'd left for her. His smoky eyes squinted at her. "I could have sworn I saw a face in the window when I pulled in just now. Maybe I'm getting paranoid."

Rivka jerked her hands and feet against the limits of her tie-straps. "It wasn't me," she garbled between chocolaty mouthfuls.

Emil shook his head and went back to key-making at the workbench.

Chapter 31

The Stakeout
Same Evening

Accepting their role as backup, Special Agent Justine Burgess, Constable Sergeant Fenton Thorwal, and their driver, Agent Willis Messenger, waited in a black Ford Bronco parked 150 yards from the post office corner. Constable Thorwal could also identify the principals in their investigation. The leading FBI agents positioned the primary vehicle, a black Chevy Suburban, on the same side of the street as the post office, a half-block away from the same corner. The two vehicles faced each other on opposite sides of the street to be able to respond in either flight direction.

Special Agent Robards sat behind the wheel of the SUV, leaning back on the headrest. Agents Bob Miller and Norm Parker sat in the back while Agent Elliot Landow took over the watch inside the building. Dan Sherman sat in the front passenger seat with a pair of binoculars, intent on picking out Everet Kanter. By process of elimination, Kanter just had to be Kravitz. He couldn't find any other explanation.

* * *

Emil encountered a different FBI surveillance agent on his third trip to the post office lobby. Full-blown evening obviously meant a change in shift. In a way, this boded well with his plans—his earlier disguises could be reused if necessary. This agent

Death Goes Postal

wore a janitor's coveralls and sat on a folding chair by the public restroom reading a Tom Clancy thriller. A mop, propped against the wall, stood in a half-filled pail beside him. The new coveralls, sharply groomed man, and his choice of reading material were all a dead give-away. As if that were not enough, his Sony boom-box beat out a rap tune quite out of step with the local country music. He acknowledged the man with a grunt and proceeded to the area behind the wall of postal boxes.

Knowing the agent couldn't possibly see or hear him at the rear wall, Emil inserted and rocked the half-fashioned key in the lock of number 191075. He partially rotated it farther in both directions to make new impressions. The removed key now bore new shiny rub-offs in the marker doping—some calling for a deeper or wider cut and others a new, more shallow groove. The boom-box music covered the noise while he took a number of coarse file strokes across a few of the grooves. He tried the key again and discovered that the angle of rotation had improved considerably. He recoated and dried the key once more and repeated the rotational process. Satisfied with his progress and certain he'd need the Dremel tool again, Emil put the re-doped key back in its wrappings and shoved it into his jacket pocket. The Dremel tool he slid separately into his hip pocket. Next he removed several envelopes from an inside pocket that he'd purloined from the office at R-J's gas station. From all outward appearances, a box holder had emptied his box and now held a letter in front of his face to read. He returned to the tow truck parked in an empty driveway around the corner—several houses farther down the block and out of view of both surveillance teams.

Using the vise mounted on the rear of the truck, a flashlight, and the Dremel grinding tool on battery power, Emil made the latest cuts in the metal key and recoated it once again. In the tight space of the truck's cab, he tugged off the coveralls and Braves cap. Grabbing a wrinkled Georgia Tech football jersey that had been abandoned on the front seat, Emil pulled it over his head, remembering to comb his dyed hair in place afterward. In the mirror he saw how scruffy his chin and cheeks looked from two days without a shave. That worried him, but there was nothing he could do about it now. He stuffed R-J's envelopes back in his pants pocket and re-entered the post office to find the agent sitting in exactly the same place. The man showed no sense of recognition, so Emil went about the business of fitting the key to the lock once more.

This time the result astonished him. The key turned completely in the lock and the door sprang open. Inside, nearly filling the space, were four thin packages wrapped in heavy brown paper—each about the length of a modern briefcase but only half its width. Emil slit open one side of the wrap on the first package and slid out a sturdy wooden chest with twenty-four tiny wood screws securing both front and back covers. He could hardly open and inspect the contents in this environment so he slipped the wrap back over the chests. He needed to take them back to the garage where he'd have some privacy, at least until some time before daybreak when R-J's son would likely return. Kravitz set the chests on the floor and relocked the postal box. Emil hefted the wooden chests, a weight he judged to be between thirty and thirty-five pounds, and boldly attempted to lug them through the rental box area and past the scrutiny of the FBI agent posted beyond it.

"Quite a load you're carrying there. You need some help with that?" Elliot Landow, the agent in janitor's navy blue coveralls, spoke to Emil in a non-alarming tone as though he suspected nothing amiss.

"Ah, thank you, no. I'm doing fine." Emil looked away from the man.

"Oh, but I insist," said Landow, getting to his feet. The agent displayed a commission wallet, with badge and ID, in his left hand and a service gun in his right pointed toward Emil. "FBI! Let's just see what's in those packages, sir."

Emil leaned the packages against the same stand-up desk where the first agent had stationed himself and slid them onto a more stable position. As a result, several stacks of certified and registered mail forms fell from the desk and toppled to the floor. He tore the paper away from the open package, revealing one of the chests.

"As you can see they're pretty well sealed. I'll need a screwdriver and a table at least to open them." Emil kept staring over the agent's shoulder. Staring at nothing—a tactic to keep the agent on edge and nervous.

"In that case, let's see some identification," demanded Landow.

"That's my name on the package label." Emil spun one of the chests around so the agent would have to come closer to read it. "I don't know what you're after, but I'll get my driver's license out."

Emil's right hand went around to his hip pocket where his wallet might have been, only it came out with the Dremel grinding/cutting tool instead. As agent Landow positioned himself to read the label, Emil grabbed the gun-hand wrist like a vise with his left hand and slammed it down hard on the table. The agent's struggling grip was no match for the cutting blade as it sliced through the trigger finger and two adjacent digits. The gun fell to the table and slid immediately to the floor, as did two of Elliot's fingers.

Shock and excruciating pain kicked in without warning. Landow tried to scream, but only a low-level groan came out. He pulled back his arm and stuck it under the opposite armpit to stem the flow of blood, all the while moving away from his attacker. But Emil, following, reversed the tool in his hand and cracked the heavy part down on the agent's forehead. The wounded agent thudded first to his knees and then crumbled to the floor, unconscious.

Emil pocketed the tool, picked up the chests, and headed for the street. Suddenly, he stopped as a thought hit him. He wheeled about and re-entered the lobby. Setting the chests down on the tall desk momentarily, he knelt down next to Landow, still out cold, and retrieved the agent's gun. Shaking free the trigger finger, he brazenly used Landow's own sleeve to wipe the Glock 9mm clean of blood, and set the safety before sticking the weapon in his belt. Bolting through the front door and down the steps, he looked in both directions, but didn't attach any significance to the surveillance vehicles parked half a block to his left and right. Moving the four chests to the tow truck around the corner became his first priority. Getting back to R-J's Towing and Service, where he could open the chests, was next.

* * *

Agent Justine saw him first, Dan next, with the binoculars glued to his face. The front door to the post office had burst open, and a man in a Georgia Tech football jersey hesitated there for a moment, looking up and down the street before bounding down the steps to the sidewalk.

"He's carrying the chests, but I can't see his face because of the boxes. He's getting away! Shouldn't we follow him?"

"Yeah," said Robards, "but not too aggressively. We *do* want him to lead us to your wife."

Agent Miller, disturbed over not hearing anything from Landow inside, cautiously stepped out on the curb side and slowly crossed the street.

As soon as their target reached the corner, Robards started the Suburban's engine, but couldn't pull out until a moving van passed. The same van, braking for a stop sign, hampered Justine's view as well. By the time the van had passed them, Emil had vanished around the corner. The Bronco turned the corner first. The Suburban followed. Nearly two minutes had passed. They'd left too much of a cushion. Neither found any sign of Kravitz or the chests.

Emil, believing that he might be followed, had dashed up the second driveway behind the post office and hidden behind a hedge just in time to see the Bronco creeping slowly by, checking each car, alley, and driveway. A minute or so later he saw the Suburban race by. Apparently, the parked tow truck in a driveway drew little attention. Finding a window of opportunity, he darted across several backyards and deposited the chests in the back of R-J's tow truck.

Miller entered the post office and immediately sized up the

dire situation within. He ran to the door to flag down the others, but he was too late. The Suburban turned the corner and disappeared from view. He pulled the walkie-talkie radio from his belt and yelled into it, "Agent down and bleeding. Need ambulance and medical assistance. Landow's still alive but he's unconscious."

Miller's frantic message reached them as the drivers of both surveillance vehicles approached the end of the block. They also heard the EMT team's response: "Ambulance dispatched…e.t.a. six minutes."

As the two FBI cars turned in opposite directions to re-circle the block, the tow truck—parked only four doors in from Eisenhower Drive—came to life. Emil drove the first block in the opposite direction toward White Bluff without lights. He'd lost them completely.

* * *

Rivka waited until she heard the tow truck leave before she freed herself from the last of her bonds. Emil had told her he'd return in forty-five minutes. She tried the office door first and found that Emil had thought to lock it. Then she remembered the overhead door switch. But at the wall where she'd seen him operate the door, she discovered that the key for the switch had been removed. He'd also taken all the fuses out of the box on the wall, so she couldn't even turn on the lights.

Rivka tried the office phone next and found that it lacked a dial tone. Tracing the wires led to a frayed end ripped from the wall box. *If only Dan were here,* she thought, *he'd know how to fix it.* There wasn't anything that resembled a fire alarm either. *Think, woman, think. You're not a dummy.* She picked up a tire iron and swung it with all the power she could muster—first at the door glass and then at the larger window. The heavy iron merely bounced off the thick plate glass like so much rubber. After a number of tries, she gave up. A small thread of a crack in the door glass went unnoticed. The only other windows were too high for her to access.

Emil had taken the car keys. In fact, the only key Rivka

could locate was stuck in a door next to the small washroom. She unlocked the door and found R-J lying on the floor unconscious, still under the effects of the drug Emil had given him. Laying her ear to his chest told her that the man still breathed. She soaked some paper toweling and placed it across his forehead, but it had no effect. Neither did shaking him. Failing to revive him, Rivka went through R-J's pockets to find a possible spare set of keys. But she came up empty. Resting his head on a pile of drop cloths, she stacked two tires as a chair for herself.

Then Rivka remembered Emil's cell phone and pounced on the same number as last time, but no response. She tried again and again until she became a bundle of tears. Just when she was about to give up, she heard Dan's voice barely—as her battery drew its last breath. Rivka closed the storeroom door and tried to find a place in the office where the signal was stronger. She kept repeating: "R-J's Service Station" until she found some business stationery with the address on it. She repeated the address in her loudest voice, with absolutely no idea whether Dan could hear her. Then the phone went dead and black in the same instant.

Rivka returned to the car and her prison seat feeling completely dejected. Thirty minutes later she heard the tow truck outside and slipped into her tethers once more to sustain her ruse. Minutes passed and suddenly, the service bay flooded with light. She waited.

Then he peered in the car window at her and smiled. He opened her door and propped the seat into the upright position. He stared into her eyes, wondering if she'd share his good fortune. "I've got Koenig's matrices and Abner's chase in my grip. The trip is a success. And I'm going to let you see them as soon as I open the boxes." He pointed to the dark wood chests on the workbench.

"Does this mean you're going to let me go soon?"

"Perhaps sooner than you think," he said, cutting the armrest strap and the chair frame strap and helping her to stand up.

Keeping up the subterfuge, Rivka waddled over to the workbench to watch him unpack a treasure he believed worthy of killing for.

Emil's eyes followed her movement. Suddenly, something dawned on him. "Hey, your straps, they're loosened—you could have escaped at any time. How long has this been going on?" He grabbed her by the arm and spun her around to face him. "You gave me your word, Rivka! Doesn't your word mean anything to you?"

There was a hurt look on his face when she stared back at him. "I had no idea you would keep your word, Emil. No offense, but I do value my life ahead of my word. I never got the chance to escape because I undid the last tie-strap only a few minutes before you came back."

"Never mind," he said as he turned and shoved her toward the workbench.

"Does this mean you're not going to let me go now?"

He rolled his eyes and said nothing.

Chapter 32

Deception and Clarity
Wednesday, June 2nd

Stepping out of the remaining tie-straps that held her legs, Rivka complained, "You haven't answered me!" There was no need to prolong this damn charade. "What do you intend doing with me now?"

Emil had turned his back to her, more interested in the chests stacked on the workbench than providing a decision. His excitement grew—a child with a new prayed-for toy. He glanced up at the clock: a little after midnight. "I'm not obligated to tell you anything," he finally answered.

Searching among R-J's tools, Emil selected a Phillips-head screwdriver tip, stuffed it into a Makitta power drill's chuck, and tightened it with the chuck key. He selected the first chest in front of him, set the drill's direction to REVERSE, and began backing each of the twenty-four wood screws out of the cover. The task's tedium worked to build his own grinding anxiety and anticipation. The drill whined in short two-second bursts. When the last screw had been removed, he set the cover aside and stared down at the contents in complete disbelief. The chest was divided into dozens of sections, each containing a half-dozen or so of the same type of screws he'd removed from the cover. No printfounding matrices and no chase. He spun around toward Rivka like a Doberman ready to pounce.

"What?" she said, bending over and rubbing her ankles. "You got your precious treasure, didn't you?" She straightened up. "Well, didn't you?"

Emil unleashed a flurry of expletives and his normally pallid face grew a blotchy red as he slid the second chest in front of him. His breathing turned shallow and rapid and both hands shook. Twenty-four screws later culminated in the same result—more wood screws.

The third chest held a pair of old horseshoes and a telephone book, supposedly the combined weight of Abner's tome and the engraved chase. The fourth—more screws. By now, Emil fumed with temper. He'd been outsmarted. He flung one of the horseshoes across the service bay, and it rang out with all of his anger as it struck a concrete column and then fell to the concrete floor, reverberating like a settling manhole cover. Staring at Rivka with fire-crazed eyes, he picked up the second shoe and shouted, "The FBI has *my* treasure."

For the second time in two days Rivka felt she was about to lose her life. She slowly backed away from him, trying hard not to send Emil over the top.

His voice conveyed the tremor of both anger and disappointment. "Mrs. Sherman, either you haven't been entirely honest with me or Abner Fraume has had the last laugh on me. Which is it?"

"I have no idea what you're talking about," she protested. "I've never lied to you."

"Well now, if that's true, I'd say that the FBI has had me for lunch. They're in possession of the Koenig matrices. What was it that you didn't tell me then? The key had a number?" He took two menacing steps toward her and she retreated again. He hesitated. "Only the third and last of Professor Fraume's letters gave any hint of the box number, and that was in my possession before you and your husband had a chance to read it. The others couldn't have deciphered it."

"But there *wasn't* any number on the key," Rivka said.

"How would they know which box to go to?"

"Which box? I'm sure they had time to try the key in every one of them."

"I take it I'm in bigger trouble now," she said, nervously, with an impish grin. "I didn't lie to you and I did help you translate all of the clues. I think that deserves some consideration. Please!"

An enraged Emil moved toward her once again with his arm raised, this time his large hand clutching a horseshoe and shaking it over her head. A terrified Rivka kept retreating step-by-step. Back…backward until she encountered a hydraulic jack, lost her balance, and, arms and legs flailing, tripped over it and landed on her backside. Her ridiculous position on the greasy floor softened his intense look to almost a smile. Emil dropped the horseshoe to the floor, and a new expression appeared on his face: one of resignation and defeat. He leaned over and extended a hand to help her off the dirt.

Rivka peered up at him, trying to discern the meaning of the gesture. *Is he really being helpful, or is he just manipulating to make me pay for my breach of trust?* Then she noticed a red dot skittering across the side of Emil's forehead. Without knowing why, she dragged him downward with all her might.

Her strength surprised him, and before he knew what had happened, he'd fallen across her body. At that moment glass shattered in one of the overhead garage doors. A small steel-jacketed missile ripped a hole clean through the open cover of an aluminum tool chest. The two bizarre sounds, glass exploding and metallic penetration, melded into one. It took several seconds to register, while captor and captive stared face-to-face in disbelief.

A sniper's bullet. Rivka had saved her kidnapper's life.

Survival instinct took over. Emil rolled to one side, rose up, and scurried toward the front of the garage bay in a low zigzag pattern, avoiding any chance for the sniper to refocus on him as a target. He lunged for the key switch controlling the overhead lights and turned it off, shrinking the entire garage into darkness.

Rivka saw and heard nothing for an agonizing sixty seconds. Then outside headlights illuminated the ceiling. Two more shots zinged through the glass and ricocheted dangerously through the work bay. She struggled to her feet and made her way to the car, seeking refuge. The open car door didn't turn on the dome light because she had placed the dome switch in the disabled position earlier. Emil's heavy breathing suddenly became apparent to her. He slid into the driver's seat opposite her for the same reason. She closed the door, and they sat silently for several minutes while he contemplated his next move.

"The only ways out of here are the two overhead doors and the office door to the street," she said. "There's no back way out. You've lost the treasure and any means of escape. What do you propose to do now? You really have to give yourself up."

"I don't have to do any such thing," he said bitterly.

"You mean you're planning to use me as a hostage?"

"I didn't say that."

"I would if I were you."

"Put someone's life in jeopardy when they've just saved your own skin? I don't think so. Why did you pull me out of harm's way? This whole nasty experience would have been finished, and you could have been on the way home to your darling Dan by now."

"Uh-huh," she replied. "But I didn't want your damn blood all over me. It stains like hell."

Emil sneered, "I think you had another reason, Rivka. Am I right?"

"Yeah, I suppose I saw you had something worth saving. I got to know you these past few days. I just couldn't see you destroyed in front of me. Besides, you actually knew I'd gotten out of the plastic straps and you did nothing about it. You may be a killer, but you're not all bad."

"Another time, another place, and other circumstances we might have been friends—colleagues in the literary critique group even. Yes, I felt something, too. I'm not made of stone. I gambled everything and lost even more—all that I lusted for and of course, all that I had. I'm asking that you get out of the car now, and if I can call upon you for one last favor from the friendship we almost had."

"If it's reasonable." She released the door and swung it open again. "What do you want me to do?"

"I want you to go to the wall switch and run the overhead door up as soon as you hear the car motor revving. Then I want you to lie on the floor out of harm's way. Okay?"

"On one condition!"

"What's that?"

"Give me your gun," she said. "And don't tell me you don't have one. I can see it in your belt. I don't know what your chances are of crashing out of here, but they're certainly not going to improve any by shooting your way out. Besides, I don't want anybody else's death on my hands. Your conscience may be warped and short lived, but I hope to live with mine for some years to come. That's my condition."

Rivka waited for his answer. He remained silent for several seconds and then removed Agent Landow's Glock 9mm from his waistband, ejected the clip, and handed it to her, butt first. She took it from him and began the walk to the switch on the concrete block wall. She heard a motor whine behind her for a few seconds. Turning, she saw Emil pushing the car around on the raised mechanic's hydraulic lift. Once the car's grille faced the outside doors, she heard the whining motor once more, lowering the lift. Rivka waited until he climbed back into the driver's seat.

"Remember!" he yelled as he started and revved the engine. "Down flat behind the brick wall. There'll be bullets ricocheting all over the place in a few minutes. So long."

Rivka never looked back again. At the keyed switch she only hesitated a moment before twisting a thumb and first finger around the key. The giant overhead doors began to move, creeping upward with a thunderous rumbling and scraping. She heard the Mercury's engine race and then, all at once, the car leapt forward. Rivka dove to the floor where she stood.

Emil saw the curbside barricade of black and white cruisers and the black FBI SUV as soon as the door cleared his line of vision. They'd left him no easy escape path. He quickly considered a narrow space between the parked tow truck and the cinder block wall next door. He couldn't see to the far right yet, but he assumed that at least one car filled that space. The searchlights and headlights trained on him, amassed into one huge flashbulb continually bursting and blinding. Already moving, he had to make the choice hastily. He opted for the questionable channel between wall and truck, and at first, it seemed he would make it clear to the street. Then came the sparks and scrunching noise as the wider second set of truck wheels wedged his rental car to a noisy metallic halt. Reverse gear burned rubber against the cement until one of the tires blew out. Neither door could open. Trapped! The windshield shattered into a massive web of cracks under the lateral stress.

 Emil opened the driver's side window and peered upward. He found himself looking into the business end of a sniper's rifle on the adjacent roof. Pulling his head back just in time, a single shot ricocheted off the door side. The smell of gasoline surrounded him. He saw smoke coming from under the hood and then a flame licked out after it. There was only a moment to decide. The crash had caused his cell phone to slide into view from under the seat. He didn't want to die in flames, so he took the cell phone in his hand and stuck it and his head out the window once more. He aimed it upward as though it were a weapon. And so it appeared to the expert rifleman on the roof. A single shot through the top of the skull ended the life of Emil Kravitz. Engulfed in flames, the car and everything within blew to smithereens. Somehow, the explosion was confined between the wall and the truck.

 Inside the garage, Rivka heard the fire's roar and felt the heat. She had to get clear of the building. Full of grime from her two trips to the greasy floor, she scrambled to her feet and ran for the office door. "Thank God! He's left it unlocked."

 From beyond the barricade of blinding light a man's voice shouted, "Don't shoot! It's the woman hostage. She's safe!"

 "Rivkaaa!" She heard the second voice from much farther

away over the roar and beating sounds of fierce flames. "Rivkaaa!" She heard it again, louder and closer. She couldn't see Dan beyond the flaming bright lights, but she knew he was out there coming to her. And then she saw him running toward her in long, athletic strides, arms out, ready to gather her in. She began to cry in heaving bursts. She fell into Dan's arms and collapsed. His protective arms pressed her tightly to him, as he too trembled and sobbed.

Chapter 33

At Nightmare's End
Same Day

Rivka slept on until one in the afternoon. Awaking with a throbbing headache, she sat up quickly in the plush king-size bed. Midday's light trickling through drawn drapes permitted her to examine the strange room with several closed doors and an unfamiliar décor. Even the nightie that barely reached her thighs looked foreign. Quiet enveloped the massive, thickly carpeted room except for a few distant street sounds. Wondering for a split second whether Emil had locked her in here and whether the nightmare continued, she then recalled the explosion and running into Dan's arms. Nothing came to mind after that—not even coming to this room. It certainly resembled a hotel room, but where?

Rivka pulled her knees up to her chest and called to her husband several times, but he didn't respond. Swinging her limbs over the side of the bed, she stood on shaky legs and tried to decide which door led to where. After finding an empty closet, her thoughts latched on to the fact that there were no clothes for her to wear anywhere in the room. Relieved to find that the second door led to the bathroom, she took advantage of the facilities. What she wouldn't have given for a couple of Tylenol right now. Now it was time to try the third and last door. Realizing it could lead to an outside hall and considerable embarrassment, she turned the knob and pulled it open a crack at first. Seeing the elaborately furnished sitting room and apparently no one about, Rivka stepped into it.

"Dan?" Rivka called—no response. "Dan!" Louder this time.

And then a familiar snore, followed by a snort, emerged from the blind side of the divan in the middle of the sitting room. Her anxious look evaporated as she rounded the divan. He lay there in his stocking feet with the *Atlanta Journal-Constitution* folded across his face and chest—he'd fallen asleep reading. She reached down and tickled the sole of his foot. In mid-snore he withdrew his foot and mumbled indeterminately. The snoring resumed. Tossing the newspaper on the floor, she bent down and kissed him on the lips—a lengthy, passionate kiss he couldn't ignore even in his deepest sleep.

Dan's eyes popped open. He reached up and pulled her down on top of him. They embraced, kissed, and caressed for several minutes, just absorbing the tangible realness of each other before retiring to the bedroom for more intense love-making.

An hour later, lying in the crux of his shoulder, Rivka asked, "Where'd the sexy nightie come from?"

"Justine brought it for you from home last night," he said.

"And just who is Justine?" Rivka propped herself up on one arm.

"Justine Burgess is one of the FBI agents on the case. She was just being helpful. Besides, she lives close by."

"Is she pretty?"

"She can't hold a candle to you." He pulled her to him once more and they kissed again.

"Good grief! R-J!" she cried, suddenly springing upright. "I forgot all about poor R-J."

"R-J? Oh, you mean the owner of the gas station."

"Yeah, I untied him and made him comfortable on the floor of the storeroom. He was still out of it from the drugs Emil gave him. I had to close the door again or Emil would have known. Tell me he didn't die in the blast."

"He's okay," Dan assured her. "The thick concrete walls of

the tire storeroom saved his life. The blast did knock out the window close to the ceiling, so he had plenty of ventilation. After the fire was extinguished, one of the firemen discovered him there in a confused but unharmed state. The hospital checked the man out and sent him home this morning. He's going to be fine. His biggest problem now is dealing with the insurance company."

"Thank God!" Rivka sank into his comforting arms as he kissed the top of her head. She buried her face in his broad, furry chest before suddenly looking up at him. "By the way, where are my clothes?"

"Hanging in the sitting room closet," he explained. "I sent them down to the concierge first thing this morning, and they were back by noon. They're clean, except for two grease spots that are hardly noticeable now."

"But I can't get on an airplane in those clothes."

"There's a nice ladies boutique in the lobby. I'm sure they'll let you in there."

"I can buy some real undies now. Gawd! Anything but that disgusting terry cloth diaper. But my purse—my life, my whole identity is in it. It's still at home."

"Your precious life is in my overnight bag. Liz found it on the kitchen counter right where you left it when you went out to the backyard. She insisted that I take it with me."

"Dear Liz. Oh my God. Liz. The store. Who's minding the store."

"Don't worry, Liz has everything under control. I called her this morning to give her the good news. Heather was with her until last evening. She needed to get back to school today, so Ev Kanter is staying with Liz today. We'll be back there tomorrow."

"Ev Kanter? Doesn't he have to work for a living?" she asked.

"Yeah. Get this, hon. Liz tells me he's an insurance investigator for the British Literary Museum in London. His real name is Andrew Beecham. Apparently, after Abner Fraume was murdered, he came to the U.S. incognito to search for the matrices and chase on the museum's behalf. Abner willed the pieces to them. I could have sworn Ev was Emil Kravitz. You know—with the same initials and all. He was my prime suspect until I spoke with Liz this morning. Now we have to wait for the forensics people to tell us which one Emil was. The explosion and fire left nothing for the police to go on."

"Then you really don't know which of the four men Emil posed as?"

"Gosh, Rivka, I'm beginning to think it wasn't any of them. Here's more news. It seems that Garry and Peggy are Abner's children by different mothers. But Garry was still in Annapolis long after you'd been taken. So it couldn't have been him. Turns out Spencer Edington is a British barrister representing Abner's estate. He was present during the entire duration of the FBI interrogatory that lasted until late Saturday night, well after you were taken. And we now know about Ev. So that leaves Vernon Levant. He showed up here in Savannah last night. Introduced himself as Constable Sergeant Fenton Thorwal of the Bath police. He's assisting in the investigation of Abner's death. And there you have it. So whodunit?"

"I know who," she said, grinning wickedly, shrugging her shoulders in a coquettish pose.

"Of course you do. So tell me already!" he demanded.

"I'm not telling."

"Oh yes you are." He rolled on top of her and began to tickle her ribs. She shrieked with laughter and shook all over.

"Stop, please stop," she begged, loving the game, sliding her hands down his ribs, wishing he were ticklish, too.

"Gonna tell me?"

"No, no way."

He bent his head and nuzzled her bare neck with his lips just above her left shoulder. It was his favorite target of affection when they were at the kitchen table doing a crossword puzzle. He also knew it was her most ticklish spot.

"Oh, please stop! Spence, Spencer Edington."

Death Goes Postal

Dan's lanky body jolted upright, "Huh? But like we just talked about, Edington was in the reading room with us the whole time during Robards' interrogation. How could it be him?"

"We didn't start out on the road until the next morning," she replied. "I have no idea where we were that night. I mean, I know I was lying on a bare wood floor, blindfolded."

Dan's hazel eyes seemed to burn like a cat's, and with pained effort, he slowly said, "Every minute you were gone, every second, I was terrified that I'd lost you. Rivvie? Did Emil harm you in any way? I'm sure he did. I'm almost afraid to hear the answer. But I want to know everything."

She propped two pillows up against the headboard and pulled up the covers, as if she needed warmth and protection to rehash it all. He took one of her hands in both of his, holding it tight, and she began with the shock of being seized in their backyard. "And he put this horrid shroud thing over my head so I couldn't see where we were going. He bound and drugged me and left me on the hard floor—I have no idea where, some house not far from ours, I think. I can still taste the rough material scratching my cheeks, my mouth. It was all designed so he could barter my safety and comfort for our interpretation of the clues in Abner's letters. I had no choice but to give him the answers he wanted. Lucky for me, you and I had already solved everything but the box number. I didn't tell him about the key, though. And the four wooden chests—boy, was he shocked to find the screws and horseshoes. And furious."

Rivka suddenly flushed from the reality of her new freedom and the recapping of the details. "But once we were on the way, he became the complete gentleman."

"Gentleman?" Dan retorted. "That's hardly the word for a killer and torturer. Besides, he had you trapped in the car in those tie-straps for over two days." He tenderly lifted her hands and massaged her wrists, still red and quite raw. He shook his head. "What you've been through…Oh, by the way, Kanter informed me that we're eligible for some kind of finders' fee from the museum. He didn't know how much, but it's usually between three and five percent of the artifacts' value."

"Brrr, it's chilly in here, I'd better put something on." Rivka bounded naked out of bed, heading for the sitting room closet and her clothes. "Dan? Darling, thank you for having them cleaned. You're a doll." She reappeared in the doorway a few minutes later with the bag. "Does the finders' fee mean I can shop for something really chic downstairs?"

"Anything your little heart desires, my love," he replied.

"How much time do we have? I'm starved."

"We're booked on the 805 to Atlanta tonight."

"And we're free until then?"

"Outside of a few errands, yeah! Let's go down to the coffee shop."

* * *

"Where to now?" asked Rivka in her new pastel pants suit, leaving the hotel's tiny boutique. She carried two more flat boxes in a fancy shopping bag.

"Well," said Dan, "we've already taken care of your empty tummy and your ravishing taste in clothes. Would you like to do some sightseeing?"

"Oh, Dan, do you know what I'd really like to see?"

"What's that, sweetie?"

"I'd like to see Abner's chase and the matrices—the real thing, not the screws. Is it possible?"

"I don't know. Special Agent Burgess is in charge of Abner's artifacts. In fact, they're being stored in the hotel vault until the museum people take delivery some time tomorrow. I think I saw Justine in the lobby with a newspaper earlier. But I don't see her there now. Let's check with the desk."

The desk clerk informed the Shermans that Special Agent Burgess was in a press conference currently being held in the Peachtree Ballroom on "Printing Artifacts from the Fifteenth Century." He pointed out the location.

Death Goes Postal

When Dan and Rivka entered the room, they noticed at least a dozen reporters and photographers seated in folding chairs being addressed by Special Agent Robards. Upon finishing, Robards headed up the aisle to greet them.

"Glad to see you're up and about, Mrs. Sherman. I hope you never have to go through anything like that again."

"In God's ears," said Rivka.

Constable Sergeant Thorwal tapped Dan on the shoulder. "Sorry about the subterfuge. We didn't know who to trust at first. But why would you want to attend a stuffy press conference after all you and your wife went through?"

"I wanted to see for myself what was so valuable that Emil Kravitz killed to possess," replied Rivka. "Also, I simply have to thank everyone."

Robards led the way to a display table at the rear of the room. Justine Burgess was there, and two local uniformed policemen flanked the table. The table lit up periodically with photoflashes. The pieces had been restored to their original chests. One of the policemen started to protest when Rivka picked up a single letter matrix to examine it.

"It's okay, Officer," said Justine. "She's earned the right."

"It's amazing," Rivka marveled, tilting the matrix mold so she could see down to the inverse letter "B" at the bottom, decorated with a floral design. "I didn't know how very skilled artisans were in those days, especially with the hard metals." She returned the matrix to its former pigeonhole and picked up the chase. "The scrolling is so beautiful, and there's Koenig's hallmark, an engraved K, an anvil lying on its side."

Dan and Rivka began to shake hands and personally thank each of the agents. When they were done, she turned back to Dan. "Well, I guess that's it, honey."

"Almost," he said. "I do want to stop by the hospital to see Elliot Landow. He's the agent Emil bashed over the head. Yeah, in the post office last night your 'gentleman friend' cut off three of Elliot's fingers at the first joints and then knocked him out. The doctors were able to sew his fingers back on, but he's going to have to wait till they start to heal to see how well they work."

Her forehead furrowed and her entire face filled with anguish. "Oh, no, that's horrible. Absolutely, let's go. I need to thank him, too. Speaking of agents, shouldn't I be telling my story to one of them?"

"Yes, on the plane tonight. Ken Robards is going back with us. He promised to hold off until tonight before he debriefed you for his reports. You'll need to recall every detail you possibly can."

Rivka pressed her lips together in grim determination. "That won't be hard, Daniel. Now, do you think we can go on happily ever after? Forget all this living-on-the-edge stuff?"

Dan tried to smile, but couldn't quite break out of the cocoon of fear—fear for her life, that had wrapped around him for two-plus days. But he made a concerted effort to be upbeat. "Like it is in all the mysteries we sell, my dear wife: The curious, the adventuresome, and the downright reckless can't avoid placing themselves in peril. Maybe I should buy a Doberman to protect you."

Her eyes lit up. "Make it a golden retriever and I'll consider it." She cocked her head. "Oh, but that won't work. They're too friendly. Besides, Lord Byron stepped up to the plate beautifully. Why don't we just keep our watchcat, and you'll watch my back."

Dan's somber mood broke into a joyous smile. "I love watching your back, especially in those pants."

END

Coming Soon

A New Dan & Rivka Sherman Mystery

Death Takes a Mistress

Also by Rosemary & Larry Mild

Murder, blackmail, and passion thrust a Hawaiian *ohana* (family) into Honolulu's dark side. Kekoa, the teenage son, witnesses the murder of his Uncle Big John and must flee from the killer. Danger erupts at a Filipino wedding; at a Maui resort; and amid the Big Island's volcanic steam vents as the family struggles to reunite and bring down the killer.

Available on Amazon.com, Kindle, and Nook.

PRAISE FOR *Cry Ohana*

"*Cry Ohana* is certainly a page-turner, and the authors seem to have a good take on the evolving concept of "ohana" and fractured families in modern Hawaii, and the action proceeds in a logical and gripping pace....The characters in this large novel are all drawn well...."   **—Burl Burlingame,** *Honolulu Star Advertiser*

"*Cry Ohana* captures the essence of Hawaii while providing a suspenseful adventure about family, redemption, hope, and justice.... The use of Hawaiian slang and references to historical landmarks adds to the authenticity and flow of the story. A thrilling Hawaiian journey."   **—Kathryn Franklin,** *San Francisco Book Review*

"Shame can tear families apart, and murder can obliterate them....A story of family and reunion for the betterment of it all, and dedicated to Hawaiian culture. A choice pick, highly recommended."
     —Margaret Lane, *Midwest Book Review*

"I was hooked from the very first page. There is plenty of suspense, intrigue, blackmail, and betrayal. The characters are very easy to connect with. The descriptions of Hawaii are excellent. A book you won't want to miss." **—2011 Gold Seal *Reader's Favorite* Award**

"Rosemary and Larry Mild bring us a struggle that makes *Cry Ohana* such a compelling story....Chase scenes and plot twists abound. We are given murder and blackmail as well as human pathos and drama in abundance. *Cry Ohana* is an exciting and poignant story rating a 9 of 10 on the Weaver meter."
     —Sid Weaver, *Mainly Mysteries*

"This book was very endearing....My heart went out to Kekoa. I was able to relate to his struggle of survival....Even the patience and tenacity Leilani had, never wanting to give up on finding her family, was inspiring....I recommend this book and these authors."
     —Nikkea Smithers, Pres., Romance Writers of America Book Club

Also by Rosemary & Larry Mild

The Paco and Molly Mystery Series

Locks and Cream Cheese—set in an old Chesapeake Bay mansion full of hidden rooms, locked doors, and secrets out of the past. A million-dollar painting and a jeweled key are the prizes, but are murder and trickery worth it? The wily police detective and housekeeper/cook are on the case.

Hot Grudge Sunday—Paco and Molly, finding love and marriage, go on a honeymoon bus tour out West. Bank robbers, conspirators, and murderers interrupt their bliss and once more they are called upon to uncover spine-chilling schemes as spectacular as Zion, the Grand Canyon, and Yellowstone.

Boston Scream Pie—A young girl's persisting nightmare leads Paco and Molly to the Boston family household, where the children churn up vicious undercurrents that threaten two families. Four deceased husbands lie in Mom's past. When another family member dies under mysterious circumstances, the clues point to murder. Paco and Molly see through the sinister connections and set things right.

Available on Amazon.com, Kindle, and Nook.

PRAISE FOR THE PACO AND MOLLY MYSTERIES

Locks and Cream Cheese

"A light-hearted book with likable characters."
—**Sandra Travis-Bildah,** *Washington Post*

"It's a one-of-a-kind upstairs-downstairs story, and it happens here on the Chesapeake Bay. I loved the book."
—**Kathy Harig, Owner, Mystery Loves Company Booksellers, Oxford, MD**

"This caper is full of surprises, a tale with love, hate, lust, and greed. The Maryland background makes a good setting for the action. A promising first novel." —*BooksnBytes*

"A Million-Dollar Painting Disappears—Curious? So were we. Especially since the painting is stolen from a museum on the shore of the Chesapeake Bay and the sleuths fall in love. Molly Mesta, a roly-poly cook, and Paco LeSoto, a retired detective, solve the museum mystery." —**Kathryn McKay,** *Washington Woman*

"How [can] any couple spend so much time together and not produce real-life mayhem? The [Milds] get along and it shows in their increasingly successful publishing ventures."
—**Joni Guhne,** *Baltimore Sun*

"Like retired detective Paco LeSoto and his accomplice Molly Mesta, the Milds enjoy collaborating because they've come up with a formula that works." —**Orly Rosenberg,** *Baltimore Jewish Times*

Hot Grudge Sunday

"The reader gets to share the sights and delights of the Southwest while sharing the puzzle with all its multiple parts that seem not to fit together. The finale of this mystery will surprise you. Rosemary and Larry Mild have a real knack for pulling the bad guys out of a hat without the reader knowing who is the real villain."
—**F.L. Swinford,** *Gumshoe Magazine*

"*Hot Grudge Sunday* takes us on a delightful action packed ride. The story is full of surprises and kept me riveted. I'm already looking forward to Molly's next adventure."
—Mary Ellen Hughes, Author of the Craft Corner Mysteries

"Working in tandem, the authors created scenic vistas, lively characters, and enough plot twists and tension to carry the reader swiftly to the finish." **—Edie Dykeman, Amazon review**

"The Wild West is a lot wilder whenever the Milds' tour bus arrives in *Hot Grudge Sunday*. Rosemary and Larry had me hanging by my fingernails throughout the trip. They also gave me an enticing glimpse of a part of America I've never seen. A great read."
—Robin Hathaway, Agatha Award-winning Author of the Dr. Andrew Fenimore Mystery Series

"I had not read any of Paco and Molly's adventures before *Hot Grudge Sunday*. That will be changing. I really enjoyed them and their adventurous spirit. I can't wait to read more! I highly recommend this book!" **—Dawn Dowdle,** *Mystery Lovers Corner*

Boston Scream Pie

"We have added *Boston Scream Pie* to our recommended reading list....It is worth picking up. There is a little of something down there for everyone." **—John Raab,** *Suspense Magazine*

"...In Chapter One I met a woman who I decided I hated immediately. And she was sleeping! The case twists and turns...and kept me glued to the pages until the end."
Kaye Barley, *Meanderings and Muses*

"If you want a light and funny mystery to read, I would definitely recommend *Boston Scream Pie*." **—***Mystery Reader*

"If you enjoy cliff-hanging, crisis-to-crisis mysteries filled with suspense, then you are going to enjoy *Boston Scream Pie*....Deftly written and highly recommended...plays fair with the reader...."
—*Mystery Bookshelf*

"....I was fascinated by a tale that had a little dab of V.C. Andrews mixed with a bit of Leeann Sweeney. But, believe it or not, the Milds pulled it off and *voilá*, it was a winner. I loved it!....This mystery sparkles 'n shines and if there is such a thing as a V.C. Andrews 'cozy' you'll love it!" —*Feathered Quill Book Reviews*

"*Boston Scream Pie* is a page-turning novel of suspense that will hold the reader's attention from beginning to end." —*TCM Reviews*

"*Boston Scream Pie* was heartwarming, but suspenseful. It has a surprise ending that will shock you....one of the best novels I have read in quite a long time! It shows a very familiar part of life; true things that can really happen to people, and was just so delightful!"
—**Gina Holland,** *Rebecca's Read*

"This mystery provides page-turning excitement without the inordinately graphic gore to make it unpalatable. Full of injuries, illnesses, and attacks, the book shares murders and mayhem in a lower key than that sung by Hannibal Lecter. This well-researched theme causes one to wonder which individuals in the story are related—or are they at all?"
—**Patty Inglish, MS.,** *Armchair Interviews*

"The Milds have whipped up another pleasing concoction in this charming series with their likeable protagonists, clever plotting, and generous dashes of humor. Paco and Molly are astute detectives and Molly's malaprops are as tasty as her kugel. *Boston Scream Pie* is a thoroughly enjoyable treasure."
—**Anne White, Author of the** *Lake George Mystery Series*

"....the plot and outcome were all carefully drawn with a resolution that I am sure will satisfy most readers. I should also note that there is a bit of sexual content as well, though nothing very graphic or gratuitous—I felt that it was pertinent to the storyline. My rating: 4.5 out of 5 stars. I recommend *Boston Scream Pie*."
—**Melissa,** *Mystery Mondays*

"A fast, charming read." —*Futures Mystery Anthology magazine*

Photograph by Craig Herndon

Rosemary and Larry Mild coauthor mysteries and thrillers. Seven of their "soft-boiled detective" short stories have appeared on line in *Mysterical-E*. Regular panelists at the Malice Domestic and Left Coast Crime conventions, the Milds divide the rest of the writing year between serene Severna Park, Maryland, and addictive Honolulu, Hawaii, where they cherish time with their children and grandchildren.

Rosemary is also the author of ***Miriam's World—and Mine,*** her second memoir of their beloved daughter Miriam Luby Wolfe, whom they lost on Pan Am 103 over Lockerbie, Scotland. Available from Rosemary, on Amazon.com, Kindle, and Nook.

E-mail the Milds at: roselarry@magicile.com
Visit them at: www.magicile.com

CPSIA information can be obtained
at www.ICGtesting.com
Printed in the USA
FSOW01n0625130315
5631FS